Across the Pond

Croften Grebe

To Mary Porter

Acknowledgments

Thanks to Solomon and the rest of the team – Roy Harper, Ron Connor, David Harper, Walter K., Ella Rose, Daisy and Jonathan, my editor for adding in the colours.

Contents

Chapter 1

Enunsha is still unsure as to what she should be introducing herself as, to all and everyone in the community. After much consternation where she is stuck between a rock and a hard place. She continues to go through all the variations in her head, Mrs. Enunsha Hubstien, Mrs. E or Mrs. Hubstien. Then finally, after sounding out all of the names, at last she came to a decision and settled on Enunsha. After all, everybody here knows who she is married to and thinks that she does not really need to remind all of them of that fact on a daily basis. Nor to adopt any of the old sounding, as far as Enunsha is concerned, the boring long surnames that are not really required anymore. She had made it her number one priority to get to know every single one of the people here. The insurgents who were affiliated with the old family ways had tried, then failed, to create chaos and destroy the whole community. Enunsha now has to be one hundred percent sure that there are no other threats lurking out there among them, on being absolutely certain that there are no more wolves wrapped up in sheep's clothing hiding amongst them, lurking in the shadows until it is time to launch another unprovoked attack. Abe, she knows is clean, now free and far removed from all of the all of the age-old honourable baggage. He had well and truly walked away from all of the ancestral aspirations, even the family insignia no longer exists on his back. Enunsha had even put him through the test of the drug-fuelled induced dream. This had firmly put her mind at ease, that he had finally, for once and for all, relinquished all of the connections from what his near and distant relations had held true. Where they had colluded and conspired from generation to generation in their unholy ambition. In their quest, to enchain the whole human race to their perceived vision of the inevitable future.

She had just sat through yet another mind-numbing session with the mother and toddler group. Where all the construction workers' wives, girlfriends and children all pretended to like each other. It wasn't easy, but nevertheless, a necessary exercise in checking that everyone was who they were purporting to be. Her seemingly innocent interaction; had only detected that all of them bar none. All sorely missed their once almost umbilically attached mobile phones with the endless list of apps. The never-ending possibilities associated with online shopping, instant nail bar appointments, one-to-one virtual reality, therapy sessions and the overly popular twenty-four-seven fast-food deliveries. Where it was possible to order any type of

American or International cuisine and then have it delivered straight to your door at any time of day or night. This generation would have to read their children bedtime stories rather than the old days of giving into them. In sealing the bargain for going to sleep by permitting the required extra half an hour or so on the latest game that had fully encapsulated their already damaged beyond-repair brain cells.

Now, with all the cleaning-up complete and all the see you next week barely touching cuddles along with the now almost irritating, mandatory fist bumps out of the way. She now had the time to reflect on the unsettling images that had almost crawled up her spine. It was not an enhanced nightmare of a dream where she had lived through every single revelation that had appeared before her. It was still a vivid apprehension and a stern warning that there are still others out there, perhaps even more ruthless than Abe's former kith and kin. It was just as well that Hubstien had slept through it all. As she had relentlessly tossed and turned all night. What had surprized her most was the fact that there was no blatantly displayed trail of evidence, pointing to sets of muddy footprints leading directly to dirty sheets and toes.

Enunsha had not thought about the Hidden for a long, long-time. Her mother had made her promise, never ever to reveal the knowledge of the old ones. To any of the tribe as it would place her in great danger. The more that Enunsha reflects, she concedes to the distinct possibility that the dream was a stark warning from the past about the present and the future. Enunsha could sit and worry about this all day long and some, but resigned herself to the fact. That from now on, she will just have to be more vigilant about her surroundings and above all else, the seemingly normal day-to-day activities of the people.

She grabs the truck keys and sets off to deliver the packed lunches. Rather than have to listen to all the insufferable gossiping and seemingly never-ending bitching. Enunsha had coerced the attendees of the mother and toddler group into making sandwiches for all the guys on the construction site. As the workers queued up to collect their packages, this gave her full access to check out all of the workers. She knows for sure that there are more than a few shady characters among them. That are hiding some deep, dark secret from their past. None of them have given off any indication that they are from the families that had sought to eradicate them. Her now alerted senses would have picked up any signs of danger.

Enunsha thinks that the guys like the homely touch of actually eating something that has been prepared by one of the women. In comparison to one of the unappetizing, possibly dangerous concoctions created daily by the alleged cooks at the site. Enunsha had not received any complaints and all the recipients as far as she can tell looked forward to the once-a-week delivery. Even the questionable cooks, Doctor Death and Poison Pete, had been overheard proclaiming, "Man, that was the best sandwich ever!" At last, when they had handed out all the food parcels to the grateful workers, she and Abe had some time alone. The site had a strict rule that during the breaks, conversations on the topic of work or any related work activities were on the banned list. They guys even had a fine system in place and Enunsha did not want to know what this entailed but as she was fully aware of construction workers banter. She imagined that it would be very crude and without any shadow of a doubt, most definitely utterly disgusting.

The surrounding area of the once below ground Kunupenny sanctuary has now been thoroughly cleansed. All the cremated remains of the previous inhabitants had been dispersed, carried away by the four winds. After the not-so-clever declaration of war on the above ground dwellers. The resident psychopathic incumbent, Cartater who had taken over the Kunupenny family's underground estate. He had unwittingly led the so-called upper echelons of society into oblivion. All the state-of-the-art technology that had shielded them from the onslaught of the disease. That had nearly removed all of the indigenous species from the surface of the planet was at the end of the day just not enough to save them.

Enunsha was now on the way home, for a change she had taken the long route. Still very much perturbed by the dream, she wanted to take another look at the place. She was surprised to see Jacksons' vehicle parked outside the doors of the underground shelter. Alighting from her truck, she moved towards the still-broken doors and announced her arrival. Abe had regularly reminded her that as they now lived in an uncivilised country, where some people harboured wild ideas. On his persistent advice, Abe had told her to carry a gun. He hoped she never had to use it, but if she ever had to shoot, then she should always shoot to kill. Enunsha, checking that the weapon was now off the safe mode and loaded, ready to fire, edged herself in through the now permanently open doorway. She shouted out again for Jackson to respond and still received no reply. Enunsha proceeded to walk inside, and much to her surprise, some of the lights were still on. She assumed that it was the emergency power supply and it was either solar or wind-powered. As there were no Kunupenny lackies left alive to operate any of the previously installed intricate machinery.

She shouts out again and this time Jackson replies, he greets her with a, "Hi Enunsha, I'm over here and if I promise not to sing. Will you promise to put the cannon away?" Jackson smiles and waves in her direction. She makes the weapon safe and then puts it away. "This is a surprise. What brings you here? To this subterranean paradise full of exquisite shopping malls and fine French antiques?" Enunsha looks at him, knowing full well that all the now abandoned floors in this place may hold some priceless items but the existence of a shopping mall beggars belief. Jackson tells her that it is as always, a pleasure to see her and enquires why she is here. On the spot, Enunsha makes up a story about one of the children teething, and perhaps there was a pharmacy still open for business in the shopping mall.

Jackson smiles and asks her if she would like to view the medical centre. Perhaps they have something that will suffice. Enunsha now with her hands on her hips, "Jackson, you were bullshitting about the exquisite shopping mall?" Jackson puts his hands in the air, "hell yeah, but there are some fine French antiques." Enunsha, now relaxed with Jackson and enjoying this game, confesses that she would be far more interested in freshly made French fries with some real ketchup. Informing him that the fancy, overpriced, pretentious furniture does not really appeal to her somewhat homely tastes.

He gives the mock bow more suitable for a maître D' from a top-notch restaurant, rather than a concierge at the shopping mall; "if you please, madam," and leads the way. He informs her that the elevators most likely still function but cautioned that if she were to get stranded inside. Abe would get upset, then probably just shoot him on the spot. Jackson insists that to be on the safe side they are going to take the stairs. Enunsha thinks that although the whole place is almost pristine clean, it still feels pretty dam creepy. She shivers at the thought of the evil people who used to reside here. "Jackson, how many levels are in this place?" He scratches his head, pretending to think. "I have been down to level five, but to tell you the truth, I never wanted to go down any lower, so can't say for sure how many floors are still left to explore. Enunsha, don't you be worrying; we are only going to level three. That's not unless you want to see the diamond-encrusted gold faucets, the finely carved Italian marble baths, the handstitched silk sheets and not forgetting all of that antique French furniture."

Enunsha laughs, not really believing him about all of the alleged splendour on display. Jackson felt that she did not actually think a single word of what he had said was true. Even added in the fact that they had a golf course down here. "C'mon Jackson, you really expect me to be that gullible?" He just looks at her and tells her that it is near where the medical unit is located and he will gladly give her the guided tour, once they find what she is looking for.

As they continue down the stairs, he informs her that they are nearly there. Jackson holds the door open and follows her in. Enunsha is amazed at the size of the place, the main corridor looks like it continues forever. Jackson acts as the tour guide, "The true size of this structure is more than impressive; it must have taken a very long time to construct and would have cost umpteen billions. The most surprising fact is that it was built in total secrecy and no one outside of the immediate family was ever aware of its existence. No planning permission, no routine inspections, and no bonding county, state or federal regulations to comply with. The migrant workers would never have been registered in the first place so they were conveniently disposable when the work was all complete."

Jackson tells her that they are here now and leads her into the pharmacy. "The computers are all still connected but as

I don't have a valid password, we will just have to look through all the shelves. I have no idea what we are looking for, so a heads up on what to search for would be greatly appreciated." Enunsha is in total awe at what is in front of her. The displayed stock would have been more than enough to supply a major hospital for like forever and some. Jackson notices her shock, "this is nothing, you should look at the actual hospital facility. It makes the major trauma unit in the city look like the practice where the out-of-town doctor hones his skills."

Enunsha suggests that they could try and locate the shelves that are dedicated to infant ailments. Jackson thinks that if it was only that simple, but nevertheless agrees to help her. With what he now considers a futile search and possibly a complete waste of time. Then at last, after wandering in and about the labyrinth of aisles complete with all the countless rows upon rows of shelves. They had located the feeder bottles and diapers but none of the elusive teething powders. Enunsha confesses to Jackson that she has taken up enough of his valuable time and that she should really be heading back home. "Why don't you come over for dinner tonight? Abe would be over the moon to win a game of eight ball for a change." Jackson nods okay and they make their way back up the stairs, returning into the real world with all its many imperfections. She for one is glad to have escaped the claustrophobic, almost sterile underground environment.

"Hey Jackson, don't forget to come for dinner. I will even make you some chilli dogs."

He looks at her, "Really?"

Enunsha looks straight at him and smiles as she says, "Okay, I am messing with you, but the house is kinda empty and we like your company, so just come over when you are ready."

She can't help it but Jackson sure as shit ain't no average blue collar construction worker, he is way too smart. In the same breath, she also thinks that he's one of the good guys and happy that at least for now, he is firmly on their side. Enunsha can't wait to whip both their asses at eight ball. Pity they no longer played for dollars. Hell, she thinks that even if she played with only one arm, her eyes closed and in the dark, she could still own them. Jackson always laughs when she beats them, often reflecting that he was sure that she was raised in one of them one-horse town pool halls. Hustling the locals out of their hard-earned currency and when that was gone, their watches, jewellery, as well as prized vehicles would soon be changing ownership.

The dinner was ready and although it was not chilli dogs as promised, she did rustle up something with a little spice.

Abe was just helping her put it out on the table when Jackson appeared bang on time. He says nothing about the changed menu and takes a deep breath, mentioning that something smells good. Enunsha laughs, thinking that Jackson is maybe one of these guys who is an expert tin and microwave dinner chef. He thanks them for the invite and as always, compliments her on the cooking. Enunsha tells him that Abe had made it. Abe and Jackson look at her, both of them knowing dam well fine that Abe could not spell kitchen, never mind being able to find his way around it. They shoot the shit and as always, love Jacksons' company.

He had brought over some beers and after all the tidying up is complete, they sup while Abe racks up the balls. "That reminds me, the community shop is running out of beer. Do you think we could maybe confiscate any supplies from the Kunupenny stock? I am sure that they will have some as they almost seem to have everything else." Abe thinks it is a good idea and as Enunsha takes the break, she informs them that perhaps they should take a full inventory of everything that is down there. She understands that it could be a rather big task, but once the hydro station is complete, there will be plenty of spare guys available. You never know what we may find down there and if she is being perfectly honest, they should really search every nook and cranny on every floor. The guys sort of agree to the idea but she guesses that the sterile environment creeps them out just as much as it did her.

Several thousand miles away, Murray for some inexplicable thought pattern and beyond any normal form of reasoning or sanity has been drawn back into the inner depths of the old world. When he was serving his apprenticeship, the young Mr. Black sometimes wondered how he would end up in later years. On the workshop floor there was quite a varied selection of examples to choose from. The ones who looked upon being as drunk as humanly possible. As the ultimate much dreamed of aspiration and perhaps even, for some, the one true meaning of life. The ones who would mortgage their souls on the nice house, with the obligatory back and front door located as far away as possible from the place where they had grown up. The ones who, having a propensity for self-destruction who would end up in the gutter. Then the ones who would rise to higher positions, ultimately forgetting their backgrounds and turning into someone who thought that they were rulers of some preposterous kingdom. Where their egos, only viewed their own opinions as valid. Frequently changing their minds that perhaps the previously offered solutions and proffered suggestions to preventable problems were in fact really quite a good idea after all. Then reissuing the sound reasoning a few days later, professing that this was their idea and their idea alone. Murray also thought that if he could miraculously travel back to these years. Disliking himself as much now as he did then, he would have no hesitation or problems in engaging in a conversation with his former self. The others, he wondered if they would have even been able to look their previous former selves in the eyes, never mind being able to engage in an honest face-to-face conversation.

The sound of the dogs baking had instantly dragged Murray and his mind, firmly back to reality. He was in bed with Cha. They are both fully clothed and he for one cannot remember climbing up the stairs then going to sleep. However, he can remember the vision that had played out in his head about theirs and the Valarons' shared and almost forgotten ancestral beginnings. The near tragic ending for what had initially been a great idea, the fresh start for their endangered species.

As he deposits the regular sized, almost healthy daily torpedo down into the depths of the great white telephone. This is the time of day that he sometimes misses the ten-minute crossword, that now so long ago used to appear in the newspapers. Murray has a smile, thinking that he never once completed the puzzle in the required time, but still he would be delighted with himself if he finished it at all. Murray laughs as he remembered the technique for obtaining an empty cubical, when he was at work. If he went into the gents and it was filled to capacity. He would calmly, without any hesitation, switch off all the lights and then walk around the permitter of the building. He would then hear the abusive shouts of the various punishments on offer if they managed to apprehend the culprit. Murray, on completion of his circuit, would just walk in and his trick, it had never once failed as there was always a vacant warm slot available for a new occupant.

Cha is in his head. She tells him that she loves him and that she will love him forevermore and some, if he could rustle up a nice morning cuppa. She also issues the standard prewarning, that if he even thinks about making a mess in the kitchen. That would require the timely intervention of a fully equipped hazmat team to clean and tidy the debris. Thus, rendering it safe again for human habitation, he was almost guaranteed with a one hundred and ten per cent absolute certainty to forfeiting at least one testicle. Murray instantly withdraws from the thought of making her breakfast, finishes his business and after making sure that Bobby is not on open display for the general public, heads downstairs.

All of the evidence from last night's revelation has been removed and much to his surprise, the place is now immaculately clean. The table looks polished and there is no tell-tale mark where the dagger with the red jewelled pommel was plunged through the surface of the finely-grained kitchen furniture. Rhubradug, Robbo the yobbo or whatever the fuck he was being addressed as today along with the dogs were also noticeably absent. Murray makes a mental note to have stern words with Charlie and Romulus about the true meaning of family loyalty.

He puts some water on to boil and after much furtive searching. In which he creates very little in the way of noise and once returning all the moved objects that could have very well been possibly concealing the ultimate prize. Murray felt very chuffed with himself, having at last, managed to locate the secreted stash of Chas favoured tea leaves. Murray if he had a choice, really preferred the bags, dunk them in, then chuck them out. When using the leaves, he has the distinct impression that some mysterious woman, with her head wrapped in a Paisley patterned headscarf and larger-than-life hooped earrings, is miraculously going to appear. Then enquire if he would like to part with an appropriate cash incentive, a cherished family heirloom or perhaps one of his children for her to foretell his fortune.

Alicia, a little worse for wear and tear, is the first to take the tentative steps, ventures into the new morning and helps herself to the freshly brewed chai. She mutters something unintelligible and not quite audible. Murray was at first momentarily dismayed, but also relieved. That there is not a snowball's chance in hell of her reading his future from the dormant dregs, now already residing at the bottom of her first cup. He puts another pot of liquid onto a boil and prepares to make a fresh batch. To replace the purloined exhibit number one which is now slowly reviving Alicia's batteries back into life to enable her to talk in an understandable dialect. She also, well... eventually notices that the place has been tidied up and is well aware that this was most definitely not Murray's handiwork. As his much tried and tested method would have simply entailed the shifting of everything to the other end of the table. Murray knows what she is thinking and does not even pause for a second on the thought of declaring that it was like this when he arrived there earlier.

The princess has now finally arrived and Murray puts his arms around her. Telling her that, as always, she looks like a supermodel and that he loves her just as much with one of her eyes open as she does with the two. Alicia tells them to get a room and if he does not shut the fuck up, she is going to be sick. Cha just ignores both of them and on restricted fifty-fifty vision, makes her way very carefully to a seat at the table. On the first sip of the very much-appreciated brew, she closes her eyes and savours the warm liquid. After several sips, she opens both eyes and looks around at her surroundings. Over the moon to be in home territory, she greets them with a little wave, a little smile and a quiet hi.

The sound of the various sets of feet now descending on mass down the stairs, announces that the others have decided to grace them with their presence. Murray thinks that they have waited until the big pot of tea is ready and somehow their collective sensitivity radars have colluded. Announcing that it is now the appropriate time to advance down into the kitchen and partake in much needed liquid refreshments. The trio stares at them, they all look as if they had just returned back to the land of the living from a lost weekend. The new arrivals, say nothing as they help themselves to the fresh pot of tea. "How about I make everyone a nice healthy breakfast for a change?" Murray is answered with an instantaneous myriad of noxious glares. Holding up his hands not in the act of surrender but to mentally ward off the onslaught of the incoming barrage of threats pertaining to him. In being at the receiving end of multiple participation on the rewarded gift of grievous body harm if he mentioned the food word again.

Murray declares to his adorable Fanclub, "Hmmmmm, I guess that Frank has a table with my name on it." He takes repossession of some of the ready rolled, chucks on a jacket, sparks one up then escapes out into the fresh morning air. Mr. Black arrived just in time and managed to grab the last available breakfast goodies just before Frank's assistants started to tidy up and prepare the lunch. Murray was starving and scoffs the lot down in no time, helping himself to a mug of tea, he positions himself on one of the benches outside and smokes. Frank takes a break and comes to join him, "Robbo, was here earlier and took Remus for a walk with your two. They sat there, not moving as much as a muscle while they waited on my pooch coming to join them, I take it he has a special way with animals." Murray just looked at him and was about to mention grand theft and family loyalty but pulls in the reins and quietly replies, "yeah, some gift I guess." He asks how Frank is getting on with his dog. Frank confesses that Remus just looks at him when he issues a command, almost giving him the 'do I really have to' look. Apart from that, Frank has no issues with the animal. He really knows deep down that he is Cat's dog and Frank has resigned himself to the fact that in the world of Remus, he is the mere second in command. They sit and chat about his antics, laughing at the dog's many previous attempts at curtailing the couple's romantic intentions.

Frank goes back to work and Murray walks in the direction of the Orangery. He very much hopes that it will be quiet up there, looking forward to just sitting all by himself, alone with his thoughts. Murray enters the building and instantly savours the scents as well as all the familiar smells as he heads towards the stairs. He likes to deposit himself on the top floor landing, overlooking the ducks. Who has prospered and grown in numbers since they had held the referendum on deciding that they no longer wanted to be a migrant species. He is surprised to find Robbo here. Before Murray asks, he informs him that he has already returned the now-tired dogs back to the house.

"I hope that you did not mind; I woke up ages ago and after tidying the place up a little, needing something to do, I took your adorable four-legged friends out for a walk," Murray replied that it was not a problem and so long as they had behaved themselves and did not embarrass his good family name nor his long-standing respect within the community, then that was okay. If it was anyone else but Robbo, they would have by now received the much practiced and unpolished. I like to come up here to get some peace and quiet, so could you now please fuck off speech, but he guessed that Robbo liked it up here also.

Robbo sparked one up and immediately passed it to Murray, then lit another one up for himself. They sat in the much-appreciated relative silence, devoid of all the hustle and bustle related to human activity. The bird noises from below were subtle and the soft quacks were almost soothing, "If I could get away with it, I would sit up here all day and then quietly blend unnoticed into the background." Robbo informed him that he understands and he himself gets an almost instant sense of relief, and the tranquillity just overwhelms him. He could go into specific details of what the Hidden had done in here. Their demise on these very grounds but thought that the recent revelation from last night's gathering was more than enough for his head to take in and absorb for the time being. Robbo was expecting many questions from the rest of the gang when they had sufficiently recovered enough to voice them. But perhaps they would just accept the shared insight from their distant ancestors that they had once held untold promises as well as many possibilities for a new beginning. A fresh start on a fresh, unpolluted world but nevertheless, they had unfortunately throughout the centuries, succumbed to the inherent unquenchable thirst and the insurmountable greed for absolute power and domination.

Chapter 2

Murray confessed out loud that he sometimes missed the crosswords. Freely admitting that perhaps it was even his favourite unofficial, paid for activity at work. When wanting to evade his less than approachable boss. He would take some much-needed me time and escape into the world contained within the black and white squares. Robbo accepted the next smoke from Murray and together, they sparked up. Robbo let it go that he did not miss his old job in the now-gone forever world. He professed that it was utterly soul-destroying, along with the disclosure that he frequently faked health issues. Just to get to fuck away from the almost suffocating, prevailing dark environment. However, he did from time-to-time reminisce about the time of the attempted robbery.

"The guy's name was Geoffrey Busby, an extremely well-spoken and I guess, quite a quiet chap. I had been the one who had presented him with his original mortgage package. One of these ones where you just paid the interest plus a little bit extra which was then invested in some foolhardy scheme. If the plan came up trumps, the mortgage was paid off and if you were really very lucky, you would also receive a cash sum at the end of the repayment period. Mr. Busby had been inadvertently replaced by a machine and lost his main source of income. Then, his wife had replaced him first with the painter and decorator, then with the alleged certified plumber. She had taken all the money out of the joint bank accounts, and Geoffrey, after donating his contribution to the court ordered maintenance schedule, was left virtually penniless. As he did not, as they say, have a pot to piss in and was now reduced to living in an environmentally friendly, recycled cardboard box. The house was in his name and his beloved ex-wife had no intention whatsoever of honouring, never mind looking at the repayment schedule. Thus, he was summoned to address this pending issue with the bank."

Robbo momentarily pauses as he relit the number then continued; "I could see that by just looking at him, he was nothing but a broken shell of the man. That I had dealt with previously and just to put him at ease, offered him a cup of tea. By the time I had presented him the default information, he was in a visibly distressed state and shaking like a leaf. If there had been a magic button to press to enable all of his debts, along with all of his worries, to evaporate instantly and miraculously disappear. I would have had no hesitation whatsoever and pressed it, but as he produced the weapon wrapped in the brown paper bag. I was duty bound to activate the silent alarm button.

"The rapid response unit, or whatever the fuck they were called in those days, had arrived very shortly afterwards. Geoffrey had just thanked me for the tea when the phone went off. As you do, I asked him for permission to take the call and Mr. Busby nodded. The officer in charge asked if I was okay and wanted to speak to the other person in the office. All I could do was hand over the phone, 'I want all the money from the vault, a helicopter to Rio-De-Janeiro and I want it all within the hour.' Geoffrey killed the call and much to my amazement, asked me what my thoughts were on the issued demands. I had to be honest with him and tell him straight up that this branch did not have a vault on the premises and to travel from here to Brazil in a helicopter would not be possible due to the vast distance involved.

"Geoffrey confessed that geography and armed robbery were not on his accredited skillset list. Mr. Busby now on realising that he was well and truly fucked had decided to give himself up. He asked me to make the call, to relay the information that he wanted to surrender. The hot phone line was still active and I told the guy in charge that Geoffrey had relinquished his weapon and was coming out. As soon as Mr.

Busby exited the office. He was immediately surrounded and then pounced upon by the armed officers. After being forced to the ground, he was cuffed and led away. The paper bag containing the weapon was placed in the evidence bag, and after a brief interview all the staff were all sent home early." Robbo laughs, thinking at that time he wished that there was an attempted robbery every single day just to get away earlier; preferably on a Wednesday just to break the working week up evenly.

"The branch manager, Mr. Greenwood had missed all the action. He had been preoccupied during the ensuing drama as he was in the stationary cupboard. Personally tutoring Doreen in upgrading her oral skills. Mr. Greenwood appeared in the local news program praising the police for their bravery and their very prompt response in normalising a rather dangerous situation. The bank staff were awarded danger money. Twenty-five quid apiece for the tellers at the public counter. I received Fifty quid for my troubles and the manager received additional company shares for his now rather expanding portfolio. Doreen was quietly farmed out, then eventually transferred to another branch conveniently located somewhere in the back of beyond."

"At the high court trial, it was revealed that Geoffrey Busby had previous convictions. All relating to the major disturbance at a national art gallery. Where he, along with the other members of the outlawed Justice and fair monetary dispensation for the divorced father's organisation. Had taken part in the orchestrated vandalism of supergluing themselves to various vegetable soup covered masterpieces to highlight their financial predicament. Allegedly, it was suspected that Mr. Busby was the perpetrator dressed as the superhero who ran a multibillion industrial consortium during the day, then after supper, fought criminals in his spare time."

"The judge gave him fourteen years for the attempted armed robbery. Geoffrey on entering the dreaded C wing at the maximum-security prison, was given a standing ovation. By all of the long-term hardened criminals for the sheer audacity in attempting to rob a bank with a courgette. The prisoner who controlled the wing, recognising that he was just a normal guy at his wits end. Put the word out that Geoffrey was to be respected, and exempt from all of the customary rite of passage, including the new prisoner ritual harassment."

Murray asked Robbo if he had made all this up. Robbo replied that for a few years he regularly received Christmas cards in the embossed HMP strange brown envelopes. Now that the smokes are finished, Murray suggested that the women should have by now, hopefully returned back to the land of the living. Adding that perhaps it was also very possible that they may have remembered the long-forgotten, age-old skill of how to speak. In an understandable language that did not require the services of a multilingual translator. Murray hinted that he could come with him and pick up the children. Robbo looked at him and Murray replied to the quizzical gaze. That he did not need to dress up as a crime-fighting superhero, well at least, not just yet.

Arriving at the doctors, to collect the youngsters, Mark and Vincent. Murray gets the distinct impression that Robbo and Cora have something going on, and to break the ice, he asks for two to take away. Robbo displays the usual charm that all women see and asks for tea for two while they are waiting. Cora, without hesitation, departs from the scene to help the children get ready while one of her assistants makes the tea. Murray, pretending to be the local priest, adjusts his imaginary dog collar then asks Robbo if he wishes to make his confession. Robbo lifts his eyes to the heavens, holds his hands upwards and declares to the much esteemed and revered Father Black. That although he is no angel and possibly regarded by some, perhaps by many, to be beyond any possible form of redemption. He has no confession to download from his mortally tortured soul. Murray was going to say something but the tea was delivered and he kept his mouth firmly closed. Cora has come out to join them. She informs Murray that the children's behaviour was impeccable, as well as the fact that she would be more than happy to take them anytime her services were required in the future. Murray still suspecting that these two have something to talk about and rather than being the onion. He tells them that Cha will be getting anxious, selects the gear lever on the baby buggy, and then starts on the walk home.

Murray is distracted by the whistle; looking back Robbo is catching up on him. Vincent had been unaffected by the sudden increase in G forces and is still sound asleep. In the past, if anyone had seen them, they would have been viewed as a pair of weekend dads. Part of the, then growing statistical trend of new marriages not making it to the one-year anniversary before irreversibly dissolving. Robbo informs Murray that all is good and he has finally surrendered to the fact that he needs urgent dental treatment. Murray asks him if Cora is a trained dentist, "fucked if I know, but I guess it is either her or vet. That unless you are offering to do it?" Murray tells him straight to his face to fuck right off, and Robbo takes that as a most definitive no.

The duo, along with their wheeled carriages, make it back to the house in one piece, both the infants are still out for the count. All the women are still seated at the table and they had, much to Murray's amazement, learned how to speak. He greets Cha with the traditional cuddle and tells her she looks a whole lot better with two eyes open. On hearing the comment, Okolo just mutters "wanker." Murray smiles and wishes her, along with all the other women present, a very good afternoon. They all display that incredibly serious look. Murray is more than positive that whatever it is, he is absolutely not guilty and had committed no offence. That could have any remote possibility of connecting him to the very frosty atmosphere in the room. "If all of you want, I could go back out then maybe come back later?" he receives no reply. "Okay then, if I have done something to offend one of you. Or if I have done something to offend all of you, then I am well and truly sorry."

Cha breaks the ice, "We were just sitting talking about last night and what the future may have in store for us. Then the subject of babies cropped up and it looks like we are in the process of having a few new additions to our extended family." Murray is perplexed as to why this could ever possibly be seen as bad news and waits for the rest of the gory details. "All the women at this table are expecting." Murray is delighted to receive the news that he is going to be a father again. He would have much preferred to have been told the great news privately, but with everything else with Cha. He expects that there is a valid reason for the public disclosure. Okolo looks at Alicia and they both look at Robbo. He is about to mention that he has super long-distance swimmers but holds his tongue. Murray catches this and thinks that the recent camping trip in the woods entailed so much more than Robbo sharing his al fresco cooking skills.

Robbo has not even displayed that dirty dog look and seems rather quite pleased with himself. Nor does he envisage any foreseeable problems with the double dunter. He will no doubt have to tell them about Cora sooner rather than later, as the children are now back in the house. Robbo and the two expectant mothers sneak outside, where he expects to receive earache in perfectly balanced stereo. Alicia does the talking, "We should move into another house." He looks at her and she nods her head. "Yes, all three of us or should I say all six of us," Robbo asks if Okolo is okay with this, Alicia informs him that it was her suggestion. He thinks about how he is going to broach the subject about Cora and just tells it the only way he knows. "There may be another one, and going by the recent track record of my super swimmers. I would say that Cora will be expecting one of my offspring. Also, before you ask, no, I do not want her to move in with us. It will be expected and I will want to take an interest in our daughter." The women look at each other and agree. Okolo takes her turn to speak; "As long as there are no other unexpected additional extras, your John Thomas is safe, but if you even dream about fucking about when we are staying under the one roof. I swear in front of my sister, that you will choke on your block and tackle during the night."

Robbo agrees to the stipulated terms and conditions. They move the discussion to where they are going to stay. Not one for waiting on a storm to arrive. He walks them straight into it and mentions that he is going for dental treatment this afternoon. He adds that perhaps it would be a good idea if they accompanied him up to Cora's. Robbo thinks that it would be much better if they just got it out in the open now, rather than let the situation continue and fester. "If you want, I will go in and tell her first rather than us going in team-handed." Both of the women instantly disagree with this idea. Insisting that it will be a team effort with no secret behind the scene conversations. Alicia pipes up, "Once we get that, then the tea and biscuits out of the way. We can go to search for a suitable dwelling for our expanding brood. There must be some semi derelict buildings requiring refurbishment in the area." Robbo tells them that he is not very good at all the building shit. Alicia along with Okolo insert the blade, then give it a twist, "don't worry, we are sure that Murray will teach you all of the skills that will be required."

Murray and the rest of them had not said much while the trio were outside. Not one of them would have dared to speculate about their friends' private matters. They had just conversed about normal subjects while they were absent. Robbo and the women came in and sat at the table. Robbo was in the middle position, with one of the women on each side. He holds up his hands and then tells them that all is good, no problems. Both Okolo as well as Alicia nod to confirm the authenticity of his statement.

Cha informs the assembled group that Beth and Debs have something to tell them. As Murray has practically adopted them, she advises him that he should take a huge fucking breath. Cha tells the girls to get it out into the open and put him out of his misery. At first, he thinks it was Robbo and he is starting to think that if he is guilty, he will kill him right here, right now, at this very table. As he was having these thoughts, Robbo voiced his plea instantly, declaring in his head that he was not guilty and these babies were most certainly not his. Murray looks at the girls and then asks them just to let it out and to please tell him if he should be at all worried.

The twins talk, they deliver the statement in their now accustomed fashion where one starts the sentence, then the other one finishes it. "It was not really our idea; the old woman in the hooded cloak had visited with us and sort of gave us the message that as we were now of age. Taking into consideration the shortage of our collective numbers. Ensuring the survival of our kind and to take full advantage of the unique opportunity that had just presented itself. I, we suppose that it was just our unbridled enthusiasm that took over and we abused Bartram then artificially inseminated ourselves with his seed."

Murray is distraught and not sure if he wants to puke or go look for the nearest river to drown himself. He stares at Robbo and asks him if he was aware of this grand plan. Robbo tells everyone that he knew nothing about it. The twins elaborated and informed the assembled that the old woman had warned them that you would all be upset. In time, you would understand and the old woman assured them that the result would not incur any additional dangers. The future offspring would be of no inherent threat to their group. This is way too much for Murray and noticeably upset he gets up and goes outside to smoke. What the fuck was he meant to say to this. As he sparks up, he can't help but notice that his hand is shaking. He just puts it down to an unexpected nervous reaction, now displaying the underlying symptom on receiving the shocking news.

Beth and Debs are now outside with him and the peace offering of the freshly brewed cuppa is very much appreciated. Beth speaks, "Look Murray, we could not have exactly asked if you thought it was okay and the old woman would never make us do anything that was dangerous." Debs adds, "We all have shared dreams and we all have had dreams in which we also do not share. This was just one of the latter and yes, of course the outcome could have been presented smother, more diplomatically correct, but what's done is done." Before he even gets a chance to reply, they both go back to their normal speaking mode and ask him straight up if he is going to make them leave. Murray tells them that they belong here and come hell or high water he would never ever ask them to leave. The twins are crying and Murray can't help it and cries with them. He steadfastly assures them that it will be all okay, but he has one condition. They look at him, wondering what is coming next and he informs them that there will be no fighting over the soon-to-be vacant rooms occupied by Alicia and Okolo. They all wipe the evidence of the bubbling session and go back in, trying to appear as normal as possible.

Cha smiles as Murray tells them all is good and there are no worries. They budge up and now all sitting at the table, the subject of the previous night's revelation raises its ugly head. Alicia just asked if it was a warning about something dreadful heading their way. They all look at Robbo for a reply and he digresses that he thinks it was just another constant reminder that their ancestors had fucked up and although the species had the great idea of starting all over again. They had inevitably lost track of the initial perceived goals, which had eventually been discarded and they had reverted back to the old ways. Murray thinks that this is a bullshit answer and that Robbo had said much, but in actual fact, he had said nothing, absolutely nothing at all. Cha says nothing, Okolo and Alicia sort of agree with Robbo and much to everyone's surprise, the twins deliver their normal cojoined speech.

"We think yes, but we also think a most definite no. If we were to look at this country, for example, pick any timeline and all you can see is unequivocal, unquestionable, manipulation and the proceeding unmanageable mess that was evidently impossible to repair. Adding to this, the Valaron had lots of issues with, shall we say, less than friendly rivalry. Take into consideration how many wars, economic downturns, famines and pandemics they had manipulated into existence. Not just to curtail the advancement of the indigenous species but also to challenge and bring to a halt some of their own species unwarranted expansion."

"This country used to hold elections every few years that were deemed by all to be fair and square. Did you know or did any of your friends or relatives actually know any of these esteemed politicians? The first thing that they did when in coming to power was to blame the previous administration for all the country's economic woes. Then purposely set about to dismantle and reassemble all the departments working systems the various governmental mechanics set up to make the country fully functional."

"If we look at the law of averages it is not possible that all the previously set up systems were incorrect and equally all the new set up systems were correct. In other words, if these esteemed leaders were running a business, none of them would have been successful as they maintained nothing and only changed everything to suit their needs and their visions of what should be and should not be. Take a look at all the media, a news outlet announces that a senior politician is about to be charged with gross misconduct. Then the next minute, the headlines in all the newspapers were announcing to the world that a famous actress with one breast larger than the other had just given birth. 'Both parents are pleased to announce that their son has normal-sized testicles.' Nobody noticed the deliberate diversionary tactics and the sad fact of the matter is that some, if not most, of the general public actually believed all this shit."

"If you think for a moment about all of the allegedly despicable leaders, from the less than honest foreign governments who pumped untold millions into the financial institutions down in the capital. If anyone started to ask questions, they were instantly presented with all sorts of legal restrictions. Which a tour bus full of legal representatives plus shed loads full of money would have taken many years to unravel. Have you ever wondered how many of our so-called honest politicians were connected to this? Again, it was all about control and manipulation. Then consider this, a ban on smoking, energy drinks, swearing in public, calling people names and all of the other trendy things that inundated all of the media platforms to allegedly correct the error of our ways to change us into a more forgiving and tolerant species. It was all just manipulation to keep us all from looking at what was really happening all around us every day in all walks of life."

"To name a few, they frequently changed the tax system from top to bottom, the benefits system, the price of petrol, electricity, the cost of living, the law, including the appeal system. I don't know about you but it seems incredible, almost impossible that none of these previous systems worked. The question you have to ask now is what was the actual true cost of continuously rearranging all of the said systems. Who stood to benefit from the changes and who suffered the most? Imagine this blatant manipulation being continuous from the very beginning of the political process, not just in this country and not just with democracy. They created havoc and convinced the population that it was their votes that counted. Then subdued them and coerced them into thinking that this was the only way forward, the only viable option available."

"If we are going to be truly honest with ourselves, then none of the governments. The political parties or the politicians really gave two fucks about anything or anybody. If they had really cared, there would have been no elections, no re-elections. As they would have been doing their jobs correctly taking care of their people and their nation. Just like all the promises that were delivered in utmost sincerity by all of them during the manifesto and election masquerades. That purported them all to be the party of choice, the party of the nation, and most unbelievable party of the common people."

"Just think if there had been a talk show in which all of the esteemed politicians across the divide were invited to appear. With the added stipulation that they all had to be wired up to a polygraph test, how many of them would have agreed to the pre-set conditions? There would have been none, and the programming of the network would have had to declare that due to the non-appearance of any of the invited guests, they were now going to reschedule and broadcast some cartoons. This at least would have highlighted to the general population that what they were going to broadcast was, in reality, not that far removed from the replacement program."

"I think, sorry we think that some of the Valaron had come to the realisation the Hidden had tried to halt this process in its tracks a very long time ago and concluded that they were indeed leading their species towards oblivion. They would never have freely admitted to themselves that the Hidden were correct and with all the in-family feuds and the almost attritional interfamily conflicts that had involved all of them at one time or another. Thus, this was their only viable option; the only way to gain complete control was by eliminating all the possible obstacles in one full sweep. The substantial reduction in numbers of the indigenous species and elimination of some of their own kind was calculated as unavoidable and deemed absolutely necessary."

"We cannot say for sure how they did things on their home planet but we are most certainly now fully aware that they fucked up the home world big time. They were left with no possible recourse but to leave or perish. This is, without doubt, an engineered rebirth for the Valaron. You can almost guarantee that we will not be invited to the big table and with that, you can be certain that our future does not have an unlimited time span."

Murray likes this explanation and nods, thinking that this is more like the truth. Robbo says that this is what he was trying to say and both statements mean just about the same, although one gives a much broader explanation than the other. Cha thinks that Murray is about to give his you are so full of shit speech, including that part where he declares that Robbo's head is that far up his own arse he cannot differentiate between night and day. She rapidly changes the subject and asks them if, they could show some unity with all the people now residing here and go over to Franks later as a group. Everyone nods their half-hearted agreement; Murray inwardly prays that there is no fucking fish and no fucking smelly seafood that he will feel sliding throughout his system millimetre by millimetre on tonight's menu.

The dinner is going to be a couple of hours away and while the babies are being fed, he along with the twins, take the dogs out. They bump into Cat, and Remus lets his presence known by running straight through them, daring his dogs to a game of chase. Charlie is not up for it and ignores her errant offspring. Romulus has other ideas and hot foots it almost on the tail of his cheeky sibling. Cat is almost quite chirpy and has a certain glow about her. Murray has not told the twins to say or not to say anything about their new maternal status. He knows that Cat and Frank are virtually wearing out their mattress in attempting to obtain another addition to their little tribe and hopes that the news to come will not upset her. Everyone thinks she is tougher than tough but Murray knows that this is just nothing other than a frequently broadcast popular misconception.

Cat thought that Murray looked sad and more than that he was almost forlorn. She asks him if he is alright. She knew that he would tell her he was fine even if he wasn't, so she took a deep breath and told him the good news. "We were going to come over and see you later. Frank and I were at the doctor's this morning and the good news is that you are going to be a grandfather." It is all too much for Murray and he bursts into tears, conscious of the public display of his emotions. He splutters out that he is not old enough to be a grandad yet and hugs Cat like he does not want to ever let go. He tells her that he is really pleased for her and Frank and he thinks that they will make great parents.

Beth and Debs look at him almost like they are asking for permission to confess their sins. Murray just shrugs his shoulders and tells them that it is their choice. Cat and the twins walk behind him as they continue on with the trek. Cat asks what is up with Murray, adding that she had never seen him so emotionally distressed before. The twins disclose that they are also expecting. Cat asks them no questions but does offer them congratulations on the good news. They all meet up at Charlie's favourite spot, and Remus and Romulus continue the chase game.

Charlie lies beside Murray, receiving what she thinks is a very long overdue tummy rub. Murray is talking away to her, telling her that he loves her as much as all his other children. He eventually notices the women arrive and sits up to give them his undivided attention. "I have done some thinking; you and Frank will be needing a new abode. The one you occupy at present will not be big enough. Do you have anything in mind?" Cat admits that they had not given it a thought yet but promises to mention it to Frank. The dogs have just returned, each with one of the multitudes of the once yellow balls that Charlie had abandoned or stashed away for future playtimes and dropping them at his feet. He is invited to play fetch. Cat takes over and throws the pair of once yellow objects as far as she can and off the brothers go, barking as much as possible at each other. Murray asks Cat, "I hope all your children are good at this game!" Cat retorts, "well, as you are going to be number one on the babysitter list, you can always train them." Murray instantly gives in and tells her, "No problem."

In their absence, Robbo has taken a brave pill and along with his ever-expanding brood, arrived at the doctors. Cora knows without being told; he guesses that it is just one of those secret woman intuition things. Cora is relieved as she had fretted endlessly about how she was going to give him the bad news that she did not want a relationship with him and she is delighted that Okolo and Alicia have laid claim to him. With the worrying part out of the way, she looks at his gnashers while the women talk about baby needs as well as baby nutrition. Okolo entertains them with the warning about tinned tomatoes, Robbo is given the ultimatum, fillings or extraction. He asks, with her experience, what is going to be the easiest and what is going to be the painless option. Much to the amusement of Alicia and Okolo, Cora informs Robbo that as she has never done this type of procedure before she cannot say for sure, nor can she guarantee any success of either option.

Robbo tells her just to take them out, and hopefully, it will not hurt. Cora asks the women present what they think, they collude then relay the message that the teeth should be preserved and they vote for fillings. Robbo asks if he is entitled to a say in this matter and they all reply no at the same time. They all can't help but laugh at his facial gestures as Cora injects, then grinds out the decayed sections. It is evident that she has done this before as she instructs her assistants to prepare the various bits and pieces required for the proposed remedial work. Robbo complains that he thinks his face is now grotesquely swollen and resolutely insists that he requires additional injections of anaesthetic. He is greeted with silence and they all laugh at him as he grips the arms of the chair as hard as possible. Almost like he is partaking on a white-knuckle ride on an imaginary vehicle. After what feels like a lifetime and some, Cora informs him that the work is complete and that the next time she hopes to have some stickers available. She also informs him that they are only awarded to star patients, under the age of ten.

Robbo now has a scarf covering his face, and the women snigger as he is still moaning about the need for some additional anaesthetic. Okolo suggests, "Maybe the next time we could ask Cora to just knock you out cold, but knowing you, you would probably want to get up and dance with the introduction of nitrous oxide into your system." Robbo swears that he wouldn't and no matter what it takes, he is not ever going to endure that level of discomfort again and they can take it from him. That if there is a next time, he is going to go with plan B, just get his dearest friend Murray to pull them all out with a pair of pliers. Okolo just says "wanker" and leads the hunt for their new abode. Robbo keeps the face covering on and wonders why none of the swamp people never once complained about the pain incurred on the path of dental rehabilitation. Then he remembered that Uno had a modified set of reclaimed dentures, Robbo was scared to ask where they originated. Tally had no teeth at all and relied on what he famously boasted was gum power. Wheels on the otherhand was the proud recipient of a dazzling smile which openly displayed the green one, a blue one and her favourite, the black one all in various stages of terminal decay.

Chapter 3

"The box, that is ours; we and our ancestors have been aware of its existence for generations. Have no fear, you will open it, do not hesitate; do not folly. It is yours by birthright and yours alone. Do not let them sway you; ignore all of their falsehoods, along with all their complete utter unadulterated pretentiousness. They are now lost beyond all hope and beyond any redemption. They have assumed that they are the righteous and that they are the chosen; Locate the key and they will suffer; they will perish forever.

"My sister, they are nearly here. Listen! Can't you hear them? Breathe! Can't you smell them? They have come much earlier than anticipated, and you and I both know that they are going to take me away from you forever. You will have no choice but to let me go and we will have to say our farewells now; if we leave it any longer, it will be too late. Take my eternal love, take my gift of life, and may you use it wisely and only when absolutely necessary. They are at the door and will not wait much longer. I am shutting down my life force, and my transference now begins. Farewell, my sister. I will always remember this moment. You must never give in to them, no matter what is presented. Whatever they offer, it will never be enough to make up for all of our indebted loss. They must perish as they have forever stained this earth that we walk upon."

The reoccurring dream had arrived again even after all of these years. For Blink, it was just as vivid as the very first time she had been subjected to the vision. It no longer freaked her out as she could now keep the voices in her head at bay. In the beginning, it would make her cry. It would make her sick, the blinding headaches confining her to a forever silent, darkened room. Her mother would have told her that she had received the same maligned message of hope and despair, just like her mother and all the ones before her. She was not the one who would provide the solution for the century's old enigma. She has not been told this; she has not been guided to reveal the true meaning. Deep down in the depths of her soul, she just knows that it is not going to be her. Blink, however, is worried about what this life had in store for her. She had suffered the same dream for as long as she could remember and it was only as her mother was passing into the next realm. That she had finally disclosed that it was infact her dream from when she was in her mother's womb just before they had extinguished her twin brothers light. Lucky had held Blink's hand firmly, told her to close her eyes, and then guided her through the story of their shared past.

My mother, your grandmother, grew up in New York and after graduating she worked at one of the big high-tech firms that had opened a new office complex in the heart of the city. In the beginning she was just one of the non-descript minions. One of the numerous blinkered desk jockeys, inputting data all day long with the multiple lines of code belonging to the various software suites that enabled the mobile phone network and all the home PCs to come alive. The company was looking for volunteers to try out as programmers. My mother was selected, and in due course, it was discovered that she was a natural. A true wizard at the ever-changing, newly evolving tech speak. In the years that followed, she worked her way up not only to be the head of the programming department but actually achieved a position on the board. It had taken many years of dedication and hard work. In that timeframe, all her friends got married. Had kids and all the other things that go with that, and she was well and truly married to her job.

By all accounts, it was just a chance meeting as they shared an elevator in a downtown firm. His eyes sparkled like stars in the winter night sky as he tried to charm her into going for a meal. She being as she was, had steadfastly refused, but he eventually coaxed her into at least going for a coffee. He took her to one of the finest establishments in the city, where he had confessed to her that it would forever torment him all the way down to the bottom of his soul that she had refused dinner. They talked endlessly and she finally gave in and agreed to accept the invitation, just on the pretext of keeping him quiet, to save him as well as his soul from suffering eternal turmoil. On returning to her office later that day, she was astounded by an enormous bunch of flowers that had been delivered to her earlier that day. The accompanying note with the seven dozen red roses just said thanks for accepting the invitation to dinner.

The tall dark stranger had swept her off her feet and the one dinner had led to many. Penny Burnette, in the space of weeks, had been to nearly every single upmarket eatery in town. When she went to these places, even though they were jam-packed, he always managed to acquire the best table available. All the other diners present, the backdrop of the ornate decorative furnishings just disappeared into the background and then faded into obscurity. She only had eyes for him and eyes for him alone. There had been many weekends away to the exotic locations and it was one of the European holidays that he had proposed. Her co-workers had noticed the new stride in her step. Her skin almost glowed, and everyone was amazed by her transition into one of the happiest employees in the building. She had been on dates before, but Penny could never remember anything remotely like this. Even her first childhood sweetheart had never encapsulated a feeling that this relationship had awakened in her. They were wed within a year, and as Penny had no living relatives, it was a very private affair. They lived in marital bliss; a nice home in the suburbs outside the city, but most of all, they were very happy.

Mr. Braithwaite, frequently had to travel overseas on business trips and there was never one day where they would not speak. He was on a trip to Ecuador, and upon reaching his destination, Martin had phoned home and checked in. He informed Penny that he would call back after the scheduled meeting. That was the last time she had ever heard from him. Penny had called and called and had only received the much-repeated message that the person they were trying to contact was on another call. Please leave a message. Penny Burnette, aka Mrs. Braithewaite, in a state of distress and desperation, had called the police department. She had only just been connected to the correct department when she heard the front door of her house being forcibly opened. The operator at the desk for non 911 calls repeatedly asked for the caller to respond to her questions. On hearing the woman scream, shortly followed by the gunfire. She immediately transferred the information onto the emergency police dispatch frequency. Over the police radio, she put out the call for shots fired and disclosed the address.

Detective Gabriella Serrano had just finished the debrief with the commissioner on the latest operation. That was firmly focused on curtailing once and for all the activities of the organised crime syndicates. She had the intention of a piping hot bath at what was already, yet another rather long and arduous day. The call over the radio had instantly broken her chain of thought and duty-bound, Detective Serrano automatically responded. Gabriella gave her a call sign, then informed control that she was in the immediate vicinity and was now on route to the location.

She had just pulled up in her vehicle and was approaching the house when the perpetrators of the alleged altercation were just exiting the premises. Detective Gabriella Serrano had just started to give them the standard warning when they immediately withdrew their weapons. As they exchanged gunfire, Gabriella had killed one of the perps, but she had also taken one to her chest.

The patrol cars had just shown up, and the other perp, knowing that the game was up, did not even wait for the officers to get out of the vehicles. He calmly put the gun to his head, pulled the trigger and blew his brains all over the sidewalk.

They had called over the network that an officer was down, informing everyone that an ambulance was urgently required. Detective Gabriella Serrano was lucky. The shot had gone straight through and although there was some damage, all her major organs were miraculously untouched. She was in pain but knew that she was not going to die, well at least not today. Lying in the ambulance, she was going in and out of consciousness and in one of her more lucid moments, she informed the paramedic attending to her. That the woman lying next to her was going to die and that her unborn child was going to die also, unless they performed an emergency c-section. The paramedic told Detective Serrano that he was not allowed to perform this operation in the vehicle and by the gunshot wound in her abdomen, it was unlikely that the baby had survived. Detective Serrano pulled out her gun and told him to check with his stethoscope and then make the call.

She had woken up in the recovery room and her colleagues from the precinct had set up a rota. To ensure that one of the team was on hand the moment she came to. Her fellow detective was pleased to see her and also very relieved to put out the call that all bets were off. Gabriella Serrano was back among the living. Gabriella was a little groggy and very thirsty. The detective asked her what she remembered about the shooting. She scratched her head and tried to recollect her recent memories. They were interrupted when the doctor appeared and started checking her over. The detective, aware that the doctor needed some space, not wanting to piss him off, left them to it and made a prompt exit.

"So how are you feeling?" Gabriella reaches for the water and tells him that she is thirsty. He checks her vitals, "You were very lucky. If the shot had been a quarter of an inch in either direction, we would not be having this conversation. You are going to be sore, and the muscles will take a few months to heal. However, apart from that, the results from the tests don't forecast any long-term side effects. I should also mention that the paramedics saved the life of the baby. I must ask; how did you know the woman was having twins?" Gabriella looks at him and asks, "What woman and what baby?"

The doctor had worked at this hospital for longer than he can remember and in all the years here, he had never known of an emergency c-section being carried out in an ambulance. The way things worked out these days with the insurance companies, the health care legal system and the various litigators specialising in suing the medical boards, it was far from the normally accepted procedures. He explains that if the paramedics had not made the call prior to drawing up in the prearranged parking lot to meet with the doctor. He as well as the paramedics would be facing quite substantial charges, most certainly involving some serious jail time. The hospital board would have incurred very heavy financial settlements via the ambulance-chasing litigators known to have stalked the hospital wards like vultures in the hope of landing a case that led to a lucrative lawsuit.

Gabriella repeated that she had no remote idea of what he was talking about. All she can recollect is the exchange of gunshots and the shiny wet sidewalk, nothing else and then waking up in here. Then, she heard her fellow detective giving the all-bets-off message to her worried colleagues at the precinct. The doctor is pleased to tell her that only to avoid the never-ending rainforest of paperwork and media attention. The paramedics had omitted the details of her drawing out her service weapon and threatening to shoot them if they did not check the pregnant woman for signs of the other infant's heartbeat. Gabriella is more than shocked that she allegedly did this and even more than shocked that she has no recollection of these events. "Hey doc, I can't remember any of this. Did the medics pump me full of drugs?" The doctor smiled, "Funny you should say that, as you had told them that you would shoot them if they even looked at a syringe!" Gabriella just said out loud that everyone reacts differently to trauma and shock.

She must have fallen asleep again. Perhaps they are secretly adding meds into her drip. Her captain is sitting in the chair and looking kind of pensive, she says hello and he passes her the container of water. "They told me that you would be thirsty when you woke up," Gabriella says thanks and slurps away, intentionally, accurately replicating noises a five-year-old would make. "Where's the flowers? I am guessing that that folder you are pretending is not here does not contain my get-well cards, so captain, why don't we just get straight to it."

"Alrighty, detective, the PIU have reviewed the statements and they are satisfied that it was a lawful shooting. With the on-scene forensics confirming that the ballistic reports all match up, they are not going to interview you. The metropolitan police board commission wanted to put you up for a civic ceremony and give you a medal." The captain stops there and confirms that he had informed them that she would point blankly refuse but he had been told to ask her anyway. Gabriella ignored the request and calmly asked for the next question.

"You will still be required to submit yourself for the psychological evaluation peer counselling and I don't need to tell you that until you get the green light, you are officially on leave." Gabriella has been through this brain-numbing process before, even though all the paperwork is correct and there are no variations in the story. She is miffed that she still has to endure a thoroughly vigorous psychological check. To ensure that she has not developed the going postal syndrome and will have to play the word association game. Plus putting up with all of the other invasive questioning to get the fit to return to duty box ticked.

"Gabriella, you have nearly twenty years in. How many times have you been injured on duty? We were lucky, you were lucky and maybe it's time for you to ask yourself the big question. You know exactly what I mean. Luck and our line of work don't exactly go hand in hand."

Gabriella asks, "So, captain, you think it is time for me to cash in my chips?"

"No, Detective Gabriella Serrano, I think that you would never be happy behind a desk and perhaps it is time to walk away from all this shit before it is too late. How many of our crew retire too late and don't last a year? Just think about all of the other available options."

The captain had left the case files for her to read, but the perps were unidentified. Their fingerprints had been chemically eradicated and their mug shots, upon being shared with all of the various law enforcement agencies, had come up a complete blank. No names, no backgrounds, almost as if they never existed in the first place. The dead woman, Penny Braithewaite, along with her missing husband were squeaky clean, not even a parking violation between them and no motive of why or how she had been murdered had ever surfaced. The crime would just end up as another statistic added on to the cold case files and it was highly unlikely ever to resurface for further investigation."

The doctor has now returned and asks how she is feeling, "just couldn't keep away, huh?" The doctor gave her a special look and then replied, "Hardly the case. At present you are our star patient and even the commissioner was calling for an update on the hour, every hour, so what do you think? I will be honest, I can't wait till you are out of here, and then you can deal with the boss. He even phoned the director of the hospital at home, so you can imagine the amount of attention you are receiving." He checks her statistics on the monitors and informs her he has to look at her stitches. She manages to sit up unaided and the wound is pronounced to be healing nicely. She is also informed that it will leave a visible scar and may itch from time to time.

Gabriella asks him about the baby, "We have named her Lucky, lucky to have survived, lucky that you were on the scene and more than lucky that the operation was carried out in time. Another five minutes and it would have been way too late." Gabriella starts to think that she is sorry that she had even asked, and the doctor, noticing her unease, asks her if she would like to see her. Gabriella asks if this is allowed. The doctor tells her that nothing about the recent arrival was normally allowed, so he can arrange a visit whenever she feels that she is up to it. Gabriella nods and informs him that she is up for it right now. She starts to manoeuvre out of bed. The doctor freaks out, "What are you doing? You are still hooked up to everything!" Gabriella hisses, "I was thinking that you, instead of bitching could unhook me and put me in a chair. If I stay in this room much longer, I think that I will go insane." The doctor realising that he will have to give in, "Okay, I will go against my better judgement and arrange a chair on the condition that on returning to your room you will behave, deal?" Gabriella, salutes "Scouts' honour."

He wheels her through the hospital in the chariot and no one gives them a second glance. The maternity unit staff just smile at the doctor as they go into the incubator room. Even though there are many infants, she knows where Lucky is situated. All of the balloons and cards sort of give it away. Lucky is fast asleep when they approach but wakes up immediately. Gabriella is smitten on seeing her for the first time and wants to take the little one in her arms. Giving her all the love that had so abruptly been taken away from her. The doctor informs her that, "She will stay here until the state orphanage system come and take her. She could be fortunate and be adopted immediately or she could end up languishing in the orphanage and then the foster care system." Gabriella knows that some of these children, through no fault of their own, don't end up with a happy ending. Lucky has not taken her eyes off her and Gabriella's heartstrings have been well and truly tugged. She wipes the tears and asks if the doctor could return her to her cell.

On returning to her room, Gabriella asks the doctor for a favour. She needs her phone and the charger, and if he could kindly dig them out for her, she promises to behave. He does what is asked and returns to his ward duty. Now with the device charging, she thinks about who she is going to call and more to the point, what she is going to say. At the first call, the commissioner does not take her call and she is put through to his voicemail service. Gabriella, knowing that there will be many, perhaps nearly a hundred messages waiting on the never-to-be-re returned call list, hangs up.

They had not supplied her with a courtesy phone in her room, but she had a brain wave and called the hospital switchboard from her mobile. Gabriella informed the operator who she was and who she wanted to contact. Not really giving them much of a choice in the matter. She had lied to them, saying that the commissioner had left a message with her captain that he wanted to speak to her as soon as she had recovered. To avert all the shit that followed, she wanted to make the call now. Unfortunately, she had lost the number and although they would be bending the rules, she asked them to help her out in her hour of need.

It had worked and after memorising the number, she called the commissioner on his private line. He picked it up after two rings. Gabriella apologised for disturbing him at this hour and not wishing to languish on the never to receive the return call list, asked him for his advice and help. She told him what she was planning and if he could somehow make the paperwork sail unhindered though the complex system, it would be greatly appreciated. He promised that he did not envisage any problems and that he would have his office look into them first thing in the morning.

The commissioner told her that he had thought that she would have come and worked for him but on the understanding that this was not really for her. He would speak to whomever it was necessary to help her out. Gabriella much relieved, thanked him and cut the call. The call to the captain was easy. She just told him that she had thought about his advice and was going to cash in her chips. In doing so she would not need to go through the psychological evaluation and as soon as he could sign her off, she was well and truly out. Sure, she would miss the guys in the department, all the teamwork, the trust and the comradery. As the captain had said, you only get lucky so many times in their line of business and no one has an exemption from dodging all the bullets. The soon-to-be ex-Detective Gabriella Serrano does not worry what she will do in the real world. She has saved some, the pension and the added in gunshot compensation will add to her funds. If she is careful, there will be no pressure to return to work. In the unlikely event that this plan fails, there are loads of companies outside that would hire her at the drop of a hat. Even though the thought of being retained as a PI or as a security consultant would bore her to tears, it was always another available option. Gabriella attempting to sleep, is thinking of the infant in the incubator who had stolen her heart. Strangely enough she never thought for one minute that she had held any maternal urges. She runs the name of Lucky Serrano through her head, almost bursting out laughing at the mobster-sounding name, and for once in what she thinks is such a long time, she goes to sleep with a smile on her face.

Gabriella is in the process of undergoing her final check-up prior to, at long last, to being finally discharged from the hospital. The doctor has finished with all the prodding, the seemingly never-ending list of questions and exercises. "Well?" The doctor replies, knowing what she is about to ask. "You can leave in the morning, and yes, you can go see Lucky before you are discharged. I am hearing that both of you are now quite attached." Gabriella admits that the baby is quite a cutie and she could talk endlessly about her all day long. "In the morning, please remember to sign the rainforest worth of paperwork prior to leaving. If not, the city's finance department will not cooperate, and my employer will give me a really hard time." The doctor confesses that she had been a perfect patient, the staff on duty in the maternity ward have been dually notified and she can go in anytime. He holds out his hand, wishes her luck, and says goodbye. He could have said so much more than that, but his pager was going off ten to the dozen and he had to leave.

She had as planned, put in her notice with the police department and had fully surrendered to the idea of cashing in her chips. She still had no real idea what she was going to do in the world outside the police department. Hopefully, the commissioner had ensured the smooth sailing, acceptance, and approval of the paperwork for adopting Lucky. Gabriella has still not received any kind of reply from the authorities in charge of the process, and fingers crossed she will be accepted. They will double-check her character references and validate that she is an upstanding, law-abiding citizen with no state or federal criminal convictions. The bank will confirm that she has sufficient funds in her account. She hopes that her squeaky-clean record and including the fact that the child has no known living relations, will be enough for the adoption approval. Gabriella looks at the huge pile of good luck cards and thinks that she will disappoint them by leaving, but although she will sorely miss them, she thinks that she has made the right decision and has no regrets.

Now in the maternity ward, Lucky has been stabilised and had now been removed from the incubator. As long as Gabriella wears the scrubs, they can touch hands and exchange private goo-goo-gaa-gaa messages. She is always close to tears when leaving and prays that they allow her to take the baby away, removed as far away as possible from the uncertain future if she was unfortunate enough to be placed into the overloaded, almost Victorian state adoption system. At last, the day has arrived and the soon to be ex-Detective Gabriella Serrano is on her way to the precinct to hand in her service-issued weapon and her badge. She is greeted to a standing ovation and after giving a short speech, jokingly detailing how much she intensely hated working with them and was forever pulling them out of the proverbial shit. Her colleagues had chipped in and presented her with the gifts. There were no secrets at the precinct, and she was very touched by the baby buggy with the added precinct emblems along with the junior uniform with her spare detective's badge attached.

After all the applause had died down, she made her way to the captain's office. He looked pleased to see her and also sad at the same time. "It's been a while since you have been here. I bet you remember the first time?" Gabriella nods, remembering in excruciating clear detail the reaming that she had received for making a mistake on her first arrest. The captain was not one for holding grudges and it was conveniently forgotten about in due time. He had soon realised that she was good honest, upstanding police officer and had promoted her then steered her through the various required regulatory exams and interviews. He hands her two packages; one is a copy of the updated case file relating to the murder of Lucky's mother. As he had gotten the heads up from the commissioner, the second package contained the recently deceased woman's personal possessions. Penny Braithwaite did not wear much in the way of jewellery and all that was in the bag was the watch and the wedding ring she had worn at the time of her untimely departure from this world. Gabriella thanked him for everything that he had done for her over the years, shook hands and exited the building for the very last time.

By the time she had arrived back at her apartment the mail man had been and gone, but he had deposited the letter that she had been waiting for what seemed like a very long time. Her adoption application had been stamped for approval. Gabriella whooped and danced in celebration, then went on a shopping spree, opening her phone and hitting all the apps that contained all the items she had looked at over the last few weeks. She phoned the commissioner, thanking him from the bottom of her heart for all the help in influencing the decision of the adoption board. He pretended that he knew absolutely nothing whatsoever about it and wished them both the best of luck in a world full of endless happiness and joy.

Gabriella and Lucky had spent most of the day watching children's movies, cartoons and what Lucky liked the most was the animal documentaries. They had a break for lunch and another break for an afternoon nap. She thought that Lucky was amazing and just loved the way her eyes almost sparkled when she opened them first thing in the morning. She wished that these days would be never-ending and last forever and ever. There was more food, more games and after a bath, it was time to read her a story before Lucky fell asleep. Gabriella would like to think that the baby liked the stories, but perhaps she only liked the sound of her voice.

The ex-detective goes through the case file, she had looked at it more times than she could count and still it did not make any sense. The perpetrators were one hundred percent untraceable, no fingerprint match. Gabriella had even contacted one of her old friends in the government agency with the famous three letters and the profilers had also come up blank. So, the bad guys as far as traceability is concerned, did not have a matching profile in any of the files connecting to all of the international law enforcement communities. Lucky's parents were more than squeaky clean. Yet somebody had wanted them taken out and had even shot Penny Braithewaite in the womb. It was almost as if their existence was to be permanently erased. The husband's background had been investigated, and he was some sort of mineralogical expert who provided technical solutions to various mining facilities all over the planet. All of the Braithwaite's belongings had been wrapped up and placed in a long-term storage unit. Through the rather expensive law firm, the sale from the house was put into a trust for Lucky to collect when she reached twenty-one years of age. The house was on the expensive side, and the firm had estimated that Lucky would inherit quite a sizeable sum. The accountants had started projecting some numbers, but Gabriella shot them down in flames and stopped the meeting before they revealed the final projected figures. She just asked them where she had to sign and who Lucky would contact at the end of the allotted timeframe. Gabriella figured that it did not matter what the final sum would be. Lucky would have much preferred to be with her parents. No sum would ever be enough to compensate for her loss, no matter how many thousands of dollars.

Gabriella looks at the watch, one of these rather expensive ones, where the manufacturer does not advertise it existence in the glossy magazines. She had looked it up online and the company only produced a limited amount per year. The timepiece was self-winding, self-adjusting and was guaranteed for life. The price was unavailable on the company's web site and could only be disclosed through a nominated law firm in Switzerland. She twiddles it about in her hand. The dial contained everything; it would tell you the current altitude above sea level and if you wanted to go under the water, it would tell you the depth in fathoms. All this information was tried and tested to allegedly being ninety-nine-point-nine percent accurate. On the other hand; Gabriella's watch could tell you the time and if you wanted anything changed, you would have to take it to a shop; where they had the proper tools or someone with really small fingers. Gabriella is still perplexed with the demise of Lucky's mother and when the baby was fast asleep, she would go over the notes, time and time again.

It did not lead her to any foregone conclusions and only ended up with the usual unanswerable questions as to who and more importantly, why. No one had come forward to claim the bodies of the perpetrators and as per the rules of the state they were cremated and their ashes were scattered. In days of old they would have been buried in an unmarked grave but due to the lack of available space and the incurred expenditure. It was viewed as being more environmentally friendly as well as cheaper just to incinerate them. Gabriella would have loved to have questioned them, but that was the strangest fact in the case. Rather than being captured and subsequently questioned the perp had topped himself without any hesitation. She knows for sure that the hit was sanctioned and wonders what the future has in store for her and the child. She holds the watch in her hand as she was looking at the pictures along with the short bio. Gabriella turned the exquisite timepiece about, and it was only then that she noticed the inscription and the numbers on the watch case.

Chapter 4

Now, in the rather ornate surroundings of Buckingham Palace, Lesqueth has summoned Olga. At the breakfast meeting, the Baroness of Kindeace-Shire listened to all of the disclosed details as she reviewed the complimentary paperwork. Olga has just revealed the latest number of infants now being cared for and nourished while they are undergoing subliminal processing during the indoctrination program. That will ultimately produce Lesqueths' envisioned future generation. She notices that Olga is looking at the item at the end of the table. Which under the artificial light, the woman in the transparent plastic coating just stares right through them. "That's what used to be the Prime Minister, taking her former position into careful consideration. I like to keep her in the loop with all of our current projects. She does not offer much in the way of a reply, but I think that it is the thought that counts. Also, I quite like the fact that, even after being removed from the hanging tree, she still managed to retain that once famous stern, disapproving glare. The dried skin and withdrawn look of death just add to her character. I think she would have been rather pleased with the results." Lesqueth points, "the gentlemen you see hanging from the rafters are the handymen who took rather a long time to complete what I really considered to be quite a simple task. It is just as well that they had trained others to carry out their job, otherwise they would start to stink the place out. In the future, you will see the results of their handy work, as it is my intention to get a couple of corpses to undergo the plastic coating to represent the ex-king and queen in all their finery."

The Baroness of Kindeace-Shire is now on a roll and continues. "It is a dreadful pity that we were unable to locate all of the last elected parliament. Just think how the House of Commons would look like with all of the now sterilised figures. Personally, I think that it would be really hard to tell the difference, well that is apart from the noticeably absent sixth-year school boy humour. I really don't think that the general public would actually be able to differentiate between the plastic-coated ones or the real ones. Olga, add this on to your list, bodies required to occupy the House of Commons, and please note that the speaker's chair is already occupied."

Now that the breakfast meeting is over, Lesqueth wishes to review the updated exhibits. She still can't resist pretending to be a commoner and in a fake accent, announces to the driver, "British Museum, Great Russel Street, gov." Olga smiles and pretends that it is slightly amusing, but in reality, she is now without a doubt, utterly convinced that her new boss is as much of a complete psychopath, perhaps even more deranged than her old boss, General Vladimir Miasnikov. On attending these morning meetings, lately she has been thinking that one of these days, she will be getting served with the axe rather than being offered the morning meal.

The keeper of the records, almost by magic, is at the door to greet them as the vehicle draws to a halt. He appears to be attempting to break his back in attempting to bow to the esteemed leader as she approaches. Lesqueth notices that it is not the same one as last time. Even though he is wrapped up in the same white-upon-white hooded cloak, she can still tell the difference. She wonders if Olga had put that in the report and informed her of Vort's recent demise, the previous holder of the title, along with the update that the reigns of leadership had now been passed over to the equally repugnant Tesporo. Lesqueth never said anything about the change and as long as all she has asked is being carried out there will be no problems. Later, when she is home, the paperwork will be cross-checked for any omissions, spelling mistakes and discrepancies. Olga up till now, had made no mistakes and she carried out all her tasks without fail. Alas, one error will inevitably lead to another. Based on the experience she gained in the past; it is better and much quicker to replace than to retrain. Lesqueth thinks it will be very disappointing to eradicate her as she had shown so much promise and dedication in the beginning. So much so, that Lesqueth had been thinking about promoting her again. "Oh well, some things are not meant to last," she mutters to herself and directs Tesporo to show her the recent upgrades.

The keeper of the records glides across the recently polished floor, almost as if a noiseless wheeled device had replaced his legs. Tesporo is surrounded by his assistants. Who are carrying pierced metal orbs that give off the sweet fragrance of incense. The swarm of acolytes are engaged in the process of desperately trying to mask the ever-present smell of decay associated with the brotherhood. A small bell chimes and one of Tesporos' assistants walks forward with the rather large pair of scissors for Lesqueth to cut ornate rope that once severed, will open the path into the new exhibits. Lesqueth listens to the speech about how their race will prosper and overcome all obstacles in fruition of the great plan laid out by their ancestors. Lesqueth gets impatient, cuts him off mid-sentence then walks forward to review the latest offerings. She presses the start button to bring the audio-visual presentation into being. As the screen gradually comes to life. Lesqueth wonders on the fact that although the brotherhood is firmly set in the much-practiced ways of the ancients. They have still managed to grasp the modern technological advances that are currently available. A deep voice booms out of the hidden speakers, curtailing the inquisitive chain of thought. She watches with avid interest as the presentation starts to unfold onto the huge, somewhat oversized display unit.

The majestic ocean liner had one thousand nine hundred and forty-two souls onboard; quite rightly so, the lower tiers of the nine decks contained the working class. Whom the captain vehemently had wanted nothing to do with. He had more than enough ex-Royal Navy men within his crew of eight hundred and fifty men. To take care of the riff-raff should they decide to advance to any of the decks above their station. The middle level he thought were presumptuous upstarts, all four hundred and sixty-seven of them. Who had thought that with a little money, along with all of the pseudo-posh voices they could be treated like royalty. They could try all they wanted but they were not going to be allowed anywhere near the upper class on the first-class section. The five hundred-odd blue-blooded thoroughbreds wanted nothing to do with the lower classes aboard the ship nor in everyday life. Some of them were genuinely bewildered at why they were given the vote never mind being allowed to breed without a valid state permit. The captain was proud of his vessel, it had left New York on the first of May and could travel at twenty-five knots all day. This was the thirty-two thousand ton, five-funnelled ship that provided untold luxury to those who could afford it and could carry more passengers than most of the other vessels of that era. The company had fought and won the transatlantic crossing competition with the help of the Admiralty who had aided with the design and with some cash to offset some of the building costs.

The UK had declared the North Sea a war zone in the autumn of 1914. The Royal Navy proceeded to blockade the German ports with the sole intention of denying access to any nation involved in exporting any materials that could be used to enhance the German war effort. On February of the following year, Germany replied to this by announcing that they were going to conduct unrestricted warfare on the ocean waves. They had placed adverts in several international newspapers warning that merchant ships carrying material to aid the UK and its allies' war effort were now legitimate targets. It was during this time that the great game was being played out in earnest. The major nations involved truly appreciated that public opinion could be manipulated and easily coerced into believing everything and anything that was printed in the tabloid press. The captain would be more than happy when this voyage was over. First of all, there was the continuous daily press reports informing the sea-going community along with the general population of the danger of the iron sharks patrolling the sea. Then there was the admiralty telling him every single day that there was nothing at all to fear and they had it on reasonably good terms that the Germans would not attack a cruise liner of this pedigree and status.

They had been traveling for six days, and thankfully, this journey was nearly over. Tomorrow they would be in Liverpool where they could get everything unloaded. The captain would be especially delighted to get rid of, once and for all the passenger in the private luxurious state room who had not once left his room nor allowed anyone to enter. Although he had paid in full and by all accounts, he had been more than a generous tipper. The captain had thought that without any doubt. Several other senior members of his staff had been given fairly large sums. To get his elusive cargo loaded discreetly into his room. He still did not like him or the fact that his secret cargo was onboard.

Lesqueth's grandfather Reginald Bretton had gotten wind that several of the American families had aspirations on global domination. In their growing relationship, they had started exchanging ideas on establishing a new world order. The Kunupenny family had money and influence among their many friends as well as numerous supporters. One of the innovators of mass production, allegedly by all accounts, was one hundred percent in favour of a new world order. He had volunteered to supply them with all his ideas along with tried and tested methods of increasing production on a massive scale. The Kunupenny clan was more than aware of the great game underway in Europe and with that in mind. They had surreptitiously contacted their German counterparts to offer them advanced ideas to enhance their war effort. The Germans had accepted this proposal with open arms and stipulated that the information must be passed through their embassy in Madrid. To keep the proposed industrial advancements far enough away from the prying eyes of the British intelligence service. Along with their ever-growing network of clandestine operators. Who seemed to have numerous eyes and ears in every port as well as every city on the planet.

The Spanish families who were and had been for hundreds of years been cold-shouldered by the Valaron Inner Council for their foray into South America. Where their conquistadors had plundered, pillaged and removed anything that stood in their way.

The roving bands had been totally ruthless in their quest for the yellow metal. As they had subsequently destroyed everything on their path. They had rather enthusiastically eradicated several of the old Valaron families without permission. The Spanish families that were ostracised, were now desperate to be allowed back to the big table. They had approached Reginald Bretton in the hope of reconciliation and forgiveness for all of their past crimes. Hoping that this gesture on their behalf would pave the way forward for redemption. The German embassy was bugged, giving them unparalleled access to all the codes used in the transmission and receiving of the allegedly clandestine diplomatic and military messages. Reginald Bretton was on his way to see the current chairman of the ocean-going company. He had made the introductions when they had needed help to win the transatlantic race. Without his timely intervention and money, they would have lost to their French and German competitors.

The ocean liner received a coded message and the captain on being notified on its arrival goes immediately to his cabin to decipher it. His instructions are to continue as normal. He is to ignore the warnings, given the route and speed at that which he is to adhere to. The Bretton family's main business was in mining and steel manufacturing in the years leading up to World War one. He had branched out and now had major share interests in several shipyards. Being the pride and joy of the British Empire, the navy envisaged great sea battles with the German navy who were also massively building up their fleet. Reginald Bretton had enough influence in the ruling parties and the various government departments to win the contracts in building prototypes and the building of the advanced submarine research facility. His group had designed every submarine of that era. These were allocated to other shipyards to be built and commissioned, even though it was his company that had initiated the general concept.

Submarines were at an early stage in their development and it was not that long ago. That every maiden voyage was almost cursed, of an almost guarantee that the crew who manned her were going to be claimed by the ocean. Over the proceeding years, things had gradually improved and life expectancy had increased. The F-seven-type submarine was a nightmare on the surface, but her teardrop-shaped hull was an innovation in manoeuvrability under the water. The Admiralty was under the impression that the prototype F-Seven E54381A had sunk and all her crew had perished. On receiving messages that the Germans wanted to expand, to have more than just an empire and were intent in achieving global domination. Reginald Bretton had taken evasive action and the prototype that was reported to have inadvertently sank without trace during the sea trials was selected for a secret mission.

The Valaron Inner Council had warned him at the meetings of the unstoppable rise of the German war machine. He suspected that many bribes had been presented, concessions and untold promises had been offered, then accepted. Reginald Bretton has no intention of letting this ever happen. The German families had been less than supportive in his families struggles throughout the preceding centuries. He declared an open season on their overseas activities, eliminating their spy networks and the associated sycophantic allies who hung onto their shirt-tails. He now had the mechanism in place to throw an enormous spanner in the works and curb their unwarranted expansion. The F-Seven E54381A had been recovered and was now in one of the shipyards on the river Clyde.

The communist party held great sway over the Trade Union which had the ability to surreptitiously close the whole area down overnight. Reginald Bretton had covertly met with the leaders several times. The first one was in a grotty little pub where they had tested his mettle against a couple of their enforcers. After he had laid them out cold, their leaders agreed to discuss what he wanted. Reginald Bretton had given them the deal of the century and at the end of the day, money talked. Even the ardent communists and trade union officials had more than a fondness for hard cash. He was not interested in the petty political squabbles between the two movements vying for the title of the great party for the people. He knew at the end of the day; all of the people would suffer no matter who won. Reginald Bretton hoped and prayed that both of them would eventually perish into the pages of history.

He offered money to be donated to the party and made the bold initiative of paying all their bona fide card-carrying members money behind the book. This was to be paid every week in cash on top of the meagre wages that they toiled for every week. In this bold move, he could never be traced and if it was ever discovered they would receive all the blame. He did not like the trade union officials and he was more than positive that they did not particularly like him but at the end of the day money is money. The modifications were carried out in relative secrecy. Of course, Reginald Bretton knew that the details would eventually make their way back to Moscow. It did not make any difference as the dead cannot talk and they would never be able to prove his involvement.

The captain was on the bridge. He had just instructed the helmsman not to bother with the zigzag course previously used in this sector of the ocean. This area had recently been used as a playground for the newly instigated German submarine group intent on avenging the blockade of their ports by the British navy. To avoid any unnecessary attention, they did not fly any flags declaring their sovereignty and had the ship repainted in non-company colours even hoping to disguise the five funnels that acted as the primary identification at distances. He checked the course, speed and then filled in the ship's logbook.

In the North Sea, the converted bulk carrier had just opened the moon bay doors and as the huge compartment had flooded. The captain had ordered a full stop and then waited until he had received the all-clear signal from his opposite number in the recently modified F-Seven E54381A submarine. The previous night the combined crews had received a huge banquet and the company had provided copious amounts of free alcohol. The finest wines, champagnes, and whiskies were all available. The sailors being sailors, had drunk most of what was on offer. There had been a few sore heads the following morning but the captains were well used to this aspect of heavy drinkers, having been surrounded by them for most of their working lives. They had set aside enough to ensure that the hair of the dog was freely available to all who wanted it and to all that required it. The captains shook hands, and the submarine crew descended the stairs into the moon pool and climbed into their vessel. The two captains had stood at attention and saluted them all. Before entering the stairwell, the men stood at attention and saluted back; nothing was said, not one single word was spoken.

Now that F-Seven E54381A was underwater, the air was already starting to turn bad. The captain imagined that the confined atmosphere would be putrid after several days in this steel coffin. No amount of aftershave or perfume would disperse the smell of pish, shit or the fumes coming from the engines into the confined space that he and his crew now inhabit. The converted merchant ship is now moving south by southeast on the predetermined course. The captain, watching it through the crude periscope, calls for loading the newly added and installed stern tube. He receives the callback, through the shouting in one compartment that repeated and then carried all the way through to him in the control room that the fish is now armed and ready. He nods, tells them to fire then presses the button on his stopwatch and watches intently as the second hand slowly moves forward.

At the appointed time, the captain of the converted merchant ship shakes the hand of the helmsman and tells him that it has been a pleasure, an absolute pleasure working with him and shoots him in the head. All the men, apart from the stokers and the engine room personnel, had been given the command to bunk up. As the torpedo hits the predesigned weak spot, the ship starts to sink immediately and the captain goes down with his ship. There are no lifeboats and therefore there will be definitely no survivors to tell the tale. The captain of the submarine having witnessed their demise through the crude periscope salutes his opposite number and the crew. He then plots the course changes for the rendezvous with the ocean liner on route from New York. He has plenty of time to spare and will be in a position ready to carry out his orders. He knows his and all of the crew's names will be added to the fallen but that is far better than being added to the forgotten or the vanquished.

Several hours later, they lie in wait approximately eleven miles off the coast of southern Ireland. On the seventh of May at twelve minutes passed fourteen hundred hours, the F-Seven E54381A launched a self-propelled torpedo. The eighteen-inch fish is the latest in submarine warfare. The hydrostatic vale and the pendulum system operate in synchronised movements, keeping the depth constant. The newly acquired gyroscope orchestrates, then continues to stabilise the fish, ensuring the direction is maintained. The torpedo explodes on the starboard side, causing damage to the structure as well as punching a hole in the steel hull. The ensuing fire had quickly spread into the cargo hold. The munitions onboard ignited as did the boxes of unlisted gun cotton. This caused the also unlisted four thousand three hundred and seventy-eight and a half boxes of three-inch shells to explode. Twenty minutes later, the ocean liner, one of the largest ships ever to be built by a shipyard in Scotland, was lying on the seabed three hundred and twenty-seven feet below the surface. Just like most liners of the day, they did not have enough lifeboats to save all the passengers. One thousand one hundred souls perished on entering the cold, murky depths. The captain did the honourable thing and as per the rules governing captaincy, he stayed onboard and was witnessed sitting on a deckchair, reading his favorite book as the ship sank. He was very unhappy at being rescued and although he had carried out his duty to the letter, saving many souls. He still felt it was his unquestionable obligation to go down with the ship.

The captain of the F-Seven E54381A submarine moved a further two miles south; he had called a meeting with his entire crew. "Gentlemen, sailing with you has been an absolute privilege and honour." Saluting his crew, he pressed the self-destruct button and the modified F-Seven E54381A exploded, then sunk to the depths of the Atlantic to join their drowned comrades of the merchant ship in the pages of the fallen.

The Spanish, on their promise and now obligated under the recent agreement with Reginald Bretton, had issued a telegram allegedly sent from the German embassy in Madrid declaring responsibility for the sinking of the ocean liner. The wire was inadvertently released worldwide to all the news agencies. The embassies in Washington, London and Berlin were now frantically sending ambassadors to and from the various ministers and secretaries of state, issuing denials and threats of acts of war for breaching the maritime code of conduct. The German Grand Admiral knew that his imperial navy had not done it, and because of the illicit tampered with cargo that would have aided their war effort was on that ship. He also knew who must have found out about it and he also realised that he was in no position to deny it. He had to find a way out of the political storm that was heading his way. The British Government had offered the cargo manifest via the registered ocean-going company. They were issuing a state of absolute denial that they were pleading not guilty to carrying any munitions to aid the war effort on the western front. He knew that this was not true and they also knew that if they had admitted it. Then carrying munitions and flying under a false flag were a direct breach of the maritime code. Thus, Germany would have been fully justified in carrying out the attack. This covert action was nothing but a ploy to get America into the war. As the international press was coercing the general population into believing that the German imperial navy had cold-heartedly murdered many innocent civilians in an absolutely outrageous cowardly attack.

The German high command was now also aware that the embassy in Madrid was now seriously compromised and had immediately sent some of their best investigators to find out who was really responsible. The British were still vehemently denying any wrong doing and were still in the process of putting in pages of lies upon lies into all of the British and other international newspaper agencies that would print them. They were adamantly declaring their absolute innocence and making out that the Germans were nothing more than cowards killing innocent civilians. The head of the high command pressurised his connections in Germany and after transferring a substantial amount of cash the Kunupenny family. They had persuaded a previously German-owned armaments company to publish a list of what they had shipped onboard the ocean liner. The list included the items that the British had somehow managed to forget to include in their previously published list. The tons of gun cotton used for propellant for long-range artillery, tons of three-inch shells and the four million two hundred thousand rifle cartridges for exclusive use on the front lines. Not one country further questioned the justification of the alleged German sinking, but the American newspapers had not forgotten their fellow countrymen who had been onboard. The media war intensified with the Great Britain feeding lies to its media outlets in the States every single week and keeping the public in a state of absolute outrage. The various senators and governors who wanted to be reselected would eventually raise this in Washington, and all of them knew that war equals money. The last thing that the Grand Admiral and his cohorts wanted was the United States with its massive industrial machine to enter the war.

Reginald Bretton kept to his deal with the communist trade union officials. As far as any member of the British government was concerned, he was doing an upstanding job for his King and country. He had subsequently arranged for the disappearance of all the shipyard workers, including the union officials involved and over a short period of time they were all quietly eliminated. Not one of them was listed as a murder, car accidents, pre-mature deaths due to chronic alcoholism and accidental deaths were fairly common in the industry that they were employed in. The authorities, albeit with an anonymous cash incentive, never investigated any one of the fatalities. The grotty little pub where the first meeting was held in was bought over by one of his untraceable companies. Two weeks later it had been mysteriously destroyed by a fire, the building was then demolished and the site lies overgrown and undeveloped to this day.

Lesqueth nodded her approval and wanted to escape the fetid smell of the brotherhood. The Baroness informed Tesporo that he had done a splendid job, an absolutely splendid job. She had especially liked the fact that his team had accurately reproduced then displayed the appropriate pages from the fallen, the vanquished and the forgotten. Tesporo could not help but notice that their esteemed leader for once is rather pleased, almost joyous. Asks for permission to speak on what is perhaps a delicate subject. Lesqueth pretends to look at the non-existent watch on her wrist and asks him to proceed.

"As you are aware, my predecessor, the late and the sadly lamented Vort is now being prepared for burial and the brotherhood would like to intern him in a manner fitting for our sect." Lesqueth waits patiently on what is to follow. Tesporo pauses then adds, "We would like to give him the proper send off into the new world with an ancient forgotten tradition, although it has been banned for several centuries. We therefore seek your permission to bring this practice back into the fold and bury him with the full honours once bestowed on the ancient keeper of the records." Lesqueth did not particularly wish to share any more oxygen with the creepy Tesporo and his now rancid-smelling brotherhood. Agrees without hearing any of the details and instructs him to deliver the requirements to her office.

She turns her back on him and exits the building. "Olga, before we have to sit through their next performance, issue them with a time limit for the presentation. I think that ten minutes will be more than ample for my nostrils." Olga takes the notes and thinks that the keeper of the records should have been permanently forgotten about and left to perish on the home planet. She for one, had never ever figured out what they do apart from muttering mumbo jumbo phrases that no one can ever hope to remotely understand.

On returning to Buckingham Palace Lesqueth, summons the footman to organise lunch for one and Olga sits as Lesqueth scrutinises the paperwork. She is reviewing the activities of the white-upon-white to ensure that Olga had indeed included the details on the demise of Vort and his replacement Tesporo. Lesqueth with the axe always seated next to her, picks away at her lunch and slowly scans the reports in front of her. Olga has no idea what her boss is hoping to find and thinks that the time has finally arrived to terminate her current employment. As much as she wanted to, she will not be permitted to leave gracefully in declaring her intention of resigning. Her severance payment would equate to a bullet in the head. Olga will just have to try and escape at the first available opportunity. Lesqueth eventually finds the details she was searching for and is disappointed that she had overlooked the prize details and will not be axing Olga afterall. Her assistant had crossed all the T's, dotted all the I's, and omitted nothing from the report. Lesqueth dismisses Olga with a wave or her hand; now that she is gone, she thinks of a suitable replacement.

Chapter 5

Miasnikov had finally received the news that all his troops are ready to roll and are now finally about to embark on the route to Hull. As he knows nothing about the place, he had tasked Anna to ask about it and all she could tell him that, by all accounts, it was just another run-down outpost on the north east coast. It had taken several months of work to clear a path throughout all of the jammed-up roads. After being on the road for so long, General Vladimir Miasnikov is looking forward to a decent hotel or a nice stately home to base his headquarters in. Anna's main task is to keep Miasnikov supplied with copious amounts of vodka. Through trial and error, she is aware of what brands he will accept. It had taken a while to get it right. As she had correctly assumed that the ones he used to chuck at her and anyone else in the nearby vicinity were not quite suitable for his exquisite pallet or refined tastes. They are nearly there. The sign in front of them states that it is only fourteen miles away. Anna wished that the sign had stated that the location was fourteen light years away and dreads what this monster is going to think of next. She was a soldier, a highly trained combat veteran and was truly sick and tired of rounding up hapless civilians. Then torturing them just for the entertainment of her hard-to-please boss.

She had thought about it many times, of abandoning her post and driving away into the sunset. Anyplace would do, anywhere at all just to get away from this endless madness. Anna had no idea where she would go, but she would undeniably depart. Her biggest fear is what will happen when her boss eventually runs out of defenceless civilians to kill. The convoy rolls into Hull, where Miasnikov has assembled all sorts of equipment to enable him to plan for any battle. He doubts that he will be able to engage the self-propelled guns, artillery and all of the tanks into the textbook battlefield scenarios they were designed for. In his drunken state he thinks, that perhaps this time, the locals will have organised an army to come and face him so that both parties can engage in a real fight. On this epic journey up north, he has seen no one person, and not one shot has been fired. He hopes that JJ has had better luck. Miasnikov had been told that Wales was just the exact same as Scotland. That contained nothing but lots of sheep and that both countries had once contained a nationalistic population. They wanted independence from all and everything, including themselves.

Now in the city centre, Miasnikov orders a halt at the civic hall. He requests that Anna send the troopers forward to check that the building is secure, then he wants his special suite prepared on the top floor with a panoramic view of the area. Anna does not argue. She could have told him that there are bound to be some nice hotels in the area, but as he frequently refuses to listen, why should she bother. Miasnikov was only in the place for one night and after all the work that his troopers had carried out to make it habitable. He had announced that all of a sudden, the substandard building should now be used for tank practice. Vladimir now insists that he is required to go to a decent hotel. Anna takes notes of his latest wish list and then sets off to carry out his bidding. There are not too many stairs, a vodka bar on the same floor, plush interiors, and possible entertainment facilities. Miasnikov puts the tanks to work as they demolish the once pride and joy of the city. By the time Anna had returned, the grade two listed building is now nothing but a smouldering ruin, but at least for the moment, Miasnikov is happy. She stands at attention and then delivers her report on his accommodation request. He nods and then tells her that she had done a splendid job. She thanks him, knowing full well that after the next bottle of vodka, he could very well be cursing her, then ordering her immediate execution.

Taking a deep breath, she shows him around his new dwelling and praises the gods that he seems quite content for now. Vladimir follows her around, nodding with satisfaction at the well-stocked bar. He is impressed with the full regulation-sized snooker table. Miasnikov crouches down and surveys the pockets from all of the various angles. Anna is not clear on what his current thinking could be devising for the future. She doubts very much that it is anything remotely connected with sponsoring a tournament with all the top local players. He had picked up the brochure on entering the premises, now seated at the bar, he quickly flicked through the contents. Anna shows him the bottle of the once unbelievable-expensive imported ultra-grade vodka allegedly contained within a handblown diamond-encrusted bottle. Miasnikov peruses the small information booklet and then asks her if she has possession of the other two hundred and forty-nine bottles. Anna tells the truth, admitting that she does not. His adjutant admits that she has some of them and will add the task of searching for the rest of the specified brand as his troopers ransack the city, rounding up any survivors. Miasnikov opens the bottle and then throws away the equally expensive diamond-encrusted cap. Anna pours him the required four-fingered measure into the crystal glass. He slurps away, almost casually mentioning that he is quite interested in the activities advertised in the hotel brochure. He mentions that if she was to locate the previous event manager's office, she could conduct a search for more information. It could be possible that they could most likely be hosting their own events pretty soon. Anna knows for a fact that he is not talking about the hen party and the advertised wedding reception functions but the other events that were listed on a different part of the brochure. "Anna, consider this, to be your next task and tell the engineering team I wish to see them first thing in the morning."

In the city known as Hull, Miasnikov had been busy. All the roads leading north have now all been blocked off, with numerous manned checkpoints installed. His troopers are rounding up the people who were not smart enough nor lucky enough to evade being captured. There have been sporadic reports involving the exchange of gunfire. These are just isolated incidents occurring with looters along with householders who had adamantly refused to surrender. The unfortunate looters who were captured alive are now hanging, swaying gently in the breeze, firmly affixed to various lamp-posts and inner-city bridges affixed with a sign blatantly advertising their alleged crimes against society.

Anna had found the details that Miasnikov had required from the event manager's office. She is now having been issued with a new set of instructions, currently on a tour of the city collecting all the said items that he has suddenly developed an avid interest in. She has been ordered to report back to him every evening to present the artifacts discovered during that day's search in sealed boxes. Anna thinks that this reminds her of an excited little boy discovering that Santa had secretly visited during the night and had stashed some presents under the tree. As the items build up, she still has the unnerving feeling that this will not finish with a happy ending for any or all of the intended participants. For the time being she can relax as she had still not been invited to attend the yet-to-be-planned event. The mechanics have been busy for days on end, and the downstairs bar has been declared out of bounds for all and everyone until further notice. She thinks that major alterations are underway, as the groups involved in the secretive work have been toiling on the project night and day. Anna did not even look at what they were preparing but the continuous noise of the construction work in progress echoes twenty-four-seven throughout the hotel.

Lesqueth had just received a message. The footman cautiously approached, not taking his eyes off the axe beside her. He had quickly put the letter on the table. Then he had stepped back immediately. She pulled out her knife then intently staring at him. The Baroness slid the blade in, then in a quick flash, her razor-sharp implement sliced through the paper. The contents disclose the current keeper of the records request for the internment of his predecessor, the equally smelly and perhaps the even more repulsive Vort. The Baroness of Kindeace-Shire wonders where the hell, they got their names from. She thinks of a now-defunct TV show where the contestants sometimes asked nicely for a mystery selection of vowels and consonants. Then on receiving their allocated allowance, they would proceed in attempting to try and assemble a normal-sounding word. Perhaps the brotherhood has changed the concept of the original game rules and has now involved the use of a Ouija board to find new odd-sounding names.

Tesporo had submitted the request, which on a closer inspection, looked like it had been originally written in blood. The somewhat now faded, once crimson red was now a pastel pinkish colour. The way-over-the-top calligraphy asked for the bestowed blessing of twenty-seven reasonably fit and healthy prisoners to accompany Vort into the afterlife. The detailed drawing, requiring her stamp of approval, included a prisoner placement plan in the crypt as well as all the materials required. Lesqueth summoned her scribe and then sent the footman to retrieve Olga. The keeper of the records had his plan stamped for acceptance and just as the scribe had finished transferring the Baroness of Kindeace-Shires' notes onto the paper Olga had appeared.

The note is now sealed with the wax stamp displaying the mythical creature grasping the flaming earth in its talons. Is passed over to Olga, who was informed that it had to be hand-delivered by her, to Miasnikov immediately. Olga saluted and then left the building. There was no detailed map supplied to reveal his current location. She was expected to perform as the resident clairvoyant and somehow guess which direction to travel in. She arrived at the motor pool and then showed the people in charge her recent order. They had hummed and hawed about the lack of supporting paperwork to enable them to issue her with one of the approved vehicles. Their decision was only rescinded when Olga had half-heartedly suggested that perhaps they would like to go and question their esteemed leader for the relevant documents that they gave in and allocated her a set of wheels.

It was quite an ugly machine, but they informed her that it should be able to deliver her to Hull. "Don't let it run on fumes before you fill it, otherwise it will suck in the scum in the bottom of the tank and will leave you stranded." Olga thanked them for the latest info. She had a quick look at the grubby map that had been in place for at least a decade to see where the fuck Hull was actually situated within the UK. The machine started the first time, then she set off, looking for the sign that indicated where to turn to lead her to the north east. Still not sure of what road numbers will take her to her final destination. Olga hopes to find a motorway shop that had not been destroyed completely. That would furnish her with a book of roadmaps that would hopefully enable her to figure out the correct direction. Olga suspected that for some reason, she had fallen out of favour with her boss as well as furnishing her with the suspicion that the letter she was delivering contained details about her future. She is sorely tempted to rip it open and then just vanish into the sunset but perhaps she is just being paranoid and the contents contained within could just be related to nothing that concerned her. Putting her survival instincts to the side, Olga concentrated on the road ahead.

As the vehicle travels out of the city, she can see some of the impending results of Lesqueth's along with Miasnikov's troopers influence on the surrounding area. In some streets, there is an almost continual display of skeletal remains of former workers or just normal people apprehended while trying to evade being captured. These are either nailed to trees or displayed in groups, lining the once pretty, neat wooden-fenced street. The now-tattered, wind and weather-beaten attire gives the illusion of clothes hanging out to dry in the distance. It is only when Olga gets closer that she realises that it is actually people. The saddest scene that she had come across was the strangely named street. The huge sign had proclaimed that it was the Avenue of Forgiveness and Redemption. Impaled figures occupied this whole stretch, all of them slumped over in grotesque figurine-shaped poses depicting their final moments.

Olga had thought at first that there must have been some very small people living in this area. It was a total shock, when it finally registered in her brain that her fellow combatants had impaled men, women and children. She had to pull over and instantly eject the contents of her stomach. This was not the deal she had signed up for. Olga wonders if this madness and seemingly never-ending cruelty had now totally immersed itself in all of her species. She eventually pulls herself together, and then after another few miles, she pulls over. On purpose Olga had dumped her weapons on the back seat. If any of the survivors had approached her, she would have gladly embraced and welcomed death with open arms as an apt just reward for her species' unforgivable sins.

On finally reaching Hull, she immediately thought that it was a shithole just like every other dull and dreary city in the UK. The human population may have diminished here, but by the sound of the screeching overhead. The seagull numbers must have increased exponentially. Avoiding the regular bombardment of shit descending like rain from above, Olga pulls up at the checkpoint. The guards saluted her, noticing her unease at the flying rats above them. They blast away with their machine guns, slightly reducing the number of them. Seemingly satisfied with the initial outcome they direct Olga where to find headquarters. A few of the wounded birds flap about on the road, indiscriminately squawking at anyone who would listen then suddenly become very quiet as she runs, accidentally on purpose, right over the top of them.

Anna is at the entrance of the hotel; she delivers a brief salute then a warm handshake to welcome her to the northern frontier. They had known each other for a very long time, both having served as combat soldiers in several of the same campaigns in what now seemed like, they belonged to another lifetime. The pair of them had been involved in fighting guerrilla groups and armed militias who had actually fired back. On one occasion they had been ambushed. If it had not been for Olga taking control of the dire situation when their commanding officer had dithered and made bad choices, they would not be alive today.

She has been tasked with yet another errand as well as receiving the usual standard warning that this was very urgent. Miasnikov has been drinking most of the day and has come up with another one of his hair-brained schemes to terrorise the hapless population. Olga joins her in the vehicle, and when they are out of everyone's earshot, she asks her how she is and if she is still enjoying her posting. There are no secret listening devices in play here, not like the old days when even the toilets were bugged in the hope of collecting subversive conversations. Anna informs her that she would not believe the stories of what the butcher has been up to, even if she had told her. "You will see soon enough for yourself. Then you can tell me afterwards what you think." Anna had never been one to speak out or complain, even in private moments but Olga senses a state of unease with her long-lost friend.

Stopping off at the nearest hardware shop, Olga is amazed that it had not been ransacked and looted. Anna just said that the premises were not touched as they contained no alcohol nor any pharmaceuticals. She produces the shopping list and they walk among the wares on display, selecting the items contained within the latest wish list. Once they loaded the bags into the vehicle, they drove around until she found one of the duty sergeants. He utters a complaint, protesting, "I don't have the items that are on your urgent request list." Anna tells him to be patient then delves into the bags to produce a couple of hacksaws and several packets of replacement blades. She hands them over with the choice words, "modification and alteration, as soon as possible, please." The Sergeant shouts out a command, a couple of troopers appear and they quick-time it to carry out the issued orders. The women stay quiet and smoke some of the disgusting English cigarettes while they await on the delivery of the package.

Olga accompanies Anna as they report to Miasnikov, he is handed the communication that bears Lesqueth's family seal. He places it unopened on the table. The general is far more interested in the bags of goodies that Anna has just delivered. Miasnikov shouts for the mechanics, informing them that he wishes to play a good old-fashioned game of English snooker within the hour. He warns them that there will be no permissible delays along with no deviations to his plans. The foremen of the craftsmen assigned to this project did not look him in the eye when he was delivering his speech. With the attributes of an accomplished thespian, the general tells them exactly what is required and with the nodding of their heads in blind obedience. They all know that the quicker they get out of his presence, the better it will be for all of them. The foremen can vividly recall the incidents where their esteemed leader had instantly lost the plot and then eliminated workers for no apparent reason.

The workers were delighted and over the moon at still being alive. They set about to accomplish his latest whim with the utmost efficiency, fully aware that failure is not a valid option. Vladimir looks at the clock on the wall and even though it does not work, he declares that they should adjourn to the snooker room. The urgent letter still lies unopened on the table, for now, as he has much more urgent tasks to attend to. The snooker table has been adapted as per his explicit instructions. He shakes the foremen by the hand, congratulating them on the achieved perfection in performing the requested alterations, then dismissing them with the wave of a hand.

Miasnikov announces it over the PA system as his henchmen stand at the ready. "If anyone has any information relating to the whereabouts of the terrorists, now is the time to come forward." The prisoners, now herded together, located on the one-time dance floor, look at each other, wondering what the fuck he is going on about. Vladimir Miasnikov relays through the speakers that this is their final warning and that if there is no forthcoming information, he will unfortunately be forced to set an example. The general nods and one of his henchmen steps forward to operate the handle that spins the tombola. When it had stopped, Vladimir reached in and picked up a scrap of paper, "I am pleased to announce to one and all that the winning number is twenty-four. Would number twenty-four please raise your hand to be identified." The prisoners had no idea why they were all numbered and now they were going to find out. Sheepishly, a woman raises her hand, declaring to all that she is indeed in possession of the winning number.

The henchmen on hand proceeded onto the once-happy dancefloor to extract the winner and then escorted her to the stage. Miasnikov shakes her hand, then with their hands raised as if she has won the star prize. He introduces her to the audience as tonight's all-time winner. Vladimir nods to his uniformed thugs and she is dragged away to the snooker room. She is seated facing the modified pocket, not quite matching the height of the alarming apparatus lying in place. The seat is adjusted, then her arms are firmly affixed to the table. Anna along with Olga wish they were somewhere else, anywhere else but here, as they witness the nails being hammered home through her limbs. The mechanism for holding her mouth firmly open is fitted and then connected to the now in place non snooker federation approved attachments.

Miasnikov assisted by his loyal henchmen, repeated the process until all of the other five pockets are connected to the now worried participants. His number selection had nothing to do with gender, nothing to do with race. It was totally indiscriminate, and the general could not care less about who was selected in the random numbering process. He calls out again for information, warning that his declaring this round to be double or quits. As no one comes forward to furnish him with the required information, Miasnikov sighs, pretending that he is sad, then selects and shouts out the next six numbers with glee.

As they are escorted into the snooker room, he shakes hands, then congratulates each and every single one of them on being selected for the runner-up prize. One-by-one they are conjoined on to the already immobile contestants who are now firmly attached to the modified pockets on the snooker table. They are placed behind the participants, with their heads now at approximately the same height, facing in the opposite direction. Duct tape is wrapped around their heads and bodies to semi-permanently attach them to their blind date partners, who are rigidly fixed at all of the pockets. Originally, Miasnikov had planned to obliterate their heads with snooker balls. He had imagined that Anna would have been dressed in the penguins' suit and would have diligently placed the balls on the spotlessly clean green baize. She would have called out the score and then cleaned the cue ball when required. Vladimir had changed the plan when he realised that achieving the magical number of the fabled one-four-seven was almost impossible to reach. Then calculating that it would take him far too long to achieve without cheating as well as the fact that it would take like forever for the contestants to die.

His next dark instinctive thought was to introduce the snooker table to golf, this time Anna would have dressed as a caddy. Standing on the table, Miasnikov would have pretended to know about the game. Then spending a lot of time deliberating over which type of club to use. He had never once participated in the game, which he truly thought was a waste of a good walk. He would have missed most of the shots and subsequently destroyed everything in the room but the intended targets. Miasnikov finally decided that he would just be making a complete fool of himself and decided to proceed with plan B.

The fruits of Annas' last-minute shopping excursion are now on display. The single-barrel shotguns have been chopped down to the bare minimum. To get them all placed within the desired configuration and within the limited space available. The stocks have also been shortened, leaving only enough wood to enable the once finely grained and decorated walnut to be attached to the table. Various brackets hold the guns firmly in place. The short barrels are firmly inserted into the pipes that are connected to the alarming apparatus, retaining the contestants' heads. The trigger guards have all been removed and various cable clips hold the connecting string in place. The gathered ends are fed through the partially elevated ring, secured at the centre of the table, and all of the now connected string terminates above on the overhead fan. Anna along with Olga, watch as Miasnikov asks if any of the dancehall audience wish to reveal the names and locations of the rebels. As no one had said a word, Vladimir switched on the fan, and twelve heads were instantaneously blasted apart. Blood, brains and bone splatter all over the room. Miasnikov is absolutely delighted with the results and requests that everyone should be served with the once-expensive vodka then to raise their glasses and join him in the celebration.

The bodies are removed and dumped outside on the pavement below via the nearest window. Vladimir Miasnikov is well impressed by the results, then parades himself about the room, telling everyone that his next show will be nothing short of being truly spectacular. Anna along with Olga on finally being excused for the evening and now alone. As she has witnessed the displayed madness, Anna asks Olga if she really needs to ask her what she thinks of her placement on the northern frontier. Olga tells Anna that it is not that much different down south and that she would have never signed up for this detail if she had known then what she knows now. Anna as well as Olga, now think that it is perhaps a good time to escape from the seemingly endless spread of insanity.

General Vladimir Miasnikov is now sober enough to open and read Lesqueths latest dispatch. He grunts then curses her, as he trolls through the elegant script. He wished that she would just inform him straight rather than make him painstakingly decipher all the rather long-winded words that could have been easily substituted with shorter simpler ones. He knows that she knows that English is not his mother language and that it would amuse her to no end. To see him struggling with all of the tongue-twisting involved in attaining the correct grammatical pronunciation, never mind the true meaning of the overly long unnecessary words that she had selected. Miasnikov thinks that she is nothing more than a manipulative bitch but she is in the seat of power, for now he has to respect this and carry out her orders no matter what he thinks.

Anna will be transferred to JJ's division, which is now most likely to be surrounded on all sides by militant sheep located somewhere in the darkest Wales. However, only once has she introduced Olga to his way of working. Miasnikov thinks that it would only take her a couple of days but with his next entertainment package in progress. Lesqueth won't mind and she does not need to know that he will be delaying the transfer for at least a couple of weeks.

Vladimir had planned to give Anna a starring role in his next extravaganza, but now due to the transition of hers and Olga's duties, the arrangements can be easily altered to include the pair. He really hopes that they will like the part that he has very thoughtfully pencilled in for the pair of them and fingers crossed the costumes will fit perfectly. He goes to inspect the construction work underway in the downstairs bar, and when entering, he clicks his fingers to attract the foreperson's attention. Vladimir Miasnikov wants an accurate update on today's progress. He intends to remove her tongue if she even attempts to use any of the long-winded or any of the associated managerial bullshit words that translate to yes, no or don't know. The general is also fairly confident that her dead or alive body will be chucked out the nearest window. Since he had walked into the room, he had noted that the atmosphere had turned decidedly frosty. Miasnikov could not care less as he thinks in the old school way of thought, that if the minions are terrified of him, they will perform much more efficiently.

To prove the point, Miasnikov calls over one of the workers and requests that they stand perfectly still in the process of pretending to be looking at the work in progress. Miasnikov boots him at full force in the stomach. It is not a case of the worker having done something wrong; the guy just happened to be in the wrong place at the wrong time. Miasnikov mutters to the man now lying on the ground, "Keep up the good work," and walks out of the bar, thinking that in the old world, he without doubt, should have been producing movies for the big screen.

Chapter 6

At the watermill they have come to terms with all the unexpected news. Murray has resigned himself to the fact that in the not that far away distant future he is going to be staying in a house full of children. With that will come the ever-present waft of dirty nappies along with the unrelenting dispersal of toxic fumes into the atmosphere that will attempt to try and take your breath away. He wonders if they will eat and then all go to sleep at the same time as well as possibly being well-behaved. He on the other hand is in no hurry to see Alicia along with Okolo leave. Murray will sadly miss both of them when they do finally depart. Although it is not as if they are moving to another continent, and to be honest, it will only be a short distance away. Over dinner the trio had informed them that they had found some ruins near the Orangery. They ask when it's convenient could Murray come and have a look to see if it is possible to reinstate the former dwelling into a habitable home. He cannot picture where it is, nor what state or repair it is in but promises to go and have a look at what they have found.

Cat and Frank have not yet bothered looking, never mind thought about a new dwelling. Frank has even joked about putting his name on waiting list for council house. Murray nearly choked at this, thinking that as far as he can remember it was almost an impossible scenario in dealing with the local council run housing department. You needed to be either a single parent with one leg who had nearly a football team's worth of three-legged mutant children or an alien from a far distant planet. That had purposely crash-landed into a council-owned property and then claimed political asylum before you even qualified, to be issued an application form by the housing committe who have taken on the role of being the unelected ruling Junta. Cha had told them not to worry about it, Murray would sort something out. Then kicking him under the table he had wholeheartedly agreed, with the required level of displayed enthusiasm to her statement.

Murray and his closest relations, including the dogs, are out hoping to find the location of the desired new dwelling for Alicia and company. They had made their way up to the Orangery, then attempting to follow the issued, somewhat haphazard directions, they eventually found the ruin. Mr. Black is stumped as all that remains of the former house is one wall as well as several piles of boulders. Cha asks him what he thinks, and Murray tells her the truth, informing Cha that there is nothing here to build upon. Nothing that he would be able to add onto then sadly delivers the news, informing her that a completely new build would be much easier. Murray knows there will be some disappointed faces when they receive his opinion. He is also aware that all three, really all six of them, will issue an appeal. "I think they should have a word with Karen. Grumpy as she is, she has more experience in this type of work and I am sure that Robbo the yobbo could charm her into agreeing to the project."

After they had a short family stroll, then giving in to the damp and cold weather, they returned to their warm abode. Murray along with all the others engaged in this disgusting, futile habit, are now banned from smoking in the house. Although he fully understands the reasons why but he does not relish the fact that he will now have to go outside in all forms of weather. Maybe he could become a seasonal smoker, winter is just about on them once again and no doubt it will bring a few problems. He could get an office, far removed from the house where he could pollute his own space as much as he wanted. If people visiting did not like the smell, they could always wear a fully enclosed suit with the attached breathing apparatus.

The children are now on their feet, they want to explore every single space as well as wanting to touch all and every single thing. Charlie and Romulus have been more than perfect with them. Murray likes the way that they let them cuddle in, even if their nappies are somewhat on the smelly side, omitting highly inflammable fumes. In the passing, he had mentioned the proposed dwelling refurbishment to Karen and then asked for her honest opinion. Robbo had been introduced to her a while back. On being continuously egged on by Alicia and Okolo he had been badgering her about going for a look at the ruined house. Karen was tempted to tell Robbo to fuck right off, informing him that when she had some spare time, then she would view the site. Robbo had even made a hint that as he is up in the orangery most days working on the feeding system for the hydroponic system. That perhaps if the ruin is not workable, then the trio could get a space inside the orangery. Cha just said that this was a most definite no and it was never, ever going to happen.

Karen had avoided going to speak to Robbo and had approached Murray to take her up to show her the place. He had duly obliged, when they arrived. She just looked, informing him that to make the wreck habitable, it would have to be completely demolished, and then it would have to be rebuilt from scratch. She did mention an alternative and took Murray to see some large sheds that were almost empty. "There is going to be lots of children, then soon enough they are going to have to learn things. The buildings here are not really used for anything and with a little bit of work, you could have several apartments as well as a school." Murray thinks that it is a far better idea than anything he could have possibly come up with. He promises that he will run it past the others.

On returning to the subject of the ruin, he had noticed that the stone displayed was almost of the same type and colour as the house where they were all living in just now. Murray asked if it was possible to build an extension with the available material. Karen nodded that it was feasible, but unless everyone involved agreed, she would not touch it with a barge pole. Knowing full well that Robbo, Alicia along with Okolo would be firmly against the idea of being exiled to the sheds. As well as the fact that she got the impression that Cat was going to be offered first dibs on the proposed extension. "You can let me know, in due time, what the outcome of the discussion is. If you have some spare time, come and I will show you what the teams have been doing to the place." Murray submits to her request; Karen gives him a guided tour of all the recent works, including the new construction projects currently underway. He is as always impressed with what she has achieved with the bare minimum of everything. Murray informs Karen that, as always, she is doing a fantastic job.

Mr. Black, now back at the house, had a turn of feeding Mark. He had tried everything to make him eat the latest offering and had ended up playing the train game. At first Mark was having none of it. He just spat the concoction out as soon as Murray had withdrawn the spoon. He persevered and felt that he should have been receiving an award for this arduous task. Okolo asked him if he wished a round of applause. Murray only said one word in reply, "wanker." This amused Okolo and she told him that it would get easier, mentioning that if it was only tomatoes that the baby wanted, then he would have her fullest sympathy. The children are now asleep, and with the meal underway, they sit and chat about this and that until Robbo brings up the subject of Karen.

Murray told them that Karen had thought it was an unfeasible project, on the fact that it would have to be demolished and then rebuilt. Robbo was not happy and asked again about moving into the orangery. Cha let it rip that this place is for everybody and if he moved in, it would not be fair on anyone. Okolo as well as sister Alicia are pretty grumpy about the whole conversation. Murray feeling the growing sense of unease at the table, offers the alternatives. None of them are interested the Karen's proposal of what they deem as the residential janitorial housing project. Without even wanting to go and view the sheds, the three of them are more than dead set against the whole idea.

On the subject of the extension, they get straight to the point by asking who is getting first choice. Murray wanting to avoid the accusation of favouritism raising its ugly head simply states that they can extend the house for all the parties involved. Murray also adds in for the record that as he had not yet broached the subject with Cat or Frank but now that they have mentioned it, he should really go and ask them. They had really pissed him off big time. Murray not wanting to sit and fume in silence, puts on his jacket and takes the dogs out.

Alicia looks at Robbo and tells him that starting from tomorrow, he should start looking for building materials, as he is going to be involved the sooner, he starts helping the better. Okolo agrees and just to noise him up adds that she along with some help from Alicia will give him a drawing of what they want along with a list of suitable furnishings. Alicia aided and abetted by Okolo start rattling off all the imaginary items that would be required, including the obligatory state-of-the-art sound system. Robbo asks if she is being serious only to receive the now-standard reply of "wanker," in stereo.

Alwyn Davies before the arrival of the great sickness had returned home to Wales and much to the understandable but forgivable annoyance of his parents. He had fulfilled his dream and purchased the family home. The devoted son had paid for it outright with one purchase to ensure that they had no mortgage repayments to make retirement financially difficult. Alwyn had explained to them that he had received a hefty bonus for his outstanding contribution to the work that his company was involved in. He was, as per the stipulations enclosed within the NDA, unfortunately not allowed to go into the specific details but nevertheless they should be proud of him all the same.

His parents had aged considerably in his absence. They had many discussions and after their, especially his father's point-blank refusals. He had won them round in persuading his parents to take a much-deserved holiday abroad. They had never been on a decent vacation. The farthest they had ever travelled was to an alleged fun-filled, holiday resort in England. He had helped them book the dream destination, the holiday of a lifetime and Alwyn had driven them to the airport. As they had never been on a plane before, he had told them not to worry. It was just like being in a big taxi and before they knew it, they would be aboard the brand-new ocean liner, cruising between exotic islands in the Caribbean. He had returned back to his research post in England and a week later, everyone had started to die off.

At his workplace Alwyn was part of the diverse multi-cultural society in and around the university area. As being from Wales and now with all the people dead, he was now most definitely an ethnic minority. On his journey back home, he had witnessed so much depravity, ruthlessness and cruelty being dished out by the survivors who had formed into marauding, almost feudal gangs. Who had pitifully succumbed into transforming willingly into being subhuman parasites surviving on the leftovers from the now-dead past. He reckoned if he was fortunate enough to make it back home to the country of his birth. Then at least speaking with the same accent would give him a much higher percentage of survival. He had witnessed all sorts of things that would have been previously considered absolutely appalling and at one time, he had even witnessed a fatal shooting for what looked like a minor traffic accident. The woman had just pulled a gun out and then shot the other woman in the head. What had freaked him out the most was that there had been no shouting, no argument. They were only talking and then the next minute bang, the assailant had calmly started walking away before the victim had hit the ground.

He had eventually made it back to the town where he was born and raised; not much had changed. The place looked more or less exactly the same as he could remember it. The family house was now empty, cold, and bare, all the neighbours were now dead and there were not any signs of life in the adjacent streets. Alwyn in searching the town from top to bottom, had spotted a stray dog or two, and at uncalculatable odds, a still alive junkie. She had taken up residence in the chemist's shop, having unlimited access to the supply of the various pharmaceuticals on display. He had found the woman on the floor, surrounded by the accompanying filthily paraphernalia. Blatantly advertising the sad aspirational goal to fulfil her rather woeful life choices.

On the counter where customers would have once handed in and received prescriptions, now displayed the discarded scorched spoons along with the heap of blood-stained syringes. The dirt engrained mortar and pestle shows signs of extended use for preparing the various experimental concoctions, that she was frequently pumping into her veins. Alwyn had tried to speak to her, but during the resulting communication process, he was unable to determine if she was purporting to be animal, vegetable or mineral. He had walked away in total disgust, at her sheer disregard for the gift of life. The woman did not want any help from him or anyone on the planet. She was quite happy going from fix to fix. It did not worry her at all, if it was her last fix, the one that would finally stop her heart working. As long as she went out on a high that was all that really mattered.

He had taken up residence in the old family home and had been holed up in there for months. Alwyn had ended up being depressed at being the only survivor and neglected himself. He would only eat every once in a while, as the weeks and then months passed by, he got thinner and thinner. His near-to starvation diet had adverse effects on his mental stability. In his state of delirium, he could imagine his parents happily dancing away to the steel band on a beautiful island somewhere in the tropical Caribbean. Alwyn Davies has decided that he has had enough; he is tired of being alone, totally sick to the gills of speaking to himself. All he can see around him is darkness. The once-happy home full of wonderful childhood memories is no longer enough to prevent the dark clouds of despair engulfing his soul.

He had lost a childhood friend who, on being totally distraught at not being able to find suitable employment, had killed himself. Perhaps it was partly due to the protestant work ethic that had been permanently installed in his brain from an early age. David had even been referred to a behavioural psychologist, and he told them that he worried like fuck about not getting a job and ending up being a down and out with no fixed abode. David also confessed that if he did actually gain erstwhile employment, he worried like fuck about if he would be able to do all the required tasks. He fretted that his subminimal reticence at not joining in with the expected sycophantic behaviour. In not laughing at the boss's jokes would lead to him being ostracised. The behavioural psychologist had listened carefully to every word and had subsequently allocated David a prime slot on the at danger list. When he had requested that he wished to be placed in suspended animation until a suitable job became available.

Alwyn had downed a bottle of whiskey, it had taken him quite a while as he thought that it smelled and tasted like old socks, but nonetheless he was intent on doing a David. His first attempt had failed miserably and all he had done, was make a huge hole in the sitting room ceiling as his weight had been too much for the light fitting. Alwyn had persevered and even in his drunken state he had eventually secured a stronger fixing. He had tested it by grasping it with both hands, then temporarily suspending his weight from it.

Alwyn was thinking about penning his swan song, but in realising that there was no one actually left to read it. He thought that it was just a pointless exercise. Alwyn finished the whiskey and calmly placed the monkey knot noose around his neck.

While he was kicking his legs about and swinging frantically in the hall, Alwyn had thought that he was hearing some voices and was thinking that it was only noises in his head. He blamed the foul-tasing liquid for altering his limited sense of reality and was starting to give in to the darkness. He had stolen his last breath, knowing and welcoming the fact that at last, it would finally be over in a few minutes.

The last taxi journey was disappointingly uneventful, no heading towards the bright light to be welcomed by long gone family friends and childhood pets. Alwyn is at ease with himself and does not panic as he calmly glides into weightlessness. His thoughts are disturbed as he hears the voices again and feels his body being roughly manhandled. He opens his eyes and then sees the people he does not know looking at him, he croaks, "Am I in heaven?" The people look at each other and one of them steps forward, "Now look here, boyo! If we were the welcoming committee in front of the heavenly gates, don't you think we would at the very least put on nice, clean clothes to welcome you through the entrance?"

His throat is a little on the sore side and he tries to speak some more, but a hand is in his face telling him to be quiet. "Here is the deal boyo! If we had found you a couple of minutes later, you might have very well ended up in heaven. My name is Gareth D and we are part of a group trying to pull everyone together to learn how to survive." Gareth looks at Alwyn's previous attempt at testing the weight load of the ceiling rose, "Looks like you have been busy, huh? Here is the deal, if you want to remain one of the living, we would welcome you with open arms and you could maybe join our group. On the other hand, if you truly, really truly wish to end it all we can give you a loaded gun and promise that it will be over in seconds. So, what you want to do?" Alwyn still amazed that there are more people, takes his time to answer finally declaring that he wants to live. "Okay people, let's get him in the truck, then take him back to camp. The rest of you finish searching for other people." Gareth D asks if he had seen any other living souls. He shakes his head and in a hoarse voice eventually revealing that there is the resident junkie in the chemist's shop.

Alwyn must have fallen asleep and wakes up in a bed, the room is clean and he can't honestly remember the last when he slept in crisp white laundered sheets. There is a glass of water on the bedside cabinet, along with a couple of what he thinks are headache tablets. There is a knock on the door and in walks Gareth, "thought you might have a sore head, whiskey can have that effect, yeah go ahead," and points to the tablets that allegedly cure a sore noggin. Alwyn thanks him and munches them down as fast as possible. "Our medic has seen you and thinks that you will have a sore throat for a few days. They also think that you need to eat more. Starvation diet? or suicide diet? Well don't worry about that for now, there are some clean clothes in the dresser, have a shower, then get dressed and we will get you some warm food. See you downstairs when you are ready."

He had showered, shaved and having been quite a while since he had washed, he had spent quite a considerable time under the warm water. This was a luxury that he had sorely missed, cleanliness is next to godliness or so they used to say, but either way, it is good to be clean again. If Alwyn was going to be really honest and declare the whole truth and nothing but the truth, it was also good to be back in amongst the living. He walks downstairs and follows the smell of the food; Gareth D sees him entering the room and waves him over. Alwyn is introduced to the woman sitting beside him, "This is Cinds' and after you grub up, she will ask you a few questions, nothing to worry about. Alwyn there is no table service tonight, so you will need to go and get your own food." Gareth points in the direction where it is located. Alwyn gets his drift and goes in search of some sustenance.

Out of earshot Gareth asks Cinds' what she thinks, "office dweller? or construction worker?" Cinds' replies that his hands looked soft but he looks kind of smart to be just pushing a pen, "I think he may have been an engineer of sorts." Nodding, Gareth just says that they will find out soon enough. Alwyn returned a few minutes later with a tray of nutrition. Before he sat down Gareth had got up and left. He has only taken the first spoonful when Cinds' had asked him where he came from. Alwyn gives her the house number, the street name, and the name of the village and includes the now redundant postcode in his reiteration. "No silly, where were you when the people started to die off?" In between the mouthfuls of food, he answers all her questions about what he had been employed as in the old world, where he had travelled from along what he had witnessed. Cinds' was very interested in his journey to get back home and asked for all the details. Alwyn asked if he had passed the audition. Cinds' calmly replied that they had to check everyone out as they all had some horror stories about what was happening in other parts of the country.

"Okay, now that you have finished stuffing your face, how about we go and get you checked over?" Alwyn asks if there is a psychiatric evaluation test involved, as he might not be quite ready to undergo that right now. Cinds' just smiles and leads the way; Alwyn passes Gareth in deep conversation with a group of people. He says hello, tells him the food was great and also says thank you for saving him. He never received anything in the way of a reply, not even a grunt. Alwyn asks her if he is always that rude. She just informs him that he has got a lot on his mind at present, but perhaps he will be more talkative later on. Cinds' indicates that they are here, knocks on the door and enters.

The scruffy guy behind the desk asks him, "Name?" He states his first and second names for the record, then gives his date of birth as well as the rest of the previously supplied information. "Okay sunshine, if you want to remove the clothes, we can check you out." Alwyn asks, "all of them?" Scruffy asks if he is shy, then barks, telling him just to get fucking on with it as they don't have all fucking day. Cinds' watches and when his chest is bare, she has a quick look at his back. Scruffy checks him out, then nods to Cinds' who seemingly has remembered she has somewhere to go and leaves the room. Alwyn is none of the wiser and answers Scruffy's questions.

He thinks it is the quickest medical ever as all he was asked was, can you see me? Then, can you hear me? "Okay, you've passed and please put your clothes back on." Alwyn does as he was instructed and when the task is complete, Scruffy does not even look up at him as he waves bye-bye and then points towards the door. He was wondering why they had made this process necessary. All it had achieved was to remind him of the frequent head lice checks at he had been subjected to at primary school. Cinds' waves him over. Gareth D holds his hand out and offers to show him around. "We had to check that you were not one of them. Your journey here was quite uneventful, you by all accounts, were very lucky. The stories I have heard from some of the other travellers you would not believe." Alwyn asks him what was the big deal at, looking at his back, "What was so important as let's be honest about this, that was the only part of the alleged examination that was relevant."

Gareth stops walking then informs him that he is more than welcome to stay and they will find something that he is good at, adding in that if everyone was as honest and straightforward as him, they would not have to do the checks. "A while back, we came across a couple of fellows who were allegedly Albanian fruit pickers. None of the details that they submitted were true and unbeknown to them, we had a couple of people who were actually from that neck of the woods. I had them listen in to the conversations and they told me straight up that their accents were from another country. The whole story that they had tried to give us was just nothing but a pack of lies."

"Eventually after, what you could say was less than friendly persuasion, they confessed. They were part of a forward scouting group attached to the new army allegedly liberating the survivors and then taking them under their wings to ensure freedom and healthy living. The tattoos on their backs revealed that they were part of the armed forces now tearing the country apart, rooting out what is left of the population. There is no liberation, all there is conscription, blind obedience or the alternative of slave labour or torture. You should really hear some of the heinous acts of barbarity along with all of the cruelty that these so-called saviours of humanity have been committing on unsuspecting civilians. Cinds' is my second in command, the go-to person when I am not around. She will find you a job that you can do and, if possible, get you trained for one that you cannot do. Anything that you once held dear and thought was important, you should forget about as it is now firmly buried in the far distant past. The only thing that is now dear and is important to all of us is our collective survival."

Gareth instructs him to jump in the vehicle and Alwyn is then given the quick guided tour. He asks Gareth why she is called Cinds' "That's an easy one, the first day I came across her, she was running about with only one shoe on." Alwyn is none of the wiser. Noticing his quizzical look Gareth adds more clues; "you know the story about the wicked step mother bordering on acute schizophrenia and the extremely ugly, pox ridden, bipolar step sisters." Alwyn nods, "okay, got it." Gareth adds, "before you ask, her real name is Gwendoline, but I would strongly advise you never ever to call her by that name as she truly detests it and there is more than a fair chance that she would probably shoot you there and then for using it."

He gets dropped off, where Cinds' introduces Alwyn to the firing range, "Have you ever used a gun before?" He replies that he never had any inclination or any reason to do so. "Well, that as you know has all changed. Take your pick." The weapons laid out in front of him are all unfamiliar and not being quick enough to make a selection, she picks one for him. Cinds' shows him how to work it and then how to position himself to discharge the weapon. She is very disappointed at his first effort and then tells him to try again and keep his eyes open as one day it might be the only difference that will send the bad guys to hell and keep him with the living. Alwyn asks to try again, but this time refrains from closing his eyes and much to the surprise of both of them he is a born natural. Throughout the rest of the day, Cinds' introduces him to the rest of the weapons on display and by the end of the training session, Alwyn can use all of them.

The next day Scruffy, who was the alleged medic, takes him out after breakfast, showing him where they make all the things that go bang. Alwyn is introduced to the team resident in the bullet building, "as nothing last forever and just in case we run out, Gareth thought it would be a good idea to make our own." A list on the wall displays the various calibres that they cater for, along with the ingredient list accompanied with all the applicable weights and measures. Scruffy asks him if he could work in here if required then leads him to the next building. Alwyn is handed a mask, "It is a bit on the smelly side in here and I have been advised not to ever enter this building without one." In here various powdered chemicals are being mixed as well as what looks like a pile of household cleaning fluids that were commonly stored under the kitchen or bathroom sink. Scruffy shouts at him through the mask, "Nobody likes working in here, but I have to ask if you are willing to take a job in here if required?" Alwyn asks, "What the problem, it is only sixth-form chemistry?" Grumpy says, "We will take that as a yes then."

They venture outside and Cinds' is waiting for them. "What do you think? Do you want to make bullets or the stuff that makes big noises and blows stuff up?" Alwyn looks at her and just tells her straight that the process they are currently using is just simple sixth-year chemistry and yes, he could work in there. "I don't know what compounds you are trying to make nor what you intend using them for, but if you were to give me the specifics along with their intentions. I am pretty sure that we could improve the process and the effectiveness on the end product." They go and speak to Gareth, "you're a chemist then?" Alwyn admits that he has done a bit of chemistry in the past and from what he had seen he could improve it. He takes the initiative, asking Gareth what his intended use for the concoctions that they are making. "I would like to blow up a section of the road and it has to be powerful enough to obliterate the military vehicles that are unfortunate to be in the wrong place at the wrong time," Alwyn tells him that would not be a problem and asks if that is all he requires. Gareth gives him his other requests; Alwyn closes his eyes for a couple of seconds, working out how to make them. "Yip, I can make these also; we will require some bits and pieces but I am assuming that there is

a DIY supplier or a hardware store in the vicinity. Cinds'
looks at Gareth, "Danger Town?" He replies, "Danger Town
it is." Alwyn looks at them, "Don't worry about it. You will
see it soon enough and then you will appreciate why we have
given it that name."

Chapter 7

Blink had never known anywhere else. This was her place of birth, her sole life experience. She had never travelled out of this tiny village and the surrounding area. They had just interned her mother; Lucky had passed away after a short illness. The village healer had tried everything possible to cure her and near the end, she had confessed that she was not going to be able to save her. She looks at the watch on her wrist, the elaborate timepiece that had been her mother's and before that, her grandmother's. Blink is amazed that after all these years it is still in pristine condition and keeps perfect time. The only thing it unable to do is accurately tell her about is the uncertain future.

The small village located on a remote section in southern Argentina had a strange history. Most of the inhabitants had Scottish sounding names and many of the headstones displayed the same shared heritage. Blink was well aware that the nation often referred to as the mother country was thousands of miles away. The long-gone souls only represented now by the weather-beaten grave markers must have travelled for weeks and weeks upon end, in almost slave ship conditions to get here. Blink thinks of all the unfortunate souls who would have perished on the crossing.

Scotland in the 1660s was by far not a very happy place to live in. The English crown was unrelentlessly carving out an empire in all parts of the known world. Much to its consternation the country situated on its northern border was still under the illusion that it could function as an independent state. The English crown, aided and abetted by the shadowy powers at be, were forever meddling in the state's governance. The appointed Scottish adjutants were blatantly transparent and openly viewed as being errant lackeys bought and paid for by the English crown and state. Bribery and corruption were the current, widely accepted trends of the day. As long as the affluent families paid the required sums to the English governmental agents, then all would be well. Those who did not want to pay were subsequently punished and then refused entry into the various sanctioned business charters set up by the state south of the border. Scotland's financial and economic status was now slowly being strangled. If this sad state of affairs remained on course. Then eventually over a relatively short space of time, the nation would, without doubt, suffocate. Without sufficient financial resources, Scotland would be expected to succumb to being ruled by the southern capital. Who would install a rather one-sided permanent political and monetary unification. If not, the country would face nationwide poverty and starvation.

The Hidden were well aware of the inherently unfair dangerous game underway throughout the British Isles. Where the rules were constantly being changed and then reconfigured, creating an unstoppable English superstate. When it was required, the Hidden made its voice heard, emerging out from the shadows to protect the ones who were loyal and true. The presumptuous, entitled ones belonging to the gang of the landed gentry, on foolishly taking on the role of being employed as a governmental agent in any guise or form. Now faced the almost certain probability of being rewarded with a slit throat or the prospect of quietly disappearing off the face of the earth. The Scotsman who had founded the bank of England and greatly enlarged the fortunes of the esteemed gentlemen in this establishment, had dramatically fallen out of favour. His ideas were financially sound and more than economically viable, but they did not want nor need him. The fortunes that they had now amassed through his steerage had been paramount in his exclusion, as well as the fact that he was just another one of them Scottish bastards.

The founder of the Bank of England had returned to his country of birth and was dismayed at the nearly dead and almost dying economy. He knew that this was being totally engineered and instigated by the crown with the blind obedience of their less-than-honest agents. In his mind, he saw his country's economic prosperity almost drowning in the water, and his nation was only going to stay afloat if it accepted the lifeline of the English state. That came attached with more than unfair monetary restrictions as well as the political terms and conditions. As his nation had been recently banned from sea-borne trade by the English Navigation Act, he devised a plan to make Edinburgh an economic hub. As equal or greater than the economic powerhouses of London, Paris and all of the other prosperous European capital cities that he could think of. The founder would set up a new colony, full of Scottish ships trading between all of the continents of Africa, the Americas and Asia. All he would need to set up this free port was hard cash; he knew an ideal location. His vision would curtail the often-dangerous navigation around the Cape of Good Horn. The plan he hoped to bring to life would allow ships to berth on the Atlantic and then transfer goods to ships berthed on the Pacific. The returning ships would transfer goods and the much-treasured luxury goods, exotic spices, fine silks to Scotland and from there they would deliver to the rest of Europe.

He had set about on the earnest task of petitioning any merchants who would give him the time of day, to outlay his plan of economic prosperity for Scotland. On hearing of his grandiose plans, the Hidden kept an even closer watch on the pending developments. The founder had now gained enough support amongst the affluent merchants and their friends to start the process of gathering sufficient monies to fund the expedition. A princely sum of one hundred and one pounds and one shilling would entitle the affluent to a share. The ones who had the available cash were clambering over each other to buy into this scheme. From as far away as Hamburg, Madrid, Paris, Budapest and most surprisingly, from various cities in England, merchants wanted to invest. The Dutch East Indies company strongly objected and then issued their demands on the crown and the parliament. Through their bought and paid for representatives to bring an abrupt halt to the usurpers attack on the English monopoly on international trade.

All of a sudden, a new law was passed that banned anyone apart from the Scottish from buying a share or having any type of monetary contract in a Scottish company. The founder was distraught that the monies that had been previously invested now had to be returned immediately to all of the investors. His plans included purchasing a sizable property in his nation's capital that would have been the company's headquarters. The name he intended to use was the Scottish International Trading Company, a slap in the face for all the established trading companies south of the border, in attempting to abort and kill off his franchise when it was at its embryonic stage.

The Hidden still avidly watched the events and sensed danger at every turn. They were very worried about the future and knew that if the founders' adventure failed, Scotland would be financially ruined. England would bail them out, but that would not be for free. A hefty price would have to be paid. Scotland would become a dependant state bowing to unconditional English rule and its people would have to pay more than homage and tax to the governing state. The Hidden knew who was behind the crown and knew that once Scotland was subjected to their rule, it would only be a matter of time before they sought to eradicate them once and for all. It could be centuries; it could be only decades away, but it was almost certain that it would happen.

The founder had been awake all night wondering what he could possibly do to reverse his dire monetary situation when his secretary knocked on his door. "Excuse me Sir, sorry to bother you at this early hour but I have a Mrs. Mary Porter in reception and she wishes to see you on an urgent matter. I told her that you were extremely busy and asked if she would like to make an appointment, but I am afraid that she is determined to see you today and is refusing to budge." The founder told his assistant to show her through and make a pot of tea. He wondered what this was all about, expecting it to be yet another urgent request demanding a refund.

Mrs. Porter sat in silence as the founder faffed about making the tea. She thought the brew looked as weak as its maker but held her tongue firmly in place. After pouring the offending almost transparent brew, he introduced himself with his full name, title, and the name of his just-about-dead in the water company. Mary waited for him to finish, then waited a couple more minutes before she said a word. "I am led to believe that you are going to set up a trading company, a free port of commerce somewhere I presume is located in the new world." The founder attempted to speak, but she put her finger to her mouth, indicating that he should refrain from opening his lips. "I am also led to believe that your plans have stalled and somewhat faltered due to the fact that you will have to reimburse the various continental and English investors." The founder attempts to speak again and this time Mrs. Porter curtly informs him to be quiet and just listen to what is on offer.

"The sum of monies involved would surely curtail your ambitions and your company would most definitely be declared bankrupt. I can arrange to have all the money you inadvertently lost, delivered to a bank of your choice today, before the close of business."

Mary knows that she now has him well and truly on the hook. "First off, our little transaction must never be revealed, under any circumstances, to anyone outside of this room. Just nod if you agree. I do not require any shares in your company. All I need is for you to take the names included on this list to your undisclosed destination, which I believe is located somewhere in the new world." Mrs. Porter hands over the envelope containing the named persons. "In addition to this, we will require our cargo to be loaded, without being inspected or tampered with, then unloaded on arrival at the unsaid destination." Mary waits until he understands, then nods in his acceptance. "Lastly the people on that list, upon arrival, will be allowed to leave the area on two tenders that we will provide. Do we have an agreement Sir?" He holds out his hand, Mary spits on hers and they shake on it. "All I need now is the name of your bank and for you to contact the list of people when the ships are ready. Good day and good luck Sir." The founder could not believe his timely reversal of fortune; one minute it was dark without any possible hope of a tiny glimmer of light and the next it was glorious eternal sunshine. He did not know anything about this woman and nor did he want to know anything about her. As there are no affordable establishments where he can build his ships in this country. He contacted some known agents to acquire some suitable vessels that were allegedly within a reasonable price range in Europe.

Mrs. Mary Porter was good for her word, and the required sum was deposited at the bank. The four ships that had been purchased in Europe were renamed and then sailed to Leith, where they were fitted out for the transatlantic crossing. The Unicorn, Saint Andrew, Caledonia and Dolphin were hardly fast ocean-going vessels of the day. He had been steadfastly reassured by the owners that they most definitely fit for the intended purpose. The founder honoured his agreement. The names that the mysterious woman had provided on the list and their cargo were loaded aboard without question or examination. The small fleet set sail on the twelfth of July and twelve hundred souls ventured into the unpredictable, frequently volatile Atlantic Ocean.

For all involved, it had been a horrendous journey. Some imagined that travelling on a Gold Coast slave ship would have been far more luxurious. The food that they provided was not fit for human consumption, and after a few days, it started to turn bad. This led to an outbreak of scurvy, dysentery and eventually madness started to affect several of the passengers and crew. Mary Porter's passengers stayed well clear of everyone, especially the gang of diehard fanatically devout Scottish ministers. Who held the unquestionable belief that anyone outside of their undeniable true faith was nothing but heathens and disciples of the devil incarnate himself. The vessels were in fact barely able to handle the rough seas. A few passengers and several of the crew had been lost overboard during the perilous crossing. One of the ardent ministers who had succumbed to insanity. In proclaiming to all that his God, the one true God, did not approve of this adventure. He wrapped himself up in weights and then much to everyone's surprise, he had jumped straight overboard on the calmest day of the otherwise nightmare of a crossing.

After several months, the bruised and battered small fleet limped into the sheltered water around the new settlement that they were going to name New Caledonia. It was November the second, and it would have been bitterly cold, overcast and damp in Scotland. This location was only a few degrees off the equator. The passengers were blissfully unprepared for the humid climate, the heat, the insects as well as the almost wall-to-wall impenetrable jungle. Mrs. Mary Porter's delegation waited onshore until all of the scheduled passengers and their supplies were offloaded. The founder was good for his word and the two tenders, along with her people, disappeared during the night.

The Hidden knew deep down that this adventure was doomed to failure and had taken the necessary action to ensure their survival in the uncertain future. With nine people on each boat, they had set up the small sails, then kept relatively near the coast. They only sailed a couple of miles to get clear of the original settlement. In the following days, they ventured southwards then continued their journey only when the weather was suitable, fully aware that their boats were only suited for small waves and relatively calm waters.

The indigenous people that they had encountered in their travels, offered them no aggression as the travellers had not offered to trade them worthless beads, combs or mirrors for the yellow metal. That the previous strangers had almost demanded at every encounter. The local tribes had noted that these people were only interested in fresh water and the identification of a place in which they had shown them a picture of. Until now, none of the tribesmen had recognised the slightly tattered pencil drawing. This procedure had repeated itself at every stop where the natives had come close enough to trust them and have an interaction. Sometimes the locals just ran away and who could really blame them for this reaction. The numerous Europeans who ventured into these territories usually tried to shoot them. The supplies were just about depleted when they called a halt to the journey. It was the general consensus among Mary Porter's travellers that they would never be able to reach the fabled destination.

They had set up their camp near the fresh water supply, then supplemented the last of the merge rations with the abundant fruit and vegetables that grew in the area. On the better days, they fished the coastal waters, through trial and error they found out the hard way which species to eat and what species to throw back. The indigenous tribe watched them but kept them away. The newcomers cooked meals for them and then left them on the outskirts of the temporary settlement. Weeks passed into months until they eventually made contact. Trust had to be earned and through painstaking long conversations where no common language was spoken, the two groups grew friendlier and equally trustworthy.

In time they would bring most of the tribe over and the settlers would prepare then cook for everyone. The locals liked how the strangers would entertain the children and give the older ones of their tribe the respect that was required in old age. The settlers had shown them maps of where they had come from and where they had crossed the great ocean in reference to where they were now. During these welcoming sessions, a pencil drawing fell out of one of the leather-bound books as one of the locals had picked it up. The native had said the name of the place out loud and all the locals bowed to their presence. The newcomers were mortally embarrassed and then explained through the now common sign language that they were not to be worshipped, informing everyone that they all should sit and eat.

The next morning, several of the tribe appeared and said the name of the place on the drawing, pointed then signalled them to follow. The newcomers who went with them travelled for several days through jungle tracks, then along the dangerous mountain paths till eventually they came across ruins that had almost been forgotten by time. The elements had almost returned this place back to what it was before it had been established. The newcomers searched the surrounding habit, deeming the area suitable for a settlement. They established, through sign language that they would like to move here. The local tribe understood then expressed that they wanted to move with them. Both parties agreed and shook hands on it, and the combined people group moved lock stock and barrel to the new settlement. All the dwellings were rebuilt, the old people of the indigenous tribe were given the first houses. Both groups learned new skills, and they all prospered. They had lived in peace for what was now centuries and nobody bothered them and they did not bother anyone else.

Blink now sits in her small dwelling. She had found the passports of her adopted grandmother and mother, understanding why they had used the fake documentation to leave the USA. She had never met her grandmother, but her mother, Lucky would tell her all the stories of the great adventures they shared when she was growing up. The knock on the door is to let her know that it is time for the ceremony to begin. Blink makes her way over, enters the circle and the single bell chimes, announcing her arrival.

The old woman and the swirling mist had appeared and they were now in unfamiliar territory. Murray and company were present to witness the sound of the first chime. They watched as the robed young woman was presented to the gathered. The old woman in the hooded cloak was especially pleased to see her and had shared grief for her recent loss. Cha along with the others were looking and feeling almost lost in the unfamiliar surroundings. This was not their native turf; it was from another continent. The plants were different, even the air did not smell the same. They watched the ceremony and the young woman was inducted into being the new leader of her group. The single bell chimed again and the humming started and they were now back beside the dead tree lying on the ground up behind the orangery. The old woman in the hooded cloak introduces them to each other, the two new faces look somewhat familiar, although they had no recollection of actually meeting. Twin bells sounded, and the old woman in the hooded cloak herded them into a circle, motioning for them all to hold hands.

"The north will join with the south; the east will join with the west; all the four points of the compass will converge and the Valaron will be punished for all the atrocities that they have committed during their unholy quest and unquenchable thirst for power."

The old woman senses danger and signals out to Murray, "Two strangers will arrive and you must grant them safe quarter, no matter what everyone else wants to do. You must do what is right."

As she is made to wait, Blink remembers all the words contained in the message from the old woman in the hooded clock. The newcomers she felt as if they were long and distant friends. Blink recognised most of them but was unable to put a name on any of the faces. As the trial to qualify for her accession is about to begin, Blink puts the message to the back of her mind. In stepping up to take her mother's position, she has to prove her worth in the arena. The tradition goes back all the way to when the strangers arrived here and had taught the local tribe how to defend themselves. Over the centuries, the techniques developed and changed. Blink would be tried and tested by the best; failure would lead to her being refused her mother's position. She felt like she had been training for this day for the whole of her life and was not looking forward to today, nor was she scared of what she was expected to accomplish.

On receiving permission, Blink walks into the centre of the arena with her head held high. Dressed from head to foot in black on black. She has no weapons and is expected to defend herself against several well-armed combatants. She knows that the ones who were chosen to challenge her ascension to claim her mother's position would have been told to give her no quarter. They would be expected to attack with all the necessary force and brutality in a real battle. Blink is made to wait again, as they purposely delay the trial, hoping to make her nervous and anxious, which could inevitably lead her to make mistakes. They start to appear, at first there is one and then a few minutes later they are joined with another. They are now eight of them all armed with long poles and short clubs. She knows each of them by name and is fully aware of all the injuries that they are more than capable of inflicting upon her body.

The adjudicators announce the test to begin and as the single bell chimes, Blink launches herself into the attack. She runs at full speed towards the first opponent. Blink has chosen Arto as the preliminary target as he is the best of the best. Just before reaching him, her hands briefly touch the earth, and she flips over the top of him, undoing the jacket and wrapping it around his head before he has time to react. Blink kicks his legs away from him, then takes ownership of his weapon. Snapping the pole in two, she backflips, turns around then runs forward. Now sliding across the ground, she takes away two of the opponents' legs and does a forward roll to escape her pursuers. Now that she has the space, Blink launches her short poles at the nearest opponents, both are direct hits. She takes on the three remaining members of the opposition team by hand and easy-out moves them as she deflects their attacks. One of them made the mistake of lunging at her with the long pole. She sidesteps the pole and increases the momentum by pulling him all the way forward, headbutting him on the way past.

Blink uses his weapon to pole vault over the remaining two and picking up a short club, she makes fast work of subduing the limping and struggling to stand combatants. Blink now attends to the two still standing opponents. She bows to them and then launches her attack in a flurry of moves that outflanked, out manoeuvred, and then outclassed them. Their attempted parries and deflective actions did little to evade her onslaught.

One was sideswiped by the pole and in a reverse action the other received a full blow to the stomach. The last attacker was held on the ground, the end of the pole positioned to her throat; Blink asked her to yield, and on refusal the pole was spun and knocked her out. Blink bowed to the adjudicators and then helped her would-be attackers get back to their feet. She did not ask for the result of their judgement; she had defeated the eight opponents. Blink was only sweating where her attackers would be bruised and sore for a few days. Blink knows for certain that she could have just as easily have killed them all, but suspected that her display was merited on what she could have done as opposed to what she had done. Blink bows to her defeated opponents, the adjudicators of the trial and leaves the arena.

Somewhere not too far from Texas, Enunsha is now awake and the latest disturbing images that had briefly inhabited her dreams was a sure sign that there are others just like her. Somewhere out there, in what is now a vast wasteland, now almost devoid of most of the former inhabitants and their mass-produced, must-have consumer goods. She reflects on the new faces. Enunsha thinks that she should know their names as she has most definitely met them all before, but unfortunately, she cannot remember where, when, and how they are all connected. It had also been long ago, much longer than she can remember since the old woman in the hooded cloak had visited her. The message is, for now, unfathomable, and it is the new people with whom she is almost cojoined with her soul that are perplexing her. Enunsha is up and notices that her feet are filthy, the soil is dark and most definitely not from around these parts of the woods. Luckily for her, Abe has gone to work otherwise, she would have some explaining to do about her soiled feet, the footprints and the dirty bedsheets. The ensuing questions could have led to serious consequences and not sure how Abe would react, she counts hers and especially his lucky stars then set about cleaning away all the damming evidence.

Thousands of miles away and across the great ocean divide, Cha is awake and goes into Murray's head to give him his early morning wake-up call. Murray is pretending that he is still sound asleep and would just love for her to say. "Good morning honey, would you like a wee long lie and when you are ready just let me know and I will serve you breakfast in bed." Cha sits up and is just about to put her hand across his nose and mouth and he opens his eyes, turns his head, "got ya!" He kicks off the covers, and they look at the dirty feet and sheets. "Well, where do you think we were last night?" Cha plays at being silly and he replies, "why honey, I was with you all night long, are you suffering from memory blackouts in your old age?" Murray just smiles at her, and tells her that as always, he loves her more than anything, offering to go and get the morning cuppa ready. Cha puts her arms around him and they get up together. Hand in hand, they go downstairs.

The rest of them are up before them, Robbo appears to be undergoing his probationary house training is washing the dishes. Okolo tells him to make tea for two, and he obeys her issued command. Murray wants to know if she had turned him into a robot. Alicia just mentioned the fact that he had lost at a board game, which is the deal that had been agreed upon prior to playing. Murray asks if he is allowed to order anything, Robbo hearing the remark, tells him to fuck off. Okolo looks at him and as per the sub-clauses in the agreement, he has just accumulated another twelve days of in-house training.

Robbo brings the tea over and he and Murray sneak off for a smoke, "They whipped my ass good and proper at some general knowledge game. Not because I did not know the answers but because they asked the questions in French." Murray asks him if Okolo can speak French and Robbo says that he did not think so, but there is no way that he can prove it. Murray just smiles, knowing that Robbo will put up with all the nonsense just to keep them happy, but he will no doubt turn the tables when the time is right and extract some fun-filled revenge. They take in the morning fully enjoying the tea with the smoke, both of them wholeheartedly agree that these two things were most definitely invented to complement each other.

They enter the smoke-free environment, now the infants are up and about. The dynamic duo has their arms up wanting cuddled, Mark and Vincent now snuggled in to watch everything around them, and their eyes follow the conversation around the table. Murray slurps his tea and then made gargling noises to amuse his offspring. Cha gives him that 'you need to behave' stare. The conversation is about the old woman in the hooded cloak and her two-part message. They all had pleaded guilty to the dirty feet as well as the soiled bedsheets. There are several theories about the compass points, and Murray taps the teaspoon on his cup. "In order to know what she meant by the four points coming together, we need to ascertain what is the centre, as otherwise, it would be almost impossible to correlate any geographical reference point. If the centre is in American continent, then Asia is west and Europe is east. If the centre point is in Europe, then the American continent is west and Asia is in the east. Alternatively, the reference to the individual compass points could be taken as individual points all acting separately but working together on the one perceived goal." Mark looks at him and says, "Dada." Murray is pretty chuffed at this and lets everyone know that, "well at least one person seated at the table likes my explanation."

Okolo has not called him a wanker, but mentions the first place they went to had almost a tropical feel to it and she thinks it could have been in South America as the plants looked different from the ones in Africa. "All we know is that we are going to be engaging the Valaron in the future and everything else is just a don't know, as in where and when. I was more intrigued by the second message, and it almost sounded like we would all disagree with the outcome, but you, Murray, would bring calm and some form of understanding. Then again, it was pretty cryptic and what can we do except keep an eye on things around us. There was no message about going to look for any of this and I propose that we should extend our patrols just to double-check that we are safe and secure for the time being."

They all see the sense in what she is saying and set about marking the map to where and when the patrols should be extended out to. Murray is pleased that all the discussions are over and tells Robbo that they have work to do if he is excused from his household chores. Alicia and Okolo nod, indicating that he has permission to leave the kitchen. Robbo bows graciously, acknowledging that he has been granted permission to leave and is greeted with "wanker" from Okolo.

Chapter 8

JJ had followed his instructions strictly to the letter, and as per orders, there is now only one remaining main usable road in and out of the forbidden dark kingdom, formally known as Wales. He had been here a long time ago and still harboured an instant dislike for the place. He thinks that some helicopter gunships and a few bombing missions would have cut months off the task of cleaning the place out, but he does not have access to that equipment. JJ watches as his troopers cross the bridge into the kingdom with all the utterly unproduceable place names. The plan is for his troopers to push out any survivors and the other families will move forward where they will capture what is left in the barrier that stretches from Hull to Blackpool. He knows that some of the rebellious people, along with some of the equally rebellious sheep will no doubt escape. Some of them will be killed, but orders are orders and Lesqueth has issued specific instructions. After the last discussion, he persuaded her to change the proposed action of the combined forces of his and Miasnikov's troopers pushing south and utilising the other families to get them to push northwards. Lesqueth had agreed the change and wants the island cleansed bit by bit until all of the dissidents had been completely purged and eradicated from this land.

Now surrounded by sheep, never-ending winding roads and a landscape that could have very easily been on some other forbidden planet. In darkest Wales, JJ has achieved very little in the way of success. For some inexplicable reason, there are more survivors here; they are better armed and are not afraid to fight back. John Josiah Aitken would never dream of admitting his losses or lack of progress to Lesqueth and hoped he could replenish the numbers by replacing them with some of the captured indigenous population. They will be offered the choice of enlisting, working or just plain old torture accompanied by a painfully slow death. The other captured people in the south of the country were more than happy to volunteer for the work camps. The offer of three regular square meals per day, copious amounts of drugs, alcohol and secure accommodation was more than adequate to win them over. In this God-forgotten, barren landscape he is not so confident that they would except anything on offer. The sound of nearby gunfire, has him and his men diving for cover. In his travels across this inhospitable landscape, there is almost armed resistance on every road, then around every single corner of every dreary town and remote village that they have come across.

He had no choice but to immediately change his tactics. Now the tanks go in first and any sign of defensive measures are blasted into oblivion. The fairly large town up ahead his been under observation for the last twenty-four hours and the co-ordinates have been relayed to the artillery team. JJ checks his watch and then counts down the seconds until the barrage commences. The onslaught begins as they shell all the selected targets, then the co-ordinates are slightly adjusted and they then fire on the adjacent areas. As nightfall approaches, the sniper teams are let loose and stealthily move forward into their positions. When daylight appears, hopefully they will be in the perfect place to pick off the remaining dissidents who are blissfully unaware that their stand against the undeniable changing future is nothing short of futile.

Sargent Mitchel and Corporal Jones have been allocated to their former assignment of collating information on the newly captured local inhabitants. Jones brings them forward one at a time; "Name? and don't give me any of this Davies, Williams or Evans shit. You all can't possibly have the same fucking names." Sargent Mitchel is totally exasperated and before the woman standing in front of him gets to say a single word, he just shoots her in the head. As she is dragged away to be dumped in the already accumulating pile of bodies, he shouts, "Next!"

An old gentleman is helped along to the processing table by Corporal Jones. "Name?" The reply is "Wilfred Ebenezer Wilkinson." Mitchel shakes his head and not very good at spelling, enters him as WW.

"Occupation?"

"Retired, professor of phycological occupational therapy." Sargent Mitchel, closes his eyes, shakes his head again, marks his occupation as unknown, and then puts him on the prison list. He much preferred this job when the people he interviewed had nice, simple jobs like welder, plater or butcher.

Over the last few days, he had to record too many fucking professors of this and too many fucking professors of that. He even asked the one who had declared that he was the executive head of the social studies department, what that actually involved. Mitchel on being informed, in-between all the big fucking words, that it boiled down to the equivalent of just talking shit all day and getting paid handsomely for it. This guy he did not shoot, and being very impressed by his sincere honesty marked him down for the prison list. It looked as if this prison intake would supply a world-class debating society, specialising in grammatically correct Middle Ages English, social studies, and including experts on every imaginable physiological and phycological issue possible.

JJ now in the centre of yet another unpronounceable town, looks around at the thoroughly depressing grey and dilapidated buildings. The area must have been dying then falling into rapid decline with massive unemployment. There is no evident industry, with only bargain shops, turf accountants, Turkish barbers, multiple takeaway food places, and boarded-up shops located on the high street. The onset of the virus had probably done the area a huge favour. A shot from a sniper only just misses him, and JJ issues orders that he wants this one taken alive. Everywhere his people go in this shithole of a country, there is always one embittered local who thinks that they are going to make a difference to this world with the one lucky shot. The would-be assassin has been pinned down and is now taking pot shots at anything that moves.

The clock tower, once the pride and joy of this town, built when coal and steam powered the empire. John Jenkins can't remember the clock ever showing the correct time or the last time the bells announced the hour and half-hour intervals. He watches from his concealed position as the prisoners are used as human shields to enable the invaders to approach and then block off his escape route. Some posh-sounding fucker has just announced that they will shoot a prisoner every minute if he does not relinquish the weapon and then surrender.

One minute later an old woman lies on the pavement. The pool of blood around her head increases in size and is now seeping through the gaps in the locally produced kerb stones into the gutter. The prisoners have now been herded into the middle of the square; he knows many of them, if not most of them by name. A few had tried to make a break for it but had only managed a few steps prior to being mown down with machine gun fire. Another shot rings out, and this time, it is a young man lying bleeding. They had shot him in the stomach, hoping to play the sympathy card, with the young man relentlessly pleading for help. Jenkins was just going to shoot him and as he fumbled about trying to unjam his rifle, another shot rang out. He can't get his weapon to work and as he has nowhere to jump from. Jenkins shouts down at them, surrenders, then throws his now-defunct weapon to the ground.

JJ is not impressed and most definitely not amused by the would-be assassins' ambitions. He is intent on making an example and hopefully this will get it finally imprinted into all of their defiant thick heads that they are being conquered whether they agree to it or not. The captive shooter is being held firm by two of JJ's biggest troopers as he watches the ad-hoc rudimentary construction work take place.

The clock face is being destroyed from the inside of the tower. The hammers and the crow bars make light work of the framed glass. One by one, the captured inhabitants of the town are led up the stairs. Then they are unceremoniously propelled out of the opening. Jenkins watches in utter disbelief as the almost medieval scene unfolds in front of him. He witnesses the screams, the pleas for clemency as the men, women and the children regardless of age, political affiliations or creed impact on the ground. The dead and dying are now all lying in a strange contorted configuration at the bottom of the tower. JJ hopes that there is still a hidden observer in the vicinity as he issues orders for Jenkin's clothes to be removed. Now standing naked, encircled by the invaders. JJ takes the steps forward and then punches Jenkins in the face. As he walks out of the circle, "feet only gentlemen and I want him kicked up and down the street." Jenkins is kicked and then stomped upon by all of the assembled troopers. By the time they are finished, even a top-grade, fully equipped forensic laboratory specialising in identifying bomb victims would have found it quite a challenge to identify the victim. The misshapen head with all the missing teeth, the shattered jaws and the broken black and blue body is left where it lies, to rot away in the street.

Scruffy is driving the SUV. At one time or another, the top-of-the-range vehicle would have been the pride and joy of the previous owner. Lovingly maintained, sparkly cleaned and polished on a weekly basis for all of the neighbours to see. As of now it just another available option in the groups motor pool. Alwyn is in the backseat with Cinds', and Gareth D is riding shotgun in the front passenger seat. There is a vehicle in front and one behind them as they negotiate the steep hills along the abundance of the very tight ninety-degree corners that just suddenly seem to appear out of nowhere. Occasionally they stop and the truck in pole position initiates a series of flashing lights to declare that they are indeed friendlies.

Gareth twists around in his seat and says to Alwyn, "If you ever need to go on an adventure somewhere, get someone to take you; otherwise, you will be shot at the first checkpoint." Alwyn nods at understanding the statement. Gareth is now out of the vehicle, heading towards a couple of chaps who look like they are from some forgotten tribe that resides in the surrounding woodland. Alwyn thinks that these are perhaps the largest people he has ever seen and that they could have pulled trucks as well as railway locomotives with their teeth for entertainment in the now and forgotten world.

The leader has returned and he is not the bearer of good news. The report he had received gave a detailed account of the recent atrocities carried out by the invaders. Gareth had retold them the story word for word, and Alwyn found it almost impossible to believe that these people actually existed. Cinds' elaborates and then clues him up on past stories and reports that had been carried by people who, unlike him, were unfortunate to have seen the horrors first hand. As they were evading the alleged liberation forces that were in the process of establishing their unquestionable rule in the land. The south must have totally capitulated and now the so-called liberators were now heading westwards. According to the recent accounts, these animals will be venturing into their homeland sooner or later. Gareth has plans to make it as difficult as possible for them to advance into their territory, without incurring any substantial losses on the home team.

They restarted the journey and on recognising the road signs for the city, Alwyn asked if this was them nearly at the place, they had renamed Danger Town. Cinds' nods, then elaborates on the home-grown lunatic who has taken to calling himself King David. "In the beginning, there weren't that many of them, but as their population increased, so did the size of his head. That steadily developed and they now have an egomaniac in charge and his brain-dead followers blindly obey every single royal proclamation that is issued. Every fully paid-up member of their community has KD and an identification number stencilled onto their clothes. King David now has quite an established settlement and has done everything like an ordained monarch in the Middle Ages would have done. Except issue his own postage stamps and currency, but I would not hold your breath on the last one."

The convoy pulls up to the prearranged spot; this time, there is no displayed light sequence. They wait and in due time a vehicle approaches from the other side. Gareth informs Alwyn that he should witness the performance otherwise he would never believe a single word of it. The first thing that he noticed was that even the approaching vehicle had received the KD and serial number stencilling. The car stops, and then the back door is opened. After the underlings perform all the bowing, the representative flanked by his numbered associates walks towards them like they are displaying all of their exquisite forms of numerological identification on a high fashion catwalk.

Gareth advises Alwyn to join in, as the representative stops to a halt in front of them. They stand at attention and all shout out, "Hail King David." Gareth hands over the list of all the items required. KD number 53 peruses the paperwork. He tuts and shakes his head slightly every once in a while. As he officiously works his way through the fairly extensive list. When KD 53 reaches the last page, he asks, "You do have the required payment?" Gareth shouts and the packages are brought forward and then laid out in front of them. In a painstakingly slow process, the representatives' assistants weigh all the gold and thourarly examine all the assorted precious gemstones. After what seems a rather long, hushed discussion with KD number 53, the rep informs them that the payment seems adequate and informs them that King David will require an audience.

Alwyn wonders what the fuck is going on, as he re-enters the vehicle with the others. They follow KD 53 to what he assumes will be the palace or whatever the fuck KD is calling his headquarters. The one thing he finds particularly odd is that there are no people on the streets and they pass no other moving vehicles. He mentions this to Cinds, and she tells him not to worry about it and resolutely assures him that they are being watched every single step of the way. Alwyn was expecting a moat filled with hungry sharks along the obligatory gilded drawbridge. That led the way to a fairy-tale castle with all the flags, banners and pretentious trimmings. There is nothing in view, resembling a forgotten medieval kingdom, not even a solitary rotting body suspended in an iron cage, displaying evidence of being recently pecked to bits by the crows.

The tenement block that once would have housed several families has been converted and extended into the flagship residence. In the immediate area, the other blocks have all been demolished and King David's castle stands on its own. Gareth's group is ushered forward after being searched for concealed weapons; they are then led up to the first floor. The overtly ornate doors are opened by KD 59 and KD 60. Gareth and company are permitted to enter by a loud booming voice. They approach King David, who waits to be greeted in a much-accustomed manner. Gareth leads the chorus of "Hail King David." Seemingly satisfied with the grovelling KD 1 asks them questions about the list and even more questions about the offered payment. The pompous usurper residing on the throne even has the audacity to inform them that the next trade will be more expensive due to unforeseen seasonal inflation. Gareth shows no emotion and says nothing in reply to the royally issued waffle.

KD 1 speaks and Alwyn is confused as the King does not appear to have a Welsh accent and is in fact one of them Scottish fuckers. King David speaks in an extremely fast manner where there is no space between the words and one sentence glides without a pause into the next one. Alwyn wonders if Gareth had been on a special translation course to understand what KD 1 was actually fucking saying. Gareth replies that all the information is correct and the invaders are now in their country, proceeding to kill and conquer all in their path. He knows nothing, almost very little about them or their alleged numerical strength, but agrees to pass on the relevant information once he acquires all the accrued details.

One of the Kings' men approaches and they have a brief whispered conversation. King David announces that the cargo has been delivered to the rendezvous. He nods his head ever so slightly to KD 23, who stamps the ornate rod on the floor twice to indicate that the meeting is now over. Gareth and his crew stand at attention, utter the last "Hail King David," and then perform the bow and leave. Alwyn on the drive home is informed that King David, via his suppliers, was unable to complete his shopping list in full, but not to worry as he had other scavenging teams out searching.

Alwyn was going to ask them what the meaning of the women displaying the 1A, 1B and 1C represented but had managed to work it out for all by himself. Gareth had filled him in on why it was called Danger Town as in the beginning there had been a few skirmishes where they had shot some of them and they had shot some of ours. "It was only when the cease fire was agreed and the boundaries set that the indiscriminate shooting finally stopped. King David is under the impression that one day everything will return back to normal and he will be in the enviable position of having lots of gold and precious stones to buy into anything available." Alwyn thinks that he will be terribly disappointed when he realises that the new regime currently ravaging the population is only interested in killing or imprisoning.

Gareth goes through his want list and, looking at the ticked-off items, Alwyn confirms that he has or has not got the appropriate ingredients to make what is required. He explains to Gareth that if he could be shown or given a more detailed description of what these items were required for then their intended usage he might, just might be able to rustle up a viable alternative. Cinds' and Scruffy are instructed to give him a guided tour of the outskirts, especially the choke points tomorrow. Right now, all Gareth is thinking about is a nice hot shower that will cleanse his skin after the meeting with the hey Jimmy bastard, who is portraying himself as a legitimate king in his own country.

King David's real name was not actually David at all, and he changed it to suit his needs. Steven Donaldson was evading an outstanding arrest warrant when the sickness arrived. Steven had the gift of the gab and soon gathered enough gullible people to support his claim. Gareth just thought that he was a dangerous loudmouth and that he was well worth a watching. After the last meeting, he ordered the patrols to be doubled.

The next day Alwyn is out and about with the not-so-friendly Scruffy and the slightly friendlier Cinds'. They are in the process of showing all the selected areas where they think that there will be a fair chance of inflicting some serious damage on the invading forces. Now standing in the middle of the road, Cinds' asks him what he thinks. Alwyn wished he had an idea of what she was talking about, "what do I think about what?" Scruffy tells Cinds' that maybe he is just stupid and she will have to join the dots for him to understand. "Okay, if there is a tank coming along this road and we want to stop it, what can you make? What can you rummage up to put it out of action?" At last Alwyn understands, "right oh!" and gets busy with his pad and pencil. When he is finished, he presents them with the ideas, Cinds' asks him if that is all he needs? Alwyn shakes his head. "We will need quite a few of these, as we will need to make as many of them as we possibly can."

Scruffy drives them to the next spot, and without getting out of the car, he points "trees!" before Scruffy gets impatient Alwyn catches on and then scribbles with the pencil. "I will need this stuff and the size is not that important. I have put alternatives in brackets." Scruffy pretends that he is dead, deaf, dumb and blind, says nothing and drives them to the next spot. The dam is the next target on the current agenda, and this time, he thinks that Einstein will be able to guess what he is supposed to be looking at as it is the only thing that is in his view. Cinds' takes Alwyn out for a closer look; Alwyn asks some questions and Cinds' is unable to answer any of them. "Well, can we get inside then?" she shouts the question, and Scruffy holds a thumbs up out of the window. Eventually, he gets out of the vehicle and very reluctantly shows them where they can gain access to the structure that holds the body of water in place.

The newcomer talks non-stop and Scruffy prays that God could please bestow and bless him with the gift of deafness, right fucking now. Alwyn jumps about, touching and then measuring out the distances in regular steps, stopping every once in a while, to jot something down on the pad. He knows there is no point speaking to Scruffy as he feels it would just be a complete waste of his breath. Alwyn just hands him the pad and Scruffy after briefly looking at it, asks a couple of questions, he gets one-word replies. Cinds' think that Scruffy is going to blow his top and suggests that they go back to camp. Alwyn is relieved to be out of Scruffy's presence, thinking that one of his old professors would have been delighted to meet him and then to exhibit him as the fabled missing link. Alwyn does not think that Scruffy would get this joke, but then he quite happily escapes out of his way and starts to mix the ingredients for Gareth's pet projects.

Alwyn has been promoted and is now in charge of making the new toys. Scruffy tried to barge in and tell him what to do. Alwyn had stood his ground and told Mr. Scruffy that as Gareth wanted these items completed as soon as possible, he should keep out of the way. If not, he could go and inform Gareth that the project is a non-starter because the fucking caveman does not understand shit and wants to be the boss. Scruffy gives him the double finger and then retreats. Cinds' comes over later to see him and Alwyn waits on what she is going to say, "I heard that you had a visitor today?" He does not reply. She knows damn well fine who was over and what had transpired. Cinds' informs him that she is over to try and ease the situation. Alwyn delivers a message that he hopes she will pass on down the line. "You can tell him to fuck right off and stay the fuck out of my face. I am not putting up with any more of his shit. How does that sound? When I am messing about in here and mixing all this shit up, it has to be right. If I mess up, it will not work and that will not go down too well with anyone. The last thing I need is Mr. Fucking Caveman breathing down my neck and asking stupid fucking questions. Please just tell him to leave me the fuck alone and keep him away." Cinds' says that she will pass on his message.

The new chief bombmaker has been summoned to go and report to Gareth. He searches about and finds him sitting in the recreation room, come food hall. Scruffy along Cinds' are with him and Alwyn wonders what on earth they will be talking about. He approaches the table and then waits until Scruffy moves his seat over before he has enough space to sit down. Gareth makes a slight cough and then explains that Cyril is a little rough around the edges but his heart is in the right place and that we all have to make allowances to get along with each other. The whole of the time that the 'let's all be friends' speech is being delivered. Scruffy gives Alwyn the fuck you look, knowing that the boss is telling the smartass to get in line and just do as he is told. Cinds' had watched the parlay and witnessed Alwyn in action this afternoon. She has the distinct feeling that Gareth will need more than soothing words to resolve this situation.

Alwyn asks Gareth who is Cyril, Gareth puts his hand to his face and shakes his head, but before he can say anything, Alwyn lets it out of the bag. "Oh, you mean Scruffy! The guy who talks to me like I am a piece of dog shit, something that is stuck to the sole of his shoes. Even though he is a fucking caveman and thinks that he should be in charge of telling me what to do and when to do it, then how to do fucking it." Scruffy chucks his ten pence into the ring, "Why don't I just take you outside then teach you some manners." Alwyn having had enough of his shit today, slaps him hard across the face and then kicks the chair out from underneath him. As Scruffy gets up Alwyn stands and slaps him again, and again, then pushes Grumpy outside. "Listen here, if you want to play, I will slap you about in front of everybody. Then we can get on with normal living. How does that sound to you?" Scruffy takes a step forward, and Alwyn slaps him several times. Then, he takes his legs out from underneath him before Scruffy has a chance to hit back. Gareth is outside now and asks if there is a problem. Alwyn looks at him, telling him to ask the caveman. Scruffy launches an attack and this time Alwyn knocks him out with a single punch to the head. As Cyril is now lying unconscious on the ground, Alwyn declares that as far as he is concerned, he has no unresolved problems and walks away.

When he moved to his research position at the precidous university, Alwyn loved the work but not so much the people with the put-on plastic accents. A fellow Welshman had told him that the best pint was in the roughest drinking establishment in town. Alwyn had had enough of the Hooray Henrys and wanted to go for a decent pint and most definitely not in one of these fucking pseudo-posh wine bars that required a mortgage payment for a round of drinks. As he was a skinny kid, his father forced him to learn how to fight. He knew how cruel the streets could be in the mining community and had no wish for his son to be another hapless victim.

On walking into the Dead Donkey, he orders his pint and several of the local yobs noticing his non-indigenous accent, took an immediate interest in him. Alwyn walked into the pool room, then sat in the corner, minding his own business and savoured every part of that first pint as it glided down, hardly touching the sides of his throat. It was indeed the finest pint that he had come across in this yuppy, fake money and trust fund-infested town. The resident yobs had started to congregate in the pool room. The other locals knew what was about to go down. They all suddenly remembered that they had to be somewhere else and had started to leave.

The young man from Wales, knowing what was about to go down, told the ring leader that if he bought him a pint, he would forget about it and all would be well. It never worked out that way and after Alwyn had knocked the shit out of all of them. He bought them a pint and another for himself, and on leaving told the barmaid that it was definitely the best pint in town, "See you next week." Alwyn had become a regular at the Dead Donkey and after the first night, he never had any problems. Scruffy, if he had any balls or any, even just a miniscule amount of grey matter between those large fucking ears, would back off then leave him well alone.

Alwyn was busy at work. He finished prepping and mixing all the chemicals and powders, then had loaded them into the various ad-hoc devices that Gareth and his team would place in anticipation of stalling and taking on the invaders. All this work had taken a great deal of time and he was just about worn out. He had given it his best shot, hoping that all his inventions work as well as he had promised. He is now sitting outside, catching a brief glimpse of the sun before it goes back to hiding behind the clouds. Alwyn notices Cinds' along the Scruffy chap approaching and hopes, really hopes that he does not need to give him another kicking.

They draw to a halt beside him, and much to his surprise, Scruffy speaks, "Look, I guess you gave me what I deserved and thing is, see, we need your help." Alwyn asks him what he needs; "we put all these things in place but really need you to show us all how we should be doing it. As if we fuck up all the good work that you and the team had produced would be a waste of time. So, could you spare us some of your time and show us the correct way of setting these up? It would be greatly appreciated, by everyone, especially me." He asks them when they would like him to look at this and Cinds' now having got the awkward part of the conversation over with. Invites Alwyn to come with them in the vehicle, they could do it right now. They give him the tour once they are clear of the various checkpoints. "These trees, we know that they need to fall in the correct direction and I think we have got that part right, but what if it rains?"

Alwyn looks at what they have done and tells them that the work is okay-ish, but they could improve upon it. As always, he has his pad and pencil with him as he jots down a little sketch. His diagram shows them an improved version of where and what angles to drill the holes at, and then on the next page, he details the waterproofing process. Scruffy utters, "Fuck me, I never thought it was that simple, how did I not see that." Alwyn adds that they have to ask the next time and he will try to help. As he realises the importance of the work as well as that if they are going to have any chance at all these things that go bang, they will have to work the first time. As there will be no second chances. Cinds' accompanied by the now polite and chatty Cyril, take Alwyn around all the locations where they have envisaged a particular form of action and defence. The trio are now reviewing the place where they think that the tanks and heavy vehicles will arrive.

They had dug under the road then placed the charges in various locations and now wanted his opinion. Alwyn looks about and then advises the precautions that must be put in place prior to filling up the holes at the side of the road. This time, Scruffy borrows the pad and pencil and writes down a flurry of notes. He whistles at the team involved in the work and then passes on the instructions. Their last stop is the dam and once they clang all the way down the metal stairs, Alwyn looks at the sight before him. He walks up to, then looks between all the numerous containers. As they are all wired up together, he asks Cyril if they have checked all the connections. Scruffy confesses that they were hoping that he would show them how to perform that task. Alwyn thought it was a good, honest and straight forward reply, rolled up his sleeves, then showed his now best pal the process.

Chapter 9

Murray along with Robbo are at work. Well, Murray is grafting as Robbo does lots of non-stop talking. Murray wishes that he would sometimes forget how to speak and then somehow instantly revert into silent mode. He chuckles as he once tried pressing the mute button while pointing the remote control in his direction. Needlessly, unfortunately it did not work; otherwise, he would have brought the said device along with him. Murray wonders if Okolo and Alicia have a secret potion to make him shut the fuck up. Robbo notices him smiling and asks if he has said something funny. Murray looks straight at him and assures him that he has said nothing funny at all. He unrelentlessly swings the Monday hammer to remove another section of the wall. In the hope that Robbo will finally get his arse into gear then start to join in and move the rapidly accumulating rubble. He eventually submits, starting to manhandle the chunks of stone over to where they will be collected by some of Karen's highly skilled workers.

They are in the middle of it, the two of them shifting a big lump of stone when the women appear. "As you never arrived for lunch, we thought we would deliver it." Robbo and Murray were that engrossed in the work, blissfully unaware that lunchtime had descended upon them. They had completely forgotten all about it. Murray is more than happy with the liquid refreshment. He had to inform Robbo, who had rapidly consumed his lunch in a world record-breaking time. Who was now in the process to devour his, to get his grubby little paws off his food. Robbo told him that he did not think that he was hungry and that rather than waste the food, he was going to scoff it. Now, admitting his mistake, Murray gives him half of it as a peace offering. They sit and chat away about this and that. The children are restrained as they want to get in and about the derelict building. Cha knows that Murray wants to get as much as possible done today, sounds the whistle, then gathers up the tribe. She tells the guys not to be late for dinner. They get back at it, almost every chuck of rock seems to be heavier than the last. All of the wall has been knocked down. They now set about shifting and then relocating all the loose blocks that are scattered over the site.

As the task at hand now dictates that they have to work together, Murray makes most of the calls, and Robbo does as he is instructed. The heavy crowbars are frequently used to force the long-abandoned masonry from their present position. The centuries of dust and weather had almost held the blocks of stone, rigidly fixed to the ground. It's only with the use of excessive force that actually removes them from their almost permanent fixture. They had been hard at it for a while and agreed to a smoke break. While they are sitting there shooting the shit, Robbo notices the patch in the ground. He points it out to Murray, "What do you think that is?" Murray notices the slightly different colour, thinking that it could have been covered over by something at one time, which would explain the slight change. Robbo goes over, then reaches down and brushes the surface with his gloved hands. "You better come and have a look at this!" Murray does not sigh or complain and goes over as requested. Now just as curious as Robbo, he joins in clearing the surface.

Murray accompanied with Robbo have arrived late for dinner. The women are engrossed in yet another deep-rooted conversation about nutritional supplements related to the well-being of expectant mothers. Murray guesses that the list they are jabbering on about will not contain and spicey food, but he is prepared to bet his ass that it will contain loads of fucking slimy fish and bottom-dwelling creatures from the deep murky depths at the bottom of the ocean. Nobody had noticed that they had not changed before they sat and joined them. Nobody had even asked them how they had got on today. The women are now talking about hair and nails. Murray along with Robbo are now thinking that to get a word in edgeways that they might have to make an appointment. Murray looks at his nails and, in a loud voice, asks Robbo if he thinks that his hair is okay today. Robbo shakes his head and then bluntly tells him to fuck right off.

Cha looked at him and finally asked him how his day was. Murray just smiles, telling her that it was fine. He informs the table that they will be going back up tomorrow as they have found what could very well be a hidden room underneath the old ruin. "Just for the record, I have to say that it was Robbo who found it first and that should stop him complaining about it later on. We won't know what it is until we are able to move the cover off, and we will have to speak nicely to Karen about borrowing one of her machines." Alicia thinks it could be anything or nothing, wondering how long it has been hiding there completely undisturbed.

Cha asks Grumpy Chops if she will be invited, and Murray replies that he would never dream of going anywhere without her. He is all sore and tired, the soreness he puts down to not being active for some time. With that into consideration, he intends to ask Karen to adopt him and give him something to do. His days are fairly long. This place is now all running correctly, along with the fact that there have been fewer and fewer problems to deal with. To be honest, he is getting bored and just sitting about doing nothing. The rest of the team are far better at dealing with all the people, and there is no hope in hell that he will be able to match their far superior people skills. Murray will run it past Cha when they are alone. While they are all sitting together, he makes the most of it. Murray, forgetting for a moment, sparks one up, realising his mistake before they all go nuts and start pointing to the non-existent no-smoking signs. He offers his sincere apologies, holding up his hands as he escapes outside.

He is only on his own for a couple of minutes when Cha comes to join him. They steal a quick cuddle as he tells her that he loves her. She knows what he is thinking, telling him that she sometimes thinks of what it was like when it was just the two of them. Pretty soon, they are laughing like school kids as they delve into their collective memory banks, remembering some of the fun they had. Charlie and Romulus have been let out and sit staring at them, full of hope that they are going for a walk.

Murray knows that it would just be plain rude to slip away unannounced. He opens the door, asking the rest of them if they would like to come on the family walk. He is surprised when they all agree, and he asks Cha to wait as the others are also coming. The children are strapped into their buggies and are fast asleep within five minutes. He does not know what it is or why it happens but these walks seem to bring out the best in all the people here. He smiles, knowing that Cha was told by several of them that he is always on his best behaviour and is always very diplomatic when Charlie is happy. Cha also told him that someone had asked her once if it was true that he is also part dog.

Charlie as always enjoys these moments the best when it's at her favourite spot, looking out over to the hills in the distance. There is no snow on them yet but the weather has started to change. Murray sometimes wished that it could be a warmer climate, but then again, the scenery is spectacular and he should not complain. His grandmother used to tell him that it can never be too hot; it can never be too cold, and you just have to dress correctly for the weather. Romulus has found another ball and wants to play; Robbo does the honours, launching it into the distance.

Murray asks Robbo if he has ever owned a dog, and he admits he wasn't allowed to. Okolo mentions that it could have something to do with the fact that the family had one animal who regularly left his scent on the furniture when nobody was looking. Why on earth would they need to look after another one? Alicia thinks that this is a little harsh but also a fair comment. Playtime over, Charlie barks as it starts to rain. At first it is just a slight drizzle but Charlies' sixth sense comes into action and she barks at Romulus as they tear off in the direction of the house. Murray and company have arrived all soaked to the skin. Charlie looks at them as if to say I told you so. The women get first chance at the bathroom. Murray with assistance from Robbo set then lit the fire. Charlie can't wait till it is on twenty-four seven, stretches out to savour the heat. Murray bids them all goodnight and after the luxury of the hot water is sound asleep. Mark snuggles in beside him and has a goo-goo-gaa-gaa conversation with his sleeping father. Cha thinks that this is the nicest thing she has ever seen. What a guy.

Cora has just had the pleasure of having Cat along with her partner in the surgery. She had only come here for a check-up and the doctor had for want of another word, been fucking dreading it. Much to her utter astonishment, Cat had been the perfect patient, nothing at all like the person that had scared the shit out of her and all of the staff during the previous visits. Frank must truly be an angel sent from heaven to tame this monster. Cat was calm, gentle, very polite and helpful, nothing at all like the feral animal that had instinctively followed every single movement and every sound during her initial visit.

The doting couple did not want to know the sex of the offspring, and so long as the baby was healthy, that would be enough. Cora thinks that Frank has tamed the ferocious beast. She had heard all the stories about her and the very scary but very nice description was more than perhaps true. Frank stayed by her side every step of the way and had also asked many questions. Cora had informed them that both baby and mother were perfect, steadfastly reassuring them that there was nothing, nothing at all to be worried about. Cora wonders what version of Cat the baby will inherit, the wild, uncontrollable or the calm and caring one.

Murray had persuaded Karen to part with some machinery and equipment. Now, in full view of his entourage, they are going to attempt to gain access to what may or may not lie underneath. Much to the amusement of Okolo and Alicia, Robbo grunts with almost every action as he assists Murray. They had cleared the possible opening as best as possible but are presently stumped as to how it could have been originally opened. Murray had tried everything from his skill book to get the stubborn covering to budge. In all his efforts it had not moved a millimetre. In frustration he had even tried surprising it, but alas, it was all to no avail.

Frank accompanied by Cat had been out for a walk. Remus barks, not at the people but at the ground. The dog does not like something and whines to get away. Cat shouts, "see you later" as they depart with the now still unsettled dog. Murray is scratching his head, still trying to figure out what to do next. Alicia comes down and pours water over several parts of the unmovable stone. Three discoloured patches appear, then working out the geometrical sequence Alicia pours some water on the next target and the fourth discoloured patch appears. Okolo is delighted and is overheard, "what would they do without us?" Murray acknowledges the remark with a bow to their alleged superior problem-solving skills. Robbo is already on his hands and knees, scraping away at the patches. One by one the metal bars set underneath the surface is revealed to all. Murray gets up off the former dwellings ground floor then searches in and about the equipment borrowed from Karen. He gives Robbo the heads up as the selected items sail across to land near his location. Robbo just looks at the slings, trying to guess the next part of the operation. When Alicia saves his embarrassment, as she motions with hand signals what he should be doing next. Murray had forgotten that Robbo had not ventured into the construction game, realising that he truly belonging in the world of the much-dreaded and totally untrustworthy pen pushers.

Robbo is delighted with himself, standing with his hands on his hips, thinking this is the correct pose for a bonafede experienced construction worker. Murray was going to ask him if he could drive and operate the machine. Cha realising the next sequence of events saved him the hassle and started up the once bright yellow monster. Murray gave her the appropriate signals; Cha obliged then manoeuvred the beast accordingly. He gives the double thumbs up sign. Cha stops then before being asked then she starts to extend the forks. Robbo finally grasps what has to happen next and stands with the end of the slings in his hand, still posing with the fake "I have done this load of times before look."

Murray slides the green things onto the forks, pushing them as far back as possible. He then delivers more hand signals to Cha, who obliges with the small incremental changes that are required. Satisfied that she is now in the correct position. He asks the showroom dummy from the tailor's window display to move out of the way. Now that it is safe to proceed, he guides Cha through the lifting process, but nothing happens. Murray resets the slings and again tries to release the slab from its firmly held position. Doing the process half in half also produces no results. Murray has one last attempt and has to reconfigure the rigging to one of the corners. The block of stone does not lift, but they have managed to release some of the dust and grime that had accumulated over the centuries. Murray gives instructions for Robbo to help him repeat the process from corner to corner and at last the slab has actually started to move. With a visible space all around the stone cover, hopefully, the next lift will release the cover, allowing them to view what is underneath.

Robbo is thinking about getting the word slave emblazoned onto his tee shirt. He got stuck in to the work, thinking that at the very least, he had done his fair share of the graft. After much hauling and pulling, they had managed at last to remove the large slab that had been preventing them from viewing what was underneath them. The covering is now secure and sitting on top of some scaffolding tubes. In the event of having to close it in a hurry, all they have to do is roll it across and the momentum will take care of the rest. There are no pungent odours emanating from the now open chamber but as it had not been open for quite some time, Alicia had suggested that they let all of the bad air out and then some good air in to replace it.

They had taken turns shining the flashlight into the darkness to view what was inside but all that was revealed was a staircase descending into the dark, empty void. If they wanted to find out what was down there, someone was going to have to descend into the dark to explore. Cha had suggested that perhaps they should just put the sealing block back in place and then just forget about it as it was an unnecessary risk with many unknown possible dangers involved, empathising if the whole process was actually worth all of the effort. Murray told her that as they had spent so much time, along with all of the effort, on getting this far, what harm could a little investigation do. She knew that no matter what she said he was going inside and she would not be able to persuade him to do otherwise.

Robbo had the bright idea of getting a canary and lowering it down in a cage to test the air quality. Okolo, in response, suggested that if he had any idea where they could locate a live canary, that would be a good idea and possibly work. Murray just told them to hold off a little, and then together, they would think of a way around the problem. Cat has arrived and delivered some food and liquid. "Frank thought that you would all be still up here and employed me to deliver these," she hands out the supplies. She asks what is happening, adding that she had never seen a canary and does not even know where they could get one. However, she does suggest a man on a rope. If anything happens, they have to pull him up and out in a hurry.

Murray immediately volunteers for the vacant position, while he is drinking his cuppa. He thinks of how they are going to rig up the pulley system to ensure a quick extraction if and when required. He finally has resolved the problem, acquiring all the required bits and pieces. Robbo was not surprised when he was allocated the task of delivering the begging letter to Karen. He was so pissed off at being the gofer, he was thinking of applying for a job in the Bank of Murray.

When he returned, he carried down all the required parts and then assisted his manager in assembling the new contraption. Time was relentlessly marching on, with the women having other things to do, but rather than just leave them here on their own. They had agreed on a rota system to make sure that there was always somebody on the outside to help if required. The guys were ready to be lowered inside. Robbo stands at attention, saluting Murray, who just tells him to fuck right off. Murray goes first, then shouts that the air is fine, allowing Robbo to follow him down. They play the beams of light back and forth, searching for any clues that could reveal anything regarding this place's purpose. All the walls are blank, revealing no clues, no symbols, and every surface that they had shined the torches on was devoid of any type of information.

"It looks like we are going to have to go downstairs. We should take it easy by only doing one flight of stairs at a time." Murray shouts out their intentions to inform the topside sentry of their plans. Okolo, who had taken the first watch, confirms that she has heard them and understands them. Down they go, step by step, stair by stair, the air is still okay. There are no sudden creaks or missing parts of masonry. On the way down, the walls are still completely blank, revealing no clues as to the purpose of this building. On reaching the bottom, Murray shines his flashlight and it looks like they have found a tomb. The area at the bottom of the tenth flight of stairs has opened out and there is shelf upon shelf of clothed skeletons. At one time, the fabrics must have been clean, completely covering all of the bodies but over time some of them are now threadbare. Where the cloth is missing, the bare white bones are visible underneath.

The dynamic duo decide that a smoke break is now required and make their way upstairs to report in. Okolo has ended her shift, and her replacement Alicia listens to what they have found up till now. She offers no comments or suggestions but asks Robbo if he still desires a canary. They smoke and ask Alicia to arrange for some more batteries, after finishing polluting the air, they return back into the darkness. The bodies have not moved and are still in the same place. Robbo along Murray give the place a thorough search and still have no idea what to look for. Murray thinks that the structure would have taken quite a while to construct even just to use it to store dead people, which is way over the top. He is positive that this was used for something else, but the problem that he is now facing is that he does not know what the something else could possibly be. Robbo accompanied with Murray continues searching and finds some of the remains had been committed to this place in chains. The clothing is different most of the inhabitants had black hooded cloaks and the ones in chains were robed with once white-upon-white. They are in a separate part of the chamber, well away from the rest of the bones.

As if they had been ostracised right to the very end of their lives. By the claw marks beside them along with the skulls displaying angst and torment. Murray thinks that these people had been entombed down here when they were still alive. He has another look, startled and as well as a little freaked out as all the chained-up skeletons all have sharpened teeth. There were no tell-tale scorch marks on the walls displaying evidence of torches every having been in use. In what they have seen, it is possible that they must have died in the dark confines of this room. All the other skeletal remains appeared calm, and the immediate area around them showed no signs of panic. Thinking that they need a fresh set of eyes down here, Murray suggests that they pull the pin and ask for reinforcements. Robbo agrees immediately, vanishing up the stairs in a flash. Even before Murray gets to the top, Robbo is already standing outside in the fresh air.

Alicia listens to the proposal and then sets off to inform the others. Murray is a little pissed off at Robbo's antics but holds the peace for now. He thinks that he could have at least waited until he got to the top of the stairs before abandoning him, so much for trust along with dedicated teamwork. Beth and Debs have been left in charge of the infants; the rest of their gang is now here to venture into the crypt to cast a set of fresh eyes on the mysterious surroundings. Without being asked, Robbo volunteers as the outside man and watches as everyone descends into the ground. He figured that he must have done something to irritate commander Murray. Not at all bothered, he sits, awaiting any instructions.

As Murray showed them the chained skeletons, the women bounce their flashlights about the place. Alicia agrees that they had been put in here when they were still living and shivered at the thought of what they must have gone through. They continue to look at everything, it is Cat who locates the doorway. Behind one of the sections is a very faint line depicting that at one time there was another exit. Murray not wanting Robbo to see, nor not wanting to invite him down to help, tries to manhandle the skeletal remains out of the way so that they can all get a better look at what is there. While he is pulling and hauling away, Cha tells him to stop and then shows him the marks on the ground. The frame has been designed to be moved in a specific direction. They now start searching for the mechanism to detach the sleeping skeletons from the wall. Alicia finds the lever and then pulls it down. Several small wheels lock into place on the bottom of the frame.

They all give Murray a hand in moving the frame out of the way, and the wheels squeak and then groan, protesting at not being used for many years. Now that the frame has been rotated by ninety degrees, they all have a clearer view of the forgotten doorway. Cha gently rubs the opening with her gloved hands, the centuries of accumulated dust start to fall off. The strange, almost alien-looking symbols slowly start to appear as more of the dirt and the grime are removed. Alicia pours and then splashes some water down over the surface. The shapes extend, fully exposing themselves. The symbols all look familiar, all of them present agree that they have seen them before. Unfortunately, none of them cannot remember exactly where or when.

Chapter 10

The keeper of the records on receiving Lesqueths seal of approval had started work on the burial chamber for the esteemed Vort. The building work was well underway and before carrying out the final construction work in sealing off the tomb, they required the twenty-seven prisoners who were destined by fate to accompany Vort into the afterlife forever. Tesporo armed with the stamped authorisation, approaches the building where the prisoners are stored. The sentry on duty really wants to tell the utterly repellent keeper of the records and his equally repulsive attendants to fuck right off. On being presented with the approved application he has no other option but to allow them in.

Tesporo leads the way and on locating what he thinks are reasonably suitable specimens. He taps him on the shoulder and a couple of his acolytes step forward to remove the prisoner. Several hours later, once he has selected the full quota. The now shackled prisoners are marched to the site of Vorts' burial chamber. All twenty-seven of them are one at a time held firmly and then operated on. Several modifications were required to be carried out prior to the ceremony taking place. The prisoner is held firm, his hand is placed on the bench then, one by one, their fingers were removed with a hammer and chisel. The process was repeated for the other hand. The prisoner is in a state of absolute shock. He hardly has time to register what is happening as his offending toes were removed in the same manner. The now prisoner who has no remaining digits left to be amputated, wonders what his torturers are about to do next. He was not kept waiting for long before his testicles were dispatched with an open razor. The soundwaves emanating from the prisoner's unsanctioned donation must have carried all the way into the afterlife.

The keeper of the records is more than well aware that the modifications could have been easily performed with the use of anaesthetics. Tesporo is of the opinion that in filling the burial chamber with screams of this strength, validity and conviction prior to Vorts' interment was indeed a blessing bestowed on them from the gods on high. The full moon would be rising soon and he desperately wanted everything in place for the interment process.

The now-modified prisoners are all shackled to the walls of their very own private little enclosures. All of the offending testicles, the now unnecessary fingers, along with the repulsive toes have all been disconnected from their owners. The operational procedures, cauterisation followed by the sewing up process of all the inflicted unauthorised amputations would not have passed an inspection by the ruling medical examination board. Nevertheless, Tesporo was confident that all would be more than adequate for what was required.

One by one, the naked detainees awake in their new surroundings, now slowly becoming fully aware that they are almost encased in stone. On recovering from the unscheduled operations, they are all having the associated pain in the areas where some of their body parts had been removed. A single bell chimes and a bunch of white-on-white figures carry a wrapped body and with great reverence. They then place Vort in the middle of the chamber. A double chime of the bell and twenty-seven are introduced to the incessant humming as the single note reverberates throughout the chamber.

A group of the white-on-white kneel beside the wrapped-up body and offer prayers to the Gods on his behalf. As the others slowly move about the chamber placing the small barbeque grills just below eye level. In this position, all of the shackled prisoners can see through the opening of their stone chambers. The humming never stops, never increases in volume and is always the one single note. Over and over, the keeper of the records along with all of his acolytes keeps up the incessant irritating noise. One by one the barbeque grills are ignited, then a small bell chimes three times. Tesporo accompanied by two of his assistants, mutters some undecipherable waffle to the gods. His assistants raise their hands to the heavens. Tesporo places the body parts on the barbeque and then whispers some more, this time an almost inaudible prayer to the gods. The process is repeated until all of the twenty-seven have had their offerings accepted by the old ones.

The screaming, along with all of the other associated pleas for mercy has started. Tesporo knows that Vort will now be starting his journey into the afterlife, now happy at the unrelentless cries and pleading. The bell chimes four times, and then each of the twenty-seven, one by one are introduced to the tube, which is inserted roughly down their throats. They are force-fed and watered. The food contains generous amounts of laxatives. No sooner than they are fed, the twenty-seven then start to shit themselves uncontrollably. The ones who had balked at the feed process are allowed to be sick, the steaming puddles of vomit adding to the pile of accumulating filth at their feet. Some of them had protested, in refusing to accept the tube. A sharp implement piercing their torso gently persuades these ungrateful protestors to encourage a rethink of their rather hastily made decision.

The incessant humming along the never-ending force-feeding, continues for days on end. The prisoners are not allowed to sleep and when the human waste is just below their knees the force-feeding suddenly ceases. The twenty-seven inmates who are thinking that their ordeal is finally over. Unfortunately, they are all going to be bitterly disappointed. The opening that the brotherhood had used to reach in and place the tubes down their throats is permanently sealed off. If any of the prisoners had fallen asleep during the curing of the waterproof cement. They were rudely awakened as the valves on the human effluent tanks above had been activated. The accumulated pish infused with the lumps of shit slowly glugs down through the interconnecting pipework, drowning each of the entombed prisoners. When the screaming had finally ceased, Tesporo hoped that his ascension into the afterlife would be just as exhilarating and a truly joyous occasion as this one.

With all the prisoners now dead, the humming stops and Tesporo delivers the farewell prayer. In full praise of his mentor as the white-on-white robed brethren repeat the sombre rhetoric issued to Vort word for word. The final act of cutting themselves and then letting their blood fall on the wrapped-up body of their former leader is performed. As they form a line and approach the exit displaying their cuts before Tesporo. The one who had cut into himself the most, along with the one who had cut himself the least are selected. The humming begins again as they string up their fellow brethren by the ankles. The humming stops then they sing earnestly together as the suspended pair have their throats cut at exactly the same moment. The once white-on-white linen covering Vorts body slowly changes into the same colour of the blood. The warm liquid gushes out from the newly opened veins and arteries, spreading its warmth along with its true unconditional devotion as it seeps along through the fine cloth. Tesporo delighted with the grand finale, leads the brotherhood out. When the last one leaves, he orders the workers to brick up and permanently seal the opening for the rest of the time.

In the northern outpost of Hull, Miasnikov is delighted. His master plan for the all-inclusive entertainment package is almost ready with all the preparations just about complete. He was going to give his production a grandiose name and then spread the announcement by placing flyers everywhere. Vladimir changed his mind at the last minute before he had even looked into the design of the leaflets. As this would have given away the secret and then it would no longer be a surprise for everyone. The general, in his wisdom, had also decided that there would be no rehearsals nor any final dress rehearsal. This performance will be strictly one of a kind, and it will be performed live in front of a captive audience.

He summons Anna along with her replacement. Miasnikov paces backwards and forwards, running through all the various scenes that are being played out in full inside his head, along with all of the broken bottles and barking dogs. Vladimir's thoughts are interrupted when the women finally arrive. He enquires if they are up to speed with the proposed changes in duty. Both of them stand immediately to attention and then give the correct salute, confirming that they have exchanged all of the necessary information for the swap over to run smoothly and efficiently. Miasnikov grunts something in reply, using his native language then indicates that they have to follow him. The transformation of the bar is now complete. Miasnikov, as far as he could remember, had always been a big fan of Western movies. Anna and Olga, look totally bewildered at the spectacle that is in now right in front of them.

The once meet and greet place for every event you could possibly imagine has been replaced by a Western saloon that you would see in a typical run of the mill Hollywood cowboy movie. Some of the horned skulls nailed to the walls were not of the same time period. Nor are they remotely connected geographically to the region, but it was all that was available. Miasnikov thinks that no one attending would be bright enough to notice the inconsistencies. The out of place Rhinoceros or the various dinosaur skulls that had been issued on a temporary loan from the local natural history museum.

His personal favourite is the gaming table. His workers had suffered more than a fair amount of pain and discomfort in getting the mechanism to work the way that he had described. Eventually after a few beatings, all the flaws were ironed out and he was happy, very happy indeed. Vladimir shows his assistants around the future production, using his finger like a revolver, he points and speaks. "Card table, roulette wheel, quick draw area, knife throwing area and this lady's is the bar."

He beams with pride as he hands over the Western costumes, "during the performance, both of you will be stationed behind the bar. Most of the time you will be looking pretty while serving drinks. However, if push comes to shove and I get into trouble, you will arm yourselves with the 9mm automatics and then eliminate any of the problems. I don't think it will ever come to this but with these people, you just can't really predict how they react to a challenge. We start in a couple of hours, so go and get changed then get used to your new surroundings. I nearly forgot, if you could put on an American accent, that would be fantastic, as it would give the whole thing more of an authentic feel."

Now with the resident-certified lunatic, well out of the way. Anna asked Olga if she had ever by chance seen a Western movie. Olga just looked at her, thinking that this was pure madness. Anna continued, "If I am thinking correctly, we have to dress up as tarts, behave nice, also have to look pretty then if the shit hits the fan, we have to shoot everyone in the bar." Olga puts on the fake American accent, "Yip homes, that's about it and if any of them God-dam mother fuckers diss you, then fucking cap 'em." Anna does not think that the slang being displayed was anywhere remotely near being authentic for the era, but she thinks that she will get the jist of it.

Vladimir Miasnikov is ready. He would have much preferred it if it was sundown. It would have given the whole experience a truly Western feel. Alas, sundown in Hull would have hardly matched the geographical splendour of sundown in Oklahoma or Tallahassee. As well as in all of the other places in the American West that he could never remember the names of. His troopers have been given their explicit instructions and if they do not carry them all out to the letter, there will be some unavoidable, rather unfortunate life-threatening accidents. He parades himself in front of the full-length mirror. He thinks he looks more than perfect for the part.

The general had even tried one of them small cigars and had posed with the stub hanging out his mouth. The smoke stung his eyes. The taste, along with the smell, was awful and made him want to puke. Miasnikov had decided that he was going to be a non-smoking cowboy. He had the full intention of being the meanest son of a bitch that had ever breathed in this God-forsaken one-horse town. Vladimir has a last practice of drawing his revolver and then blowing away the pretend gunpowder residue, "go and get em, cowboy," he says to the handsome chap staring back at him. Then living the dream inside his head, at sunset, he rides alone along the dusty trail. The tumble weed drifts aimlessly through the deserted street, and a lone wolf howls crying out in anguish somewhere in the untamed wilderness as Freddy Fast Fingers journeys towards his unavoidable appointment with destiny and fate.

The curtains open, as per his orders the bar is almost full. The players all have drinks and religiously keep to their parts within the script. They whoop and holler with joy when they win at the wheel, on cue the two resident town drunks have a punch-up at the bar. Anna as well as Olga have surpassed his best expectations, in looking perfect for the part. Freddy approaches the bar and then orders whiskey on the rocks. He gets a glass of the liquid, ignoring the fact that ice is the rocks and that he has not received any. Freddy Fast Fingers walks around the bar, watching as they play cards and intends to partake in the game of chance on the roulette wheel. All the money is real, the word was out that if they win, they will be allowed to keep it. Miasnikov can't think of what they could possibly spend it on, never mind anyone alive who would accept the now worthless pieces of paper. Vladimir admittedly had to give them some inspiration, even if it was a total pack of lies that he had filled their empty heads with.

Depositing himself at the wheel of chance, Mr. Fast Fingers places some of his hard-earned cash on the table in exchange for some of the gaming chips, and then places his bet. He does not win and proceeds to place another bet, this time when he does not win. He accuses the wheel operator of cheating, and then in a loud voice, Freddy demands to speak with the manager. The prisoner had been dressed for the part and had been held in the office until the manager was called. One of Miasnikov's troopers opened the door and then forced him out at gunpoint to face his audience. The bar had been extended, allowing all of the prisoners who were not given a part, to be located in the new seating area, which gave them all a bird's eye view. Guards were seated at the ends of the rows and also in amongst them, just in case they had any silly thoughts about non-participation along with any escape attempts.

"My name is Mackenzie, and I am the manager of this fine establishment. What seems to be the problem sir?" Fast Fingers was delighted that the prisoner was playing to the script, even though he had changed the plot at the last minute without informing him. He still thought that his performance was riveting. "This wheel is rigged and you have been cheating. What kind of establishment is this? That takes an honest man's money through deceit and trickery." Mackenzie, the manager, does not know what to say as this part was not in the script and in reply, mutters something incoherently. Fast Freddy drags him by the lapels then shows him the switch under the table, which when activated, alters the spin and then changes the house odds to win, win and win every single time.

The would-be manager protests that he does not know anything about it, then desperately pleads his innocence. Freddy Fast Fingers pulls a quick draw and shoots Mackenzie in the head then turns quickly, working the trigger with the palm of his left hand, he shoots the other people at the wheel of fortune. All four of them had also received a forty-five slug in the centre of the head. He is not as good at shooting with his left hand so he shoots the other six people in the chest. Freddy picks up all of the now blood-soaked chips and then calmly walks over to the card table.

All the seats at the table are full. Fast Fingers places the revolver on the head of one of them, "I believe this is my seat," then pulls the trigger. After he pushes the body and lets it fall on the sawdust-covered floor, Miasnikov reloads his weapons. The empty brass casings bounce off the table and everyone in the bar watches as they spin almost in slow motion on the floor. He puts on his mean poker face and then watches carefully as the cards are dealt. Freddy does not look at his hand but bets anyway. He increases the sum every time it is his shout. The players whittle down to just leaving the two of them in the game as Fast Fingers make the call.

His opponent unveils three jacks and two aces and looking at what Miasnikov has in front of him, he reaches over to rake in the now sizable pot. "Not so quick partner!" as Miasnikov declares to all that he has the winning hand, "Tallahassee quadrouple cheeseburger with fries!" The guy with the full house of jacks over aces, calls him a cheat for calling out the unregistered hand, which in reality is nothing more than seven high, and then asks for a duel. In the script that he had read, he was perfect. The notes had stated for the record in bold in your face, underlined capitals that Miasnikov would not shoot him. They take the position and make snake eyes at each othe. As suttle a hand grenade, Freddie delivers the prearranged signal. On que Olga pulls the lever behind the bar and suddenly the trapdoor springs open. The true winning card player falls into the deep hole full of spikes. Freddy Fast Fingers looks down at his fallen opponent. The dead man has been pierced several times, well impressed he gives Olga a ten out of ten.

He accuses the rest of the players of being nothing but low-down cheating scumbags and carpet baggers. Fast Fingers sets about killing them. Some of them pulled their revolvers and fired. As they are only loaded with blanks, Freddy acts as if he has been mortally wounded only to miraculously recover and now that he has regained his strength, continues to murder them. At the end of his performance, he had impaled one of them on the rhino horn, two unfortunate souls dangled on the pronged dinosaur skull, and the rest he had shot or strangled. Freddy Fast Fingers reloads and then instructs Anna and Olga to join him in a curtain call. The troopers positioned in the front of the audience, produce cards along with their weapons to encourage the hostages to clap loudly and very enthusiastically as the trio take their second curtain call.

Fast Freddy Fingers, still full of adrenaline, fires his weapon into the now applauding audience, killing three hostages and two guards in the process. Absolutely delighted with the whole experience, General Vladimir Miasnikov informs Anna that the next time they should have a horse in the show. Anna, unable to deliver her true honest opinion, agrees straight away, replying that she thinks that it is a splendid idea.

Miasnikov is still on a high from his recent performance, thinks that everyone who witnessed it should be, without a doubt, asking for his autograph. He had found out that one of the detained people was a painter in the old world. The woman had tried very hard to explain to him at length that she was a painter and decorator and on the rare occasion, an interior decorator. Vladimir refused to listen to anything that she said and insisted that she should paint his portrait in view of his recent, five-star Oscar-winning performance.

He had gone to great lengths explaining what he wanted in the painting and throughout his vivid descriptions. She had once again tried to tell him that portrait painting was not her true forte. Miasnikov still had on his cowboy clothes and told her to watch as he posed, looking mean with the revolver drawn. "This is how I want to look; memorise it and I will come and review the results of your labour of love sometime soon." Vladimir tips his hat to the lady, then walks away. He has to get changed back into his normal clothes. The instructions from Lesqueth still have to be addressed, as it would not look good if she paid a surprise visit and noticed that her last instruction had not been carried out.

He shouts out for someone, anyone to go out and locate them. Both of them appear to find him with the painter. Miasnikov is perplexed. He had requested a full portrait, given a vivid description of the pose he wanted, along with the details of the imaginary landscape that had to be captured. The scrawl of the matchstick man on the matchstick horse was less than inspirational. The small circle with the eyelashes on the top left corner depicting the midday sun was hardly a representation of the truly epic Western scene that he had desired. The image that he intended to call Freddy Fast Fingers rides again. What was now in front of him, was more like a gift from Artistic Annie the Amputee. Vladimir flies into an uncontrollable rage, grabbing her by the hair, and as she struggles, he tightens his grip then rams the unused paintbrushes up her nostrils and sticks one in each of her eyes. Then, for good measure and to apply the finishing touches, he pushes one into each ear as far as physically possible. The general shouts for his guards to remove the portrait painter and add her to the accumulating display on the pavement below. He sets the picture on fire, thinking that a blind primary school kid with no fingers or toes could have done so, so much better.

Now addressing Anna, he informs her that she will be transferring to JJ's attachment on the western reaches of this unforsaken Godless land. "Thank you for all of your hard work and dedication and if you happen to come across a painter, ask JJ to send them over. Olga you will be in charge of the escort. Please give JJ my finest regards when you eventually find him." Both of them are delighted to be dismissed. They had discussed in private their escape plan and the time had finally, at last arrived for them to release themselves from the clutches of this mad man.

Olga fires up the engine and signals her group to move on out. Miasnikov would have liked to have changed the place name to Dodge. As no one knew where the fuck Hull was, then they would have had absolutely no chance whatsoever of locating Dodge. She switches off all thoughts of her soon-to-be ex-leader, changes gear and accelerates out of whatever he would like to call this fucking God-forsaken place. Her only passenger has no regrets and she knows what she and Olga must have to do. At last, finally being able to escape as far away as possible from all of this madness. Where they will be escaping to, she has no idea, nor does she think that it will be a pleasant and carefree existence. Whatever lies in front of them will, at the very least, be certainly free from the barbarism and all of the cruelty that the leaders have seen fit to bestow upon this once green and pleasant land.

The convoy draws to a halt at the first checkpoint. The sentry nonchalantly approaches them and orders everyone to switch off the engines and then to have the appropriate paperwork ready for inspection. Anna thinks that this will be the first time that she has ever been stopped and the first time that she has ever possessed the correct documents. None of the soldiers are recognisable, and she surmises that these new faces must have been dispatched from the families down South. The patches displaying the insignia are new, but the lettering above still registers the distinct same four letters that every company displays.

The one in charge looks at the paperwork and then looks at them, he asks how long they expect the journey to last. No one can give an estimated time as none of them are aware of the road nor the static traffic conditions. The sentry blurts into the conversation and forces the issue. She throws her hands in the air to remonstrate, "two days? three days? a week?" Olga would just like to shoot her in the head right now but holds back and tells her that it will take them approximately seven days, allowing for the jammed-up roads. She also adds that if the roads are clear, they will do it in five. The sentry seems happy with the answer and replies to all that this is why our great leader has promoted more women to senior positions, as only women can lead their race to the final victory. She salutes and the one in charge, with a flick of his hand, indicates that they are now free to go.

Olga asks Anna what she thinks that was all about, and without even looking, she replies, "One very lonely brain cell, crying out for a bullet and a long, long, lonely sleep in a dark field." Olga is sorry that she had even asked her the question, kills the conversation and concentrates on the road ahead. They continue on with their journey and with only a couple of hours of daylight left and as the road in front of them is pretty fucked up. Olga issues the call and the convoy slows to a halt. She gives out instructions to find a suitable place to rest, telling them that

Miasnikov is not here. They do not need to be residing in a former tourist guide recommended five-star establishment. Anna is now awake and guesses that this is their first overnight stopover on route to sunny Wales. She forces herself out of the vehicle and then stretches to rid her body of all the accumulated aches and pains. She sees Olga heading towards a few shops that stand out like an oasis in the foreboding concrete jungle.

Anna stands guard and smokes while Olga is inside rummaging about. She does not have to wait long as she appears with an item from the shop, Olga hands her the gift. The title is "Places to visit when in Wales, volume 8" Anna thanks her, telling her that this was the one book that was required for the full collection. "I am thinking that you never just went in there just for this and that you actually got a road atlas." Olga tells her that when the grunts are resting, they will have a look at it later and at least now they will know some of the names of the places in their escape up north.

The underlings have found a place for them all to bunk down for the night. It was once a bed and breakfast establishment. The outside has some visible signs of damage, but they are both assured that inside it is cleanish and is more than good enough for one night. The crew set up who was sleeping where, Anna and Olga selected to share the one-bedroom downstairs, letting the others decide who was sharing and who was not. Olga informs them that she will cook just as long as everyone contributes something out of their secret stash. Miasnikov did not believe in the ration system, thinking that in this land of plenty, there was an abundance of food available as all you had to do was find it and then eat it.

Various tins are presented to her, ignoring the bashed ones she is left with four with labels and three with still-to-be-identified contents. Olga opens the ones without labels first. The first one is dog food, which she chucks straight through the closed window. The others are some unidentifiable vegetable mixtures and she is not sure of the name of the industrialised meat product in the other ones. Everything is emptied into one pot; she sprinkles in a few spices to add some flavour to make everyone pretend that it is actually edible. Cooking was never one of her strong points but none of them need to know this. "Grubs up" on hearing the news, the crew appears armed with their bowls and plates. She does not let them help themselves, otherwise the person at the end would be getting nothing. She delves it out as equally as possible. One of them asks what it is and Olga bluntly tells them, "How the fuck should I know? I only opened the fucking tins." There are no other questions from the hungry troopers and all is scoffed without any comments or any issued complaints.

Olga had sorted out the duty rota and now that they are alone in their billet, the atlas is produced and they work out where they are and, more importantly, where they are going. Initially they had planned to escape tomorrow after the next stop. The only problem is that there is no guarantee that there is going to be a next stop. Anna asks Olga, "What do you think? Why don't we just go tonight? No one knows where we are and it will be days before they notice that we are gone. If we do it right, they will think that we are dead and will not even bother looking for us." Olga looks at her and replies, "Funny you should mention that." She asked if she had noticed that they had their food had been delved out first. Anna had noticed nothing, "I ground up a large bundle of sleeping tablets and masked the taste with some of them exotic sounding Indian and Asian spices. Give them half an hour and they should all be sound asleep." Anna nods, confirming that she fully understands.

Chapter 11

Murray and the team have called a halt to the investigation in the recently unearthed chamber. Now with them all sitting around the table, Charlie is upset about something and won't let Murray out of her sight. This is not like her and even though the fire is on, she has not taken up her regular spot in front of the hearth. She had even followed him to the toilet and then waited patiently outside for his return. Murray does not know what is the matter with her and even though he has tried and tried again to console her, it has made not one bit of a difference. Cha and everyone else had noticed the change in Charlie's demeanour, but even though they all have also attempted to coax her over, she is refusing to leave Murray's side.

They are now in possession of several rough sketches relating to the configuration of all of the mysterious markings. Alicia and Cha had made a fair attempt to copy what was displayed on the secret door opening. All the artwork was now displayed on the wall, complete with all of the ornate swirls and the strange interconnected letters. They were placed in an almost identical configuration, representing the sealed entrance. Murray had added Cha Black age five to one of the sketches when no one was looking and he was the only one of them who thought it was remotely funny. Cha on seeing the added little extra, told him that he was being very childish. Then to rub salt on the wound, using that you should know better tone, she asked if it was possible for him to behave like a mature adult as this is a very serious matter.

All of them had looked at the pictures for a long while, constantly racking their brains in trying to remember where they had seen them all before. Then finally it dawned on them, that these symbols had appeared on the trim of the old woman's hooded cloak. It did not help them unravel the enigma but at least all of them agreed where they had previously seen them. Cha had suggested that they examine every artifact that is now in their possession for any associated patterns that could possibly help them unravel the mystery. One theory that they have come up and is now the conversation playing around the table is that the strange symbols are all separated by lines indicating that they can or were able at one time to have been pressed into the wall. If they worked out the correct running order then perhaps the door would open. The only possible problem would be that if the sequence entered was incorrect, there would surely be a fail-safe in reserve. To deter them or perhaps eliminate any uninvited guests attempting an unauthorised entry.

Every single artifact that was related to the Hidden had been collected and then placed on the table. After carefully examining all of the precious items, they still were still no further forward in solving the mystery. Murray thinks that the pile of necklaces looked like the proceeds from an illicit late-night visit at the local jeweller's shop, all they needed now was a fence. Alicia interrupts their thoughts "We have been through everything, looked at all the items from every conceivable angle, there is nothing there, no indications and no clues. Perhaps it is something that we are not meant to know, somewhere where we are not meant to venture into." Murray shakes his head, "Then why did we find the opening in the first place? If it was not meant to be found, I am sure that they could have easily obliterated all the clues that led us there. I think there is a sequence. We just can't see it." Cha is deep in thought; Murray asks her if she wants a penny for them. Smiling she looks at him, "Yes, I am sure that there are clues to be had and this will be the only true way to proceed forward. I dread to think what would happen if we tried to force an entry."

Okolo is about to say something, when there is a knock on the door, it is Rebecca, still resplendent in full makeup. Murray thinks that she looks like a warmed-up corpse out searching for someone to take her picture in a more than fair exchange for not devouring their soul. She delivers the message to Cha; she reads it quietly, then informs them that Dean has just passed away. He was not one of their favourite people. Most definitely not that easy to get along with, but she thinks that some of them should at least show a little respect and turn up for his funeral. She asks them if they want to go, and Cha asks Cat to speak to Frank to find out if he wishes to attend. The funeral will be the next day. Much to her surprise, all of the team, with the exception of Beth and Debs, are willing to attend.

As Cora and Karen are part of the inner circle in their community, they have been asked and then accepted to go along. Cha along with sister Okolo are more than happy about leaving their precious bundles in the care of the twins. Beth and Debs are well aware of their routine. Freely admit that they are looking forward to reading all the stories, plus the song and dance routines that they intend to share in entertaining the children.

The next morning Murray along with the gang arrive at the Farmhouse community. Mark and Ellie are there at the gate to greet them. Cha speaks for all of them, "Sorry that we are meeting in these circumstances. We always meant to come over but you know how it is." Mark tells them that he understands, thanking them all for coming to see Dean off. Cha sets out to find Emma and give her all of their condolences for her loss. Murray as well as Cha had remembered the first day that they had all met up in the supermarket. Emma thanked them for coming, knowing fully well that Dean most certainly had his moments, but even with all his many faults, she did love him. As they are all gathered at the graveside, Mark delivers the eulogy adding in a few policeman jokes to break the sadness. Emma followed up, thanking everyone for their presence, stating that Dean would have been chuffed to bits to see all his new and old friends here together to remember the good times and overlook the not-so-good ones. Murray along with Cha have been allocated to hold a cord. Ellie says some nice words as the coffin is lowered into the ground.

Mark had laid on a spread and led the way, holding Emma as he guided her towards the wake reception. Cora is in deep conversation with the trainee vet and he does not believe her that Cat did not hiss like a wild animal when she had undergone the last examination. He just happens to notice her at the other side of the room and does not know whether to pray or go into a deep extended hibernation when she delivers a friendly wave and smile. Frank is now chatting to Emma as they talk about the times that they had shared, in what now seems like such a long, long time ago.

Murray and Mark now having sneaked outside to smoke. "I know that Dean was not on your Christmas card list but it was really something that you all turned up for Emma, thanks bud really appreciated." Murray said it was no problem at all, empathising that the good times and the bad times are intermingled and sometimes you just have to forget and then overlook the other not-so-good ones. Mark informs him, "You will need to go and see the repair team. If not, I will be on the receiving end of never-ending earache." Murray thinks that they must now be holding their own as he no longer receives any requests to come and help or advise, but he does agree to visit his former trainees. Ellie has kidnapped Cha, Alicia along with Okolo and can't wait to show them what the children get up to when the grown-ups are at work.

The first stop is the nursery, where the pre-school kids generally play and almost habitually make a mess. Ellie stresses that it is important that children get to mix and interact at an early age, "After all, we don't want any of them to end up like Murray." Cha thinks that Mark and Vincent would love it being in among this lot and as they are now all sleeping, they leave them to continue on the guided tour. In between all the laughter, mostly at jokes about Murray. Ellie tells them that life at present is good; their community is growing almost monthly, and fingers crossed, they don't have any major problems with roving armed gangs trying to take everything away from them. The children are on a break so they are allowed to have a sneaky peak in the classroom. All the desks are very neat and tidy, but it is the artwork that has them speechless. There is an almost near identical display of the sketches that Cha had posted on the wall in the kitchen. They would be the same except for the fact that these sketches have been allocated marks out of ten for their effort and artistic prowess.

At the farmhouse, Ellie was wondering what was going on with her guests, if she had said something wrong or perhaps even offended her friends. All she had done was to show Cha and the other women from the watermill the exhibition of the latest drawings produced by the children. They had all went quiet on her, standing motionless, staring at the displayed pictures. "Have I said something wrong, something to offend all of you?" Cha replied that she could never say anything offensive to her or any of the others and promised to explain if she supplied them with some pens along with some paper. Ellie supplied the required items, then watched as Cha and Alicia scribbled down a rough copy of all the pictures that were now staring them all in the face.

Cha offered a reasonable explanation, "You are aware that Ruby and I had this unbreakable connection relating to an age-old mystery. That neither of us fully understood and therefore, we could never properly explain." Ellie nods, remembering the bequeathed letter and necklace. "We recently uncovered a room that, as far as we are aware had lain undisturbed for centuries. Imagine our utter surprise when the symbols that are on display here are identical match the symbols on the doorway. It is just too much of a coincidence to be ignored, we could not for the life of us fathom out the correct sequence and I think, we think that with the added numbering could very well be the solution to the problem." Ellie asks them to be as quick as possible, copying all the information that is required as the children will be back soon and she does not want them freaking out.

Alicia informs them that there is not enough time to copy everything and asks if they could come back later. Ellie tells them that will not be a problem, "It will be almost dark when the children finish, so I should go and make arrangements for the overnight stay." Cha and the women walk back to the reception. Cha had asked Ellie to keep the latest news under wraps for now and she will try and explain it later to Mark. Ellie just smiles, knowing that she and her gang will be asking questions about something she does not know anything about. Cha finds Murray with Mark in the repair shop; they are sitting laughing at the various posters that appear on the walls. "Murray would do this!" and the one they are very amused at, "Murray would never do that!" Cha much prefers the graffiti, with one secret artist adding, "Who the fuck is Murray?"

Mark greets her with his customary charm, asking if everything is okay. She tells them the news and Mark is none of the wiser. "Once the funeral reception is over, we will meet in my office later where we can talk about this. In the meantime, I will have to go and show face." Murray and Cha go with him, although Murray absolutely hates all the small talk with a vengeance. He had promised to make an exception and will make a conscious effort in attempting to partake in communication with anyone he meets. Cha had warned him before they had left that he would be expected to mingle, adding that perhaps he would even be required to make a small speech. He had escaped the public speaking part but had now to go and work on his "Hi, how are you? Wonderful weather for this time of year."

On arriving at the reception, Murray grabs a cuppa then activating his search and evade radar, he finds a secluded spot where he can partake in a sneaky smoke. Cha along with the women has sorted out the sleeping arrangements with Ellie. He sees them in the corner explaining to Cora and Karen some reason for staying overnight. Murray would just like to tell them the truth but the insurmountable questions that followed would be unbearable. He much prefers to tell things straight, but perhaps it is just better to keep things as they are without adding in any unnecessary complications.

Frank had not been over here for a very long time. He never had thought about it or Linda, who by all accounts is now the number one tractor driver in the community. Cat had shown no interest in knowing or asking anything about her. She thinks that what is in the past can stay firmly in the past. The vet nearly had a heart attack when she approached him, then had very politely introduced him to her other half. He could not believe how charming and warm she was compared to the previous version. In which she was a hissing feral animal. That should have been given an extremely dangerous, do not approach notice. Then had her name, along with her description, added to the top of the dangerous species list. After their brief conversation he had several stiff whiskeys to calm his nerves which was really quite something, as right up till that point he was strictly tee total.

Cora had noticed his predicament; she delivered the open confession that Cat is actually quite nice when you get to know her. It is just the getting to know her part that is the ultimate challenge. The vet has calmed down and wholeheartedly agreed with her statement adding that Frank must be an angel sent down from heaven to calm the wild beast that resides within her just beneath the surface. Cora smiles and promises never to repeat his comment. Karen approaches informing Cora that the others are staying overnight and they will be travelling back with Frank in about ten minutes. Cora wishes the vet well, reminding him that if they need anything, all they have to do is ask.

Murray has had a change of plan and along with Cat, they have decided to go back home. He is worried about Charlie, not wanting to leave her alone. There is a bit of a squeeze in the car but as it is only a relatively short journey, they can endure the slight discomfort. Cat has fallen asleep wrapped in Frank's arms as soon the vehicle started to move; Cora thinks that if it was possible to take a picture it would be the ideal present for the vet.

Charlie is going nuts as soon as they open the door, Cat fusses over her as Murray checks that the young ones are settled. When he is free, he takes over and, as Cat puts the water on to boil, Murray has a gentle word with Charlie, "if only dogs could talk, then it would all be so easy." There is still something bothering her. He wishes he could help her; he can't remember her ever being this unsettled. Murray puts on the fire and although she takes up her normal position, she still watches his every movement. Cat asks him what is up with her. Murray wishes that he knew. He thinks that it has something to do with the underground chamber, as she was fine until then. Not quite knowing what to say, to ease his worries she suggests that they could go out a walk with all the dogs later. Murray agrees, reminding her to make sure he lets the twins know; they had done a great job of looking after the infants. They had found them all upstairs; the floor was littered with children's books and the four of them were all sound asleep. Mark is not quite ready to walk up to Charlie's favourite spot. Murray is looking forward to all the father and son conversations that they will have during these glorious days. Murray sadly did not have any of these conversations with his father and he has every intention of talking non-stop to his son.

Murray had unintentionally amused Cat as well as the twins to no end with his baby's somewhat unusual feeding routine. Charlie along with Romulus had watched with one ear up and one ear down wondering what all the fuss was about, after all food is just food. Murray was pleased that Charlie had calmed down a little. He thought that the recently uncovered hole in the ground had most definitely spooked her some. Charlie had never liked it up there. The inside of the orangery was fine; they had played in there loads of times but the more he thinks about it, she never ever really liked certain areas around the outside of the building.

Cat had brought over Remus earlier and unless he was getting some of the baby food. He was most definitely not interested and now lays flat out in front of the fire. Murray gets himself Vincent and Mark ready. Cat clicks her fingers and Remus springs to attention. "So, you have been working with him?" Cat replies, "No, he knows that if he is good and does everything that he is ordered to do that he will receive a miniscule piece of cheese." They both laugh, thinking that their animals would do absolutely anything for a piece of cheese, no matter how small. Murray jokingly lets it slip that he had tried a similar technique with Cha but he had ended up in hospital. He holds the door open and the children are walking this time. The dogs' sense this, almost behaving like they are the retinue of personal bodyguards as the children take their first tentative steps outside. Both of them know that they will not walk the whole way, but it is great to see them try.

Mark speaks sometimes and his most frequent words are Cha-Cha, which translates to both Cha and Charlie. Charlie does not leave his side and the infant happily shouts Cha-Cha, at which Charlie wags her tail. Vincent gives up first then holds his arms up for Murray. Mark soon follows suit and gives up on the idea of walking, holding his arms up where Cat dutifully obliges and the dogs now noticing that they are free from escort duties, spring into action, chasing and barking at each other.

Mark now in Cat's arms, sticks his fingers in her face, exploring all of her features along with attempting to remove her nose. "Don't you wish that all days could be like this?" Murray wholeheartedly agrees but they both know that sooner or later, the bad guys are going to come back. They had trampled these very grounds in the past and it will only be a matter of time before they finally figure out that they are here. "If you are not too busy later, we could have a look at the maps and see where we could extend the patrols too. The bridge is covered, anything from the direction of the farmhouse is covered and we only have to look at the areas out within these locations." Cat replies that she will come over later and noticing the yellow ball at her feet, kicks it to Murray who much to Charlie's delight, throws it for her to fetch.

They get to his dogs' favourite spot and then notice that there is now snow in the distance. Murray thinks that it is once again early this year and it could be a cold one. Cat smiles, thinking that they may have a few chilly days but she would not exactly call it cold. Where she came from the dry winter winds would almost cut you in half, making you feel so cold that you would want to cry. The weather here had never made her cry, and the only tears she had shed here were tears of joy and happiness. "Murray, thanks for looking after me since I have been here and making me feel welcome." Murray asked her where that had appeared from, "I thought it was just time that I told you." Murray smiled, replying it was time to get the wee guys back home for bath time and then bedtime stories. "I don't think they listen to a single word I say, but I do like to think that they both like the pictures and my animal impersonations."

Chapter 12

Upon arriving back at the house, Cat left him to it and took her dog home. Remus didn't leave her side, always ready to pounce on anyone who strayed too close or approached too quickly. She had heard some of them say the scary but nice woman with the big scary dog. Murray got on with it, entertaining Mark and Vincent, who decided it was time to wake up and have more food. Mark just turned his head away from everything that was presented to him as if Murray was offering him roasted insects coated in regurgitated dog food. Vincent on the other hand would eat anything; he laughed at this, remembering pulling him away from Charlie's bowl on several occasions. Eventually, he found something that appealed to his selective palette and had them fed and bathed by the time Cat arrived. She had brought some food as she knew that they would not have bothered to make anything for themselves. It was only sandwiches, but they were grateful for the gift and scoffed the lot in seconds. Murray placed the open map on the table, and the twins, along with Cat, went through what they could and could not do.

At the farmhouse, the children had now left school for the day, and now with no chance of freaking them out; Ellie had taken down all the pictures and brought them to Mark's office. Now, with them taped onto the wall, they were the focal point for the watermill investigative team as they scrutinized the evidence before them. Cha explained to Mark what was happening, and although he did not have a clue what they were talking about, he told them that he would help them in any way he possibly could. Alicia went through the pictures and explained that what they could see here was precisely identical to what they could see there. "The point is who put the marks on the sketches, the four out of ten, etcetera? was it you, Ellie?" Ellie replied that they were there when she put them on the wall. She had asked the other teachers, amusingly, and they mentioned that they did not do it and thought she had done all the marking. Okolo asked, before anyone else, if she had any examples of her mother's handwriting or if she recognized the script style. Ellie told them she would return in a few minutes and then disappeared on an urgent errand.

Mark requested more tea, then told the assistant that they didn't have to bother bringing any of the preggie biscuits; as they looked at him, he confessed that Ellie had told him the good news. Robbo, who had been silent throughout the impromptu meeting, didn't even mention his super swimmers; if he had, Alicia and Okolo would have probably clobbered him. Ellie had returned with some letters; they looked at Ruby's handwriting and then compared it to the fine script on the children's drawings. It was, without a doubt, a one hundred percent identical match.

Alicia had taken control of the room, and they all paid attention as she tried to go through the imagined sequence of what symbol to press first.

"We have ten squares or ten symbols now with a selected numerical identification," said Alicia, expecting a response. She looked at Robbo as he stared at the wall, finally noticing that Alicia was waiting for a response.

He replied, "Yup, that's a Rodger Dodger."

Alicia gave a strange look and continued, "So here are the represented numbers."

Robbo interrupted her and said, "I have a question. You have ten pictures, but if I am counting correctly, there are fifteen squares; how does that work?"

Okolo muttered "Wanker" and then told him to shut the fuck up, insisting that he at least let Alicia finish before asking any more questions.

Alicia took up from where she had left off, "In front of us, we have ten symbols with the code of ten numbers in which each number relates to a particular symbol."

Robbo, thinking that he would be asked if he understood what had been explained so far, shouted, "Got it!" before he was even asked anything. Alicia shook her head, "Four of the symbols have been allocated with the same double mark, so they must be pressed at the same time but in the correct sequence. The additional symbols with no allocated number do not come into the sequence and are likely just a ruse to confuse the chain of thought into trying to work out a non-sequential process."

Alicia nominated Okolo and Robbo to assist her in the demonstration; Robbo was going to bow and give a short speech, saying that this was the first time he had appeared on stage, but he changed his mind at the last minute. Alicia positioned them in front of the pictures; she went through the process, pointing to number one, and Okolo touched it. Alicia then pointed and touched number two herself and went through the whole process, empathizing that the double numbers must be pressed simultaneously. Cha wondered about the numbers on the associated pictures that have not been selected. Then, asking Alicia if this was another possible ruse to overlook the intentionally unused symbols and if it was the case. It would relate to an entirely different sequence of events. With a tone of honesty in her voice, Alicia admitted that she did not know if she was correct, but going by their information, she couldn't think of any other way of doing it. "We could try it, and if it does not work, we could try something else," Alicia spoke.

Cha was still thinking and agreeing with what she was saying, but she also thought that if something went wrong and some device came into play with the incorrect sequence inputted, they could be in grave danger. Alicia understood Cha's thinking but countered that they would face the same unseen, unknown, dangerous situation if her alternative sequence were incorrect.

Mark and Ellie had carefully weighed all of the pros and cons of what they were proposing; he informed them that puzzles were, unfortunately, not one of his strong points. Mark decided to leave them to it but asked if they wanted some food along with something to drink to be delivered. He thought they would be working out whatever they had to figure out until the wee hours. Cha thanked him for the use of his office and for the food. Mark told her that he wished he could help them solve the puzzle. He wished them all goodnight and the best of luck in solving the seemingly head-numbing enigma.

They are all sitting facing the enigmatic puzzle in front of them, just staring at the alienesque symbols on the wall. All of them thought about the various scenarios that were issued both by Cha and Alicia. There was a knock on the door, and the provisions were delivered; Ellie told them to eat it while it was still hot, then wished them all goodnight. Robbo asked if he would play the vicar and then poured the tea. As they shared food, Robbo chimed in, suggesting they take some time out while eating. They had all been so intertwined and engrossed in the mystery that they had just plain forgotten to eat anything, and now realizing their mistake, they get tucked into the splendid fare on offer.

Robbo has been warned not to make his usual mess once they finish eating. At the very least, they should gather all the used plates and utensils and place them outside the door. They drank the tea. Almost in competition with Okolo, Robbo rolled up a couple of bangers, and they smoked while reviewing the current information. Robbo was deep in thought as he performed like a machine making the numbers. He had been quiet for quite a while, with no jokes to make them laugh or annoy them. Cha, almost hearing the cogs whirr non-stop, churning the grey matter in his brain, asked him outright what he was thinking.

He stepped up to the floor and started his little speech, "Any of the messages, as well as any of the images that we have all received from the old woman in the hooded cloak, have never been straightforward, and they also have never been crystal clear. Without a doubt, every single one required extra thinking to piece together the parts of the story. I think this message about the symbols is the same: we have not been given the straightforward A, B, and C to solve the problem, and even now, we are still left with the seemingly unsolvable, enigmatic puzzle."

Okolo was looking like she wanted to either tell him to shut the fuck up or just get straight to the point. "I have listened to all that has been said, paid attention to every theory along with every variation on the said theories." Robbo then pointed at the pictures on the wall, "What if the puzzle is in two parts? Perhaps there is an ordered sequence along with an unordered sequence to consider. And given the agreed-upon fact that there could be danger if we make an error, we should definitely keep that in mind," Robbo stopped, asking if they were following him; the women nodded their heads and asked him to continue. "Therefore, the sequence here could be the one that eliminates the danger, and the alternate sequence that Cha has proposed could be the one for opening up the hidden doorway. I know what you are going to ask, and as for which one is first, I would hazard a guess in saying that the one discovered here is the first sequence, followed by the straightforward sequence of the missing numbers, just to be pumped in the way they appear."

There is now nothing but silence in the room; it was so quiet that you could hear a church mouse fart. The women were astounded by what Robbo had proposed; they wondered if it could be that straightforward and simple. Okolo, Alicia, and Cha joined him at the picture display, asking him to go through the whole sequence from top to bottom. Robbo's eyes lit up with a spark of realisation as he launched into the discussion, laying out his thoughts with unfiltered enthusiasm. "All of the squares are initially, or for the purpose of this demonstration, numbered one to fifteen. The symbols that have been numbered in the school are not part of the numbered sequence and have been selected in accordance with their place within the first sequence." He repeated Alicia's initial theory, leaving the following untouched symbols to be pressed in the order of lowest to highest. "Therefore, if we punch in the numbers six, seven, nine then eleven to fifteen, then maybe the secret door will open and reveal the mystery hidden within."

Robbo was quite chuffed with himself and added that if this does not work, then they are fucked as he can't figure it out any other way. "I had run this through my head while you were all discussing the variable processes involved with all the feasible parameters. This is the only envisaged working scenario that I could think of." They all agreed it was worth a try and now needed to decide who would actually take on the challenge.

They had been talking all night and realised that the restaurant was open; they tidied up Marks's office, remembering to open the windows to rid the place of the lingering smell of smoke. As they were all hungry again, they unanimously voted that breakfast was more than a good idea. They found Mark sitting on his own, and after loading up, they asked if it was okay to sit with him. Okolo thanked him warmly for everything he had done, especially for allowing them to use his office on such short notice. He emphasised how much they all appreciated his kindness and generosity. Mark gracefully accepted the gratitude shown to him, informing them that if it had been the other way around, Murray would have done exactly the same.

Beth and Debs were up before the larks and drinking tea, waiting for Murray to make his grand appearance. They had not slept much, constantly worrying about just how they were going to break the news to him. It was not possible yesterday as the appropriate time was never available. The more they thought about it, the more they would have to tell him straight out. Hopefully, the rest of the gang should be returning from the farmhouse today; the twins would like to get the news out in the open before they all arrive home. The dogs had been fed and watered and now lie, pretending to be fast asleep or dead in front of the fire. It was only their ears that gave them away. Every time they thought they heard something, their radars moved in the direction of the new sound. Having been fed, the children watered, changed, and changed again were now happy, clean, and sound asleep upstairs.

They could hear Murray moving about; a fresh pot of tea was ready for his preferred start to the day as they anxiously awaited his appearance. As always, he bounced down the stairs and greeted them with his customary cheerful good morning.

Murray poured the liquid and apologised for oversleeping, thanking them for looking after the young ones. He went outside to smoke, and the twins followed him out. Murray had just sparked up, and sensing they wanted to say something, he told them to just spit it out. "When you and the rest of the gang were attending Dean's funeral yesterday, in between feeding and sleeping times, we were playing games and entertaining the children." Murray sensed there was more to their story and patiently waited for them to share the rest. Beth spurted it out, "We had shown the simple game of passing the ball."

Debs finished the sentence with, "They cottoned on to the game pretty quick, except they could move the ball without touching it!"

"We did not get the opportunity to let you know yesterday and felt that we should tell you in private."

They continued in their normal speech, one starting and the other finishing the sentence. "We're definitely not making this up; we've seen it happen. It might relate to the dream we all shared that night with Robbo. Some of the people had special gifts. If it's alright with you, we'd like to leave it to you to break the news to

Okolo and Cha." Murray didn't know what to say; sometimes, they all could get into each other's heads, but as far as he was aware, none of them had ever tried to move anything by the power of thought alone.

"Okay, keep it quiet for now, and I will broach the subject with Okolo and Cha." They returned inside the house; Murray poured a refill, and the twins were more relaxed after having aired the important news. They had not been at the table for more than ten minutes when Charlie barked, announcing the arrival of the rest of the gang. Cha entered first, then straight away put her arms around Murray. She had only been away for one night, but to both of them, it felt like far too long. Robbo seated himself at the table; he had not been seated for a minute when Okolo and Alicia both mentioned that a cup of tea would be more than welcome.

Taking the hint, he asked if anyone else wanted some then set about preparing a fresh pot for all of them. Okolo and Cha had gone upstairs to check on their offspring, and Alicia had opted to shower and change. Murray asked Robbo if they had found a workable solution to the problem, and while he clattered about in the kitchen, he replied that they thought they might have something to go on. Robbo added that if they waited until the team came back down, he would fill him in on all the details. He mentioned that if he tried to do it now and got any of the information wrong, he'd only end up with a severe earache in stereo. With the fresh brew now ready, both of them seized the opportunity to escape outside for what they hoped would be an extended smoke break.

Murray had forgiven Robbo for fucking off and leaving him alone, down inside the underground chamber. Robbo started apologizing, and Murray told him not to bother, based on his firmly held belief that the other day was the other day and that life was too short to hold grudges.

With that out of the way, they just shoot the shit the way they used to. Robbo is relieved that things are back to normal, these people had more or less adopted him, and he did not want to piss them off as this was now his home. Murray informed him that Karen had started work on the extension, suggesting they could all go to look at the works later. Karen will no doubt need some more building materials, "I think it would be a good idea for us to offer her some help or, at the very least, volunteer for this task."

Robbo agreed and then asked him about the underground chamber, meaning that they could not explore the chamber and search for building materials simultaneously. Murray replied that they should prioritise the extension and that any possible underground exploration would have to wait. "It is getting colder, and it would be better for everyone if the work was completed before the onset of the bad weather." With the smokes now finished, they returned inside to join the women seated at the table. The device in front of him was new. Murray pointed to the empty box, and Cha filled him in. "That was a present from the vet; it is one of the old-fashioned baby monitors that will work without an internet connection. It just required batteries; it will let us know when they wake up or require any immediate attention."

Cha had just finished her explanation when they all heard a clatter of something falling on the floor. Murray was first up the stairs to investigate; both of the children were now awake. They were not displaying any signs of needing urgent attention or even expressing unhappiness. Vincent and Mark looked at him, smiled, and went back to sleep. Okolo and Cha joined him and asked what noise they had heard downstairs. Murray informed them that he thought that the children did not like the monitor and were just proceeding to let them know their feelings about the new device.

Okolo was just about to deliver her favourite word; Murray stopped her in her tracks, letting them know what the twins had observed while they were watching over them. Cha along, Okolo listened and could hardly believe what he was saying. Murray offered them a solution; he removed the monitor from the floor and then placed it back on the chest of drawers. He ushered them outside as they waited and listened. The trio only had to wait a few minutes before they heard the bang of the device, contacting the floor. "Looks like, for now, they don't like being listened to. We could leave it on the floor because if it is put back up on the furniture, I think they will play this game all day long." Cha and sister Okolo ventured back into the room; the children were sound asleep and displayed huge smiles.

They went back downstairs, telling everyone that all was okay and that there was nothing at all to worry about. Okolo could tell

Robbo and Alicia what delights were in store for them when the next little bundles of fun graced them with their presence. As promised, Murray took Robbo on a guided tour of the work in progress with the extension. Karen was on active duty; Murray asked if there was anything that she required to finish the project. "I thought that you were going to ask that as she hands over her current wish list," Robbo informed Karen that she and her team were doing a great job. Robbo freely admitted that he was more than fucking hopeless at anything to do with his hands or tools. Karen just smiled and went back to work. Murray handed Robbo the list, telling him they would be busy for a couple of days.

In the kitchen, they were in mid-discussion regarding the still-to-be-explored hidden chamber. The marks displayed on the farmhouse sketches had been added to the ones on the wall. Murray listened intently to the latest theories about the proposed sequence required to gain entry into the next chamber. He did not have a problem with the sequence order but thought that they should thoroughly clean the wall and the surrounding area. He interrupted the flow of the conversation, "This place has lain untouched for at least hundreds of years. We should clean the wall containing the symbols as well as the area around it. We could be very well missing something, there could be other symbols on the floor, and as it has lain there for hundreds of years undisturbed, a little clean will at the very least help it to open."

Murray explained that it would take a few days. During that time, Robbo and he could be out foraging the building materials required for the building in progress next door. Alicia thought that a clean-up was a good idea and asked who would venture into the unexplored chamber once they got it opened. "As Robbo and I are the only ones not having a little bundle growing inside us, we would be the first choice. Anyway, we can think about that. What if it does not open? Even if it does open, there is no guarantee that we will find anything. For all we know, it could just be another room with more dusty skeletal remains. Until it is open, we will just have to wait and see, but please consider what I have said, as each and every single one of you is very important, and so are the children you are carrying."

Chapter 13

Alwyn was thinking about his parents, smiling to himself, and although he knew it was implausible, it was almost impossible. He still likes to think of them having a great time drinking exotic cocktails. As they danced away to the steel band on a sun-soaked paradise island somewhere in the Caribbean. The noise abruptly beams him back to reality as he regains focus on the road in front of him.

Gareth had seen something in Alwyn, and after some intense one-on-one training, he had been taught the rudimentary techniques of guerrilla warfare. Alwyn had been promoted; he had thought it strange that Scruffy was the first to congratulate him and also the first to step forward in volunteering to be in his squad.

The invaders are now moving towards them, coming in from the east. They had been receiving reports of their activities and King David's point-blank refusal to align their forces under one command for weeks. Gareth and his team were sadly left on their own. He had no armored fighting vehicles or artillery to defend the people, but this was their territory. Like many of the others who grew up around here, Gareth knew this area like the back of their hand. Alwyn intently watched the progress before he waited for the right moment to give the signal. JJ had halted the convoy and then ordered a patrol of troopers to scout out the area up ahead of them. He had done this exercise previously, and his troops had found nothing to report but in view of his mounting losses. He had to recheck every single mile of this sheep-infested countryside. Cinds had her people in position, ready to strike; she was waiting on the appropriate signal to either attack or withdraw.

Alwyn waited until the troopers had advanced further down the road; when they were out of sight of their fellow troopers and commander, he gave the order. The devices were Cyril's idea; in the old world, he had watched just about every medieval historical epic imaginable. He had run the various contraptions through Alwyn and, in turn, had thought it was a brilliant idea. Not only would it eliminate the intruders, but it would also scare the living shit out of them.

Cinds, upon receiving the order, had her team of saboteurs ready. As the first troopers approached, she told them to hold steady, and when they reached the exact spot, she issued the command. The rope had been sliced clean through, enabling the suspended old rotting tree trunk to crash through the trees noisily. The branches obstructing the incoming log's forward movement alerted the troopers to the noise, causing them to all duck out of the way. As the momentum ceased, the troopers returned to the standing position to examine the failed device. As they stood there, chuckling at the feeble attempt, the troopers did not hear the incoming projectiles approaching them from the sides. These were tried and then thoroughly tested, with all the overhanging branches removed from the flight path. This ensured a smooth transition from just overhanging weights to free-moving objects. They were killed and then wounded when they came into direct contact with the troopers. The surviving soldiers watched as the tree trunks with the metal spikes smashed into their fellow combatants. Now fully laden with the dead and dying troopers, they swung back and forward, spraying blood and guts all over the road.

One of JJ's troops spotted the naked woman ducking behind one of the trees; as he alerted his colleagues, they began the pursuit. No matter how brief, any glimpse of her prompted them to discharge their weapons. Despite their frantic shooting, not even a single shot hit her as she moved quickly in and out of the trees. Now, they are very frustrated at the death of their comrades as well as almost being taunted by the fleeing assailant. They charged forward, disregarding all their basic training. Fully intent on capturing the woman who had lured them into the woods. The first one to fall had dislodged a holding peg, which had activated the release mechanism, and then propelled the frame with all the foot-long knives out of the ground and then straight into his chest. Now full of fury, the others sought revenge for their fallen comrade and charged forward, oblivious to the danger. The next one, not seeing the branch used as a stop, ran straight through it, dislodging the huge blade that sprang out of nowhere and then instantly decapitated him.

The two remaining pursuers stopped in their tracks and looked at their fallen comrade, wondering what the fuck was going to come out of the dense woodland next. They had not spoken; they had not even reached the point of making any decision on a hasty retreat when the arrows struck home. One of them was pierced through the heart, and the other had taken one in the stomach. Cinds' and her team hoisted them up on the ropes; it did not matter if one of them was already dead, it was the fear factor they were counting on. The one with the arrow in his gut kicked his legs and tried to evade the inevitable. Cinds' and her crew set the next trap and retreated silently back into the dense woodland.

JJ had heard the shots and ordered the advance; the convoy soon came across the log on the road, displaying the impaled figures draped over the other still-suspended trunks. He issued orders to locate the missing troops and very soon was notified of their demise. JJ told his men to stop in their tracks, not to move a muscle as he surveyed the scene. The men now hanging from the trees were both now dead. JJ follows the direction of the rope. He orders his men to stand back, and once they reach a safe distance, he asked for a rifle.

He shoots at the rope where they would have cut down the hanging men. As the rope is cut through with the bullets, the men fall to the ground, and so do the rocks and the various weighted sharpened implements. Anyone unfortunate enough to have stood in the immediate vicinity would have been severely wounded. JJ said a few words as they buried the dead before moving forward. Alwyn watched from a safe distance as the convoy advanced. JJ slowly realised that this might be the war he could not win; he could not see them, and he could not find them, as all they did was play hide and seek. He did not have to think too hard about what stroke the defenders or the terrorists might make next; around the next corner, the road was completely blocked.

JJ took the lead, directing his men to advance forward; he checked for explosives hidden amongst the abandoned wreckage. All the batteries had been removed, but he suspected that it would not be that simple. A mechanic is brought forward to investigate. A short time later, he confirmed that all of the engines had been filled with coal dust and cement. It would take them most of the day to drag the dead machinery out of the way. His force had only advanced two miles today, and now they were stuck in the middle of nowhere. JJ posted the sentries; through his binoculars, he scanned the area around them, where he knew that the rebels were watching his every move.

He barked out an order and waited for the weapon; the rocket launcher had thermal imaging, which could be selected to home in on the detected heat source. JJ unpacked the weapon and waited for it to become active, scanning the area where he thought the prey was hiding. He searched the terrain, finding no target; very disappointed, he deactivated the weapon and then handed it back to the trooper. These toys were about ten K a pop in the old world. They were not designed for removing terrorists secluded in rocky overhangs but were the ideal weapon of choice in this situation. If he had managed to locate the spotter and fired the weapon, his troops would have been given a much-needed morale booster. JJ now feared that they were dreading every step in this seemingly unforgiving landscape with some form of resistance and hidden danger lying in wait around each corner.

As they were not going to be able to clear the road today, JJ issued the order to set up camp, dispatching additional troopers to double the perimeter patrols. He thought that tomorrow would be different, and then perhaps, if he was lucky, he could change the dire results of his campaign. JJ walked around the camp, chatting to his troopers but basically shooting the shit and not talking about anything in particular. JJ just wanted to let them know that he was here with them, not secluded in some far away heavily guarded fortification issuing orders from his comfortable surroundings. On the first explosion, he had raised the alarm; the trees were now crashing down around them. Most of them were outside the camp's perimeter, which was just another scare tactic to create unease and fear among his troops. The damage was minimal, and no injuries had been inflicted.

Alwyn had volunteered for the job and skulked about like an avid cat burglar in the woods, setting the timers. Armed only with the bag full of rechargeable batteries, he had taken a deep breath before setting every timer. All it needed was one mistake, and he would be blown apart along with the trees. His mission was a success; he could hear the shouts coming from the encampment in the distance. Cinds' had the next part of the plan ready and signals her team to get prepared. JJ could smell a change in the air; he shouted out for his troopers to take cover just before the flaming arrows descended upon them. JJ cursed them out loud, and with no ensuing casualties, he ordered his men to put out the fires. This has just been another blow to further demoralize his trooper's morale, who would now have to endure another sleepless night wondering what surprises would come next. Alwyn, Cinds' and their followers had scarpered into the night and were now sleeping comfortably, getting a whole night's rest prior to attacking the invaders in the morning.

JJ thought that he had made some progress today; they had accrued no causalities, and no one had thrown anything at them or even tried to kill them today. The road to this town was obstacle-free, and although the advance patrol had searched everywhere, it was almost as if the local rebels were having the day off. If only every day was like this, or perhaps the locals would have given up, realising that defeat was imminent and they had just moved to another area. In reality, he did not think so, but it was nevertheless a nice thought. As usual, the town had an unpronounceable name, but it was unusual that they had found no living soul there, not even the complimentary stray cat. This was perplexing, and JJ ordered another search. It was a fruitless exercise, only confirming what had already had been reported; a double guard was posted, and he ordered his troopers to find somewhere suitable to bed down for the night.

Gareth had originally thought that Alwyn was certifiably nuts when he had presented the initial idea. As he listened to more of the proposed plan in detail, he thought it was a good idea and wished he had thought about it himself. It had taken days to assemble all the required parts and another couple of days to set it up. A dress rehearsal was required for this exercise. When it was complete, they had to tidy up all the evidence to leave no revealing clues of the pending surprise for the invaders.

Just around midnight, the signal was given, and the catapults loaded with the demi-johns encased in clay were let loose, and the projectiles started raining down in the town centre. At first, the troopers thought the locals were only hurtling glass at them. That was until the second salvo followed immediately afterwards. The burning objects streaked through the air and then exploded on contact, igniting the previously sticky petrol-laden demi-johns that had distributed their cargo all over the town square. JJ was sound asleep when he was jolted awake with the bad news that five trucks had been destroyed. The only relief was that there were no casualties to report.

He ordered out a search party, as the range must be fairly limited; they must be close by. The replica ancient machines had been located; all the operators were long gone, but they had left a postcard. It was a picture of the village in happier times with the wording, "wish you were here." JJ was furious and gave out the order that they were moving out at first light. Taking a stance that he knew Miasnikov would have firmly approved of. JJ shouts out that he wanted them all dead, there will be no prisoners taken, no quarter given, and from now on, it was a strict shoot-on-site policy with no permissible exceptions.

After yet another sleepless night, they are all ready. As dawn approached, the convoy moved out; on the road out of the town, JJ scanned the places in the surrounding hills. The RPG with the thermal imaging sensor picks up a target hidden within a rocky outcrop. He discharged the weapon and then immediately sent a detachment of troopers up to investigate the carnage. They returned quickly, reporting that the sheep must have been placed there deliberately. JJ was about to ask them where they learned these uncanny powers of deduction when he was presented with yet another picture postcard. He shook his head, now fully aware that they were playing with his head; he silently vowed to eliminate every single last one of them. JJ ordered the convoy to move, and they slowly snaked along the winding road. Snipers scanned the hills around them, hoping to find something to shoot at. They see no one, not one living soul, only sheep, sheep, and more sheep.

The convoy came to a halt, and JJ wanted to know why. They pointed to the enormous flock of sheep completely blocking the road. "Just drive over the top of the fuckers if they won't move!" JJ snapped.

He ordered them to advance forward. The driver of the armored car continued, obeying his last instruction, and depressed the horn to try and disperse the woolly animals in front of him. Some moved out of the way, and some didn't even budge a muscle. He was just going to have to run over the top of them. The explosion took out the armored car, and the debris that once was part of the vehicle was all over the field, mixed with the various sheep parts. The explosive had been placed inside a few modified sheep carcasses fitted with a motion sensor detonated when the vehicle came into contact. The road was damaged, a fairly large crater had appeared, and the convoy would have to bypass it by driving on the field. JJ ordered the men to shoot the sheep and then directed the required diversion.

The convoy did not get very far as the ground was sodden, and the weight of the vehicles only bogged them down into the wet earth. JJ ordered his men to find where the water was coming from; he knew that the bastards had blocked off a stream or river and rerouted the flow down onto the field beside the road. By the time he sorted all this shit out, that would be another day wasted. JJ moved through the chaos, commanding his troopers to clear the traffic by any feasible means. They filled the hole in the road with whatever they could find and, after considerable effort, managed to get the convoy back on the move.

The obstacle had no sooner been cleared when another explosion was heard that time, one of his tanks had been blown up. The crater was twice as wide and twice as deep as the previous one. It must have taken the locals weeks and weeks to dig it out and then plant the enormous quantity of homemade explosives required to create this amount of devastation. This one must have been detonated by sight; JJ orders his men to search for the tell-tale wires that will hopefully lead to the perpetrator responsible for this act of terrorism.

After a thorough search and finding no wires, JJ concluded that a timer must have controlled the device. The bastards, he realised, had just been lucky. "Well, boyos' your luck won't last forever," he said out loud to no one in particular. The convoy moved onwards, and they then found themselves entering yet another valley, steep hills at both sides and with no rocky outcrops to camouflage any would-be assailants. JJ thought that there would be no more sneaky attacks. A series of explosions totally destroyed the road in front of them, making it impossible for all his transport. Through the binoculars, he saw the terrorists fleeing. He immediately ordered everyone to dismount and pursue them into the quarry. "We have got them now, a special reward to the trooper who kills the most; let's go, men, after them."

As ordered, his troopers dismount from their vehicles and then charge after them. JJ thinks that his troopers were competently trained soldiers chasing after the inbred farmers and the illegitimate offspring of unemployed militant miners. This should be nothing but a child's play. JJ looked forward to the body count at the reward ceremony later that day. He scanned the horizon, and unbelievably, the fools were heading toward a fortification at the top of the valley. If they thought for one minute that this was going to save them, they had another thing coming. JJ thought that he would save a few and then hang them from the structure as a permanent reminder to all and sundry that the old days were gone forever.

He spurred his men onward, with sporadic fire exchanged in both directions. Though a few of his men had fallen, he urged them on relentlessly, encouraging them to show no mercy and eliminate as many as possible by any means necessary. "C'mon guys, let's do some good old-fashioned indiscriminate killing!" Gareth watched as his people ran as fast as they could, evading the onslaught of the invading troopers. His men had shot a few of them but nowhere near enough as they lay out the covering fire. His people had not yet reached him, and if they did not hurry, he could not save any of them. Now within hearing range, he shouted at them to get a move on, "For fucks sake, hurry up, you bastards." JJ forces were gaining on them and started picking off some runners. He ordered his best shots to aim at the invaders who were standing still, killing their brothers and sisters. As the distance closed, the shooting intensified, and casualties increased on both sides.

Finally, all of his people who were going to make it were there, and Gareth gave the order. Alwyn had spent weeks in this building going through the original blueprints and then supervising the required modifications. His team had spent days and days drilling into the massive steel-reinforced concrete structure. They only had one chance at this, and if it did not work, then they would be facing death and would be joining all of the other countless innocents that the invaders had eliminated.

At the very last minute, JJ noticed that he had been duped into believing that this was to be the last stand by the terrorists. This place was nothing but a mere facade, with the walls only strengthened enough to make it look impregnable and defensible from a distance. JJ heard the explosion, then realised that he, as well as all of his men, were well and truly fucked. Alwyn had laced the inside wall with loaded pipes and then interconnected them all together; the rest of the building was stuffed full to the brim with homemade explosives packed into every container imaginable. The first explosion severely weakened the inner wall; then, the second one blew it entirely apart. The dam suddenly released millions of tons of water that had been held back. With nothing holding the massive volume in check, it burst through the opening, sweeping away everything in its path. The massive blocks of concrete crushed any lifeform that had managed to survive the onset of the deluge, along with parts of the wooden make-believe stockade that was now rushing down the valley. JJ now lay dead at the bottom of the valley along with all of his men and flocks of the famous rebellious sheep.

Gareth and what was left of his crew sat at the top watching the water cascade down the valley, destroying anything that came in its path. He was just about to congratulate Alwyn on his groundbreaking plan, but as he was now entwined in Cinds' arms. He could hold off for now, letting him know later that the boys from the valley had done good and that luck had fuck all, absolutely sweet fuck all to do with it. Gareth had lost many of his crew, but they had eliminated all the invaders. There would surely be more to come, but that would be King David's problem.

Gareth and what is left of his crew are on their way to the coast. He had thought it would be foolish and reckless if they had gone east. That would surely have only taken them into direct contact with more of the invading forces once the so-called liberation forces had discovered the fate of their comrades. There would be no negotiations nor a peaceful transition of power. The invaders would be hell-bent on seeking revenge and retribution for their fallen brethren. Gareth thought it was a good idea to get out of the immediate area and try to link up with another group. He was not one hundred percent certain that there was another group, but he at least had to try and find out. They could not be the only ones who had stood their ground and battled with the would-be oppressors.

Once they reached the coast, it was his intention to find a ship that could take them all north. Going south or east was out of the question, leaving them with limited options. Their only choice was to travel north to the land where it was rumored, they still ate their young.

Alwyn and Cinds' were now a couple and were almost joined at the hip. Gareth had put them in charge of the scouting party to travel ahead, hopefully finding a suitable vessel. He was only worried that none of them had ever been in charge of a sea-going vessel. The limitations of their pooled experiences only revealed that not one of his crew of land lovers had experienced anything larger than the rent by the minute tubs at the local council-run cesspit.

Gareth knew for sure that they would be able to get the engines to work, but sailing the fucker would be another matter altogether, perhaps even a nightmare. He hoped that there he would find other people on the way, some of whom would be ex-sailors who have ventured on tidal bodies of water greater than the tranquil boating pond in the local park. Alwyn along with Cinds' were now viewing the harbour through the binoculars.

At first, they did not see much in the way of movement, but as the day continued, so did the activities. They had counted about twenty armed bodies going about their day-to-day business. A fishing boat had just arrived; there was a fair bit of hustle and bustle as the fresh cargo was unloaded. They sent word back to Gareth that they had found some people and then continued watching as they awaited his arrival.

Gareth had eventually caught up with the forward patrol. Alwyn and Cinds' had passed on all the relevant information they had gleamed about the area during their clandestine observation. The trio shared the binoculars; Gareth asked lots of questions as they directed him to view specific points of interest. "We can't just waltz in and demand a boat; I don't want to fight them. I think we will either have to go to them or get them to come to us." Gareth thought for a while, and when he finally formulated the plan, he gathered them around. They all listened intently about how it would go down, along with the part they would be expected to play. Scruffy asked what would happen if they didn't want to talk. Gareth simply replies that they would just have to kill them all and then steal a ship. None of them wanted it to end up this way; maybe it would just be this once the people on the other side would listen rather than just start shooting.

By dawn, they were all ready, everyone was in position, and Gareth took the lead. He set up his tent outside the harbour town on the small hill overlooking the area. Gareth then lit the fire, making a grand show of struggling to get the wood to catch alight. He exaggerated his efforts, puffing and blowing as if the flames stubbornly resisted his attempts. The performance was clearly meant to entertain and draw attention as he finally succeeded in getting the fire going. To make sure that they would notice him, he added some ferns and damp moss-covered sticks to create lots of smoke. Gareth did not think it would be too long before the visitors arrived and started preparing breakfast. He heard the sound of the approaching engines and stood up, giving a friendly, welcoming wave. The vehicles came to a sudden halt, and several tough, dirty-looking individuals confidently stride towards him.

The woman with them stepped forward and did the talking; the other ones just pointed their weapons at him. "You can give up your weapons; then you can tell us who you are and what the fuck are you doing here." Gareth calmly pointed to the little red dot that had just suddenly appeared on the chest of her biggest companion. "I thought that we could discuss that over breakfast; the red light on your buddy is the laser sight attached to the high-powered rifle. I could just have all of you killed and eat the breakfast on my own, but as they used to say in the old days, it is good to talk."

"So, for starters, please lower your weapons so that we can eat as we talk," Leena ordered her team to lower the weapons, informing Gareth that she would listen. He told her that the breakfast was ready and that he did not want to waste the food. "I am now going to sit down; we are then going to eat and talk; my team has weapons pointed at all of you, so if you don't mind, no sudden movements." Speaking directly to Leena, he asked her if she was in charge of this outpost; if not, she should send someone to go and retrieve them. Leena let out a slow breath, confirming that it was she who was in charge; giving in, she sat beside him.

Gareth hands her half of the cooked rabbit, "I caught this one this morning not my favourite breakfast but still more appealing than all that tinned shit. The so-called liberation army invaded us. That is now scouring all over the country, flushing out all the ones who had survived, then either torturing them, enslaving them, or just killing them. We have defeated the contingent that had been dispatched to our neck of the woods. The people in charge will eventually notice that they are gone and no doubt will send more forces to eradicate or enslave anyone that they come across. What we know is that there is only one road in and out of Wales; the south and west of here are under their control."

Leena admitted that she had heard some stories about the alleged liberators' activities but wanted to know why he was here and more to the point, what he wanted. Gareth smiled and told her that it was easy to explain.

"We wish to travel up north and hook up with other groups to fight the invaders. Because all the exits by road are blocked, we need to acquire a boat or a ship to take us there." Leena asked him if he thought that her group was just going to give up everything and then just walk away from all that they had built. Gareth sadly informed her that the so-called liberation army would not hold any talks on the transition of power nor any discussion on the ensuing placements and the required subservience to the new brutally enforced rules.

Gareth spoke for a while about some of the atrocities their common enemy had carried out during their unchallenged expansion of this country. "You have what? About thirty people. I don't think that you would be able to hold them off for more than five minutes. The first item on their agenda was the artillery strike. Any resistance that existed after multiple sniper teams took them out, then they rolled in the tanks. Everyone would be thoroughly questioned; those who were lucky enough and managed to survive this process would be given the following options. You can enlist in their army and be the cannon fodder for the frontline troops. Be detailed to a work party, slave all day, and be chained up during the night. Lastly, not being selected for the previous two options, you would be imprisoned and eventually selected for one of the many freely administered gruesome endings on offer."

Leena was thinking about what he had told her, "At least you have the same accent; we have heard about the King David guy and all his crazy ideas." Gareth took great delight in revealing all of his dealings with the pseudo-royal usurper. Especially at his idea that everything would return to normal, and he would be in the unenviable situation of having bucket loads of gold and precious stones to buy all and everything available.

"All we want is a chance to join another group who is going to fight and to be honest, we cannot achieve this here," Gareth explained if someone from her group could steer a ship and take him and his people along out of here. "Another possibility is that you and yours could come with us. King David had refused to see reason and would be left to face his bad decisions and unfathomable reasoning on his own. Leena, why don't you think about what I have offered? I will even let you take some of my people back with you, and your people can chat with them. We don't want to fight with you or yours, but we really need to leave this area. Take up my offer of asking my people questions, come back in the morning, and let me know what you want to do."

Leena replied straight away, "So, what you are saying is that even though you have more weapons than us, you are willing to send some of your team to come and talk." Gareth nodded and told her that just about summed it up. Leena agreed she would put the ideas on offer to her people and then return in the morning. Leena was about to leave when three of Gareth's people came forward to join the talks; she told him that there was one condition.

He asked what condition that was, "I will supply the breakfast as I have to admit that scorched bunny is not one of my favourite ways to start the day." Gareth hoped for the best possible outcome as he watched Alwyn, Cinds' and Scruffy step away with her. He was sure that his people would be unharmed; all he wanted was a boat that would take them out of there before the reinforcements arrived to take up from where the so-called liberators had finished.

Chapter 14

Somewhere south of Texas, Enunsha had been putting pressure on Abe, insisting that once the power was back on. They should be taking stock of everything that was stored away in the underground facility. "You were quite happy to go and plunder to more than adequately replenish the beer supplies. Hell, who knows what we could find down there that could be as useful." For some reason, Abe was not keen on venturing into the bowels of the Kunupenny subterranean kingdom. "You have about two weeks' worth of snagging to complete before the first test." Abe nodded, waiting for what she was going to come out with next. "In three weeks, we could be finding out what we can take out of there and then use up here to make a difference for the people. Jackson told me that the computers are all still connected, and the system they had is still alive." Abe knew this was all true, but they couldn't use it because they didn't know the password.

He replied, "Jackson thinks that they could have some sort of detonation sequence installed, and it could activate if the defense system were alerted to any form of attempt to hack into the network." Enunsha, not backing down, asked him how many people he knew had written their passwords down on a piece of paper.

They were always afraid of forgetting them and did not want to be subjected to the audible sighs of despair issued by the holier-than-thou people manning the I.T. helpline. "Someone in there must have jotted down something; all we have to do is look. The bottom line, baby, is that I think they would have had educational departments, and if I am right, at the very least, we could have some of the young ones' training to be doctors."

"You may not have noticed that the guy currently masquerading as a trained medical technician is nothing more than a snake oil salesman. Who would have not been out of place in some touring medicine show selling elixirs that allegedly cured every possible ailment known to mankind. He is not getting any younger, and people are more than genuinely afraid to go and see him as he is fucking charlatan. We now have a growing population, and kids get sick, kids break bones, and kids at one time or another need to be treated by a proper doctor." Abe finally took her point on board and promised to act on her plan once the lights were switched back on.

Abe thought that air conditioning, freezers, and all the other equipment for the cookhouse could be switched on. He also thought that some of Enunsha's mother and toddler group would want microwaves, hair driers, curling tongs and all the other stuff left behind in the old world. He pretended that old Smokey would be wired up and made fully functionable, but there would be no point if they did not have any crimes or criminals. However, Abe had made a promise about the cinema and would have to honour that. However, he dreaded what movies they would want to watch. Abe thought that you could only watch a movie so many times. All of the lists he had seen until now were full of movies that made your mama cry. He would try to avoid them, but they would at least keep the people happy once a week or once a month, which should be enough for the time being.

Enunsha had come to the point of dreading these weekly gatherings but faked all the smiles and warm welcomes as all the regular mother and toddler group attendees advanced into her home. Most of the time, she thought the conversations were brain-numbing; sometimes, she felt like screaming and running away just to escape the continuously banal topics. She would never have met any of them in the old world, let alone had the misfortune of sitting in their company. Then she listened to the sometimes-never-ending verbal diarrhea, which reminded her of the relentless repeats of quiz shows that used to run back-to-back on all the various media networks.

They know the power will be switched on in the next few days. Enunsha thought some of them had been puffing away on some seriously strong weed. They were under the impression that the mobile phone network would return to normal service. She has had just about enough as the ladies engage in a seriously vigorous debate about the type of service that will be available. Enunsha, as gently as possible, broke the bad news that the technology used to enable the network was no longer accessible.

A little miffed and disappointed at hearing the sad news, one of the women offered her help as she used to work in a shop that specialised in selling state-of-the-art smartphones. Enunsha was going to educate her on the technology in place when one of the other women explained that without active and constant satellite coverage, the phones, no matter how smart they thought they were, would not work. On a brighter note, they could use hairdryers, straighteners, and all the other associated shit. In their previous life, they used to alter and manage their hair. "Hey, I'm sure we would have enough homegrown skills to open up a hairdressing salon. I don't know about you, but I would love to get pampered occasionally." The change in chit-chat had lightened the mood in the room. The subjects aired soon evolved into microwave ovens, fridge freezers, and the much dreaded, sadly missed almost stadium-sized home entertainment displays.

Enunsha told them that everyone would get a fair chance of receiving an equal share of the available juice to switch on the essentials, and fingers crossed; hopefully, that would allow for air-conditioning in the summer months. This idea was greeted with several 'hell-yeahs' and the obligatory hi-fives. Enunsha would be happy enough if they all got enough electricity to work as many appliances as possible to keep them quiet. "Okay, ladies, it's time to make the packed lunches for the guys out working. You all know where all the stuff is kept and how many we need to make. Lastly, who wants to volunteer to deliver it today? We all know that you single ladies have been eying up some of the single guys except for Poison Pete, AKA Peter the Creeper, so come on, who's going?"

Later that day, Abe had just received word that they were finally ready to throw the switch and deliver electricity to everyone. It was a huge deal for the community; someone had suggested that they have a communal countdown, and he reluctantly agreed. Everyone was outside; they were all set, getting ready to call out the numbers. It was just like New Year at Times Square, except there were fewer people here and no outlandish costumes. Someone shouted 'ten,' and everyone took the prompt to announce the decreasing sequence.

Jackson had wanted a trial run but was outvoted. Abe countered, "We've run all the checks numerous times and walked through the entire system from top to bottom. Let's just go for it." Jackson had been offered to throw the switch to bring the power online but politely declined. He emphasised that all the guys had worked hard on this project, suggesting they should pick one of the guys and give them the honour. They drew lots; Poison Pete won the draw, along with another new name, Peter the Meter. He pulled the lever, and the water surged down the penstock.

The force of the water started rotating the turbines then, and all of the other equipment and machines were now all online. When the first electricity was produced, there were lots of hell-yeahs and even a few hallelujahs brother emanating from the gaggle of construction workers. Fully engaged in self-congratulating themselves on the results of their hard labour.

Enunsha was out on the street with the rest of them, and one by one, the community's houses, cabins, and ramshackle dwellings started to light up. One of the mother and toddler groups had rigged up a portable sound unit and had just shouted "team dance" when all the lights blinkered one by one and then shut down.

At the hydro station, there was a flurry of activity as the workers ran about shutting down the turbines. The horrendous sound of metal grinding upon metal filled the hall. "Close the valves, then get someone up to close the gate, gotta get the flow stopped before we can do anything." Jackson and Abe were in the midst of the action; they jumped about like headless chickens directing the work, hoping to avert the damage occurring inside the workings of the turbines. Number four has been shut down, but the others are damaged. Unable to close the valves, the mechanical tearing and friction brought the turbines to a dramatic halt. Abe called out for the bypass on each feed to be opened once the main water supply had been isolated. Jackson, accompanied by his gang, went around shutting everything off. The hopes and dreams of having an adequate power supply for the community were now well, sadly null and void.

Jackson and Abe grab a quick moment to discuss what happened. "Everything had been double-checked; how did we manage to overlook this?" Jackson was puzzled and then added, "We never overlooked anything; everything was checked and double-checked. I think that we are looking at sabotage."

Abe was dumbfounded, "I know it wasn't you, and I know for sure that it wasn't Enunsha or me. So, who do you think would be able to do this?"

Jackson told him to hold it right there, "I think it is more of a question of how this action could have been carried out without any of our guys noticing it. We are going to have to drain the system and then pull this rig apart piece by piece to find out if we can fix it."

Abe and Jackson rigged up a rudimentary bypass and finally managed to run off the water supply feeding the turbines. The construction workers were currently undertaking the task of dismantling all the pipework intakes. Once that was complete, they would be able to view all of the damage. After climbing down the vertical shafts to gain entry into the penstock, the first port of call is the control gate. The apparatus was complete with no visible signs of damage or sabotage. Abe scratched his head, "Jackson, you know that this means the damage was set up from inside the power station." Jackson admits that it could be possible, but they could only confirm his theory once they had checked everything out.

They walked all the way down the penstock, and it was clear that both of them were surprised by how clean it was. Jackson pointed out that there were no tell-tale marks of debris leaving scratches and tears on the smooth surface; he admitted that Abe's thesis could actually be correct. Abe was going to ask him if that meant he would be receiving his promotion to detective sergeant, but now, having finally gotten to the bottom and faced with the uphill slog back to the entry point, he said nothing. They finally surfaced, squeezing out of the hatch that welcomed them back to the real world above ground. Abe had thought it would be a good idea to keep the guards posted here twenty-four-seven until they had carried out a full investigation, and Jackson had agreed. He, for one, was deep in thought, calculating how long it must have taken the saboteurs to plan out and then arrange all the equipment to malfunction. The most perplexing item on the agenda was how they carried all this out without any of their crew noticing a single damn thing.

As they entered the turbine hall, Abe couldn't understand why all the construction workers were just standing about doing sweet fuck all. One of the foremen noticed them and walked towards them. "We thought you should see this; I ordered the guys to stand down and do nothing until we were given the go-ahead to resume work." They gather at the disassembled works in front of them. "The filters had been removed, received a bastardised modification, then refitted. The various bolts and pieces of scrap metal had jammed in the valve, rendering it completely inoperable." Just when they thought the news could not get any worse, "The turbine blades are damaged way beyond repair, and the once fine tolerance has been shredded to bits with what looks like coarse diamond cutting paste."

Abe asked if that translated that the machinery was fucked. Jackson confirmed his acute observation with the comments,

"Well and truly." Abe told the guys to take an early lunch break, leaving just the two of them alone. Abe asked Jackson if he now agrees with him and that someone was fucking them over.

Jackson confirmed his theories, mentioning the time and planning undertaken to achieve this amount of disruption. Enunsha thought that she would have to pacify some of the rather irate members of the mother and toddler group at not having their much-missed electrical appliances in operational mode. Abe wondered what problems they would all have to face when he gathers a meeting and inform them that an act of sabotage had curtailed their hopes of a regular electricity supply for the foreseeable future.

The construction workers were all now back from the extended lunch break to continue pulling apart everything that had been meticulously bolted together. At the end of the day, the bad news is that three of the turbines were now dysfunctional, but the good news was that one of them would still be able to operate. This would not supply all the power needed to enable all the households to plug in and switch on every conceivable device imaginable. However, it would give them a power supply for some of the sadly missed appliances. Abe thought there should be enough power to get the promised movie night up and running, which should, at the very least, keep one of his promises.

Jackson posted a guard detail inside the hydro plant; they were not expecting any more problems but had not expected the last one. Taking into consideration, it was better to be overly cautious than to be bitterly disappointed. He wandered over to see Abe and Enunsha with the intention of delivering the update on the power situation. Jackson had not intended to stay for dinner, but the pair of them insisted on his company. They did not play eight ball as they discussed the serious implications of the recent sabotage. During the deep conversation, they concluded that it was a distinct possibility that the saboteurs could very well be hiding out in the subterranean kingdom. Abe and Jackson would now have to search the Kunupenny family's underground estate from top to bottom, every nook and every cranny, as none of them had ventured below the fifth level; who knows what surprises they would find or flush out down there in the hidden depths.

Abe collected Jackson as they headed out the following day towards the power station; much to their surprise, there were no guards on duty.

"Perhaps they are still asleep?" Abe pumped the horn several times, and no one came out to meet them. Jackson, fearing the worst possible scenario, had his weapon out and was ready to fire before exiting the vehicle. Abe followed closely behind him, covering Jackson. He moved slowly, ducking in and around various parked vehicles and machines as they approached cautiously. The building was completely empty; there were no visible signs that the guards were there and no signs that they had left. No tire marks, no signs of struggle, no scrapes on the ground, no spent cartridges or bullet casings, nothing at all. Jackson now had to freely admit that someone was fucking them over.

Abe looked around the turbine hall, "I am sure we put that valve in there yesterday. Had it been all buttoned up; it would have been ready for today's trial." Jackson confirmed the validity of his statement, and with the valve now absent, they were not going to be able to operate the power at all. "For all our guards to vanish without a trace, plus the fact of the disappearance of the valve, there must have been more than a few people involved in this operation." Abe nodded, adding that they had sentries posted in the town, and no one left or entered during the night. "Do you think we missed any of them Kunupenny people? Maybe they are up to no good during the dead hours." Jackson replied that it was possible but doubted it as he never thought that the leadership was that smart. "If it was them, why did they not just fuck us over right at the very beginning? I don't think it was them and think that something else is in play here; I just don't know what or what direction it is coming from."

They agreed that the hydro station without the required valve was inoperable for now, and the number one priority at present is to locate their missing people. "We need more people up here; it is too big an area for the two of us to cover; we could be playing hide and seek all day and see nothing. Abe asked Jackson to go and round some up, but Jackson, point blank, refused.

"If you are up here on your own and go missing, what will I say to the people? Let's be honest about this; the first question is, why did I leave you alone?" Abe got his point and altered the plan, with the two of them now going to have to go back to town, where they are going to call a meeting and tell everyone what has happened.

What was going to be the highlight of all the hard work that they had put into this project had just turned into a momentous cluster fuck!

Abe and Jackson will have to devise a plan and at least try to provide answers to all the insurmountable questions that the township will throw at them. Enunsha will have to be informed first, and then they will need to do the decent thing and go around the missing guards' partners, informing them before anyone else. This was not going to be a pleasant experience, but there was no way around it; they will have to show their people some respect and dignity.

Enunsha knew most of the missing guards' partners, and once Abe and Jackson had briefed her on what they knew, the trio went to every single one of them to deliver the bad news. The first visit was hard, and none of the subsequent visits were any easier. Enunsha, having superior people skills, did most of the talking; Abe and Jackson only spoke when it was required. As with the first visit and all the others, they explained that they did not know all the facts nor all of the details but tried to reassure them that they would work non-stop to find out why and how this had happened.

Everyone then gathered; Abe could feel the tension in the air. The people wanted answers; he only wished that he had them.

"As you all know, several of the guards have disappeared, and the hydro station has been damaged beyond repair by an act of sabotage. We need volunteers to help with the search and investigation to resolve these issues. I also understand that you, just like us, have lots of questions, but please take into consideration that we are asking for help because we do not know any of the details that we all seek. If any of you have seen anything suspicious or think that you have witnessed something that you think was not quite right, please come forward. We must empathise that none of the people here are under suspicion; these acts have been carried out by others who still remain unknown."

The questions started to roll in, and most of the replies from Abe and Jackson were polite, mostly saying, "We do not have that information to share with you at present." Search parties were organised, and the first one involved a detailed search of the hydro station; they searched every building, every room, and all around the site. At the end of the day, there was no sign of the intruders, nor had there been any sign of the guards dead or alive. The power station was locked up for the next foreseeable future. It will now be guarded day and night, with the patrols required to check in at various intervals. Jackson thought setting up the rota would be a real pain in the butt, and a lot of people would continuously bitch about it, but it was absolutely necessary.

Enunsha couldn't believe what Abe and Jackson wanted her to do. At first, she thought it was so unfair, and they were being downright unreasonable. "Just because I can read the sign and, if we encounter the great tribe, am I the only one who can communicate? Am I the only one who holds any sway with them?" Abe replied, informing her that they had gone through all the people on the list and she was the only one capable of doing all that was asked. Jackson pipes up, "Enunsha, it was a concise list, and that list had only one name on it. Nobody else in our community has your unique skillset." Enunsha stared at him and curtly replied that she used to like him.

Abe took a deep breath and then spit it out, "While you are out searching for a valve and the replacement parts, we will go into the Kunupenny underground facility and search it from top to bottom. I do not want ever to have to spend one night apart from you. I'm honestly, truly one hundred per cent sorry about all of this, but needs must." Enunsha is still far from happy about the whole idea. As far as she is concerned, she has been given the shortest stick in the whole deal.

Abe pushes his point across, "By the time you get back, we will have sorted out any of the problems. The bits and pieces you return will enable us to switch the power on, which will make the difference." Enunsha shook her head, "We don't know how many levels are still left to be explored down there. How could you possibly know that you will have it all sorted by the time I and my intrepid explorers return." Jackson admitted that they still do not know all the answers or all the problems they will face, but they are still going to have to face it head-on.

She eventually gives in to their idea, admitting that the underground facility completely freaked her out. "Just promise me that you will be careful, and if you need to, just blow the place up,"

Abe promised to be careful, and Jackson assured her he would look out for him. They had selected a list of people to go with her on the material search party. "I am giving you a couple of the construction guys who know what parts to look for, as well as some of our best shooters, in case you run into any trouble."

Abe and Enunsha didn't sleep much on their last night together. Both of them were worrying about each other and how long they would have to wait till they were back together. The morning arrived, and Abe saw her to the convoy, cuddling her, telling her she would be back before she knew it. Abe told her that he loved her then waved her off. Enunsha convoy was left en route to the once industrial hub up North. Abe and Jackson watched until they became a tiny speck in the distance, and then they gathered all their people together.

They went through all the things they were going to do, along with all the ways they were going to go about it. Jackson had the section leaders accompanied by their second-in-command around the table, going through all the textbooks' moves. He took it step by step. If they faltered or didn't understand, he went through it all again until they fully understood what was expected of them and the routine, they all must adhere to without any exceptions. "We don't know what to expect down in the hole, but either way, we have to be prepared for any outcome. Okay, grab your people and weapons, and let's move it on out."

Jackson had them all assembled. All stood ready in their assigned groups, prepared to enter the Kunupenny underground facility. Abe took the lead, and his group was the first to cross the threshold. They assumed the predetermined positions and waited for the second group to enter and move ahead. One group covered the other as they moved into the building in mass. All the exit and entry points on this floor were covered, and Jackson and his crew took the lead to start searching. He had warned them that if they came across something that did not look right or anything remotely suspicious, they must call it in. Jackson drummed it into them, saying that they have to be really careful and check everything that they come across.

"These bastards were devious mother fuckers, so don't be shy in saying you don't know what something is." After searching for several hours, they found nothing that was remotely suspicious on the first floor. Then, by the numbers, they moved down the stairwell to the next floor.

Enunsha had been driving for what felt like endless miles upon miles, and they had not seen a living soul. The roads were almost devoid of any stationary traffic, and what really surprised her was that she had seen no recent signs of the Indian nation. Enunsha called a halt for that day and directed her people to pull into the gas station in the middle of nowhere. She drew her weapon, assisting in the check to ensure the place was safe enough to rest for the night. All that they found in the place were a couple of long-dead bodies. The flesh and the putrid smell were long gone. All that remained of them were the obligatory checked shirts, cowboy boots, and white bones.

Once they were all settled, she marked the spot where they were located on the map and then calculated where they hoped to travel to the next morning. As they drove towards the city, she thought that the stationary traffic could be a problem, which would no doubt add extra time to their journey. Hell, if this was in the old days, she was more than sure that they could have ordered all the parts online, paying a premium rate, and they could have been guaranteed delivery within 24 hours. For now, they will just have to do it the hard way; there was not even a pool table in this place. Come to think of it, there was nothing in this place. It must have been plundered and then plucked clean quite a while back. The team organised the rota for the sentry duty; although she offered to take her shift, they told her that it was not necessary as it was all covered. They ate their fill, and fortunately, Poison Pete wasn't among them, and after eating, she bunked down for the night. One thing was certain: this was the last time she would venture out into the long-gone world. It was not very appealing to her even when everything worked and was normal. Now, with everything dead and gone, it held nothing of interest to her; what was gone, in her opinion, was gone forever.

Abe, Jackson, and their crews had worked all the way down to the fourth level. They had found many goods that would be useful to them in their world outside, but nothing at all indicated any possible sign of danger. Jackson had told Abe that he did not like the situation that they were in and maybe they should just seal the fucking place off forever.

"Take what goods we can use, then bury the rest." Abe disagreed, reminding Jackson that whoever had fucked them over could be hiding down below, waiting to come back and get them when they least suspected it.

Jackson argued the point, "Every time we go lower, we have to station more guards to cover our retreat. How long will it be before everyone is on guard duty, and it just leaves one guy to go and search. Abe, I have a horrible feeling about this place; the hair on the back of my neck have been on end since we walked in here. If push comes to shove and we see anything at all that jeopardises the future of our people, then without any hesitation, I want to leave this place like an earthquake zone. Some army bases near here could supply all the explosives required, and 'Et voila,' there would be no more sleepless nights. Abe, I am deadly serious. I don't think exploring this place will come with a happy ending."

Abe had point-blank refused his request, and his team took the lead on entering level four. They entered the doorway, fanned out, took up their positions, and waited for the rest of the teams to catch up. Jackson couldn't prove it, but he was positive that they were being monitored every step of the way. Now that everyone was in place, they started to search, room by room, corridor by corridor. The computers were all still connected to the power, and Jackson thought about what Enunsha had said about the dreaded IT police. He foraged in and around the desk, even lifting the keyboard to see if it revealed that magic sequence. Jackson hoped it would allow him access to the restricted hidden world within the guarded realms of the information technology department. He thoroughly searched every single workstation and looked under every keyboard, but the elusive key to the magic kingdom was not located. Jackson thought this place must have been swept clean since he had never seen a cleaner office in all his investigative work. The trash cans looked as if they had never been used; none contained as much as a single scrap piece of paper, no bare naked confectionary wrapper, no crumpled cheery or sombre sticky paper notes, absolutely nothing.

He had not given up on the idea that they were being watched every step of the way, so he took a step back from the PC station and surveyed the room from various angles, thinking if he was placing secret cameras, where would he put them. Jackson grabbed a chair and placed it on the desk. He climbed on top, attempting to push up the ceiling tile, but it did not budge; he got a few guys to help him, and they set about finding one that would move. They found not one tile that had not been firmly set in place. He was like a dog looking for that elusive prime marrow bone; Jackson knew the cameras were definitely somewhere. They would be everywhere and hidden in plain sight, looking like everyday objects, except they would have the secret device concealed inside.

Abe had sent word back that this floor had been checked, and he was intent on going down to the next one. He wanted him to stop. Jackson had pleaded with him but to no avail. Abe wanted to go down into the very bowels of this place. If only he could find the god-damn monitoring devices watching every move they made. He took another final look around, looking for something unusual, and found nothing–nothing at all.

He found Abe at the entrance that led down to level five, "I know that you are not happy about us doing this, but whether you like it or not, it has to be done." Abe did the countdown, and as the numbers descended and reached number one, they opened the doors to proceed inside. There was no inside; all that lay before them was a solid, impenetrable wall. Jackson shook his head and went down a few flights of stairs. There were no more doors to the next level; all there was at the bottom was yet another solid wall. The walls revealed no signs of any recent work, no damp or drying stonework, no scrapes on the surfaces around it, and most definitely no tell-tale signs of cement or sand particles. "I guess that we are done for today, then?" Abe asked Jackson if he still thought they should blow the place to smithereens.

Jackson replied, "Hell yeah. Just think about it: who builds a doorway at the bottom of two flights of stairs that do not have an opening? And better than that, who built another two flights of stairs that go straight to nothing? I think that we are definitely getting fucked, big time. If you want the real truth, I think we should just pack up and get the fuck out of this whole god-damn area."

Abe asked Jackson if he was okay; he had never seen him this deflated before, but he was always buoyant and full of hope and enthusiasm. Jackson held his hands up, "Abe, that's it; I have had enough; I will be leaving in the morning." Jackson turned his back and started to climb up the stairs, not stopping until he reached the very top. Abe had told his guys that they were finished in here for the foreseeable future, and they all followed Jackson out.

Chapter 15

Olga and Anna had dragged the now fast-asleep sentries back into the house and then unceremoniously dumped them in the former sitting room. When they were relieved of any ammunition as well as weapons, prior to the women slitting their throats, as they bleed out, Anna dumped the ammo along with the weapons by the front door and then followed Olga up the stairs. As all of the soon-to-be ex-comrades were in dreamland, they did not need to creep about like church mice. Starting at the top landing, they repeated the process with each and every single one of them. The spoils were placed into their vehicle. The duo pillaged then removed the batteries, fuel containers, along with anything else that could be put to good use from the other vehicles that until quite recently belonged to their now dead team-mates.

As they waited for dawn, they perused the book of maps in the kitchen, working out their approximate position and then the route they would take on their adventure up North. They prayed that the proposed path would not bring them into direct contact with any of Miasnikov's outposts. Olga looked out the window, noticing that the light had started to change, letting Anna know it was time to depart. Starting on the top floor, they doused everything in petrol, working their way down to the bottom floor. Olga ignited the liquid and then left the door open to allow the breeze to waft the flames, helping the current of air to flow through the house and exit via the partially open windows on the top floor. The vehicles that belonged to the others were doused in petrol and then torched. The women set off driving through the deserted streets, looking for the farmland that, by their calculations, would bypass any checkpoints. If they were lucky, it would eventually lead them to the road going north. After a few starts and stops, they finally found what they had been looking for. They worked fast in cutting the wire fence and then removing a few fence posts that just happened to be in the way.

After crossing more than a few mucky fields, a bump-laden track led them to a farmhouse; with the process of sequential elimination through the complex unlisted farm tracks, the women finally ventured onto a minor road. The vehicle stopped at the first available sign after checking the place names along with the designated road number in the book of maps.

Anna drove while Olga called out names of the next place they would encounter, directing where they should turn. These country roads were almost empty, unlike the jammed-up routes that almost plagued the towns and cities they had encountered in their previous journeys. They had made good time. The odd vehicle had to be manoeuvred around, but it was nothing serious enough to make them double back to choose an alternative route. Having been up most of the night, then driving all morning they pulled into a quaint little village with the intention of stocking up on some much-needed supplies and resting for a while.

In the plan to escape, they could not pack a change of clothing as if any of their compatriots had noticed. It would have raised too many unwanted questions if the non-military attire had been observed. Anna had stopped the vehicle, waiting for a few minutes to make sure that there were no signs of life before they ventured out to explore. A new set of clothes and a set to change into was first on the shopping list. This town did not even have a resident stray dog, and the discarded weather-beaten litter was the only evidence relating to any previous lifeforms present on these cobbled streets.

Anna and Olga spaced themselves out as they looked for a clothes shop situated outside of the city. They hoped to find a suitable retailer that provided attire for the affluent country set. They were lucky, and four shops down, they found the place. Anna gently pushed the door open, and the women stepped inside. The shop was dusty, with no prevailing smell of the dead being present. Jones, the country outfitter, kindly supplied everything that was required. Olga and Anna took it in turn to rid themselves of their uniforms. The boots were a bit on the fancy side but would be comfy enough once broken in. They could not find a suitable bag to place the change of clothing in, but they did manage to find some plastic refuse liners to stash the spare clothes in for the time being.

Anna checked that the coast was clear; once satisfied, they donned the attire worn by affluent country women and made their way back to the vehicle. Olga noticed something was not quite right, so she secretly signalled Anna, which decoded to be prepared. Olga had only delivered the message to Anna when they had appeared. "Hello, my lovelies, what brings you out here on this fine day? Have you perhaps come to visit some long and forgotten distant relative? I think that by the appearance of the new outfits, you have been stealing clothes from one of my shops?" Anna could smell the cheap gut rot cider that, with the prevailing stench, must have been seeping out of every pore on their bodies. All of them looked like it had been a very long time since they had been tempted to use some soap and water.

With all honesty, they were all stinking; the layers of the encrusted filth would need to be removed with a power washer, and then all of their clothes would need to be incinerated.

"You have placed me in a rather difficult situation. Here is the question, my lovelies. As I suspect you have not left any cash or your card details on the counter in exchange for the new clothes. The way things are just now has placed me in the unenviable position of maintaining law and order. Let's be honest about this: we can't just have people marching in here, helping themselves with anything they fancy. In the good old days, stealing was a hanging offence, with no fines or the woefully inadequate probation system, just a plain old rope, as we would like to think of ourselves as a fairly civilized and modern society. In view of us being fairly considerate gentlemen, we could be persuaded to forget all about the hanging if both of you could offer us some kindness in a fair exchange for our most generous offer of forgiveness."

Olga and Anna had a fairly clear understanding of what their version of a fair exchange would entail and started unbuttoning their jackets. Keith Jones and his mates were all smiles, and there were a few boisterous remarks of "Nicely done, Jonesy" until they were replaced by, "We were only messing; we did not mean any harm." As the women had unbuttoned their coats, the surprises on display were not the womanly delights they had expected.

The compact machine guns had been nicely concealed underneath the slightly oversized jackets. Now, with the weapons pointing at them, Jonesy told them that they could keep the clothes and consider them a free gift. These were the last words he said and the last words that Jonesy boy, along with his seven companions, heard before they were all gunned down and left to bleed out on the cobbled street.

Anna, accompanied by Olga, had left the quaint little village with the now blood-soaked cobbled streets. They had driven several miles further north, then settled in a dusty old farmhouse for the night. They thought it was safe enough, far away from everything, to light the fire. The last couple of days had taken a massive weight from their shoulders, and after all the thoughts about leaving, they finally decided to walk away from all the madness.

Anna was worried that Miasnikov would send people after them. Olga had told her that he would be so drunk that he would not even notice that they were absent without leave. Anna informed her that Miasnikov pretends to be stupid, adding that he was quite cunning and a very dangerous specimen. Anna added, "At an early age, he had murdered all his brothers and all but one of his sisters in his ascension to being the head of the family. It takes a special form of barbarity and cruelty to eliminate all of your kith and kin; I think he had just seen it as another sporting event where he stipulated and constantly altered the rules to suit his needs. If you think that he is nuts, by all accounts, his sister is way off the scale and should have been committed before she attended kindergarten." Olga thought that there was nothing at all to worry about. They would just travel as far away as possible from the mayhem and find somewhere quiet, well out of the way, to raise their children.

Olga had seen first-hand the row upon row of numbered cots. Lesqueths envisioned future army, and that was enough for her to decide to leave. She had seen some of the indigenous population with their children. Their way of raising the young did not involve subminimal indoctrination, polluting their minds from an early age, with all of the associated barbaric practices bestowed upon them from the leadership that were part of the expected infant learning curves and were viewed by all as perfectly normal accepted practices. They had never discussed what names they would give their children; they had never discussed as to what sex they would be. However, what they did think was important was that the children would get the chance to grow up in a happy and healthy environment away from all of the killing, all of the atrocities, and the prevailing madness that had almost devoured their people that were now so immersed in this culture that she wondered if they would ever return back to normality.

Anna was taking her turn to drive, and in between her little naps, Olga kept an eye out for any imminent danger. They were slowly progressing north; the vehicle had been changed twice. Once due to an unsolvable mechanical breakdown. The other time, when the road became so impassable, they had to walk for several days to escape the endless sea of dead and abandoned vehicles that stretched as far as they could see beyond the horizon.

Their pregnancies had advanced, and both of them were aware of the expanding waists that they almost had to make adjustments to their clothing almost on a daily basis. In the next town they encountered, they had put a shop at the top of the list that either catered to large-sized women or expectant women like themselves who required loose-fitting clothing. Olga had announced that she was hungry. Anna thought they had just eaten about an hour ago, but it was no surprise. Olga was at the stage where she could easily eat them out of house and home. Well, that was if they actually had a place to call home. All they had been doing of late was going from one dirty, grotty hovel to another of the same standard. It was not yet living in abject squaller, but as far as she was concerned, every one of the places they had holed up in all required a thoroughly good clean.

Anna had mentioned to her on more than one occasion that they would have to find somewhere habitable before they gave birth. If not, the newborn would be exposed to various infant diseases that would inhabit the various ex-communal squats they were presently frequenting. Olga had joked that she would try harder to locate a reasonably clean five-star establishment with a functional mother-to-be suite suitable for their inhabitation. Anna was far from happy about this witty remark, empathising with the importance of her statement regarding a clean environment in which to give birth, "Have you had any previous experience of delivering a baby?" Olga replied that she had not and believed she was the resident expert. Anna further added, "I guess we will have to add a bookstore for us to cram up on the subject. It would be terrible if we had escaped the madness and had stumbled at the last hurdle. By the way that you are scoffing down everything in sight, I think you will have your baby first, so the sooner we learn how to bring the little bundles of joy into this world, the better."

Olga said, "Anna, I thought maybe we should hole up somewhere until the babies are born. Prepare all the things that we need, rather than searching like lunatics at the last minute to find somewhere suitable."

Anna continued to drive but agreed that it was not too bad an idea at all. "Perhaps once we cross the border, we should head west to escape the sure-to-be congested main roads. Then, hole up in one of those tranquil little villages or towns on the coast. We could even go fishing for our dinner?"

Olga asked Anna if such a place existed in reality, the land where they still allegedly ate their young and if she had done any fishing before. Anna answered, "For the first part of the question, I honestly don't know. For the second part, I thought you would teach me!"

It was Olga's turn to drive; there had not been much in the way of conversation as Anna had been sleeping most of the time. She announced the crossing with a fanfare introduction and a pseudo-posh-accented news bulletin when they crossed the border. Anna had not even raised an eyebrow and was still dead to the outside world. They were now avoiding the main roads that were almost impossible to negotiate through and were now taking the tourist route. She thought that the roads were shit, noting that the planners had set out on purpose to include as many steep climbs and double bends as humanly possible. Occasionally, she had to slow down to bypass the odd abandoned vehicle. Olga had to cut open a section of the fence and then remove a couple of offending fence posts on several parts of the journey. Anna had also slept through it all. Now that she was getting hungry, Olga intended to pull over at the next suitable place for some rest; some food and putting her feet up for a while already sounded more than appealing.

Up ahead, she spotted some cottages situated off the main drag; turning off as carefully as possible, she drove up the untarred dirt track. Olga parked their vehicle, grabbed her weapon and checked to see if this location was uninhabited and safe. Ten minutes later, after checking for any other squatters, she set up the camping stove and started heating up some food. The all-in-one tinned breakfast had lots of spiel, informing the would-be purchaser that this was a genuinely wonderful meal to start one's day. Olga thought that canned dogshit would not look that much different. Anna had decided to join her; she apologised for sleeping and asked where they were.

Olga asked her to retrieve the bowls and spoons, and she said she would go over the map with her when dining. Olga said, "We crossed the border a while ago, so welcome to Scotland." Anna thought it did not look that different from the country south of the border, just as bleak and, by the looks of the surrounding area, just as cold and damp.

She looked at what was being warmed up in the pan and, seeing the empty tins dumped on the floor, she admitted to herself that this was something that she would never dream of buying or trying, but at least it would be warmish, possibly even filling her up. If they were going to rest for a while, she would light a fire; the smoke would undoubtedly display that they were in residence, but as the locals would say, she thought it was 'fucking freezing.'

After Olga dished out the nosh, they looked at the map. She pointed out, then declared that they were about here and that maybe tomorrow, they should start to look for a place to settle in for the winter. "Somewhere that is reasonably close to the coast, as I don't know about you, but I really don't want to eat out of cans daily. Even if we caught or shot something, we could mix it in with some of the tinned shit; at least it would be a little healthier, even slightly more appetising." Anna agreed with her statement; she could already taste the fried, freshly caught fish as well as the rabbit stew.

Anna, almost in a secret competition with Olga, had eaten almost non-stop, and now, sitting at the open fire, they repeatedly perused the map displayed in front of them. Olga had worked it out that by tomorrow or by the next day, they should be just about halfway up the west coast of Scotland and find a suitable place to, at the very least, hole up until they give birth.

"If we hold out any longer, we could be caught in the middle of nowhere, and I don't know about you, but the thought of wobbling like an overstuffed penguin trying to do things really does not appeal to me." Anna agreed and couldn't imagine trying to shoot anything when she was fat, as well as not being able to jump about into the various firing positions that, not so long ago, they had both trained for. A list of all the things that will be required had been started and then restarted. Now that they agreed on the basics, both agreed that they must acquire another vehicle that would enable them to begin gathering the required essentials by tomorrow.

Anna, for one, was sick to death of humping about the spare battery, along with changing it out on a daily basis to keep it energised enough to start another vehicle. Olga was now fast asleep, and Anna covered her with the cleanest blanket available in that ramshackle of a house. The next one would have to be cleaned from top to bottom; she went back to the list, reviewing everything and double-checking that they had omitted nothing from the required bits and pieces. This was mainly the multiple items needed for the soon-to-be arriving infants. Anna had never displayed any inclinations or ambitions regarding the prospect of motherhood; it was just something she had never experienced. The only thing that she was sure of was that she would not be a cold-hearted bitch like her own mother, who had shown her no maternal love nor displayed even the remotest sign of emotion that every child needs. Anna thought that the only thing her mother truly loved was vodka; she had loved it so much that it had eventually killed her.

She built up the fire with the wood that had been, until recently, part of the threadbare furniture conveniently placed throughout this house. Anna placed the chair behind the front door and jammed it in, then settled in on the once big, comfy one opposite to the now snoring Olga. As always, she placed her weapon beside her; lately, she was waking up in the middle of the night, and the first thing she always reached for was her trusty 9mm automatic. Tomorrow was another day, and soon, they would be settled; she was more than happy at the prospect of no more driving for the next few months.

Olga was at last over the moon at not having to travel in the vehicle for hours on end. She was sick of the steep hills and hairpin bends and was tired of driving. They had arrived in this little hamlet and discovered that she and Anna were the only residents after searching the few houses around them. The only disadvantage was that there was no shop and the nearest supermarket was five miles back and forth. Anna had worked it out so that they could do four trips a day, and soon after, about a week later, They would have accumulated enough supplies to last a while. There was a plentiful supply of wood for the fire; when that ran out, they could always go and chop some trees down in the surrounding woodland. Anna had bagged a couple of rabbits and had promised to make her famous stew. Olga was about to ask what it was famous for, but no matter how bad it tasted, it would make a nice change from the canned food they had been surviving on until now.

The only shop was a small sports shop that mainly catered to the lost tourists. Olga imagined that there would be some rods, reels, and all of the associated tackle that would enable them to catch some fish. She did not care what kind of fish they caught; just as long as it was not tinned fish, she would be happy. Anna finished in the kitchen and came through with the meals; Olga finished hers in no time and went for a second plateful. When she returned, Anna was out for the count; both of them were exhausted, and she thought they really needed to take it easy to at least try and recharge their batteries. Her biggest fear was that they would not be strong enough to survive childbirth, and that was really not that far away. Olga checked that the doors were secure, then laid out on the couch, falling asleep thinking about what she would give for a nice, clean, comfy bed.

Chapter 16

Lesqueth was trying out a replacement for the recently transferred Olga and subsequently was putting Memo through the ordeal by fire. Unless she shortened it, his name was one of those long, almost unpronounceable ones. Any and all of their conversations would never start or have a middle or an end, as they would never get past his name.

They were en route to the British Museum, and she had not bothered even attempting this time to pretend that she was one of the commoners. Memo would probably laugh at her frivolity even though he did not know what she was saying or even who she was pretending to be. Tesporo had dispatched the note with the usual ornate calligraphy, displaying the pastel pink colour that had very recently flowed through someone's veins or arteries. She wondered if he drew it out of his own supply or perished at the thought of someone hanging upside-down in the stationary cupboard readily available to donate refills. She wondered if Memo did not work out as a suitable replacement for Olga, then perhaps, he could be nominated for the next candidate for the position of stationary refill.

The current keeper of the records, Tesporo, along with the still repulsive and abhorrent followers, were lined up to meet her. As she entered the building, they threw themselves on the ground to welcome her. Tesporo informed her that it was their way of showing the greatest respect and admiration for the most generous gift of the twenty-seven prisoners who accompanied his predecessor on his journey into the afterlife.

Lesqueth was quite touched at their display of gratitude and, out of character, informed him that should they require another batch, all they would have to do was ask. He led the way to the new display, keeping up with the once overtly pompous British Museum theatrics. Lesqueth cut the ornate rope with a huge pair of scissors. Tesporo glided across the floor almost as if he had no feet and had undergone a secret operation in which his feet were removed and then replaced, connecting him permanently with some wheeled device.

The new section displayed all of the former prime ministers of this once much-overrated nation. Tesporo had pulled out all the stops on this one; the former incumbents of this country had been removed from their caskets, and now their bones were on permanent display. Lesqueth nodded her approval but noted that one was missing, "Ah yes, that one; we think that she had really offended many people during her tenure, and after some extensive enquiries, we found out that her grave had been dug up, some of her bones were subsequently fed to a pack of stay dogs, somewhere in darkest Scotland in retaliation for punishing them with the poll tax along with other various attempts to curtail any additional breeding. The rest of the bones were allegedly taken to

Wales, where it had been rumoured that the bones were now an integral part of the filtration unit housed in one of the main water treatment facilities. Lesqueth thought that she would have liked this woman, no matter what the rebellious Welsh militants or the equally rebellious Scottish peasants thought about her.

Lesqueth walked along the display cabinets, smiling at the ones she remembered and laughing at all the crimes they had not been prosecuted for. All of them had been guilty of taking money that had been allocated to grand houses, shady business deals where they themselves or their offspring or sometimes all of their intertwined families would be the primary beneficiaries. It always amazed her that the privileged were so easily swayed into looking the other way or simply doing as instructed. Her ancestors had kept records of all the transactions. On more than one occasion, the ruling parties had to be subtlety reminded of their previous transgressions and prompted to carry out the latest request without any question. Lesqueth thought and knew for sure that there was not one of them on display who did not like being in possession of a sparkling penny or two secretly stashed away for a rainy day. As far as she was concerned, this lot would not have been known, nor would they have ever contemplated the prospect of earning an honest penny in their whole working life.

The revolving display showed all of the faces of the former Prime Ministers and their declared income along with all of the taxes they paid into the system; this had been set up to take the appearance of a slot machine, complete with all of the flashing lights. When the button was pressed, all the undeclared monies flashed as the vast sums were displayed and then calculated. There was not one notable gentleman or one of the notable ladies on the list who did not have millions of pounds, dollars, or a vast reserve of gold bullion secretly stashed away. The contents of the display even showed which country had all of the ill-gotten gains hidden away. Along with all this, there was a display of the major companies they either owned outright or had a controlling interest in, all registered in an assumed identity.

As she continued to walk about the displays, Lesqueth complimented Tesporo on yet another outstanding addition to the museum. The Baroness of Kindeace-Shire particularly liked the former prime minister, who had to be reminded that although his loyalty to his brothers in the Freemasons was highly commendable, it was them who called the tune. If he wanted to survive, he should realise that their orders are neither requests nor open for parliamentary discussion or debate. She beamed at the next one; if she remembered correctly, this chap had nearly had a complete breakdown. The organisation was reliably informed that he was ready to confess publicly for all his sins. The gentleman in question had to be taken aside and then warned of the consequences that could come into play if he even attempted to bare his soul. The promise of untold dollars in the after-dinner speeches circuit all over the world had been the clincher that had ensured his silence.

Lesqueth thanked Tesporo for delivering some brightness in what would have been yet another rather dull day. Tesporo accepted the compliment and asked if it was possible to receive another twenty-seven prisoners soon, "Our astrologer has just informed us that a comet is arriving soon. It has not been seen for 50,000 years, so long ago that it was last seen when our ancestors had just set foot on this swamp-infested planet. We were thinking of putting on a display to commemorate this event." Lesqueth thought that twenty-seven prisoners would not be enough, and when he sent the request, he should at least double the required numbers. Tesporo and his septic brotherhood could not help themselves, and on hearing the great leader's approval, they all lay flat on the floor, a testament to her greatness. As she left the museum, Lesqueth thought that the almost cult-style adulation was very touching. She also thought that the brethren stank to high heaven and that perhaps they should seriously consider showering in undiluted industrial disinfectant.

Lesqueth summoned Memo and made it known that she desired to review the current status of the ongoing works in the House of Commons. She had supplied the tradesmen with the full list of the required details a considerable while ago, and after receiving no feedback on the current status of the project, Lesqueth decided that it was about time for an unannounced personal visit.

On entering the building, the Baroness of Kindeace-Shire was less than impressed with the displayed results. The cleaner fixed to the speakers' chair with the knife had been covered in the transparent coating; there were no other completed works or any work in progress on display.

The workmen claimed on the precious souls of their nearest and dearest, that when they ran short of the ingredients for the see-through plastic coating. They declared the shortage immediately and sent an urgent SOS for an urgent resupply. Lesqueth questioned them on who they had informed and when they had been told to expect the new materials; the tradesmen could not furnish her with any suitable or convincing replies. Lesqueth calmly asked Memo to beat them black and blue but empathised that he mustn't kill them. Memo duly obliged, punching then kicking the employees with questionable work ethics. The great leader sat on one of the benches, then smoked as she directed the assault underway.

The Baroness of Kindeace-Shire summoned the guards and gave the one in charge of the detail a list of items that had to be sourced and then delivered as soon as possible. Lesqueth now joined Memo, where they take turns to kick the shit out of the workmen who were now lying still on the floor.

The Baroness was not angry but was bitterly disappointed that these work-shy, lazy bastards had not even tried to accomplish the work. It was not a hard, complex task and if they had only told someone that they were short of the required materials, things could have been so much different. They really had given her no choice, and unfortunately, sometimes, one has to set an example of what happens when you do not do what is requested. Now tired of kicking them about, Lesqueth sits beside her old friend, the cleaner. She lights up another one of her little cigars, and she whispers, "Hope you don't mind me smoking." After exhaling Lesqueth puts her arm around her, "How have you been? I have not seen you for quite some time, and I hope you will fully appreciate the upgrades that I am going to get carried out as soon as possible." The guards arrived back in quick time with all of the required materials. She stubbed her cigar out on the cleaner and then informed the assembled staff that they were going to be busy for as long as it takes.

On her command, the first worker was dragged into a sitting position. His mouth was sealed with an industrial stapler, and a section of small-bore pipe was inserted into each nostril. The quick-drying cement was evenly applied onto his head and shoulders. Lesqueth inspected the work, and after asking for a small alteration here and there, she requested the blowtorch. The Baroness of Kindeace-Shire twisted the control knob on the torch and is just about to ignite the propane gas. She stopped and informed Memo that if he did not turn the gas on at the cylinder like right then and now, he would be the next one to undergo the process. Memo jumps to it, turns on the bottle then rushes over to supply a light. The torch was working as it heated up the cement. The noise that it made was very similar to that of a jet engine, filling the entire chamber.

She did not know the name of the worker nor where he came from. It did not really matter now as he had been elected to reside in a seat in the House of Commons forevermore. He tried to struggle as the heat on his head and his shoulders started to intensify. To calm him down, she called for a knife and then stabbed him in the guts; Lesqueth did not push the blade all the way through and only inflicted enough damage to keep him still. Once the head was dry, she directed the next part of the process, and the guards clamped his legs in the sitting position with some strong wire and tape. Satisfied that he was seated correctly and he was not slouching. They start to apply the cement to the front of his body and legs. The torch was ignited, and the heat was directed at the newly applied coating. At certain points in the process, he was accidentally set on fire, and as he was burning, he started to try and struggle. Lesqueth calmy and deliberately placed her fingers over the ends of the small-bore pipe, and when he stopped attempting to move, she permitted him to breathe again.

When the front of him was dry, she directed her assistants to turn him over and then repeated the required process on the back of his body and legs. Lesqueth gave him a quick inspection once the process was complete and, to her satisfaction, smoked another cigar while she ran the propane torch across the wet cement to heat him up and dry him quicker. As she inspected the final product, Lesqueth had noticed a small mistake but she could alter this. She issued a small change to the existing procedure and asked for some help to place the now redundant worker into his final position.

The worker was seated where she guessed the prime minister would sit, then applied the mixed three-part industrial glue that would hold him firmly in place. Lesqueth asked for the battery-powered drill with a hole saw bit without the centre drill attached and bore out the holes where she thought his eyes were situated. She was very impressed with the result, with the now visible large eyes that directly stared straight back at her. "Now listen up, people, the invertebrates who sat on the side of the house were very fond of the red colour, and the ones who sat on the other side were big fans of the blue colour. Don't be too worried about mixing them up as some of them changed their affiliations that often you would think that the House of Commons had a fucking revolving door."

The last step of the process that the Baroness of Kindeace-Shire had to demonstrate was the painting. She wanted it perfect and told her assistants to gather around and watch carefully. Lesqueth asked for a grinder and cut away the excess length of the small-bore pipes that protruded slightly out of the end of the worker's nose. She told the nameless exhibit that she was very impressed by his inquisitive eyes as she plugged his nostrils with some cement. A quick heat with the torch dried up the newly applied cement and gave the rest of the torso a preheat.

"Now, please try not to make a mess and keep all the painting as neat as possible." The red paint was applied and dried out in minutes. Her test piece was now dead, and Lesqueth asked for someone to glue his eyes wide open and give the wonderful set of eyes now on display a coat of varnish to preserve that special haunted look forever.

The other worker had just started to stir, and going by what he had just witnessed, he wished that he hadn't. Lesqueth points to him, "This one I would like in the standing position; please remember to keep his eyes visible and don't put any cement in them." She instructed her guards to hold him firmly at the desk, then applied the already mixed three-part industrial glue to his hands and feet. He was held firmly in place until the glue had firmly set. Lesqueth inserted the small-bore pipes up his nostrils, then told her assistants that as this gentleman was on the other side of the political divide, she wanted this one painted blue.

The Baroness ordered them all to pay attention. "The next time I enter the building, I would dearly like to see all these seats filled. I have already informed you about all of the blue team and the red team. The other teams within the minority parties can be painted in green for the eco, whatever the fuck they were known as. Oh, last but not least, we better not forget the nationalists they can be painted with a mix of red and blue, fifty-fifty straight down the middle. Lastly Memo, if this is not done to my explicit requirements. I will be putting you forward as the next candidate for the keeper of the records resident in-house blood doner, where you will see out the last of your days' suspended upside down in their stationary cupboard. If you require more guards to complete the work, go and get them. Take the people from the gardening details, the prison, from anywhere you want. If anyone objects, supply me their names, and they will also be seated in this building. Enjoy your evening, ladies and gentlemen; please remember, above all, to have some fun."

The Baroness of Kindeace-Shire was far from happy; both of her generals, JJ and Miasnikov, had, shall we say, been a little on the shy side of posting an up-to-date report. She did not think that it was too much to ask, and all they had to do was, well, in the case of Miasnikov, to scribble some notes down on a piece of paper and send someone down here with the information. Lesqueth shouted for Memos' attention. She really did not know what to do with this one; he was about as dim as a one-watt lightbulb and struggled with words longer than two syllables. The Baroness dictated a message to both her seemingly forgettable commanders. The scribe was told that she required an immediate update and for them to send down a couple of their troopers who could read and write. English would be an advantage, and she did not care where they were from or whom they were related to.

The number of times she had been presented with the runt of the litter from a notable family truly infuriated her. "He is related to such and such, or your will know his father from bla, bla fucking bla." She thought back, and even Bartram had been guilty of this despicable crime. Lesqueth smiled, thinking of the disposal of the one who he had valiantly protested to save, citing his family's long and distinguished service. She had not heard a squeak from her cousin in a while either and set the scribe frantically constructing an urgent reminder that he had to keep her up to date on his and the demon spouses' activities.

Lesqueth thought that he would still be spending his days looking at the truly fucking awful private art collection. The one that he was under the full impression of– being a truly magnificent example of modern art seen through the eyes of the once primitive bipeds. Personally, if the artist had approached her with the alleged works of art, she would have had no hesitation whatsoever and removed his fingers with a meat clever. Memo had at last appeared, perhaps he was sleeping, perhaps he had gotten himself lost again. It was not that important; as soon as his replacement arrived, she would transfer or execute him. Most likely, she would entertain him with a private exhibition of what the axe beside her was actually used for. The scribe had finished the letters and as soon as the Baroness applied the wax, stamped the impression of her family's emblem. She handed them to Memo, "I would like you to go to the transport section and instruct them that I wish for these here letters to be delivered as soon as possible."

"Memo, on the way back, if you manage to lose your bearing and end up getting lost again, don't bother coming back." She did not think that he even understood this command as he stood at attention, presenting her with a salute. As he strode away, full of self-assured importance, she wondered how long he could hold his breath for. The display in her little quaint water garden was in urgent need of a refurbishment. Perhaps he could be rewarded with a permanent placement there.

Lesqueth had decided that another visit to the House of Commons was required. The last time she had been there was initially very disappointing. She hoped that the newly adapted working method was far more appealing and that the work had actually progressed. Memo had not returned from his previous mission. Well, that was not quite true. He had returned but unfortunately, he was two hours late, proclaiming his innocence and begging for clemency as he had lost his bearings and ended up through no fault of his own getting lost. The Baroness of Kindeace-shire wondered if he was capable of finding the toilet without losing his sense of direction.

She had not killed him but had supplied him with an urgent dispatch that he was to deliver by hand to the keeper of the records. The Baroness had stated that the brethren were to keep a hold of the bearer of the letter. In block capitals, she had insisted that when the time arrived, they required a replacement blood donor to replenish the now dry source for their preferred writing fluid. They were instructed to hang up Memo by the feet and then drain every available ounce of liquid from his veins.

The transport department had kindly supplied her with a driver. Lesqueth walked into the House of Commons and was mildly surprised by what was on display. The blue team side of the house still had the majority, resplendent in the sea of royal blue upon royal blue. They displayed many of the alleged characteristics belonging to that party. Several of them had wads of the once-plastic money half in half out of their pockets. Some of them even had briefcases full of the stuff blatantly put on display in front of them. The Baroness of Kindeace-Shire chuckled at some of the names displayed on plates, the "We don't really care about anything, committee."

"If you don't have millions in the bank, don't bother asking committee," and her personal favourite was the aptly titled. "Why did we allow the working classes to breed, never mind allow them to vote committee."

On the other side of the chamber, the red team had received the same treatment; they had the same amount of cash on display. Their committees had the names "Too drunk to care committee,"

"I am only here for the cheap beer and free overseas jollies committee." The nationalists among them all are a group within the "give me lots of cash, and I will jump ship committee." The one sole member of the Liberals has been awarded. "Open to a cross-party alliance committee." Several members of the House had copious amounts of empty bottles scattered by their feet, and Lesqueth thought the team had done a great job in immortalising what the general public really thought about the various parties that once governed this country.

Chapter 17

Cha and Murray were having some time to themselves, along with Charlie and Romulus. It had been ages since they were alone and not had to contend with everyone being around them. They were up in among the woods behind the Orangery. The dogs had given the area with the recently uncovered chamber a wide berth. It had been quite a while since they had ventured into these parts. Charlie and Romulus ran about, sniffing at the new smells marking their territory as much as possible. Cha asked Murray if he was at all concerned with the latest development in the children. "If it were serious changes, where they could move massive objects, then of course I would be worried. This could just be a childhood thing that will fizzle out, possibly coming to nothing. The Eastern Europeans could be a little upset about it. Let's be honest about this bunch; they are really quite a superstitious lot." Cha laughed, thinking about all the times she had seen them making the sign of the cross behind his back. Murray asked her what was funny. Cha explained, and he remembered all too well when he allegedly had died, then returned back to the land of the living during the thunderstorm. "We will just have to keep an eye on them. I think that idea about them mixing in with the other children at the farmhouse school is a most definite, not going to happen." Cha agreed, "I will tell Ellie that rather than bus them backward and forwards every day, we are going to set up our own school."

Murray nodded; she asked him why he looked so happy about it. "Oh, nothing really. I was just thinking there for a second that if Okolo was doing the teaching how the lesson would go. I can see her standing with her hands on her hips, all serious-looking. "Pay attention, class. The word for today's children is wanker!" Cha told him that he was unbelievable, informing him that she would tell Okolo the next time she saw her. Murray still thought that it was funny, and he was sure that Okolo would laugh at it, too. Both of them really liked her, and at first, they were pretty sad at the fact that she, as well as Alicia, were going to move, but as it was only next door, there was nothing to be sad about. "Do you think that they will be good neighbours? You know how you used to see the stories in the media. The neighbour from hell, how I had to murder my neighbour, and all the other seemingly unbelievable stories that populated the gutter press from time to time." Murray shook his head, "I think that they will all be great neighbours. Just one thing, though!" Cha looked at him and said, "he is not taking the dogs with him." They had been out walking for quite a while and it was the dogs that were barking to let them know it was time for lunch. Murray and Cha walk back to the house. If anyone had seen them, they would have thought that they were just a courting couple out on a nice morning stroll with their dogs.

Arriving back at their home, the dogs, as usual, had beaten them to it and were now all over Frank. They said hello and stole a quick heat from the fire. Robbo, still on house duty, gave them a cuppa without being asked. Frank just came straight out with it and informed them that he had been sent over to ask if they could hold a community event at Christmas. Murray couldn't help himself, "Just as long as I don't have to dress up as Santa? it has to be Robbo's turn to do the honours!" Frank replied that no one had mentioned Santa and that the event was just to celebrate being alive. "Nothing serious, no religious ceremonies or incantations of any kind that are linked to any of the multiple faiths that some of the community believe in." Murray enquired as to why he was being asked this in the first place. Alicia reminded him that he was elected as the leader and it was part of the job to agree or disagree to proposals issued from within the community. Murray admitted that he, for one, had no objections to a gathering as long as it was non-religious. He added, "For the record, I think it is time that we have another vote to select a new leader." He paused while they all looked at each other, "All those in favour say aye." There was not one word coming from the assembled. Alicia told him that without a new vote and without a show of hands, everything was as it was, and he was still the elected leader. Murray asked if he could have an appeal against the decision. Cha asked him to whom he would address the appeal, as they had all refused his initial proposal; they could not possibly– except his counter-proposal.

Robbo congratulated him on the renewal of his tenure in office, asking him if it was for one year, a four-year, or a lifetime term. Murray thought that he had been set up and had walked straight into the trap. "It is not really fair that you have refused to let me resign. In the old days, I could have pleaded guilty to misappropriation of community funds, dereliction of said duties, and also guilty of being a general asshole. As none of you are even registering my wish to be replaced, do you think that I could get an office sometime in the future?"

"We have spoken to the building department officer; she has informed us that once the extension is complete, you are next on the list." Okolo bows and asked for permission to go outside and smoke. Murray thought that this was a great idea and was all for going to join her. When they were standing outside smoking, he told her about the conversation about the children. On the part about the "word for today." Okolo laughed and told her as a punishment; she would find some music that thoroughly irritated him, promising that her choice would piss him off for hours on end when she and her gang were installed next door. "You wouldn't do that, would you?" Okolo smiled and informed him that she wouldn't, but she suspected that Robbo could be persuaded to do so. This time, he laughed, and Murray confessed that he would miss her, but not too much as it is only next door. Okolo told him he was still a wanker and went back inside. Murray was now back among them, "As I have agreed that the Christmas gathering is going to go ahead, I hereby declare that Robbo has been voted in to play Santa." Robbo thanked him and replied that as he had not been good throughout the year, he would not be getting sweet fuck all in the way of presents.

"Okay, Santa, we should really go out and search for some of the items on Karen's list. We will just be going to rummage about in local places if any of you lot want to come, you are more than welcome." He grabbed another cuppa and informed them that they were leaving in ten minutes. Okolo and Cha had opted to stay at home to keep a watchful eye on the infants and their newly displayed gift. Murray arrived with the vehicle and gave the horn a pump to inform them that their chariot awaited them. It was only a short journey; Murray could vividly remember some farmhouses up on the back roads that could be suitable for the purpose. They arrive about twenty minutes later, "Well, what do you think?" Robbo looked at the houses, and they were all white and thought that Murray was either nuts or had gone colour-blind. "I know what you are thinking," and to prove his point, Murray took the large hammer and thudded it against the wall. The old painted coating came off the wall easily, exposing the same type of stone that was being used on the extension. "If we knock down the three of these houses, I think that we should have enough for the new build?" Robbo just agreed, guessing that they would be starting the demolition in the morning.

Along with the twins, Murray went in and about the buildings; these have lain unoccupied for quite a time they are all dirty, cold, and damp. Robbo was rummaging about outside and called on them to have a look at what he had discovered. The twins and Murray followed Robbo's finger as he pointed out all of the solar panels that had been erected in the field. "Do you know anything about solar power?" Murray disclosed that it was fantastic in the Middle East, but he was not aware of any benefits that it could have provided in not-so-sunny Scotland. "When I was still chained to a desk in the bank, I had to do the loan submissions, and I had to look into the feasibility studies of bank-funded solar farms. The technology, in the beginning, was nothing but a huge rip-off, mainly being the provider of handsome tax breaks for the rich and famous. As the years passed, the tech changed. The new panels worked on light, not just rays from the big yellow thing in the sky. I can't see much in the way of wires connecting the panels to the grid or the house, and I suspect that the installation was never completed. There could be some information lying about the houses, hopefully with some of the details about what stage the installation was at. It could be worth having another look, and if it was possible, we could have an additional source of power." Murray had listened, agreeing to have a look, but on the subject of it being a feasible or not project, they would have to discuss it with Karen. No sooner than he had finished speaking, Robbo was inside ferreting about, sniffing out the information pamphlets, installation schedules, invoices, and correspondence from the contractors.

Murray had sent the twins to help Robbo, and he went into the attic to give the roof and the supporting framework the once over. He checked it all out, no signs of rot or dampness; it would be suitable for the extension. The tiles of the roof were identical; therefore, the community would not be on the receiving end of an irate non-conformity notification from the local planning office. He had finished his survey, now outside, having a smoke while he waited for the ferrets to complete their mission. The twins appeared and walked across; they were laden with a rather large bundle of paperwork. Murray just looked at them as they dumped part of the rainforest in the back of the vehicle. He was going to say something but they did not hang about, having returned to assist Robbo in what he hopes is the last house. Murray made the most of it and rattled one up; he knew nothing, absolutely, about solar power and had no intention of looking at any of the associated gumph now residing in the back of the vehicle. Murray was nearly sleeping when the trio returned with even more bundles of paper, "Got everything you need?" Robbo replied that he hoped so.

Murray had persuaded Karen to part with some of her construction team and he is joining in demolishing the farmhouse cottages to enable a supply of building materials for the extension. They start on the roof, carefully removing the tiles, trying ever so hard not to break any of them. He tried to be careful and had to be shown the technique that the other guys used. Murray's method was creating way too much wastage. Robbo was absent, and he thought that after Karen had dismissed the idea of solar panels, he was in a huff. He had not shown up for breakfast, and he did not think that he was dead, as someone would have already informed him by now. Murray had not seen Alicia or Okolo this morning also, so it is possible that they had all overslept. All the gumph relating to the solar panels had been dumped in their house. Murray had told Robbo to find somewhere else for it, or all the paper would be used to feed the fire.

Robbo had harped on about this technology for so long that even Charlie was holding her paws over her ears in the hope that Robbo would lose the gift of speech. He had said that Karen had offered no explanation nor reason why, and it was just a straightforward no. Robbo was very disappointed and declared to everyone that he was going to master the skills required to enable him to put it together. Okolo had cruelly reminded him that he could not wire a plug without looking at a diagram. When the laughing had subsided, he had just calmly told everyone present that he would have to master that skill also. Karen had told Murray in private that the panels had lain there for so long that the fine surface was most likely corroded. The batteries used for storing any electricity that they produced were probably dead, beyond resuscitation as they had never been used in the first place. Karen did admit that it was a good idea but she could not undertake the huge project as it had no guarantee of success. Murray had told her that when he saw him, he would try and explain her reasoning and, if it was okay with her; if he could find a solar system that works. She would have a look at providing some form of help. Karen had reluctantly agreed, but only to keep the peace. All the roof tiles had now been removed; Murray did not need to be shown how to remove the wooden structure. He happily got stuck in prying off the prefabricated frame that had kept out the wind and rain for only God knew how long.

Cha had appeared, and with the twins in tow, he told the other guys he would be back in a minute or two and jumped down to say hello. They had a quick cuddle, and she wanted to know if she delivered lunch and how many she should make. Murray told her it was very kind of her to offer, but as they were only ten minutes away, there was no need as if he was allowed, he would come home for lunch. Cha and the twins laughed at his portrayal of being the stray dog that was only allowed to come home because it was cold and wet, and they felt sorry for him. Murray told her that he loved her and he was sorry, but he had gotten back to work, or they would be calling him Robbo number two.

Murray was informed that the trio had just surfaced. Seemingly, Robbo had been talking well into the night about solar power and the wonderful concept of green energy. Murray thought that, for sure, Robbo needed a few of them fucking mushroom concoctions to firmly bring him back into the realms belonging to the normal world. When he finished his part in the deconstruction of this dwelling. Murray would take him on a guided tour of how the watermill produced power, enabling them all to have lights and a fully functioning medical facility. He thought that he would be wasting his time, but you never know. Robbo might just listen. No doubt he would have been in bending Okolo and Alicia's lugs into persuading him to help him out on his special project. Murray, after speaking to Karen, thought it had little chance of success.

However, Murray would give him a fair chance to prove everyone wrong. Hopefully, Robbo would not turn up in a suit and tie one day with a compulsory white hard hat displayed on full view on the back shelf of a vehicle.

Robbo had no real excuse for not turning in to today; all the work underway was being carried out to furnish him with a suitable dwelling. If it were not for Okolo and Alicia, he would just have been offered one of the spare buildings that was situated around the community. If that had displeased him, he could always move to the farmhouse where life would not be so easy for him down there. The more that he thought about it, Robbo had to change, and even if he was as fucking useless as he made out to be, it was better to fail than to be noticed for not trying at all.

The vehicles appeared, and it was lunchtime already. If he had not mentioned to Cha that he would be home for lunch, he would have just gone with the other guys. He entered the house, and Robbo was awake, now holding court on the new project that he was firmly set on adopting and making his own. Murray sits at the table and clears away a path through the myriads of paperwork that has taken over every space available. Robbo tells Murray that he was working with the paper, and Murray replied that he had been working outside all morning on demolishing an old house to get sufficient materials that would allow them to build an extension for him to move into before it got too cold.

Cha had plum forgot that he was coming home for lunch and had been busy looking after Mark. Murray told her that it was not a problem, he would go over and eat at Frank's. He gave her and Mark a family cuddle and went back out. Murray did not slam the door, but if he was going to be honest about it, he could have quite happily ripped it straight off the fucking hinges. Somehow or another he had lost his appetite and just walked back to work. He had nearly smashed all of the building down singlehandedly before the rest of the guys arrived back. All his clothes were firmly sticking to him, and he had calmed down but only a little.

Murray had laid his cards on the table that night, and in his unpolished finesse, he had told Robbo that he was a work-shy, lazy bastard. His head was that far up his own arse that he was amazed that he knew how to differentiate between daytime and night-time. He could not give two fucks if it had created an uproar in the house or not. Murray had informed him without swearing and shouting that there was a squad of workers toiling away on acquiring materials for the extension that he was going to live in, and he had not even bothered to go and say hello. "Definitely a slap in the face and most definitely a display of a fuck you all attitude." On the subject of green energy, he asked if Robbo thought that the watermill was petrol or fossil-fuelled, cause as far as he could remember, it was fucking rain and then water powered. Robbo asked if Murray wanted him to leave. Murray replied that he just wanted him to do some fucking work for a change and stop making half-arsed excuses for doing something fucking else. "If you want to go and play with the solar power things, then go ahead; at least you will be doing something. Honestly, if it works, if it does not, I really could not give a fuck, but at least be showing all the people out there that you are not just a fucking tailor's showroom dummy." Cha had never really seen him angry, and Murray had never seen himself that angry. "At the very least, you should go and thank the people who are working on your new abode, maybe offer to help maybe offer them a cuppa, but don't just ignore them. That is not what we are about."

The next morning, after breakfast, Murray put on his leadership hat, then banged the table, opening up the meeting, "Thank you all for attending; the purpose of this meeting is to discuss what we are going to do about the recently underground chamber. I have been thinking about this for a while and now that I have some spare time on my hands. I am proposing that I go down and attempt to open the next elusive doorway with the newly thought-out and agreed sequence." The meeting was interrupted by a knock on the door, and Frank had sent over the four bags of provisions that Murray had requested earlier.

Cha asked him what the bags were for, "You never thought that I was going to go down there on my own, and if it comes to it, it is just another room full of skeletons. I thought that we could go for a picnic with the food packs. But... on the other hand, if the opening does lead to somewhere, we don't know where it will end if the opening closes behind us and lastly how long we could be down there." Okolo wanted to know who was getting an invite. Murray looked at Robbo, replying that he was open to reasonable suggestions. As Cha and Okolo had young ones it would be either one or the other as the one who was not going would be looking after Mark and Vincent. Alicia informed the table that she should go as she thought she could come in handy with any additional puzzles that could spring into existence along the way. The twins declared their interest, and they were the ones who should be going in the first place. "We want to contribute and prove our worth; you took us in, gave us everything when we had nothing, and we want to be involved."

Robbo surprisingly had said nothing as he knew, and Murray also knew that he would not be invited anyway. Murray asked Cha if she was okay with the twins, Alicia and himself going into the hole. Cha looked at him and asked him why he was asking her that question. Murray informed her that she was and will always be his better half and he would not do anything that she was unhappy with. Cha told him that she was okay with it and that if they did not go down, it would always bug them in the future. "For all we know, you will all be down there for about five minutes, the next thing we will hear is that none of you want any dinner because you are all stuffed full." Murray tapped the side of his cup and announced that they would go first thing in the afternoon and that the meeting was over.

Murray asked Cha if he could take her out for lunch. He knew a place near there that he had heard on the grapevine had just received a fresh batch of fish. Even before he had finished the sentence, they were all getting their jackets on, heading out on mass across to Frank's. Murray hoped that there was something non slimy on the menu for his simple, viewed by some as uncultured, unrefined tastes. As per the norm, Murray thought that Frank's place was fucking stinking of the bottom-dwelling ocean creatures as soon as he opened the door. He asked how Cat was feeling; Frank informed him that she was at the being sick stage. Murray was all for going to see her, but her other half told him that she had been up most of the night, and he had checked in on her a few minutes ago. Both she and Remus were out for the count. Frank said that she snored louder than the dog, but if Murray were to repeat this, even under torture, he would deny that they ever had this conversation.

Everyone in the place was fished up, and Murray settled on a wholesome plate of fries. He did not know what type of fish they were all eating, but he was delighted that he did not have to fucking eat it. Murray was finished first, informing Cha that he would wait for her outside; he stole a mug of tea and happily savoured the fresh air. Robbo was out next, asking Murray if they were cool. He nodded, indicating that he had said all that he was going to say on the subject, and they could talk about anything, anything else but solar fucking power.

Robbo wished him good luck, telling him that he hoped to see him soon. Murray thanked him for the comment and he hoped that it would be soon also. Alone now with his smoke and tea, Murray had no idea what they were going to encounter nor how long they were actually going to be away, but at least they had to try and see what had been hidden away for all of these years. Alicia and the twins had been delegated to collect all the items that were required, hopefully, they will not need anything out of the ordinary.

Cha had now come out to join him. She asked if he had seen Robbo. Murray told her that he had spoken to him on the passing. She asked him if there were any harsh words said, and he told her that Robbo the yobbo had wished him luck and hoped to see him soon. "Is it worth asking if you think you were a little harsh on him?" Murray replied that he could have been a lot harsher but he had to consider Okolo and Alicia's feelings also. "Well, for what it is worth, they agreed with you one hundred percent and have been trying to persuade him to get more involved for weeks now. Between you and me, they are going to hit him with a nookie ban." Murray put his hands to his ears and did not want to know any more about it. Cha was sniggering when she had told him and was now laughing at his antics. Cha put her arms around him, telling him to be careful and not to take any unnecessary chances as there were three members of his fan club awaiting his safe return. Murray said that he would be back before she knew it, telling her not to worry. "Can you pop in and see Cat later? Frank told me that she is not feeling great." Just at that moment the rest of the explorers' club arrive, informing him that they are ready to go. Murray put his arms around Cha and said see you soon. "Oh, you will see me sooner than that, Okolo, me and all the small people are coming up to see you off."

As they stand there, all suited up and wearing their backpacks, Murray steps forward and salutes Cha. She put her arms around him and told him that she loved him. The four of them waved and descended into the opening, arriving at the wall displaying the symbols. Murray shone his torch on the wall, illuminating the surface, and Alicia, with her notes at hand, directed the twins on the required sequence of which panels to press. The first part was performed perfectly. The twins had pressed all the double and single blocks the exact way that she had indicated. Murray had suggested that for the next part, they should stand closer; he did not know why exactly but somehow thought that it was a good idea. Alicia shouted out the ones to press. The eight remaining symbols were pushed in at first, they thought that nothing had happened. The twins felt it first, indicating that they could feel something happening beneath their feet. Another stairwell opened up below them as the stone floor slowly started to separate. Murray flicked the torch around them, and a large block of stone was now blocking off the stairway that they had used to enter the room. The unsettled dust that he had captured with his flashlight had given the surprise away. The movement had made very little noise as it almost silently glided down from the ceiling. They were now faced with little choice of which direction to travel. Like it or lump it, they were going to have to go down the recently exposed stairwell.

Chapter 18

Enunsha and her team had been hard at it. They had started at the top of the list and were now working their way through the required tasks. Some of the roads were so severely fucked up that they had spent lots of time ploughing the stubborn obstructions out of the way. Her team had never complained or even asked any questions about what they were actively involved in. Enunsha had specifically asked for the best mechanics, and now they were proving their worth. The concrete facility had lain abandoned since the onset of the great sickness and they were now in and about all the neglected machines. Ascertaining which were and which were not suitable for urgent resuscitation. She had not been supplied with an accurate figure of how many that were required, just the sub-heading of as many working machines as possible.

She had helped out where she was allowed, freely admitting to anyone who would be prepared to listen that they should have brought more people with her group. Enunsha heard the roar of the next engine sparking back into life, which gave them a total of two working machines. The yard in front of her was full of the same type of vehicles, all parked up nice and neat ready for the next bulk order. Row upon row of them, almost waiting patiently for things to return back to normal.

Enunsha was still worried as she had still not found any new signs of the Indian nation passing through. She had travelled many, many miles and had thought that, at the very least, she would have located a sign displayed from a recent scouting party informing anyone who could read that they had passed through this area. This was not normal; the next time she saw her father, she would have to inform him. For all she knew, there could be a more than valid reason why the scouts had not passed through here, but as they were her people, she was more than entitled to worry about them.

Another machine coughed and then spluttered, almost deciding whether it was going to work or not. Then coughed again, this time with a huge belch of black oily smoke announcing its' rebirth. The newly brought back-to-life machine was driven up and down the road, ensuring that when it was required, it would either be able to start on its own or accept a jump start via the extended umbilicals attached to another machine. The reinforcements should be on their way to her, and then they would carry out the rest of the tasks required for this dangerous mission. Enunsha took the bull by the horns, asking the mechanics to quickly teach her the rudimentary tasks on how to drive one of the mechanical beasts. "All I have to do is drive it up and down the road a few times until you tell me to stop and park it up. What can be hard about that? Guys, it will free another mechanic. You really don't expect me just to stand about and watch all day, do you?" One of them started to mention what Abe and Jackson had told them before they had left the community. Enunsha interrupted him midsentence and kindly informed him that if he looked about Abe and Jackson ain't here today, so she was calling the shots. The mechanic muttered, "Fair enough, c'mon, I will give you the quickest driving lesson in history." Absolutely delighted to be allowed to help out, Enunsha jumped into the cab. She got the hang of it pretty quickly, happily driving up and down the road for the required time to give the batteries a much-needed charge. Enunsha had followed the implicit instructions to the letter. With the task now complete she parked up the monster in the required spot. As she approached, the mechanics had another one ready for her. Enunsha asked if she had to give the reactivated vehicles a name. The mechanics looked at her as if she had gone bananas, ignored her completely and got back to the next task at hand.

That day alone, they had reinvigorated and then parked up fifteen monsters, all ready to roll out when required. She was chuffed to bits at what they had accomplished, beaming with pride for each and every one of her team. Abe and Jackson, by her reckoning, all going well, should be arriving there the next morning at the latest. If, for some reason, it did not happen, she would have to stop all the activities and go to plan B. Enunsha hoped that it did not come to this but had agreed on the required action if the initial plan faltered and failed. As the light was starting to fade, she gathered her gang and told them that work was over for the day. She apologised for not having a special reward for them all but promised on her soul that she would never forget all that they had done for her today.

Enunsha had a sleepless night worrying about what the next day would bring. It was not a bargain that she had agreed upon with Abe and Jackson; it was more or less a promise to make things right if the plan went tits up. She did not know very much about the weapons they had described, but she thought it would just entail point-and-shoot. Albeit these would make louder than loud noises, they would only be used as the very last resort. She thought that she had only had about a couple of hours of sleep max when the sun announced that it was the start of another day.

As per the norm she was one of the first up and had started making the breakfast for everyone. She had apologised that Doctor Death and Poison Pete were unavailable for this expedition. However, she was happy to announce that they should be arriving later on today and hoped that all of their breakfast dreams, along with all their culinary aspirations, would finally come true. She rallied her troops, informing them just to start back where they had finished off yesterday. It was now mid-morning, and they had just parked up monster number twenty; at last, the reinforcements had started to arrive.

The trail of dust in the distance reveals that the convoy is heading their way. Enunsha was worried that the first part of the plan was going to fail and leave her a widow. Now delighted with the news, she tried to tidy herself up in the cab mirror, laughing as she had accidentally smeared her face with a streak of engine oil. "Oh well, can't be a monster trucker and a good-looking wife!" She said to no one in particular. One of the mechanics waved her down, reminding her of the deal that he, as well as the rest of the team, had made with Abe and Jackson. It would save them a hell of a lot of earache if she was to jump out of the cab before they arrived. Enunsha understood his impending predicament, obliging him with the request.

As she walked back along the road to the makeshift headquarters, a vehicle drew up beside her. Abe got out and put his arms around her, informing Enunsha that they were never going to spend time apart like this ever again. She returned the hugs and kisses and agreed to the declaration of intent. Jackson had now joined them, pointing at the parked-up monster machines compliments her along with her crew on the work that they had already accomplished. "I know they did great over the last few days, and I promised them that you would be barbequing some of them special steaks for them real soon as a reward." Jackson pretended to hand over Abe a twenty spot. As she looked at them, Abe told her that they did bring some fine A1 beef and he had told Jackson that you would know without being informed. "We bet twenty on it." Jackson couldn't figure out how she knew, guessing that it must be one of them secret husband-and-wife things.

As they have nowhere to store and keep the meat fresh, Abe organised the barbeque. They were all going to be more than very busy for the next few weeks, fully exposed daily to Doctor Death and Poison Pete's as yet unclassified, experimental cuisine. Jackson thought that it was a great idea and went to help the guys find where they had stashed the beer. Although they were now situated miles from where they had established their community, it was still necessary to post a guard detail. Abe informed the first batch of sentries that it would be based on a rota system, and not one of them would lose out on the special meal. Enunsha helped everyone with the setting out of the temporary accommodation. She warmed her co-conspirators, the gossip mongers from the mother and toddler group, that those arrangements would not be forever, so put a plug in the complaining and bitching for now. "Ladies, if you would all now like to follow me, I will show you where you can set up your pitches for the time being."

The barbeque was, as always, a huge success, and there were no unruly incidents or hitches. As a community they had come together but not in the expected way. Most of them had thought by now that they would be living in relative luxury with air conditioning and all the other wonderful accessories that free electrical power can provide. Jackson reckoned that they had tried so hard, put everything in that was required, only to be pipped at the post. It had taken a long time for him to persuade Abe that they had a problem that needed to be addressed. At first, he had refused to believe him, giving in only when Jackson had shown him the irreputable proof. That someone was pissing down his back, then telling him that it was raining, did he finally give in and start to listen to then plan to strike back.

The hair that Jackson had Abe surreptitiously stick on the elevator doors and the sealed entry point at level five had finally helped sell the deal. He could not prove one way or another that they were being watched and recorded every step of the way inside the underground complex. If he had forced this issue to prove it, they would have lost more of their people. They had lost more than enough, and he was intent on losing not another soul to emphasize that his thinking was correct. The plan that he had laid out in front of Abe and Enunsha was all verbal, as he had insisted on writing nothing down. On the last visit down the stairwell, the conversation between Abe and himself had all been staged. Abe had informed him that Enunsha was having a disturbed sleep pattern, waking up in the middle of the night again and listening to Abe rehearse his parts. Jackson had to admit that he had found this hilarious, and it had put a smile on his face for days on end.

At the same time, though, he had to resign himself to the fact that if the next set course of actionable events was an unmitigated disaster, then they were well and truly fucked. He took a slug of beer. Abe had finished cooking and joined him. Jackson clinked the bottles together, welcoming him,

Abe told him that he looked as if he had a toast in mind. "Funny you should mention that. How about fucked if we do and fucked if we don't." Abe nodded, not fully comprehending the full implications, and simply replied, "Yip, I will drink to that."

Enunsha had now joined them, asking them if all was okay as they looked rather forlorn and serious. Both of them assured that all was good in their world and that just enjoying a beer or two before all the work started. Jackson indicated that his bottle was empty, and he wanted to go and get some refills. Enunsha told him not to bother, signaled one of the M&T group and held up three fingers, "No panic required, Jackson, the cavalry is on its way." He nodded at her outmanoeuvring him and thanked her for everything that she had done. They waited until the beer had arrived, then reassured each other that all would go ahead as planned. "As the sneaky bastards that live somewhere in the bowels of the former Kunupenny kingdom don't know that they are coming back, I hope that all our efforts will be a nice pleasant surprise for them." Enunsha raised her bottle, "I will drink to that," and they all clinked each other's bottle.

She told them that it would be a good idea to go and mingle with the rest of the group. The guys agreed and followed suit. Abe told everyone he met that it was his wife's idea to have the barbeque, so she was the one they needed register their complaints with. Jackson stayed in the background, hoping that they wouldn't lose any more of them in the dangerous days to come. He quickly blended into the background, having just about reached the limit of his beer intake sneaked off to at least try and get some sleep. He had persuaded Abe that there was no need and no purpose to unveil any of the plans to the people in their community. The guys and gals would only worry and then talk about it. If the word got out and managed to reach the underground dwellers, then they would be stopped in their tracks before they even got started.

Jackson was still worried by the fact that he did not know any of the details of the subterranean people. He suspects that they are another group with no connections or affiliations to the now-deceased Kunupenny clan. If they had been associated with them in any shape or form, Abe and his community would have been wiped off the face of the earth a long time ago as to the million-dollar question of whether they are just located in this region or have other established outposts throughout the former United States of America. He unfortunately just did not know the answer to this question, perhaps he never would. Either way, he intended to teach them a lesson that no matter how well they were hidden, no matter how well they concealed and disguised their subversive attacks upon them. There was only one way in, only one way out, and pretty soon, all going to plan, there would be none.

Enunsha welcomed him to the makeshift breakfast galley. Jackson just asked for a coffee and if possible, a sandwich to take away for after. She told him no problem, then handed out his order. He took a seat and thought of the day ahead as he quietly sipped the awful brew, which tasted like it had been filtered through Doctor Death and Poison Pete's sticky socks. When all the people started to move on, he took his place beside Abe. They went through all the allocated groups and the various outlined tasks.

Now that they were seated, Abe and Jackson go in among them, giving them the specific details of what they must do. "Okay, group Alpha, here is the skinny: you will need a flatbed truck on which you will locate five welding machines of the type used by pipeline welders. Johnny, I am led to believe that you are guilty of having previous crimes of being associated with this fraternity." Johnny nodded pleading guilty to all the said charges. "Okay, so you know what we need. The machines need to all be fuelled up and checked that they are in full working order, got it." They all nodded, confirming that they understood. "Now, the welding cables, we require these in set lengths." Jackson handed over the list, "These have been measured in foot's steps, no feet and inches and no metres, centimeters or millimeters. Link all the cables together as per the allocated grouping and check that they work. Once you have done this, break all the connections, tie them in a Texas loop, reconnect them then tape up all the connections. Johnny you okay with all this so far?" He nodded, indicating that all was good. "Now, as you can see, we have three different lengths. The shortest will be connected to welding machine number one the next to number two. Leaving the longest one, that should go to number three. Have you all got that because this is important to get right the first time, and if any of you don't understand, you have to say it now!" there were no questions so Jackson continued.

"Machines four and five are spare machines, and with that, you can add in some spare cables. These are included on the list and also have to be checked that they are in good working order. Lastly, we need boxes of welding electrodes; the type, the amount required, and the size are detailed on the list. Okay, people, that's it; go over what we have discussed; if you have any questions, please ask. Yeah, nearly forgot; here is the map. The company is circled on the map. I have been informed that the road is relatively clear."

Jackson thanks them for their undivided attention and asks them to go through the plan among themselves until it is time to move out.

Abe was in the middle of the planned action on the concrete industrial facility, and as it is the largest group, he would be in conversation for quite a while with group Bravo. Jackson hunted down the Charlie group, and he found them sitting huddled in the corner. "Hope you didn't think that I forgot about you. I didn't, so let's get on with it. I need you to gather round the table and we will get through all of this in quick time." Jackson placed the map on the table, and with a pen, he pointed to their destination. "This we are calling "shoppers alley." It is not an alley; you will be shopping but not for what you are thinking. Your task will be to gather, collect, and then load as many shopping trolleys as we can squeeze onto a modified car transporter as possible. I have not worked out the exact numbers, but there will be hundreds of them fucking things. The mechanics' group will be arriving and delivering five modified transporters. All you have to do is load them up. You have all at one time or another seen the guys moving these things around, the way they jam them all together and wheels them about like a train." They all nodded, understanding what he was describing. "You will wheel them five at a time, ten at a time, whatever you are comfortable with on to the transporters until they are all full. They will need to be secured for the journey ahead, and all you have to do is tie them off to stop them from falling off. All easy-peasy, with nothing complicated or dangerous about it. Just nod if you understand and discuss it quietly among yourselves until it is time to go. If you have any questions, feel free to ask?" Jackson thanks them all for listening.

Delta group was sitting outside catching some fresh air and generally shooting the shit until he arrived. They got ready to stand as he approached, but he told them to cool their jets as there was no need for that type of formality. Jackson placed the map on the table, asking them to gather around. "Okay, guys and gals, here are your tasks. I say tasks because you are going to be split into two groups. Group one," he nods to their elected spokesperson, "you are going to beg, borrow, or preferably steal five car transporters. Once you have located these vehicles, you have to get them working, then floor them out with them plywood or whatever the fuck they are called multi-something boards. You can secure them with ropes as they will only be carrying lots of shopping trolleys, as with the rest of the groups, I have been reliably informed that the road there is clear enough. If you have any questions, let me know before you set off. The second group, you have to find and make these plates." Jackson supplied them with the drawing and another map. "They don't have to be perfect, but the closer you get them to these sizes, the better it will be for the end users. As you have all carried out this type of work, you will know the types of tools that you will require to do the job. Hopefully, these will be near at hand where you locate the said plates," but just in case, he handed them over two tape measures and some French chalk. "Have a look at the drawing and the map, and if you have any questions, let me know or somebody know before you set off." Jackson thanked them for their time and went to see how Abe was getting on with the bravo group.

They were in mid-discussion; not wanting to disturb or interfere, he went to speak to Enunsha, who had the Echo and Foxtrot groups. He said hello, and she displayed a large smile and nearly laughed as she reported that the Echo group would be going back to what they were doing yesterday in performing the various sequences of the magical resuscitation involved in bringing the mechanical monsters back to life. Jackson, not expecting anything less, informed her that they had allocated her some more mechanics and helpers.

"Group Foxtrot has been hard at it all morning preparing all the provisions for all the groups to take with them. Doctor Death and Poison Pete had asked me to let you know that they have included several new recipes into the menu and hope that everyone enjoys their new creations." Jackson was at a loss as to what he was supposed to say to this remark. He had to stop himself from laughing as he informed her that he would pass on the message; he was sure that all of the people would be delighted with the new savoury delights.

Abe had finished with group Alpha, and with the word out, he addressed the town hall meeting. "Okay, folks, that's about it for this morning. You have all been allocated your tasks, your maps, and the details of what is required. If you have no questions, then I wish you all happy hunting and will see you all very soon. Good luck, and please remember the emergency safety protocols. Thank you to everyone for doing this." There were no whooping, high-fives or fist bumps. Everyone just got on with what they have to get done. Soon, the place is nearly empty. Abe asked Jackson if his group had a name, and he informed him that he had just plain forgotten.

They shook hands, and Jackson gathered his small crew, and they set off. For this one, he needed no map or detailed itinerary. Abe had been tasked with the security detail and thought that he had been unlucky in being awarded the now-unemployed sandwich makers to beef up his numbers. On a brighter note, if they encountered any trouble, he thought that if Doctor Death and Poison Pete were to give a cooking demonstration. Instead of a good old-fashioned gunfight taking place then would be bad guys having been instantly revolted, would surrender or run away.

Jackson had reached his first scheduled stop. The DIY emporium was massive and catered for everyone. All the handless home fixers who spent a small fortune on all the best kits available for home extensions and repairs. Then, all the certified tradesmen came around to fix all the bodged jobs for a handsome fee. He asked one of the guys to see if there were any suitable forms of transport available in the near vicinity. Jackson told the other guys to each grab a trolley, letting them know that they were going to all be happy shoppers for about an hour or two. They all paraded throughout the huge building like a bunch of uncoordinated tourists on an unintended mystery tour; Jackson followed the signs akin to reading a long-lost treasure map. The guys with the accompanying trollies snaked their way down the aisles and intersections, stopping off at various points where Jackson had told them to haul up. "Six packs of the grey stuff, five rolls of the thin red and white wire. Plus, a couple of pairs of heavy-duty bolt cutters." The last stop did not have the quantity that was required, so he redirected them to follow him to the warehouse.

This was a completely different kettle of fish; there were no hints or any clues to reveal what was stored where, and they would have to search the hard way. Jackson had purloined a few examples of what was required at the last scheduled stop in the main section of the emporium. He shared these and suggested that they spread out, "Whoever finds them first, shout out loud and clear, and the rest of us will come to you." They all walked away, some of them wondering why in the fuck did he want this shit. Jackson was never asked; therefore, he did not really see why he had to explain why they needed this stuff, and that is about all he would have told them if they had actually bothered to enquire. The search continued for most of the day until late in the afternoon, some smart ass shouted out, "Bobby Bingo." All the group assemble where the finder is located, and someone asks how many tubes are required. Jackson replies, "Just put as much as you can into the trollies, and that should about cover it."

Jackson was reading the manufacturer's stipulated guidelines on the back of one of the cans, working out in his head the total accumulated volume that would be discharged from the pressurised cans. He reckoned that a couple of van loads of this shit should just about be enough to accomplish the task he had in mind. The trollies were headed back out front. After the vans were loaded up, he told them that there was even a bed department in here. "We are going to bunk up here for the night. Any snorers among you who can keep the dead awake should keep out of my hearing range. I am a little grouchy when I don't get a full night's sleep and liable to shoot you if you snore like the devil." The guys were not sure if he was joking or not. It did not really matter because, just as they had found the bed department, Jackson was out like a light, and the guys thought that he snored that loud he could wake up all of the dead for hundreds of miles all around.

Chapter 19

Abe was on tour checking that all allocated work groups were safe and if they needed any help or assistance. He had just spent some time with team Charlie. They had just about secured all the shopping trollies that would be required. A modified car transporter had just arrived as he was leaving as they had started to load on the first batch. He had been constantly checking that the roads were clear, and the spotters he had hidden across the city had observed no unauthorised traffic. His next port of call was the delta group. The guys and gals have seen him approaching but have not stopped working. The mechanics were swearing at the next-to-be-assigned car transporter which was proving to be a little on the stubborn side. Abe asked what the problem was, "Well, we were having issues with the mechanism. We replaced the perished seals, refilled them with hydraulic oil, and now we are just putting the son of a bitch through the process. We think the problem is only because it has not been used in a while and will eventually function as required." Abe nodded, not knowing shit about how this fucker worked, told them thanks, then moved on.

The other team with this group had found the plates as well as all of the equipment that was required. As they saw him approaching, they waved him over. The woman in charge points to the first cut and cleaned section ready to be loaded. "These fuckers are real heavy pieces of shit; I think you will need to feed whoever is going to carry these babies some raw meat," Abe asked her if it was possible to carry them, she nodded adding yeah, as long as they have some big guys to do the hauling. Abe replied, "I will speak to the guys over in Alpha group to come and collect them on the way over to the checkpoint." The woman told him that would not be a problem, then went to help her guys figure out how to use a measuring tape. Abe looked at her; she just said, "Men, gotta be good for something?" He did the honourable thing and happily retreated to his vehicle without comment.

Alpha group was in and about a cloud of smoke as they tried and get the huge wheeled welding machine to start. The group already have three of the machines stationed on the low loader. Abe did not see the cables and asked if they had checked out that the machines were all fully operational. Johnny, the group's leader, confirmed that they were all good to go, adding that all the welding rods required were already in the cab.

"We have got packets of the motherfuckers still in the factory-sealed boxes. We will need to give them a little gentle heat before they are sparked up." Abe nodded, thinking that johnny was describing the welding process and did not want to ask any more questions.

"Johnny, when you have finished up here, on the way over to the checkpoint, could you pick up all the plates from the delta group." Johnny gave him the double thumbs-up signal, letting Abe know that they should have enough space left on the low loader to accommodate the added, last-minute request.

At the last stop was the bravo group, and they were not doing too well by the looks of things. The silos that reach up into the sky, as the woman in charge put it across, were well and truly fucked. She thought they had spent more than enough time coaxing them back into life. Even if they could get the engines to fire up, it would not make a blind bit of difference, as she had just been informed that they were just about as solid as frozen shit. "Don't worry, Abe. I think we have a working alternative. C'mon, and I will show you what we can do," she pointed, "There are three piles of stuff over yonder. As you know, the big one is the sand, and the other two are the aggregates. One of the mounds is made up of three-quarter-sized gravel, and the other is three eights size. I am guessing that for what we are going to do, it won't make any difference, and we can use any one or both." She waited for him to give her a yes or no.

Abe noticed her waiting and just said, "Yeah, I guess that will be okay."

"Some of the guys and gals are out stealing some of them big fibre plastic bags that the builder merchants used to deliver sand in. We can load these up with the stuff from the piles, lift them up, and feed them into Enunsha's trucks." Abe couldn't quite see it, looking at the piles of shit and scratching his head, trying to work it out. "The team will put the shit into the bags with help from the excavators or the back-hoe loaders, whatever you can steal first." Abe then nodded, just managing to grasp what she was saying. "Then the telehandlers will lift them and hold them over the truck opening. All the team had to do was slit the bag, shake it about a bit, then let the contents pour down in through the vertical hole."

Abe thought it would take much longer than estimated. She told him that if he had a better solution, he should shout it out now.

"Abe, we don't have any other way of doing it, and all the crew know that they will have to work through the night to get it done." He looked worried, asking her if she would need more people; she thought that she would need double what she had right now. "We could work them on a dayshift and nightshift pattern to accomplish what is needed."

Abe had no choice but to agree, "Okay, do what you need to do, then send word when you need the trucks. I will start sending you other people as soon as they are available." He was just about to walk away when he remembered that he had not seen any of the grey-coloured material. Abe asked her; she told him that they have a warehouse full of that shit, then reminded him that they will need to source a couple of tankers for the water supply.

He was then worried that it was going to be a tight race to the finish line. He would have to run all this past Jackson, adding all the details to the final plan. It all boiled down to availability and delivery times. Abe did not remember seeing the pumps that would be needed for the final touch, but as she had never mentioned them as a potential problem, he, for now, would assume that she had that issue firmly under her control. His last stop was the echo group. At least Enunsha would be pleased to see him. Abe told his guys where they were heading next. Then, deep in thought, he allowed one of his crew to drive for a change. He had all sorts of numbers flowing through his grey matter with all the associated calculations, and he thought they would be working nonstop for at least forty-eight hours solid.

When he got some time, and whether Jackson agreed or not, he was going to have to put all of this down on paper. If not, his head was surely going to explode.

Start times, holding points, watering points, the list was starting to increase by the minute. Jackson should be back the day after tomorrow. Abe hoped he could offer him some good news on what they had ready for the big surprise. Abe for sure knew that they won't have everything, but they should have enough of the items ready and available to make a good start.

Abe had arrived at station Echo, finding Enunsha out in the middle of it all, directing the trucks with as much flair and panache as a jet fighter marshaller on the flight deck of one of the gigantic aircraft carriers that used to prowl the ocean waves all over the planet. He looked at all the trucks that her group had brought back to life, now all lined up, ready for the next step. Enunsha got one of her people to take over and quickly went over to speak with her hubby. "Hi Abe, we hope to have forty trucks ready for the end of school today. All the guys are doing great. I honestly can't praise them enough. What about things with you? All going well, I hope."

Abe gave her the highs and the possible lows. "Well, at least they decided to make something work rather than standing by for someone else to make the hard decision for them. It will work, just taking a bit more time than what we originally estimated, but hey! Look at the overall progress everyone has pulled together on all of this, and they have not even been informed of the grand plan."

Mr. Hubstien knew that, as always, she was right in what she was saying. "Yeah, I know what you are saying, but I never thought for a minute that the silos would be fucked up big time. I blame myself for not thinking it through properly, but considering that we started off with sweet fuck all. I guess that we are not doing too bad in the overall scheme of things and we will know by the end of tomorrow what we have and don't have to play with. Enunsha, I think that your team have done truly wonderful things in coaxing these fuckers back into life. Really a remarkable achievement." She shook her head and confessed that one of the mechanics had told her that this place ran a really tight ship here and programmed a rigid preventative maintenance schedule that was adhered to every single working day. "I guess that we were pretty lucky, and let's be honest about this. It was about time we had some of that."

Over at DIY world, Jackson was the first to get up and had brewed some of the awful shit that someone in their wisdom had decided to call coffee. He had thought long and hard, then carefully penned a list of additional items that were then required. The rest of his team were starting to surface. After the obligatory moans and groans, they all grabbed a coffee. Not being one of the breakfast people, Jackson let them fend for themselves by rustling up some grub. They had offered him some of the various delicacies that were being conjured up but he had politely declined all and any of the offers. He informed them that he would find some bits and pieces they would need. He also made up a list of additional materials they could source while he was away. Jackson guessed that he should be back for the morning, all the items on the additional list should be available within this store.

He had told them he would return as soon as possible, empathising that it had nothing to do with their snoring. That comment had left them a little confused as they had thought that all the dead in the various graveyards in the immediate vicinity had emptied out overnight with the uninterrupted orchestra worth of snores and shouting that had been broadcast from Jackson's comatose form. Jackson had just forgotten to tell them about his sleeping habits; he smiled as he drove away, heading towards the place he hoped would furnish them with the specialised items not normally available for sale in the local DIY stores.

The guys would be busy enough with the list that he had left them to get on with. Hopefully, they would have found and completed the shopping list before he returned. Jackson had to relive his past when he arrived at his next destination. He was not one hundred percent sure that the place he was going to would still be secure and untouched. Jackson had never been there, and it and the other similar places existed. It was only a brief memory of attending a long-ago agency seminar where he and other people of the same ilk were introduced to the theme. *"If everything, turned to shit."* Jackson doubted if that was the official stamped and approved heading, but nevertheless, that was what he and his fellow agents were told. That's what it was called.

They had been informed and enlightened to the fact that if their beloved country was ever overrun and taken over by a foreign power. That they were the people who would orchestrate, then deliver fear and terror upon the usurpers. Along with all the others, he had trained for years, spending most of his working life thwarting and eliminating potential terrorist threats. Now, they had been informed that should the unthinkable happen, they were to dismantle it within. The subsequent training course had been an eye-opener, to say the least.

If the bad guys had thought they had the upper hand at inventing devices to create mayhem and destruction, they were sadly mistaken.

If the scenario ever took place, the current government and the previous ones have placed a failsafe for the future. They had built these seemingly innocuous buildings in every state and province that looked like normal family homes to the untrained eye.

The white picket fence and the wooden porch with the accompanying rocking chair were all just some of the obligatory props to disguise the secret hidden hardware contained within these premises. All he had to do was find one. They had been made to recognise the everyday signs that would be placed in the various neighbourhoods. The powers to be had hoped that this would direct the ones who had evaded capture to prove that America was still alive and willing to fight for what it believed in.

Jackson had found the residential housing estate that he believed would reveal the whereabouts of the secreted stash of items that he sought to acquire. He thought that some of the ex-leaders of his country would approve of his intended use, but maybe not all of them. He saw the poles and the tattered flags blatantly displaying the declaration that God blessed America and all her loyal subjects. Jackson just had to locate the correct configuration.

He had, on purpose, slowly driven around the area and recounted everything that was on show. If the postal service was still operable, he would have purloined an appropriate vehicle along with the obligatory uniform complete with the hat to create a viable disguise. In his previous occupation, he had several stints overseas and his little hack to keep normal was to send postcards home. They all contained the same wording, "Hi Mum, hope you are doing fine. The weather is great, but the beer is better."

These were just a little reminder, and he had accrued quite a collection over the years. It was not the pictures that were displayed on the cards. For him, the franked postage mark reminded him of what he had done and the colleagues he had lost in service to his country. Jackson found his first clue; all the signs stated, 'Your country thanks you for your service' and a small picture of the flag. It was not the wording; it was not the emblem. The serial number on the top right corner contained the coded message, directing him to the whereabouts of the stash.

If he had failed to remember the method of reconfiguring the displayed numbers, he would have wandered for days, possibly weeks, until he had located what he was looking for. His training had saved him, and how could he forget the endless hours of mind-numbing mental calculations he was forced to perform. Jackson counted out the five up, four across to the right and two down. As no residents were around to object, he abandoned his vehicle, walking through the once-perfect manicured gardens until he found the house he needed. Jackson decoded the veteran's sign on the front of the house to confirm that he was at the correct location. This time, when he reconfigured the code, Jackson walked towards the double garage, which was identical to every other garage in and around the surrounding area.

At the side entrance, he reached up and located the key. Jackson closed the door behind him, then waited to ensure that the building was empty and that no one was following him. On purpose, he had deliberately not locked the door. He had thought that he had heard something in the background. Whoever they were, they were good but not as good as they had thought. Jackson set up the step ladder, climbed into the rafters, pulled up the steps behind him, and waited for his not-so-secret followers to arrive. He thought this was the hardest part; many of the guys he trained with had sweated at this stage. Jackson controlled his breathing, stayed as silent as a dead church mouse and listened to all and everything around him.

There were two of them; his weapon was out and ready to eliminate them as soon as they entered the garage. They would look all over the place and like ninety-nine-point nine percent of the portrayed results of the statistical analysis relating to failed intrusions. He thought it was improbable, almost a given certainty, that they would fail to look above them. The dynamic duo had advanced slowly and was now at the door. By the method by which they entered, he was aware that they were once in the armed forces, but as they were not wearing a uniform, he could not guess which service or unit they once belonged to. He let them come in, and as they looked around the place, Jackson adjusted his weapon to maintain the kill zone of the possibly intended targets. "How the fuck did he manage to escape? I swear that I saw him come in here." The one who had never done the talking put his weapon down and told his buddy that they had been completely outfoxed, and the guy was up in the roof space behind them. "Mike, I am not shitting you, put your weapon down, and we might be able to walk out of here alive."

"Mister, I know you are there, so do you wanna talk? you are the first living person we have seen in a long time." Mike spurted out, "I don't think that there is anyone there, and you have just freaked me out about nothing." Jackson told Mike that if he even thought about going for his weapon, he would shoot both of them. "Okay mister, what you want?" Jackson asked them why they were following him. "We have been sort of staying here in this area, and like I said, you are the first person we have seen in a very long time."

Jackson ordered them to drop the side arms and kicked them along with the machine guns into the corner, then lie on the ground. While they were doing as they were told, he replaced the step ladder on the ground and then climbed down from his perch, never taking his weapon off them at one moment. "Now I guess we have a problem where I need to decide if I am just going to shoot you, tie you up or just let you go."

"First, I need you to take your tops off and show me your back. No funny moves, no excuses, just do what I am telling you. Nice and easy as if you were going for a shower." One at a time, they removed their clothes and proved that they had no tattoos relating to the secret people on their backs. Jackson told them to put their shirts back on. "I really need to know why you are here; why are you staying here and not in some cabin in the woods away from all the dead and decaying remnants of the old world." The Mike guys disclosed that this was where he grew up, it was a nice community, and it was home. The other one had told him his name was Perry, and he had nowhere to go. After the onset of the disease that wiped out all of their company, he had just sort of tagged along with Mike. "We tidied up the place, buried all the people and like I said, this was my one-time home, and what else do you want to know."

Perry spoke up, "Mister, I think I have seen you somewhere before, maybe Fort B and a few years back, you were the spook who came to give us a lecture before we were deployed to that hot place full of sand and fuckers that ate lots of fucking goat meat. I also remember that you actually came on a mission to collect one of the bad guys. You looked a bit different then, but it was definitely you." Jackson asked him about a few people's names and the places he remembered, and Perry's story checked out.

"How about I let you go, and if you are tired of tinned food and MRE's you could come with me. We sure could do with some guys like you. I am not saying it will be easy but at least you will be back among the living, and at the end of the day, a ghost town is still a ghost town." He told them to stand up and chucked him his keys, "Mine is the black one, he rattles of the number plate. Think about what I have offered, and if you want, grab your shit chuck it in your car and bring mine around." Mike wanted to know if that meant he was not going to shoot them, "Listen, sonny, if I were going to shoot you, I would have done it by now," Perry told Jackson. They would go and talk about it, then brought his car around shortly. Jackson nodded and let them go.

Now, back to being on his own, he opened up the key box and removed the back panel. Jackson placed his right palm on the reader and pumped in the memorised ten-digit number he had gleaned from the sign outside. He heard the mechanism chunking away, and then the workbench elevated slightly and moved out of the way. Jackson switched on the lights, went down the stairs, pressed his palm on the reader, re-entered the code, and opened the door to the secret stash.

He quickly looked at the place, and he confirmed that it held everything he needed. Jackson checked the first package, and it was still fit for purpose. He grabbed several boxes and then hauled them up the stairs. He chuckled, thinking that some of the crew back at the DIY emporium would think he had a profound fondness for almond paste. The PE 2AX5 was almost identical to the nut extract, but it was absolutely not suitable for enhancing the taste of any type of cake. When he had finished shifting all the plastic explosives, Jackson moved on to the timers along with the required detonators. The batteries that powered these devices were specially made and not available to the public. These items were invented during the space programme when they sought a power source that would last longer and held its charge without self-depletion when placed in long-term storage. Jackson had just finished checking that they were still functional when there was a knock on the door.

He shouted for them to come in. Perry stood before him in his uniform. He stood at attention and saluted. "Permission to present the rest of the squad, sir." Jackson was once lost for words and just nodded, telling him to proceed.

Perry opened the door, and ten guys marched in, all in uniform, and even the fucking dog had a camo necktie on. Perry ordered them to stand and remove their shirts. One of the troopers asked if the white-headed eagle on top of the letters of the USA was acceptable, and Jackson replied that he could bet his sweet ass that it was more than acceptable. They put back on their shirts, and Perry introduced them by their names and any specialist skills they possessed.

"Hey guys, you can stop calling me sir. My name is Jackson, no first name, no last name, just Jackson. There are some bits and pieces that you may find useful in the storeroom down the stairs. You could start by loading them into your vehicles."

Jackson was handed back his keys and, with the aid of Mike and Perry, loaded the PE, timers, detonators, and all the space-age batteries into his vehicle. It had been quite a day, and with the sun starting to go down, he told the new members of his team that they would be moving out at first light. He is persuaded to come and stay at where they had made their temporary billet. He was asked if he liked chilli dogs; Jackson had thought he had just been awarded an all-exclusive ticket to the Superbowl final. He thought, even with all the material he had unearthed there, Abe would be more than over the moon at the prospect of him being able to find someone who could make the perfect dog.

Over dinner, the guys asked him many questions about where he had been, more importantly, where they were going and what they would do there. Their dog had an all-over off-white colour, and its name was Spotty. The dog only sniffed at him once and never asked him any questions.

Chapter 20

Murray had told them not to panic as there were no immediate signs of danger. He shone his flashlight into the new opening and then checked carefully for anything out of the ordinary. As all he could see in another flight of stairs, he checked his weapon and then took the lead. Alicia was counting the steps; the twins were behind her as they all tentatively went down step by step. The flashlights bounce about the interior of the stairwell, illuminating themselves as strange-shaped, oddly distorted silhouettes. All they had seen was blank upon blank walls with no display of any encrypted symbolism. Not even a solitary directional arrow indicated where they were going, nor the name of the final destination.

They had finally reached the bottom. Murray shone his flashlight, and in the artificial light, all they could see was a very long, almost endless corridor. That stretched beyond the extent of the displayed beam of light that he was bouncing off the ceiling and floor. Murray suggested that they should take ten before moving off, and while they were at it, they might as well have a cuppa while they plan what comes next. The twins have all the makings and the flasks out in a jiffy.

Alicia advised that they take their time and be extra vigilant for hidden surprises. Murray was curious as to why the air was relatively clean. There was some dust, but it was almost as if the place had never been used. There were no signs of human traffic ever having ventured along this passageway, not one footprint, absolutely nothing at all. Murray must have had asbestos lips as his tea had vanished. "Once you all finish stuffing your faces, we will move forward in a single line. Don't stray off my path. Please don't be tempted to touch anything. We don't know what is down here or what this place was used for. If anything were to happen to you down here, I would be in very big trouble, so please do what I have asked."

The items for used for the tea party were placed back into the bags, and Murray took the point. He moved the flashlight around, checking the floor, ceiling, and walls before every single step. Alicia and the twins followed closely a few steps behind, as requested, trying not to waver away from his footing. Alicia asked Murray if he had brought any breadcrumbs, and he replied that he had not bothered to request any as he figured that they would have scoffed them all en route.

They walked for a few hours, and the scene in front of them never altered or changed. It was just an endless corridor devoid of any signs or markings, anything that would explain its intent and purpose. The only thing he was sure of was that this had been carved out of the solid rock. It must have taken years; with no fancy singing and dancing machinery, it must have all been carried out with handheld tools. Small marks on the surfaces indicated the usage of chisels and suchlike, but no tell-tale signs of the drilled holes associated with the placing of explosives. Whoever had undertaken this engineering marvel had lots of people and time. Murray calls a halt, suggesting that they have a break. They had walked for ages and were still none the wiser. By what was displayed in front of them they were going to be walking for quite another while yet.

Murray thought they had all been down in here, walking along this passageway like forever. They had continued taking precautionary measures, shining the beams of light from their flashlights in case they had spotted any signs of danger. That could have been a partly displayed mark on the floor or something odd, even discolouration on the walls, but there had been nothing, absolutely nothing at all. In front of them was another endless stone corridor that stretched as far as the furthest point of light emitted from the handheld torches. The flasks were just about empty. Murray was dismayed at this fact, then horrified that no more tea would be available after this stop, and they would have to drink water or canned juice.

He savoured every sip and thought that if he was ever unfortunate to be placed in front of a firing squad, his response to any last request question would be a cuppa, and just frighten it with the milk. Alicia thought that they were travelling in a westerly direction, but with no natural light, Murray thought they could be in outer space. He had never really been underground for this length of time before. If he was ever in a situation where he had a choice of taking part in this sort of foray into a dark subterranean kingdom. His reply would be most definitely placed under the no thanks column. He had not wanted any of the food and had told the women to share it amongst themselves. Murray had finished his brew and then had sparked up; Alicia had given up for the time being, so he never even offered to share.

The twins had started to put everything back into the bags, and Murray had offered to help. Alicia had thought it was hilarious when they had replied that if they used his tried and trusted method of stuffing everything in, it would take twice as long as they would have to unpack everything and start again. Murray had just replied that it was impossible to be good at everything. They set off again, slowly and surely checking that every step of the way was safe and danger-free. Alicia had spotted it first, announcing that there was a doorway up ahead of them. Murray hoped this one was a simple device that did not require a top university quiz team. To debate the enigmatic symbolism in front of them for hours on end, to finally take an educated guess on how to try and get the fucker to open.

With every step, it got a little closer, till finally at last, they all stood before it. The door displayed no handle or any other sort of attachment to push or pull in the hope of being permitted to exit. The twins suggested that it could be held in place with some sort of centre pin, and they had to push it. Murray and Alicia thought that it was a plausible explanation and he nearly passed out as the door gently opened with the minimum of applied pressure.

On the other side, they had yet another stairway. Murray hoped this would lead them outside, eventually connecting them with the real world, where a sky was above them. He took the lead and went stair by stair. They ascended to the top. The doorway was of the same type, and on opening it with the same method they had applied to one downstairs. The only difference was that one side was smooth, and the other was rough. Murray told them that he could smell the sea, and they proceeded forward in what seemed to be part of a cave system.

Some writing was displayed on these walls as they near the exit, but they did not require deciphering any of the displayed graffiti. It was all fairly modern guff about the various football teams the now long-dead artists had supported.

Then, they saw and witnessed the waves crashing into their exit point. Murray hoped that it was tidal as he was not what you would call a confident swimmer. The structured form of the cave walls did not allow them a good look outside, and as well as it was now dark, with not being able to see any distinguishable landmarks, he had no idea where they were. "We might as well get as comfortable as possible as I don't know if the tide has just come in and when it is going out. We will just have to wait it out, as well as that I really don't fancy getting wet."

They took turns going to check. Murray got comfy and was asleep in minutes. Alicia was of the opinion that they had just discovered or proved that this was an emergency escape route for the Hidden.

Murray had just received a gentle prob via someone's boot that it was time to wake up. The tide was now ebbing, and as soon as it was light outside, Alicia had decided that it would be safe enough to move. The women had all eaten them and finished the supplies of drinking water. Murray always carried a spare tin for emergencies. He cracked it open and finished it in a couple of gulps. Alicia and the twins noticed his hand shaking uncontrollably. Murray informed them that it was just morning sickness and nothing at all to worry about. He chucked the empty tin in his backpack, had a quick pee outside and then, agreeing with Alicia's decision, picked up his kit and asked them if they were coming.

He was not exactly sure where they were as he was more of a forest person; beaches and watching the sea were just something that he had never had any interest in. Murray advised them to tread easily as some of the rocks were a little on the slippery side. The slimy horrible green stuff that some health nuts actually ate made for treacherous footing and should be avoided at all costs. Mr. Black acted as the unofficial tour guide as he led them along a sometimes wet but safe route though the mass of seaweed that almost moved every time you looked at it.

There was no break in the cliffs. He constantly scanned, looking for a break in the rockface where they could climb up and view the surrounding landscape. Murray eventually spotted a path alongside an old, dilapidated concrete gun emplacement that belonged to one of the world wars. He pointed over to the direction that they were going to travel in. Murray informed them that when they reached the top, he thought that they would be near the vicinity of the farmhouse and panicked that they were not lost at all. The track was just a well-worn rut that the locals had established over a period of time.

Prior to the onset of the disease people from the area would have come down here for all sorts of reasons. Teenagers would have headed to the disused world war gun emplacement to drink their carry-outs, courting couples, married couples with their kids and dogs in tow would have had adventures on the beach in the summer months.

Now that there was a small distance between them and the twins, Alicia, straight to the point, asked Murray how long his hand had been shaking.

"That is nothing, and it started ever since I noticed I was pregnant," Alicia warned him. She cautioned him that it could be something serious and that he should go get it checked out. Murray simply stated for the record that if he ever decided to go and see Cora, what would she tell him?

"Well, Murray, it is life-threatening. Sorry, we don't have the machines or the specialists to try and figure out what it is, but how does a cup of tea sound." Alicia thought that he was being selfish and had no consideration for others. Murray asked her if he was being utterly inconsiderate and selfish for not making people worry.

Alicia was first to the top, followed closely by Beth and Debs. Murray, being the dedicated tour guide, ensured that he was on hand every step of the way to lend a helping hand where and when it was required.

As they looked back down, the tide started to rush back in. All of the rocks that they had recently crossed over were soon hidden beneath the water. Murray did not think they could have made it to safety if they had been unfortunate enough to have been caught on the beach with the changing tide. He spotted the tractor and announced to everyone that he was fairly certain that the farmhouse community was over that way.

He pointed to reinforce what he had been saying. After the steep climb, he persuaded all of them to take ten to catch their breath. Murray refused any of the remaining juice tins and let the women consume them. He figured that in their condition, they needed to replace the fluid levels more than him.

After recovering his breath, Murray said, "I think we are at the rear of the farmhouse as the landscape is not the same as this. It makes no real difference as entering in via the rear or the front entrance will still lead us all to a fresh, warm cuppa." Murray, having finished his smoke, was up and ready to move. They finished drinking and then loaded up, ready to follow his lead.

Not wanting to upset the tractor driver by walking across the newly ploughed fields, Murray displayed a more than nice friendly wave as they proceeded to take a slightly longer route by going around the edge. They had not been walking for long when all of them noticed the agricultural machine and its attachment drawing to a halt. They expected the occupant to display the same welcoming wave; however, this was not the case, as they were diving for cover seconds later when the first shot rang out. As the shots rained out, Murray roughly pushed them into the drainage ditch, then jumped down beside them. Alicia looked angry, and the twins were not chuffed at being covered in mud and slime. Whoever was doing the shooting was not very good, as they were continually firing upon their last known position.

Murray dumped his backpack and then checked that his weapon was still functional. He advised them to do the same and follow him. "Keep out of sight. It is going to be dirty and smelly, but if they can't see you, then they can't shoot at you." Murray scurried away, crouched down, holding his weapon away from contact with the grime and slime as he followed the route of the drainage ditch. He could still hear the shots ringing out and had the occasional look behind him, checking that his friends were keeping their heads down and that they were all unharmed.

The ditch he was moving along deepened as he arrived at the junction. Ignoring the smell, he turned into the new channel and then increased his speed. After about ten minutes, he popped his head up for a quick reccy. He had not travelled far enough yet, and the tractor and the shooter were still ahead of him.

He dropped a gear and went as fast as possible. Then, thinking he had made up the required distance, had a quick peep, and was now behind the would-be killer, he charged across to their position. The shooter was still firing at where they had last sighted the alleged trespassers. Murray closed in and as the last shot had been fired, he at last reached them. With his weapon in hand, he pistol-whipped her over the back of the head. The shooter dropped instantly and lay motionless in the mucky field. Murray picked up the rifle and then shouted for Alicia and the twins, informing them that the danger had been subdued.

As the women climbed out of the ditch and moved towards him, Murray turned as he heard and then saw the oncoming vehicles approaching. He loaded the weapon, positioned himself behind the tractor and got ready to shoot. The three vehicles stopped, and the occupants got out; he thought he recognised a few of them. A voice from their direction shouted out, "If you surrender now, we will not shoot." Murray replied that if they did not stop playing at being silly buggers, he would never come back and repair anything, and all certificates that he had awarded them would be all null and void.

Another voice sounded out, "Murray, is that you?"

He shook his head, "Okay, guys, put the toys away. I'm coming out." He put his weapon away and waved to Alicia and the twins, indicating with two thumbs up that everything was good in Murray land.

He walked across to the vehicles. Murray did, in fact, know most of them by name.

Murray exclaimed out loud, "What the fuck was all that about? No questions, no warning shots, just some fucker trying to kill me and my companions."

One of them went over and informed anyone who wanted to listen that Linda would need to go to the vet. Murray put his hands in the air and pleaded guilty to all charges, "By the way, guys, I hope she is better with the tractor than what she is at the shooting. I guess that she had contacted you by firing a flare to indicate that she was in some sort of trouble."

Murray was grumpy now; he was happy they were all still alive, but it could have easily been so different.

They were full of apologies and offered to take them to the farmhouse to change, freshen up and have some warm drinks. Murray thanked them for the offer, but he and his companions would appreciate it if they would take them home.

The one in charge allocated a vehicle, and before they left, he told them all that he was really sorry for what happened. Murray did not even look at him and replied, "Yeah, me too."

The drive back to the watermill was carried out in total silence, and all of them, including the driver, were relieved when they arrived home and got out.

Murray opened the door and shouted, "Hi, dear, I'm home." Charlie and Romulus rushed towards him and howled like wolves. He talked to them and clapped them, but they retreated and headed back towards the fire after noticing that he was stinking.

Cha looked at their state, "How many times do I have to tell you that if you are going to play in the dirt, then you have to put on your old clothes?"

He bowed his head and said, "Sorry, mama, I promise not to do it again."

Murray took a step back and told her they were all more than manky and that Alicia and the twins should first dib at the hot water. He confessed that he would quite happily sell his soul for a hot cuppa.

He went outside, not wanting to leave a filth trail or stink throughout the house. Alicia and the twins stripped off in the kitchen, then raced off to get clean, to rid themselves of all the dirt and now encrusted slime. Murray puffed away and thought he had won a triple rollover lottery prize when Cha presented him with the perfect cuppa. He closed his eyes and savoured the first sip. He thought that it was truly wonderful, perhaps mankind's finest invention.

When he opened his eyes, Cha looked kind of serious; he asked her, "What's up?"

She pointed to the pool of blood at his feet and the blood running down his arm. Cha wanted to know why he did not tell her that he was bleeding. Murray told her that he had never noticed; he continued smoking and drinking. She helped him off with the jacket, and it was then that they both noticed that he had been shot.

Okolo was asked to look after Mark; Cha took him up to see Cora. Murray had not wanted to go before he got washed and changed, but Cha had none of it. She had tried to get him into the vehicle, but Murray, not wanting to make a mess, climbed into the back. He banged the side of the cab, pretending that he was actually in charge. They had not seen Cora for a while, and Murray was shocked at how big she was. He told her that he was sorry to bother her, and ordinarily, he would have tidied himself up. Cha shut him down in midsentence and informed Cora that he had been shot.

Cora shouted for her assistants, and she called for the emergency trolley as soon as they appeared. Murray could not figure out what the emergency was about for the life of him and then passed out.

Cha was politely asked to leave, and Cora promised to keep her up to date but insisted that she give them room to work. Murray was hoisted up onto the bed, and they cut off his clothes and examined the wound.

He had been shot in the chest a few inches down and off-centre from his shoulder. Cora cleaned the area around the wound and examined him; as he was still out of it, she did not bother asking any questions. Murray was still bleeding, and she would have to operate.

She noted that, for the record, he had been the smelliest visitor to date.

"Prep him ready for surgery!" Cora shouted in an emergency.

Cha was still outside in the waiting room; Cora informed her that she was going to have to operate and she should go home. She knew she was wasting her breath but still had to let her know what was happening.

"I have to go now and prepare." Cora would have liked to sit down with her and reassure her that everything was going to be okay. In the old world, Murray would have already been in several medical journals, and she did not know what she would find in opening him up.

Now that she and her assistants had scrubbed up and had the masks on, they entered the operating theatre. Murray had been partially cleaned, and they had to insert needles and connect the attachments for the monitors.

He had been given the pre-med shot, and Cora delivered the general anaesthetic into the first available vein. She checked the reading on the monitor, and being relatively stable, she marked the incision. Cora had never done this type of operation before and did not have the time to do some reading up on the subject before commencing; she just had to go for it. The bullet had nearly nicked the external iliac artery and another couple of millimeters, and he would have bled out.

Cora thought that he had been more than lucky. It was probably the jacket that had saved him, slowing down the bullet just enough to stop it from penetrating any further inside. She was now carrying out the hard part of the process of extracting the bullet without causing a nick to the vein. It took her an hour to find the bullet and then extract the lump of metal. Luckily, it had not fragmented; otherwise, finding all the small pieces would have been a hit and a miss. Cora checked the area for any foreign matter, cleaned the wound twice, and then sewed him up. She requested her assistants to hook up some fluids and antibiotics. Cora thanked her team and went to tell Cha the news.

She expected to find her sleeping, but Cha sprang to attention when Cora opened the door. Cora showed her the small metal object in the bowl, another two millimeters or a larger caliber bullet, and told her that there would have been nothing they could have done to save him.

"I have given him a sedative, and we are most likely carrying out the biggest bed bath in history. I am going to calm myself down with a strong coffee. You are more than welcome to join me. They will be washing him for a while yet, and you can inform him, or I will tell him; either way, he is in for the week, even if I have to chain him to the bed."

She went in to see him and smiled, thinking that if he was awake, he would be truly mortified at being washed down by total strangers. Cha took up Cora's offer and joined her. The doctor was now calmed down enough to inform her that she had never removed a bullet before. Most, if not all, of her previous patients, had not survived due to the extremity of their injuries and the lack of a modern hospital with all the advanced technical teams and technical staff.

Cha could not really say much in the way of a reply. "You know that he will be a nightmare of a patient if you keep him in here for a week." Cora simply replied that if she had to, she would drug him. Cha laughed, not really believing her.

"Cha, the truth is that we have to keep an eye out for secondary bleeding and infection, and that boils down to a safe, clean environment with no strenuous work," Cora said to highlight the importance of rest.

"Let's be honest about it. Everyone knows that he is a workaholic. I have never actually seen him sitting about relaxed, calm and happy doing nothing. So, he can like it or lump it. He is here for the week."

Cora was going to ask what had happened and how come he had managed to get shot in the first place but guessed that sometimes it is better just not to know.

Cha thanked Cora for everything and expected they would wonder where she had gone. She made her way down to the house and hoped that Alicia and the twins could tell her what happened between them. The strange thing was Murray had never mentioned anything about it.

She did not announce anything as she opened the door; Charlie and Romulus got up and came over to see her, and the rest of them were sitting at the table. Alicia said hi and told her that they were wondering where you had gone. Cha informed them all that Murray was going to be staying with Cora for a few days to recover from the gunshot wound. Amazingly, Alicia and the twins knew nothing about it, as Murray had not mentioned anything about it.

They were with him the whole time, and he honestly never said a single word about it. Cha asked them to run through the whole story, but she changed her mind and asked them just to go straight to the part where the shooting happened. She listened to the whole sorry episode and thought that the farmhouse had some strange rules where they were shooting without asking any questions.

It could also be a simple mistake, but one that could have cost her dear; she thought that Mark and Ellie would be over in the morning full of apologies, saying that it should never have happened. He would know that the incident would have pissed off Murray more than big time as he never even went to see him. When Murray would return to the land of the living, she would ask him how he wanted to play this. She knew that he would not want to start a war, but he wanted to know why it happened. When they had all mentioned the tractor, Cha knew that Linda would have been involved, and not being the brightest star in the sky, she could have panicked and then started shooting without thinking. She understood that all these situations were different and that sometimes there was an exception to the rule when you had to shoot first, but not when someone was being very considerate and walking around the edges of the newly ploughed fields, giving you a more than a nice friendly wave.

Cha was still in deep conversation with Alicia and had now joined with the rest of the gang. She just couldn't believe that Murray had just not mentioned that he had been shot. She doubled over in pain, clutching her developing bundle. Okolo noticed the liquid that had formed in a puddle at her feet and shouted desperately, "We need to take her up to Cora's right now!"

Alicia went to get a vehicle, and Okolo instructed the twins to hold the fort and look after the children. Robbo helped Okolo take Cha to the waiting vehicle.

Cha repeated to herself, "It is too early; it is too early." She was bundled into the vehicle, and Okolo strapped her in and told Alicia to hit it. Arriving at Cora's, Alicia was straight out and was banging on the front door. Okolo was in the process of pulling Cha out of the back and shouted for Alicia to come and assist her. Between then, they managed to carry Cha to the door; it opened just as they reached it. There were no questions and no forms to be filled in. The woman on duty pressed the emergency bell, and Cha was carried to the treatment room.

Cora appeared a few minutes later. She asked them what had happened and quickly examined Cha.

"Looks like the baby is coming too early, but you try telling that to the baby! Okay, I need you to leave the room," Cora said urgently.

Alicia and Okolo were ushered out. Cora told Cha that the incubator was being warmed up and that she had to push when the time came. One of her assistants took her pulse and counted the minutes between contractions. Cora smiled. She had not had a patient for weeks, and now she had one recovering from surgery and another one about to give birth to a premature baby. She reached down and told Cha that everything would be okay; the baby would be smallish in size, but all would be fine. Cha was closing her eyes; Cora told her that she had to stay awake. She slapped her across the face, "Your baby needs you to stay awake!"

Her nurse shouted out the information. Cora took over and shouted at Cha to stay awake, saying that she needed to push as hard as possible. Nothing was happening; the baby was not coming, and Cha was struggling to stay awake. Cora did not want to pump any drugs into her. She did not want to give her anything that could affect the child, but more to the point, she did not have any of the drugs in the first place. Cora thought that the baby was breached; she examined her again and told her that this was going to hurt a little. Cha screamed and hissed something that Cora thought translated to, "I hate your fucking guts!"

Cora turned her hand and reached in further, turned the baby and told the now constantly hissing Cha to push with all her might. Cora held out her hand for the spreader and informed Cha that she could see the baby's head, "C'mon, you need to keep pushing. You're nearly there! C'mon, push for Murray."

Cha hissed out in English this time that she hated that bastard as much as she hated her. Cora was now able to help pull out the new guy; the cord had wrapped itself around his neck. She cleaned any obstructions around the baby's face, the nurse cut the umbilical cord, and as Cha passed out, she did not see Cora desperately trying to resuscitate the newborn.

The doctor put her mouth over the baby's mouth and gently breathed, but the baby did not want to cooperate. Desperate, she picked her up and rushed out the door, hoping that the sudden change in temperature and the baby's introduction to the cold weather would make him take his first breath. The dogs sensed something was amiss and had patiently sat outside the medical facility. As Cora opened the door and rushed out, Charlie and Romulus howled at the infant. Cora could not believe it, and the newborn took his first breath and smiled at her and the dogs. Cora cried not just at saving the baby but thought that no one would believe what had just happened. Alicia and Okolo immediately rushed out after her as she darted past them, and they also could not believe what they had just witnessed.

Mark and Ellie arrived at the watermill, but neither of them knew where to start. They were shocked that both Murray and Cha were now in the medical facility. Across from them sat Okolo and Alicia; both were displaying looks that could instantly turn mortals to stone.

"I don't know where to begin, but I am. We are truly sorry for what happened. Linda just freaked out and forgot all about the emergency protocol; she was meant to fire the flare and return to the compound. For some inexplicable reason, she started to shoot."

Alicia and Okolo looked at each other. Alicia delivered the first message, "Murray was delivering a friendly wave with no weapon on display. What was she thinking?" Okolo asked if Linda wore glasses or if she needed glasses and when was the last time, she had her eyes tested.

Alicia then continued, "Murray was millimeters away from dying. Cora was worried about the bullet moving. Otherwise, she would not have performed the operation."

They both knew and could see that Mark and his partner were really devastated at what had happened. However, they could not speak for Murray. Alicia informed them that before the first shot was fired, Murray was looking forward to a chat and a warm welcome from his old friend. Mark intended to invite all of them, including their community, for the Christmas celebration but had thought it might not be the right time. He asked if he would be allowed in the medical facility to see him.

Okolo pointed out that at the present time, not even the dogs were allowed to go in and see him, Cha, or the new addition to their family. Ellie asked if they would keep them informed and if they could do anything to help. All they had to do was to ask. Okolo hissed that an urgent appointment with the opticians for Linda would be a good place to start. Mark and Ellie got up to leave, and Okolo and Alicia didn't even bother to show them to the door. They were angry, and neither one of them was good at pretending otherwise. They talked about it after they left and thought that Murray would take the piss the next time, he visited the farmhouse and would probably run about with a target on his back. But in all seriousness, they would back him up one hundred percent despite his decision.

Robbo had been busy working with the team on the extension and had popped in for lunch. They placed the offerings on the table and told him that this was one of Murray's favourites. Robbo looked at the label on the can and told them that he would settle for a fresh cuppa. He confessed that the contents reminded him of frogspawn's sperm, and Murray could eat it later. They had not asked him to help out with the work. He had decided that with the new addition's arrival, it would be better to give them some space. Robbo was allocated to do the simple tasks; all he did was remove all the white cladding from the stone. It was monotonous, and Karen thought that even he could not manage to fuck it up. He was, however, on a different plain of thinking. In the future, when all of the fuss and hubble has gone. Robbo has every intention of trying his hand at some sculpturing. The way he sees it is that every strike of the hammer and every angle he creates with the chisel. Is only a practice, until he can get his hands on a sturdy piece of workable stone.

Chapter 21

Jackson was not up the first this morning when he finally arrived back to the land of the living to welcome this new day. The new guys were all there on hand to deliver a standing ovation. He was formally presented with the noisiest sleeping bastard on this planet award. Perry told him that they would have all vacated the surrounding area if they had known that he made this much noise. Jackson gratefully accepted the award and made a short speech informing the assembled that he would cherish this day as one of his most treasured memories forever and ever.

Mike shouted out that if they gave him a chilli-dog would he shut the fuck up. Jackson replied, "Gladly," and the guys whooped and hollered as he was awarded the food as a complimentary prize.

Now, with the festivities over and the loading complete, Jackson was going to take them over to the DIY emporium and introduce the new intake to the group, who should have gathered up the remaining items on the list that he had left them with. Spotty was barking at Jackson, and he did not know why; Mike informed him that the dog did not like sitting in the back and required a front seat. Jackson gave him the thumbs up, and Spotty followed him. Then, he sat patiently, waiting for the passenger door to open.

Once inside, Spotty barked again, and guessing that this translated to an open window, he pressed the magic button and the demanding passenger squeezed his nose up to the window. The dog fell asleep soon after they moved off and then snored for most of the journey.

On reaching the vicinity of the DIY mega-store, Jackson got the new guys to wait. As a precaution, he went ahead and alerted anyone who was trigger-happy at seeing the additional vehicles approaching.

He explained to the guys that they had some new team members and said, "This is Spotty, the dog barks, wanting out to say hello."

Jackson waved at the stationary vehicles, and on receiving the signal, they drove towards them. He introduced everyone to each other, and Spotty jumped between them all, sniffing out the friendly souls. Then finally having enough, he went back and lay down beside Jackson's vehicle.

The guys had completed his additional list, even managing to pack away all the items. In order to get the new guys and the original crew to get to know each other as well as fully integrate them into the idea that they are now all on the same side as soon as possible, Jackson suggested they swap everyone about to make all the driving a joint effort. Spotty had not moved an inch, thinking that sitting in Jackson's vehicle was part of the same plan.

The convoy headed back towards the temporary base. Abe was there with Enunsha. At first sight of the extended convoy, they wondered which team Jackson had stolen all the other drivers from. As they drew to a stop, he waved to the couple to come over and introduced them to Spotty and all the new guys.

"I found these waifs and strays along the road; seeing as some of them can make reasonably decent chilli-dogs, I thought that perhaps you would like to adopt them." Spotty barked and now was sitting in front of Enunsha, "Looks like the dog has abandoned me, then adopted you!"

She was delighted, and as she returned to her tasks, the dog followed her like it was her shadow. Abe got one of his team to show the new guys where they could bunk up for the time being.

Now, they were alone. Abe was just about to go into all the details of what they had and, more to the point, what they didn't have. Jackson stopped him in his tracks and then handed him something wrapped in aluminium foil, "Just in case you thought that I was bullshitting you! Whatever bad news you are going to deliver can wait until you eat the best dog on this side of the great Mississippi."

Mr. Hubstien could not believe his good fortune, thinking that Doctor Death and Poison Pete would have to be transferred immediately to another group as far away as humanly possible from the cooking facilities. Jackson grabbed a coffee and sipped away while Abe was munching; before he asked, he told his friend that he wouldn't let Enunsha know that he had just ate her chilli dog.

Abe got down to the nitty-gritty, "Bravo group had a problem with the silos, so now they are going to handball all of the filling material into the available trucks supplied by Enunsha's group. The alpha group has two low loaders set out with all the welding machines as well as all the cables required. Another one is loaded with cut-to-size and prepped plates. The list we gave them only mentioned one, but for some reason, they thought you meant two; either way, I told them to go ahead."

Jackson nodded, agreeing that he was fine with his decision.

"Charlie's group has loaded up five converted car transporters, and they figure that they have about at least two thousand and something shopping trollies as they are located at the staging point along with the welding machines and the plates. I have sent the crews over to the Bravo group to help manhandle all the sand as well as the other stuff. Echo group had about fifty working machines at the last count and figured that they would have a hundred by the day after tomorrow. We still have to find the three industrial pumps, and due to the inactive silos, we have sourced half a dozen water trucks, and they are also all loaded, ready to roll at the holding point."

Jackson had taken no notes on the updated information and considered what was to come. He thought out loud, "So all we need to find are the industrial pumps, to load up a hundred trucks, establish the running order and then we are good to go?"

Abe nodded but wondered how on earth he could remember all of that without jotting something down. Abe finally added, "It looks like we will be going for it the day after tomorrow?"

Jackson spoke, "Abe, group Bravo, have they checked every building for the pumps? Could you get them to recheck? We can get the new recruits, plus my old team, to help out with the search. For all we know, maybe there is a factory there with a load of brand-new pumps straight off the assembly line, waiting to be taken away. Lastly, we need someone to go and steal a fire truck. Assuming that we are going to locate the pumps, we will need water to prime and then clean them."

Abe asked if there was anything else that he required. Jackson told him that was all he could think of for the moment, but if he came up with anything else, he would let him know. Perry appeared, asking if they had anything for his team. Abe informed him to get his guys saddled up as they were going shopping.

Now left on his own with a head full of details, he bummed a packet of cigarettes along with an accompanying lighter from Doctor Death with the obligatory pot of coffee to keep him company. Jackson went through the plan, move by move, measure by measure, in his head. He would double-check every possible outcome, then work on any possible contingencies where and when he thought they were required.

Jackson thought he was missing some of the finer details and started going through it again. He had tried the first stage, where the heaviest items were moved first. This was the normal way, but sometimes, on rare occasions, there were exceptions to the rules. Jackson put the heavy items to one side of his brain and rethought the first plan through again with the alternative option. It was not the length of the various cables or the weight of the nine thick plates. It was the space that had to be kept fluid, and if they got jammed up, that would be a problem. Without asking, Poison Pete had replaced the coffee pot, "It's free automatic refills on Fridays!"

Jackson did not think that it was anywhere near Friday, but Poison Pete had switched on an idea with his brief comment. Jackson drew a shape on the table with his fingers, imagining that he was looking at a schematic of the stairwell. In his head, he superimposed people at various points from A to B.

The first movement would require twenty people to be placed at predetermined stations from the top floor all the way down to the doorway on level four. The master stroke that Poison Pete had clued him up about in a roundabout way was that they do not all need to come back up. Only the four guys on the lowest section were required to move. The others were already almost automatically in place for the next set of cables. The four guys who came up from doorway four would start to move the nine plates into pole position. It would be the same manoeuvre for level three. On completion, they would send another four guys up top. They would, again, almost automatically join in moving the heavy plates into the staging position. Jackson thought that he owed Poison Pete a beer as he envisaged the last stage, almost like placing the last piece in the jigsaw. As the team moved up from level two, he would have eighteen team members who would then split into nine pairs.

The two spare guys would switch on the welding machines as the plates were being hauled downstairs. All the erection methods, tacking and welding would be identical. The doorway on level four should be completed first, and at approximately fifteen-minute intervals, three and two would each follow suit. Jackson thought that after that, it would all be relatively easy; he thanked Poison Pete for his great idea and the coffee.

Needing some fresh air, he walked down to the staging area. Everyone was busy, and he was more than happy that they all ignored him as he viewed the growing collection of mechanical machines. He thought they had one in every colour, and the only thing missing was the outlandish modified vehicles with all the spikes and flamethrower attachments. That used to appear regularly in the various movies depicting the much-preferred mode of transport in a post-apocalyptic world.

Jackson had caught a glimpse of Enunsha. He walked towards her and Spotty. The dog ignored him and turned his head away; he was now Enunsha's dog, and anyone seeing them together would have thought they had been lifelong partners. No one would have ever believed that they had only met each other a couple of hours ago. She caught his eye, and he waved, letting her know that he was coming to see her. Enunsha and the faithful Spotty came to meet him at the halfway point.

"Don't tell me, you have located more shopping malls that have unlimited wares of all descriptions on display, and they are open twenty-four seven!" Jackson just looked at her and, showing no reaction, handed her a package wrapped in aluminium foil.

"I had to hide this from Abe. I don't like to hide anything from him, but sometimes there are exceptions to the rules. He also received the same gift but very nearly bit his fingers off as he wolfed it down, savouring every bite."

Enunsha shared hers with Spotty. Jackson told her that one or two of the new guys could cook, and it would appear that they used a completely different set of recipes. "Word is that they attended a different establishment, to where Poison Pete and Doctor Death had learned their less than rudimentary culinary skills."

She showed him what her people had achieved, and Jackson asked where were all the trucks that he was told were ready to go. "The ones you see in front of you are all ready to go and the others are, as we speak, getting loaded up, down at the batching plant."

"We should have seventy-five all ready for the grand opening the day after tomorrow and another twenty-five in position to be loaded up." Jackson did the calculations in his head; he didn't think it would be enough, but it would give them a good start.

"Tomorrow, I am going to get everyone to rest up for the day, everything should be checked and ready to roll by then. When we start this, we are most likely going to have to work straight through until it is complete. Lots of people working through the night and that's why we should give everyone a complete rest."

The noise interrupted the conversation. Abe had just returned with two fire trucks, and strapped on two low-loaders were the elusive pumps. Jackson and Enunsha went and met them and reviewed the newly delivered machines. There were six pumps, all bearing the same unpronounceable German name. The Europeans, in their wisdom, did not make it easy for anyone. They all had decided to give all the common vowels a different sound. Abe, then beside them, asked if they would be suitable for what he had in mind. Jackson nodded, adding that all they had to do now was find someone who had operated them in the past. Another truck came in, and they were informed that this contained all the hoses required, plus lots of spare ones. The machines were all brand new and had never been used; Jackson asked them to put out the word for the vacancy of senior pump operator.

Now that they had almost everything required for the payback. Jackson realised that it was now going to take much longer than he had initially estimated, but they would get a result. He needed more coffee and asked Abe, Enunsha, Spotty, as well as Perry to come and join him. Poison Pete had the coffee on the table before they asked; Jackson lit a cigarette. Abe and Enunsha had never seen him smoke before, and he just told them that he partook in this vile and disgusting habit every once in a while.

Poison Pete overheard the conversation about the urgent requirement for a pump operator. He said sorry for butting in, then asked them what type of pumps they were talking about. He informed them that he could operate these machines but thought that he would not be able to help them out as everyone would go hungry and miss his food. Jackson asked Perry to please go and get a couple of his team who were artists in the kitchen to take over from the very soon to be promoted resident head cook. Pete offered to stay and give his replacements a quick run-through of all the tasks and all the culinary delights that he and Doctor Death conjured up for the population. Abe thanked him for the offer, but it was more important for him to get him comfortable with his new machines. Enunsha told Pete to grab all his shit, and she would take him over and then introduce him to his new toys. "It looks like he will have a new name!" Jackson closed his eyes and shook his head as Abe mentioned the new non-deplume, Peter the Pumper. He could imagine all sorts of verbal abuse that was sure to follow in the wake of the new title.

Perry had returned with a couple of able bodies who would take over the cooking detail. He sat back at the table and then informed them that the changeover was all sorted, and he did not think that there would be any problems or complaints. Jackson gave them the jist of what he was thinking.

"Tomorrow, we get everyone to rest up for the day. That is, everyone who is not involved in the cooking or the patrols needs to rest up. Once we start, we will have to work all the way through for however long it takes to get the work completed. The crews will, at some point, be mixed and matched to provide twenty-four-hour cover. It is not going to be easy, but I don't see any other way around it. All is going well; I think it will take about three days if we are lucky."

Jackson explained that he had gone through the complete sequence time and time again, and had fingers crossed all the movements would fall easily into place.

"I have not told or discussed it with anyone, but the more I think about it we are going to have to move. These people move about like ghosts and after we hit them back, they are not going to forget about that. What if there are more of them, and they are all connected, we would just be hunted down. Once we get things up and running, we can let everyone know what is a possible danger in the future, and to avoid that we should move to another area. Just leave everything behind, making it look like we just got up and then left in the middle of the night."

Hubstien thought that it was a tall order, and he was not sure if their people would agree to the new proposal. Jackson disagreed and if they wanted to stay alive, they would. "You can think about what I am saying. We should now go for a drive around all the teams and give them the heads up about the rest day."

Abe asked if they would be going to see how Pete the Pumper was getting on. Jackson shook his head, and they followed him out to the vehicle. Perry had not been informed of all of the details but guessed that he would be filled in with what he needed to know, when and where required along the way.

Jackson had accompanied Abe on the guided tour, and on viewing what they had available, Jackson had asked for some minor changes and a couple of additional pieces of equipment. All the vehicles were staged in order, every single one of them was checked and fully loaded. In amongst the cloud of smoke, Pete the Pumper was in his element and had the six machines all fired up. Though a brief open window in the mad made smog, Abe got the thumbs up from him, indicating that all was well. The Bravo group was a hive of activity, with the silos being non-operational; this was going to be the most labour-intensive part of the planned action. Jackson asked if the light towers had all been checked out. Abe replied that they were all fuelled up, ready to be switched on. All the groups they had inspected today had been informed that as tomorrow would be an early start, they had to knock off early and relax for the rest of the day. Jackson and Abe had taken it in turns, informing everyone that there was a new cook on camp and they hoped they enjoyed the new menu. The last guy on the list was Perry; Jackson had a quiet word with him and told him to get his guys ready to move a couple of hours before dawn.

Enunsha along with Spotty caught up with them; she grabbed a coffee and listened to the plan. Jackson went through it all from start to finish, and Abe was still amazed that he had done all this in his head and had nothing written in front of him in the way of notes or prompts. Enunsha wanted to know why they would have to move, and Jackson coldly informed her that if they didn't know how many of the bad guys existed, then they couldn't fight them.

"They stay hidden all of the time, coming out and performing complex operations that require large quantities of men and machines. They leave no trace and disappear; we don't know if they are just active in this area, just in this country, and that is why we have to move. I was thinking about going down South, I always had this dream of retiring and growing avocadoes in my old age. Now, I would just be happy to stay alive. Please tell all of your people that once the underground forces are aware of what we have done, they will want to extract some form of revenge."

Jackson informed them that he was going to try and get some rest. He would meet them just before dawn at the entrance to the subterranean world that the Kunupenny clan used to rule over. Sleep did not come easy for him; his mind had been more than overactive for the last few days. He tossed and turned, after what felt like a lifetime or two, he eventually closed his eyes. As he got up, Jackson thought that he had stolen about two hours' worth of shuteye. The guys who were now manning the food station were open for business, and he gratefully accepted the fresh coffee as well as the pack of cigarettes.

Chapter 22

Perry was already there with his team, and like Jackson, they sat pensively thinking about nothing, just waiting to go into action. All the vehicles they would require to take with them on the first stage of the plan have been checked, and the contents secured. Jackson took the last draw and drained the last of his coffee, then told the team that it was time to saddle up. They followed him out the door and entered their allocated vehicles. The convoy drove throughout the early hours enroute to the underground facility. Jackson arrived first, and he abandoned his vehicle out of the way, ensuring that it would not impede the scheduled flow of expected traffic within the next few hours. Perry ordered the perimeter guards to take up their position, and they placed the landmines in the prearranged areas, then took up their defensive positions.

The truck equipped with the thermic lance was reversed into position, and the guard detail assigned to the building entered by the numbers and performed the required checks. When Jackson received the all-clear, he signalled the operator to remove the front doors. Almost immediately after giving the order, streams of sparks flew into the darkness, briefly illuminating everything around them. The thunderous roar of the oxygen being forced out at high pressure from the end of the lance filled the early morning with the undulated noise. The tightly packed pig iron rods were forcefully pushed out, cutting with relative ease, through the massive hinges that held the outer doors in place.

Once the doors were finally freed from the mechanisms that held them firmly in place, chains were attached to the truck that delivered the thermic lance. Jackson gave the signal, and it drove forward, pulling the massive doors well out of the way of the expected soon-to-be-arriving traffic. As the truck drove away, the next vehicles on the list arrived, and twenty guys and gals pulled off the longest welding cable and then descended the stairs to the lowest selected position.

Once the cable had reached its final destination, the fourteen crew members maintained their position to haul the next cable down to the double doors on level three. The six guys who had become free untethered the next cable and started to run it out to the start of the stairway. As this part of the scheduled operation was underway, the plastic explosive that closely resembled almond paste was unloaded and passed hand by hand to the huge elevator doors. Jackson suspected that these had been in operation in moving the vast amounts of manpower and machinery during the furtive clandestine operation in rendering the hydro-station inoperable.

Perry used a pair of scissors and cut the blocks into strips; a couple of his guys then pressed them into the huge double doors. The second cable, now terminating at level three, released another six guys who raced up to the top and stood ready for the next part of the rehearsed operation. Perry and his guys continued cutting, shaping, and forcing the malleable explosive compound into every available nook and cranny in and around the massive doors of the elevator.

As the last welding cables were being drawn into position, the trucks were signalled, and they reversed into position. The twenty guys and gals who had handballed the welding cable down the stairway to each of the offending doorways were on station, ready for the next move. They split up and reassembled into three groups of six; each group contained two welders, with the two remaining members manning the welding machines. The first group pulled off the three plates that were required and made their way over to the stairs. The second and third groups followed them down, and as they all reached their allocated work areas, the welding machines sparked into life. The welders had been pulled aside prior to the operation commencing and bluntly informed that there would be none of the following shit associated with their trade allowed. The juice had to be set before they went down, and it would be a one-juice setting to cover all of the welding positions. None of the normal whinging, two up, five down shouted to the operator on the dial on the remote-controlled current selector. They were also informed that if the welding gap was too big, just jam in some rods and block it out. The last segment of the speech that they received was directed at the final appearance of the welding, "I want plenty, not pretty!"

Perry and his team continued shaping copious amounts of the almond paste-like material and stuffing it as far as humanly possible into every available space around the double doors. Down below, in the various levels of the stairwell the pre-cut and prepared plates were being hauled into position. As per the staged rehearsals, they were tacked in place; once they had all been stitched accordingly, they were welded as per the sequence that had been drummed continuously into their head until they could recite the instructions in their sleep.

The twelve guys and gals, now free from moving the plates, started and shifted all the once-designer office furniture that was clinically spaced throughout the sterile floor. All the items were relocated into pole position to be chucked down the stairwell at the first available opportunity. The welders having remembered the bonus mode with the previous piecework contracted in the now-and-forgotten world. Operate the process as quickly as possible, keeping the time of releasing the end of the spent electrode from the whip and replacing it with a new one without lifting their helmets. A quick glance down through the space between their chest and the edge of the helmet saved precious time.

Jackson had calculated that once the welders on level four had finished, the next teams would finish at fifteen-minute intervals. He checked the progress with Perry and looked at the time displayed on his watch. The next group should have left the staging area and now be en route. The first two welders appeared at the top of the stairs. They joined their original group, waiting to install the designer furniture down the stairwell. As always, it was the waiting time that took the longest to pass. Some of the crews were sitting smoking some were anxiously pacing up and down. Jackson was counting down the minutes and then calculating all the next moves in progress.

Perry waved and signalled that his team had placed all of the plastic explosives. Jackson acknowledged his signal and nodded, giving him the go-ahead to wire it all up and lead the cables out to the control box. The second set of welders made it up the stairs and joined with the rest of their group. Jackson was still counting: fifteen minutes for the last weld to finish, seventeen minutes to start loading the stairwell, and after that, thirty minutes to complete and proceed to the next stage. It was the next stage that could be the stumbling block; all the moves had been planned with the doors being blasted open in the first move. If this failed, they would have to slowly cut them apart with the thermic lance, which he was not looking forward to, as the build-up of fumes and smoke would curtail all of the other scheduled activities.

At last, the final pair of welders reached the top of the stairs; they moved straight towards the truck containing the welding machines. The rest of their crew started to roughly place the office furniture down into the stairwell. Jackson had told them only to haul it down two flights of stairs. The guys and gals had split into pairs and passed the chairs and tables down the line. They quickly started to fill up the space, the chairs, tables, and now all the rest of the furniture started to reach the top landing. The monitors and keyboards were added to the mix. Every item was another piece that helped to increase the mass of obstacles. Should any of the underground dwellers breach the now-sealed doors and attempt to come charging up the stairs.

The leftover remnants of the designer furniture were left in a pile in the middle of the floor, and the welding cables were dragged across the floor then unceremoniously added to the debris now blocking the stairwell. Perry, having finished the required preparations, raised his clenched fist as per the signal, and everyone evacuated the building. The bare wires were connected to the control box, and the system was checked and then charged. As everyone took cover, Jackson was asked if he would like the honours. He refused, "You go ahead, son; the honour is all yours."

Perry shouted fire-in-the-hole, and the detonators inserted into the malleable plastic explosives that had been prodded and poked into every available space on the elevator doors. Simultaneously released the small charge, and there was a momentary flash followed a split second later by a huge boom and a massive rush of hot dusty air and smoke.

Jackson thought on a positive note, and while they waited for the smoke to clear, he directed the team to manoeuvre the large plates on the back of the trucks into position. Perry anxiously awaited on viewing whether his handiwork had been successful or not and smoked a cigarette, while waiting patiently for the smoke to clear. Jackson told him not to worry it would be fine. They had used ample amounts of the almond paste-like material and thought it would be a successful operation. They still had more of the stuff available should they have to repeat the process but Jackson hoped that they did not have to rerun the exercise. He thought that as the next trucks would be here shortly and still waiting for the smoke to clear, he told the crew to put on their masks and push all of the welding machines into the building. Five of them came straight off the first truck. The other five required to be gently guided across the plate, providing a temporary connection. With this complete, the trucks were manoeuvred out of the way to make space available for the next vehicles. The plate that had been placed to allow the wheeled welding machines to easily enter the building was now hauled about with brute force and ignorance, transforming it into a makeshift ramp.

The smoke had dissipated enough to enable a clear view of the destruction; both of the doors had been completely blown off and had descended into the void of the lift shaft. Jackson gave the signal, and the welding machines were each manned up with four of the crew and were pushed over the edge of the lift shaft as quickly as possible. The leftover office furniture in the middle of the floor followed the path of the discarded welding machines, and five minutes later, the next deliveries started to arrive. The first converted car transporter drew to a halt and was reversed into position. The next crew alighted from the minibuses and immediately removed the wooden boards from the other truck and laid down a track to the doorway now with the temporary ramp. Jackson watched the progress, still counting the minutes and seconds, constantly recalculating everything in his head.

The shopping trolleys were unloaded, and as per the rehearsal, they were shoved forward five at a time. The bunched-up units were passed between the groups, one passing to the other until eventually they entered the building. The crew inside, five groups of two, advanced forward as quickly as possible, and the trolleys were sent to join the growing pile of debris congregating at the bottom of the shaft. This was almost a continuous, nonstop movement as one group followed quickly on the heels of the other. They rushed forward and separated as their charge sailed into the open space that was once the elevator doors. Then, returning down the righthand and lefthand side resumed their position in the queue for the next available consignment.

Car transporter number one had disgorged its full cargo and was moving out of the way. The second modified unit took its place immediately when there was enough free space available. The crew jumped to it and started unloading the next consignment as soon as possible, and the process started again. Jackson was now at the stairwell and listened carefully for any sounds being emitted from down below. He got several uninterrupted seconds of relative silence in between the batches of the carts that were once used for the weekly shopping trip, banging and clanging down the lift shaft. He stayed there, making doubly sure that there were no uninvited guests, slowly attempting to dislodge the displaced office furniture that had been placed deliberately to curb any attempts to advance quickly up the stairwell.

Perry informed Jackson that the perimeter was intact and there was absolutely nothing to report. He looked at his watch and figured that they were five full minutes ahead of the schedule. Abe had arrived with a flask of coffee along with a pack of cigarettes; they went outside and watched the events unfolding in front of them. The fire trucks had arrived, and they were directed into their assigned parking spot. They caught a glimpse as they watched Peter the Pumper as he lubed up his new toys, ready for action. He was almost displaying a facial gesture associated with sexual gratification as he smeared the sticky solution onto the parts of his partially dismantled machines. Jackson looked quizzically at Abe, and he shook his head; like him, he did not wish to make any comments about it.

The shopping trolleys rained continuously down the lift shaft, bouncing off the inner walls as they joined their brothers and sisters at the very bottom. Jackson had no idea the true depth of the vertical shaft, but he knew for sure that all the soon-to-be-disposed-of carts would not be enough to fill it to the brim. He had made a rough calculation when the welding machines were wheeled over, and at his estimated count, it was well over nine hundred feet to the bottom. Maybe he had placed the decimal point wrongly, but for all the items they had dispatched down the hole, there were still more than a few seconds until the items sounded out, indicating that they had reached the bottom.

Now that the second modified car transporter had deposited its load, the machine moved out of the way to allow number three to get into position. Jackson sent out a message for Peter the Pumper to move two of his new toys into position. A couple of minutes later, the telehandlers picked up the machines and slowly but surely moved them into position. Once in place, Pete's crew dragged the preassembled hoses into position, and Peter the pumper adopted his favourite facial gesture as he applied the lube on the connecting ring and flexible hose. The parts were manhandled together; then, the holding clamp was hammered home. Jackson poured a coffee from the flask and had a cigarette as the next set of shopping trolleys were offloaded then sent on their short but necessary journey.

Up till now, everything had almost gone without any major hitches; even the welders had not bitched about anything. Now having some time to spare, he signalled to catch Perry's attention. He finished the coffee and walked him and Abe over to the transport that he had helped him deliver on the first day that he had arrived here with his crew. Jackson opened the door and asked Perry to get some help and unload all the boxes out of the van. He poured another coffee and, sticking his finger into the cup, drew a rough diagram of the items he wanted made once they had the available space.

"Everything you require is contained within these three vans." Perry nodded that he understands what is required. Jackson sipped the coffee then looked at his watch; he thought Enunsha would be just about ready to start rolling out her trucks. They walked back over and viewed the ongoing operation; the last modified car transporter was shedding its contents. Once that was done, Jackson would change out the crews for the next scheduled event. He poured the last of the contents out from the flask. It was not as hot as the last one, but all the same, he chugged it down. He motioned Abe to come with him, and they watched the final batch of shopping trolleys getting pushed into the shift. Abe asked him if the subterranean dwellers were aware of what was happening. Jackson thought for sure that someone somewhere would be recording what was happening, and if not, they would be terribly disappointed when they were unable to operate the elevator or use the stairs.

"Perhaps they are stationed somewhere else; for all we know, there could be a vast underground network of interconnected tunnels spreading out everywhere. At the very least, we have blocked off one of their entry and exit points."

Jackson heard the noise coming from outside. They went out just in time to see the last modified car transporter moving out and the rest of Peter the Pumper's new toys being manoeuvred into position. He and Abe avoided looking in his direction as he lubed up his machines, getting them all ready to perform the largest operation of the plan. The teleporters moved about slowly and precisely, putting the machines in the exact prearranged locations. The lines of preassembled hoses were all connected, and the spare lines, along with the spare fittings, were placed in the required area. Several crew buses had arrived, Jackson along with Abe thanked the outgoing crew for all the hard work and effort. The incoming crew were welcomed as they got into their positions, ready for the next batch of trucks. The extra crew with them took over the last shopping trolleys and sent them into the void. Abe spotted them first as the almost continuous line of trucks headed towards them. Pete the Pumper had all his machines fired up and ready to go. All of the drivers had been reminded about the ninety-minute rule prior to leaving the base, and as the trucks manoeuvred into position to line up with their allocated pumps, they started adding the water to the dry mixture onboard. The same as the welders, they had been informed of the quantity over quality request, and considering that, none of them checked the dials on the output panel on their rigs. Peter the Pumpers' guys were inside to monitor the output from the hoses; he did not care where it went as long as all the disgorged contents trickled down the stairs. The last of the shopping trolleys had left the building, and now having the available space, Perry and his crew started to shift the boxes inside the building. The first truck now had its chute extended, and its cargo slowly started to empty into the feed box on one of Peter the Pumpers' machines. He called for more water to be added, and the sludge mixture of the sand, aggregate and cement was pushed out of the pump into the hose.

Abe and Jackson were like schoolboys as they rushed inside the building and watched as all the hoses gradually came online. The grey-coloured liquid spurted out of the open hoses and cascaded down the steps. Sometimes, it appeared that the mix had stopped moving as the levels in front of the discarded office furniture increased in height. Then, the build-up suddenly decreased as if some hidden force had reached through and pulled it downwards into the stairwell. Jackson requested a water hose to be placed inside the building to discourage any future build-ups. The first truck had fully emptied its contents down the chute. The driver washed his tank and emptied the weak mixture to Peter the pumpers machines hold tank.

The truck drives forwarded, and with the minimum space required, the replacement truck reversed into position, and as soon as it come to a halt, the chute was lowered, and the contents started to flow into the already wet feed tank. Jackson was pleased with the concentrated effort and still thought that it was going to take a few days of continuous work to fill the stairwell and the lift shaft. As this was going to take hours of work before any visible signs of progress were displayed, Jackson told Abe that if there were any problems, he would let him know and told him that if he wished, he could go and see how Enunsha and Spotty were getting on.

"Abe, if you decide to come back, some fresh coffee would be nice." Jackson thought that Abe was okay, and although he was meant to be the one in charge, Jackson had just sort of taken over. He never meant him any disrespect, and it had just sort of happened.

Jackson had been awake most of the night, and they had still not filled the stairwell with concrete. The six pumps were working nonstop, and he thought that they had emptied forty-five truckloads into the feed tanks. He knew it would all take time; this was all he had to work with, and the more he thought about it they could not have done it any better. A couple of the hoses feeding the slurry had bunged up, and rather than separating, cleaning, and putting them back together again, they had just been replaced. The ones that were jammed up were chucked down the lift shaft to join up with all of the other debris. Perry had started to glue all the boxes together in the configuration that Jackson had asked for. Now Perry had a rough idea of what Jackson required; he and his men got stuck in sticking them together, forming the required shape.

Abe had arrived with Enunsha and Spotty in tow as they, along with others from the newly formed catering company, dished out food and hot drinks to everyone. Jackson thought that his energy was starting to flag and he awarded them ten out of ten for arriving at the right possible moment. He thought that, at some point, he would be found sleeping in the corner. Jackson gave them an update, and as they looked down at the stairwell, they all saw the mucky grey semi-liquid starting to get thicker and heavier. Jackson issued a request to one of Pete the Pumper's crew to fire a few blasts of pressurised water at it from the fire trucks. They watched and noted that the growing blob of the grey stuff did not flow away. Jackson reckoned that another fifteen truckloads and they would be at the top.

Enunsha informed him that the Bravo crew was working around the clock loading up the trucks that had been emptied and returned for reloading. She asked him how many trucks in total they required to complete the job. Jackson confessed that he did not know the exact number, but he would let her know as soon as they finished. The volume of the lift shaft was massive compared to the stairwell, and he did not have the heart to tell her that they would need hundreds of them. They walked outside, observing that Peter the Pumper was in his element. All of them were pleased that he was so much better at this than his old job. All the pumps were set on the maximum setting, and he talked to them like they were all his girlfriends. One of the guys had told them that he had given them all names before they left the staging point. Jackson thanked Abe and Enunsha for delivering the food and beverages. As they departed, he went back to work.

Perry and his team were still sticking the boxes together, and Jackson had another peek at the stairwell; he could now clearly see the grey gunk rising in amongst all the discarded designer furniture. He calls one of Peter the Pumpers' crew and requests a small change to the proceedings. Three of the pumps were temporarily closed down, and their hoses were rerouted to the lift shaft. Jackson called Perry over, and they watched as the grey goop started to ooze out of the ends of the open hoses and fall into the lift shaft.

"In a couple of hours' time, can you and the guys bring in the sticky tape, the rope, the rest of the almond paste, and the bits and pieces that go with them?"

Perry told him no problem and went back to his other job. Jackson was almost fascinated as the mixture of sand, aggregate, and cement splurged out of the hoses and dropped soundlessly into the shaft. As soon as the stairwell was full to the top, the other three hoses would be transferred over, and then all they had to do was wait.

Chapter 23

The mist had arrived, and as it swirled around their feet, the old woman in the hooded cloak asked them all to hold hands. This time, she introduced them all by name, and all of them thought that the new faces were familiar. They were just having the feeling that they had met them somewhere before and not in the context of a dream. Blink and Enunsha were invited to shake hands, and as they exchanged the greeting, the old woman in the hooded cloak told them that the comet was coming, and with that came great changes. 'Blink, you and your people will have to move North, as Enunsha and her people will perish without your help. It will involve some difficult choices, but they must be made.' Murray was signalled out again and was informed the two women would be arriving soon; they would come to you from the sea, you must protect them and their children. 'Like before, you will face objections to this, but I implore you that it was necessary. The old woman in the hooded cloak and the dream started to fade, but her last words rang out clearly: With the comet comes change, and change, changes as it changes...'

Murray and Cha were now awake in the medical facility, and there was a strong possibility that they would have to explain the dirty sheets, the soil-encrusted feet, and the mucky footprints on the floor. Cha informed him that there was now a new addition to their family, and he had another son. He laughed as she blamed him for shocking her into giving birth early. Murray wanted to know why he was not in the room with them. Cha informed him that the new one was so impatient to come and meet his stubborn father that he had opted to arrive much earlier than expected and was now in the incubator. Cora, she remembered, had told her not to worry; the baby was small but healthy. They had both fallen back asleep after the brief conversation. One of the nurses had popped in to check on the patients and found them both still sound asleep. She had noted the footprints on the floor and assumed that they had been visited in secret by someone not wearing shoes.

In the morning the rest of the dreamers from the watermill had met up in Murray's house and wondered what was coming their way. Okolo was the only one concerned by the repeated mention of the two women and the children that Murray must protect. She thought that the old woman with the hooded cloak was telling Murray to protect them from her. That feeling of the hair standing on the back of her neck had returned, and as in previous occasions, this equated to some form of danger heading her way. Robbo confessed that he did not know what the message meant and he must go to work; if he was late, Karen would give him a hard time for the rest of the day. The twins, as always, were tied up in knots about the cryptology, analysing what had been said and always empathising with what had not been said. Alicia wondered why the women were arriving from the sea and thought that there could be a valid reason for this. Cat had not shown up this morning; she was going to try and persuade Cora to grant her an exception and let her in to see Murray and Cha. Alicia had wished her good luck on that one, but Cat, being Cat, was determined to try.

At the Watermill medical unit, Murray was now fully awake and looked over to the occupant in the adjacent bed; Mrs. Black was pretending that she was still asleep. "If you are still sleeping when the breakfast arrives, can I have yours?"

Cha was now sitting up, staring at him, "I have just given birth to our new son and now you want to steal then devour my breakfast? Which would have helped my body recover from the arduous task of giving birth."

Murray proclaims to the world that he would have got up and made her a meal fit for a queen, but as she can see he is all fully connected up and unfortunately not allowed to get out of the fucking bed. Cha is about to wind him up with feeble excuses when the Doctor arrives.

"And how are my star patients this fine morning," Murray issued a grunt, and Cora informed him, "You will be fine, and before you ask you are in here for the full week. Get over it."

Mr. Black was not given any time to respond, and Cora sat beside Cha. "You are looking great, my dear; I hope you slept well. Sorry, the other patient snores like an intercity transport bus with a faulty exhaust manifold, but if you wish, I could have him transferred to another ward. If it was at all possible, I would have no hesitation transferring him to another hospital if you requested it."

Cha and the Doctor laughed as both of them poked fun at Murray. Cora helped her up, and together, they went to see the newly arrived member of the Black family. They had not decided on a name yet, but Cha looked in through the covering of the incubator, and already the baby had the famous Black stare. Cora also recognised that look and informed Cha that there had been lots of people trying to get in and visit, but she wanted to give them a few days on their own. Cha thanked the Doctor for everything. Cora just replied that it was her job, telling Cha not to worry if the baby was anything at all like his father; he would be wanting out as soon as possible.

As they re-enter the ward, Murray was overheard, "I can assure you that Mrs. Black asked me to look after her breakfast, and if there was the slightest chance of it going cold, she had given me express permission to eat it."

Murray was at, and there was no one else in the room. He waved to them, "I am starving, and I am not even going to ask if I can smoke in here." Cora totally ignored him.

She helped Cha get comfy, then took her breakfast order and left the room. The doctor did not even look at Murray, who now thought that he had become invisible. "Well, grumpy chops, we will need to decide on a name pretty soon, and everyone is going to start asking."

Murray mumbled, "I was thinking of calling him hungry."

Cha looked about her to find something to throw at him, "You can be so immature sometimes, so why don't we just call him

Extremely Grumpy? Then, we can tell everyone that he is named after his father. Who goes under the name of Eternally Grumpy?"

Murray gave in, "Okay, I'm sorry. I was going to ask you about the name, I can't think of one at present and just wondered if you had any thoughts on the subject."

Cha did not get time to reply as the Meals on Wheels lady arrived. Much to both their surprise, it is Cat, "Frank told me that I had to come and give him a hand today as he was short-staffed."

Murray ate everything on the plate and listened while Cat gave them the updates. "Mark and Ellie were over, and as you can imagine, Okolo and Alicia were less than welcoming hosts. They wanted to come up here to visit both of you, but as you can guess, there is a waiting list."

Cat wanted to see the new addition to their family, but Cha her she would have to wait. "Cora is not too happy about anyone going to see Alfie as he is still in the incubator."

Murray had pretended that he did not hear the name, but in his opinion, the name was fine. No Alfred, no Alfonzo, just plain Alfie sounded good to him. Cora was now back in the room, watching as Cat packed up the plates and left. The Doctor had spoken to Cat at length and had informed her that there would be no visitors for a few days. "I had to tell her that I had alarmed all the windows just to put her off trying to break in to come and see you both. Once you have both recovered enough, I will let people in to see you, but only for one hour at a time."

Cha informed Cora of the baby's name, thinking that at least it could be added to the clipboard hanging on the end of the incubator. Cora told her that she thought the name had a nice ring to it. Murray knew Cora was winding him up again. He heard her whispering Alfonzo Black in an Italian accent as she passed. Cha was up out of bed and informed Murray that she was allowed to go and shower and he would be getting another bed bath. She left laughing at Murray's acute embarrassment, knowing that he would be mortified to be washed again by complete strangers. Cha popped her head back in the door as the nurses arrived, "Murray, remember cleanliness is next to godliness."

He stared at her; she winked, blew him an air kiss, and Murray replied with stereo magic fingers.

Murray was wondering what was for dinner and prayed to all the gods of every known religion, as well as some that he had just made up on the spot, that it was not fish or anything related to the smelly species that lived in the murky depths at the bottom of the ocean. He had asked Cora when he would be allowed to see Alfie; she had told him that once he has healed enough, then when he is strong enough, she will allow it. Cora had also told him that she knows he is dying to see him but he has to be patient and wait it out. Cha was allowed to go through to see him as often and whenever she wanted. She had been tormenting him, saying that Alfie would definitely be a mama's boy. Murray had told her in reply that she was a cruel, mentally unstable woman with no regard for his feelings. Cha had replied, "Feelings? You could not even inform me that you had been shot!"

Dinner had arrived and it had been brought to them by both Okolo and Alicia. Okolo had confessed that Frank had told her that Murray might require to be sedated before you commenced with the spoon feeding. Murray told her that she had somehow forgotten to mention the fish part of that sentence.

Mr. Black got stuck into the food; he knew that they were only here to see Cha and asked about their new addition to the family. Cha and the women talked nonstop. They let it out of the bag that Robbo had been promoted. "He is not very good at anything, but he is good at telling jokes and keeping all the other workers entertained."

Murray had a picture of him wearing a shirt and tie with the obligatory white hard hat in the back of his car. To keep the peace, he enquired how the build was progressing; Alicia and Okolo took it in turns to sort of describe what stage the project was at. Apart from that, all he could really decipher out of the gobbley-gook was that the outer walls were now complete, and they were making lots of noise inside the new building.

Mr. Black beaming with pride, told them that Alfie was going to be an architect or maybe an astronaut. Cha disagreed and told them that he was going to be the head chef in a world-class restaurant. Murray retorted back he would teach his son to cook all of the meals that the Black family is famous for. Okolo made them call a truce and agreed that as long as he was happy, he could be whatever he wanted to be. Alicia informed them that young Mark wanted to learn to read and kept pointing at the books. He had said his first clear word and no one was surprised to hear that it was Charlie. Okolo told them about the dogs' performance when Alfie had taken his first breath. Cha thought that Alfie was just as stubborn as his father and revealed to the world that Alfie had already mastered the famous Black stare. Murray told them all that his son was just like him, much preferring animals to people. They laughed and made fun of him, but as they were in Cora's kingdom, they tried and kept it down a little.

Okolo mentioned the recent dream and got straight to the point about the two women who were going to arrive from the sea. "I swear it, Murray, it was almost as if the old woman in the hooded cloak was telling me that I was the one you would need to protect them from."

Alicia did not get that impression but added that he never truly knew what was in those dreams. "Okolo has had more dreams than any of them, and the old woman has protected her from danger on numerous occasions."

They all knew that Murray, more than any of them, saw Okolo as a kindred spirit and would never do anything that would hurt her. Cha closed the subject and said that they would deal with it, no matter what it was, when the time came. They heard a cough in the background and that was Cora being polite in letting them know that the unofficial visit was over. Okolo gave Murray a huge cuddle before she left, telling him he had to get well soon and that she missed him.

Cora came to see them and allowed the pair to go and see their son. She informed them that Alfie would be in there until he reached the minimum body mass. On hearing this, Alfie did not cry; both Cha and Murray would swear that they had witnessed the famous Black stare. Alfie watched everything around him; Cora interrupted the proceedings and informed them that they had to leave as it was now feeding time.

Murray declared to the world, "I think he has my eyes!" Cha hoped that Alfie had not inherited his father's sullen moods. Murray wanted to go outside now to personally deliver the news to Charlie and Romulus. Cha told him that they knew already, adding that just maybe they were waiting to meet the new addition to their family and not waiting on bated breath to reacquaint themselves with Mr. Grumpy. Murray put his arms around her and told her that he was only grumpy when she was not around. "Away you go and see to the dogs, go on, be off with you." Murray did not even bother to take any smokes with him, hoping that this would earn him some bonus points from the captain of the guard, equating to an earlier release date.

Opening the main door, he found the dogs lying outside. Charlie and Romulus barked excitedly and licked him to death. Murray told them the good news: Charlie had one ear up and one ear down, looking at him as if he was nuts. Romulus just looked at him as if to say I already know. Murray told them that they had to go home now and he would be there as soon as possible. He gave the command, "Home," then pointed; Charlie delivered a single bark and begrudgingly sauntered along with Romulus in the direction of home. Murray felt like shit for having to dismiss them.

Cora had watched the event from the window and wondered if he had always talked to animals like this. She had heard all the stories about Murray and what he had done in the past, but no one had mentioned his natural affinity with animals. Alfie had been fed and was now sleeping; he wanted to double the normal amount during this feed. Cora thought that he was going to be as stubborn and determined as his father. The Doctor delivered the good news that they were now allowed visitors, and she had taken the liberty of passing the news update to his household. Murray and Cha hoped that someone would do the needful, bringing Mark up to meet his new brother. As always, Murray was getting peckish, wondering what delights would be on offer today. As he was going to be in here for a while, Murray thought that Frank should have supplied one of them with coded multiple-choice menus, and if he did manage to translate one, he would have added the words no fucking fish in block capitals.

Okolo had arrived with the very much-appreciated food parcels. Mark had also arrived; as soon as he entered the rooms, he almost ran and climbed in beside Cha. Okolo updated them on his antics, adding that he talked almost non-stop. Mark must have heard them and said mama out loud. Murray asked him, "Hey, what about me?" and pointed to himself; Mark said the word 'wanker' and cuddled into Cha. Okolo blushed and confessed that she had no idea where Mark had picked up that from. Murray suggested that the source was most likely to have been Robbo, "Is he still busy with the building work?"

Okolo nodded, "Karen keeps him on his toes, and I think she actually likes him being there. He is not too good at any of the work, but he keeps the workers entertained. Karen says that he is the number one goffer. The outside work is nearly finished and Alicia and I are going to send him out looking for the bits and pieces of furniture that we will need soon. We really want a decent sound system; Alicia said that you would somehow know where to find one locally."

She handed Murray the paper and pen, and he obliged by jotting down the directions relating to the long-dead hi-fi enthusiasts who may have the required items.

Okolo continued, "Robbo likes just about anything and won't really get much of a choice in what we play. However, he has asked for a list of music that pisses you off, just in case he decides to have an evening of annoying you."

Murray informed them that the walls are thick and solid, "If he were to try and create a volume that would penetrate the walls, he would suffer bleeding from his nose, ears, and eyes, so tell him just to go right ahead."

Mark whispered 'wanker' in Cha's ear and cuddled in some more. The Doctor was on the prowl and asked if they wanted her to prepare them some food in the future. Murray was aware that she was not a lover of his acquired tastes, and no doubt she would be trying to wean him off the spicy foods, trying and convert him to the slimy stuff. Cha attempted to save him and mentioned that it was a very kind offer, but she had done more than enough for them. Cora replied that it was not a problem and that she would start to supply the meals in the morning. Murray couldn't wait, and noticeably, Mark did not support his thoughts.

Cha asked if they could introduce the boys to each other. Cora agreed with the idea but told them to try not to disturb Alfie, and she thought he would be as grumpy as his father if he did not get the full allocated afternoon nap. Cha held Mark in her arms, and with Murray, they went for a quick look at Alfie. Mark was squirming in her arms and desperately wanted to touch his younger brother. Alfie was still fast asleep but smiled and raised his hand; Mark reached out to let him know that he saw him. Much to everyone's surprise he said the word Alfie loud and clear. The parents, not wanting to overstay the quick visit go back and see Okolo. She had gathered up and packed the things to return to Frank.

Okolo delivered the last of her news, "There is quite a waiting list of people wanting to come and visit. How do you want me to address this issue on that list? We are receiving a daily request from the farmhouse. Mark has been over every single morning, asking for a convenient time. Who do you want to see first, and what do you wish me to say to Mark? He is more than very worried about what happened." Murray and Cha discussed who was where on the list and agreed that they would not leave Mark hanging out in the cold the next time he came over just to send him up. Alicia was more than welcome to come up anytime, and the same went for Cat and the twins.

Murray had very itchy feet and wanted to escape from the confines of the medical facility. Every day, Cora examined him, and every day, he asked to leave. It did him no good as he received the same reply, "You can leave when I say that it is okay to leave." Cha had informed him that she would only leave when Alfie was allowed to go home. Doctor Cora had started to feed them, and Murray was thinking about going on a hunger strike. It was not really that long ago that his staple breakfast consisted of a longish homemade cigarette and a tin of the last man on the planet. The fizzy energy drink was sadly no longer available in any of the local shops, and he had replaced his once favourite tipple with copious amounts of tea. Cora was trying to convince him to eat oats and fruit for breakfast; Murray complained bitterly informing her that the last time he had looked in the mirror, he did not look like a horse. Cha, of course, had seen the validity in the Doctor's sound reasoning and as far as he saw it, it was two against one. As he was confined, almost a prisoner in here, he really did not have much of a choice. Murray prayed daily that the God of the Red Cross parcels would hear his urgent pleas.

The twins were the first visitors today, and they were blushing as they handed over the present for Alfie. They had made him some clothes; Cha thought that they were beautiful, and Murray thanked them for being so kind. When Cora was out of earshot, they spoke in their usual fashion of one starting the sentence and the other one finishing it. They informed them that Mark and Vincent were winding them up on purpose and had been moving objects bigger than the monitor. "Oh, don't get me wrong, they are not shifting the furniture from one end of the room to the other. But they can definitely make things move about; the other day, I put the cups down on the table; I had only turned my back for a few seconds as they were at the other end of the table. I know it wasn't me; the cheeky wee monkeys were pretending to be asleep and only gave it away when they started to laugh."

Cha asked them if they had informed Okolo, "We did inform her but she said that it was not possible to discuss it with you as Cora was about."

Speak of the devil, the Doctor was now back in the room on her way to feed Alfie. She apologised for interrupting them and let it slip that Alfie was now on a double feed at every meal and was gaining weight by the day. Murray and Cha thought that this was great news; perhaps he would be allowed out sooner than expected. One of the nurses had now come in and told them that they had another pair of visitors waiting outside. As they only had a limited time for each visit, the twins had to leave before the next pair was allowed in. Murray thanked them big time for the clothes and for taking care of Mark. "The next time you catch him at it, tell him, just wait till your dad is home."

The twins looked at him as if he was nuts, "That was the first thing we tried and both Mark and Vincent nearly wet themselves laughing." Beth and Debs gave Cha a double sisterly cuddle, then left.

Mark and Ellie were a bit on the sheepish side as they entered. Murray noticed their predicament straight away and gave them it straight, the only way he knew how. "Look, the both of you are more than good neighbours and no matter what befalls us in the future, we will always be good friends. So, you can lift your chin up and stop looking like you have come to report to the headmaster."

Ellie laughed, but Mark was deadly serious. "I really don't know where to start except to apologise from the bottom of my heart for all the unfortunate circumstances along with the pain and worry we have put the both of you through." Cha told them they had to stop blaming themselves, "You make it sound as if it was you who was actually pulling the trigger."

Ellie piped up and told them that they had installed a new procedure to make sure that it never happened again, and Linda was now the proud owner of a pair of glasses. "I marched her down to the vets, and she had long-range vision problems. Linda said that she had never noticed the deterioration of her vision as the extent of her viewing range was only limited to an area around the tractor."

Mark confessed that it was Okolo who had instigated the eyesight test, "I think that Okolo is very protective of the both of you and in a different situation, she would have quite happily shot Linda on sight." Murray laughed, agreeing that it was so much more than possible.

As visiting time was nearly over, Ellie asked them if they were going to bring everyone over for Christmas. Cha sadly informed her friend that Alfie was underweight and she would not be going anywhere until he was allowed out of the hospital. Cara had stolen a bell from somewhere and let it ring loud and clear to inform everyone that visiting time was over. Mark's fist bumps Murray and Cha received another sisterly cuddle.

Cora had popped her head in and confessed that she had deliberately cut the visit short. As Alfie was awake, she thought that they would like to see him before he snuggled down for a post-feed nap. "I think this one is half-human, half-mattress."

Cha immediately retorted, "He must get that from his father's questionable gene pool." Murray, for once, was speechless; here was the woman who lit up his rather woeful existence, frequently informing him on numerous occasions that he was far from perfect. Alfie, wanting out of the incubator, squirmed in delight at seeing his parents; they stood over him, making all the goo-goo baby noises. Murray declared to anyone who would listen that Alfie had definitely got his eyes. Hands-on her hips, Cha bluntly said that she hoped Alfie had her brains.

The Doctor ushered them out of the room; when the time was up, Cora showed them the weight chart; both of them were very impressed that Alfie was eating his way to freedom. The Doctor reckoned that it would be at least a couple of weeks before he was allowed home. Murray wiped the tears from her eyes as she asked if she thought that the baby would be home for Christmas. Cora just said that they would have to wait and see.

When they were on their own, they discussed the prospect of their community going over to the farmhouse for Christmas. Murray thought that they would have too many newborn babies and too many tired first-time mothers to make the journey. Cha was thinking that perhaps they could invite them all over here. Murray asked her if she thought that the medical facility would be able to hold all the people. Cha told him that he was a wanker and rolled over and went to sleep.

Murray had just received some good news; Cora had checked him over and informed him that he had healed enough to be discharged from the hospital. Alfie had double his weight, and it was possible that he would be discharged tomorrow morning. Both of the doting parents were delighted. Murray had been warned that he had to refrain from working; if he had to come back and see her, she would keep him here for two weeks. Murray had promised to obey her strict instructions to the letter.

He was sad that Cha would not be coming home with him, even though it would only be for one night he would miss her terribly. Cha cheered him up no end, by ordering him to clean the house from top to bottom. She was only noising him up as she knew that it had already been clinically cleaned to a sterilised state of perfection by Alicia, Okolo and the twins. Cora also informed

Murray that she would not be awarding him any gold stars as they were only given to star patients, and as Cha had been more than perfect, she had given her a double amount. It was cold outside, and it got dark early in the evening, but Murray thought that he was the luckiest man alive and couldn't wait till they could all partake in the family walks. Murray thought that Mark would have loads of fun with his younger brother Alfie, and the best part was that they would be friends for life. Murray and Cha were allowed to go in and see Alfie, the youngster was fast asleep. Cha was crying as Murray said goodnight and 'see you tomorrow' to their son. He put his arms around her, holding her close, reassuring her that everything would work out fine and she did not have to worry. The dogs were waiting for him as he left the medical facility. Charlie was just one of the super-smart dogs that was always there when she was needed. He gathered them in close, telling them that tomorrow would be a great day and now they were going to go for a walk to their favourite place. Charlie and Romulus barked giving their seal of approval to the deal.

Mr. Black never even bothered going into the house for his smokes; he felt that he would be betraying everyone, especially the dogs, if he kept them waiting a minute longer. They had been so good and well-behaved that he had to be reminded from time to time by Cha that they were not his children and were just dogs. Murray had responded by informing her that she should wash her mouth out with soap as he would always treat the dogs with as much love and affection as their children.

Murray could hardly believe it; yesterday had just almost vanished, and he was on his way to the medical facility to pick up Cha. He hoped, with fingers crossed, that Alfie would be coming home too.

He was thinking that everything was indeed going to be fine; as he parked the vehicle, Cha was waiting with their wrapped-up little bundle cuddled into her at the door.

Murray had Mark strapped into the baby seat in the back, he had also been telling him like forever that they were going to collect his mama and brother this morning. Murray went out, helping Cha into the car; he then went into the boot then delivered Cora and all her staff the biggest bunch of flowers on the planet, thanking her for everything that they had done for them. When they had arrived back at the house, Murray had arranged a quiet welcome home party. All the usual faces were there; Murray had taken the liberty of inviting Mark and Ellie. It was his way of saying that there were no hard feelings between them, and they would always be welcome in their house.

The house, as expected, was clinically clean, and Murray had even washed the dogs. There were flowers everywhere, and Cha was so happy to be back home, even though the experts had informed her that she would never have any children. She was over the moon that She and Murray now were the proud parents of two beautiful boys. Cha just couldn't help showing tears of joy and had a little cry; everyone here had been so kind she was just truly overwhelmed with joy. Murray had told her a long, long time ago that she would have children, and she went over to him, put her arms around him, thanking him from the bottom of her heart for everything. Murray's face went bright red, but he could not care what anyone thought; the only person he could clearly see in this room was Cha.

Christmas had arrived, and there was a flurry of activity. Most of the people from the watermill had accepted the invitation for the inter-community get-together at the farmhouse. The notable exceptions are all the expectant mothers. Cora was the first to go into labour, and Robbo's ears would have turned red if he had heard the vile, abusive words she had used to describe her current opinion of him. His ears would have fallen off if he had heard what Okolo and Alicia thought about him. Murray wondered if there were enough flowers available in the Orangery to buy him even a temporary stay of forgiveness.

On the other hand, Cat and the twins were all very calm; surprisingly, Frank only received praise and kind words from Cat. He had fainted and passed out in the delivery room and now had a scar to show for it. All the mothers, along with all the newborns, were all fit and healthy; Murray had been ushered in to deliver the meals. Cora had prepared in advance a menu with all the meals that she thought were suitable for the new residents. With fish or seafood featured in nearly every option, Murray was considering wearing a gas mask to shield himself from the more than unpleasant odour.

Chapter 24

Blink had been up for a quite some time; she had meditated then performed all of the required exercises. The training was one thing, but unless you kept your body in tip-top condition, able to bend and adapt. All of the training in the world would just be a total waste of time. She closed her eyes, breathed deeply and prepared herself for the meeting with the elders. Blink had previously witnessed these closed sessions and the elders could be cruel and unforgiving, but they were there for a purpose. They were set up long ago to ensure that the madness that had wiped out so many other settlements in this continent had never ever gained a foothold in their community. Not once had their population ever been hoodwinked into worshipping the gods of the wind, sun or the moon. All the imposters that had come before had them left with their tails firmly between their legs. Some had been sentenced to death, and others had been exiled for all of eternity. Still, she had to go before them and present her case; her mother had told her never to fear them, to look them straight in the eye and always, above all else, tell them the truth.

She waited outside the chamber as the sun beat down upon her face, and she thought of her mother and grandmother, asking for their wisdom and guidance on this day of all days. Blink heard the small bells chiming indicating that she may proceed inside. The five of them sat, all displaying no emotion whatsoever. The one in the centre indicated with a well-practised hand gesture for her to approach closer. So that they might hear her clearly, so that they might see her along with all of her facial gestures. She took a deep breath, then walked forward and stood, waiting for the nominated speaker to address her. Blink knew that they were deliberately keeping her waiting; many of the would-be charlatans would betray themselves at this stage as they would perspire profusely and shake uncontrollably like a rabid dog.

Blink stood firm and stood proud; she thought that if they wished her to stand like this for days on end. She would oblige them without question or judgement. This was only part of the process they had practised over the centuries to reveal the true purpose and evaluation of the claimant that stood before them. Still, they kept her waiting. She thought they knew why she was there. They had been informed that this day would come; it had been written down in the secret history of their tribe, and it was her place to inform them. At last, the speaker rang the small bell, "Blink, daughter of Lucky, granddaughter of Gabriella, come closer to the bench and present your request."

She was well prepared, remembering the phrases word for word. Along with all the actions the old woman in the hooded cloak had taught her, Blink stepped forward.

She banged the bench three times with her clenched right fist, "I, the daughter of Lucky, granddaughter of Gabriella, approach you to inform you that the mother of mothers has spoken to me and revealed that the time has come. The green comet that heralded our ancestors' first steps in what is now known as the long journey. Once again will be displayed in the heavens above. The time that was recorded in our history a long time ago has come. The greater good has summoned me to stand against them. To finally bring the ending to the ones who would have sought to eliminate me and all of my kind since time began. To prove my claim and to prove my worth to all who sit and judge me forevermore. The old woman in the hooded cloak told me to present you with this to prove the authenticity of my declaration, which you have written down in the secret history."

Blink asked for permission to retrieve an item from her pocket, and the elder in the middle seat barely nodded to approve her request. Blink placed the wrapped-up item on the bench and stepped back, bowed her head and kneeled before them.

The elder seated at the centre of the bench gently unwrapped the package and showed the ancient relic to the other elders. They said nothing, and Blink was requested to stand before them. "Blink, daughter of Lucky, granddaughter of Gabriella, we grant you permission to leave. By the wisdom of the mother of mothers, we pray that the old woman in the hooded cloak will guide you and protect you and your warriors on the dangerous journey ahead. We will feast and celebrate before the next new moon, and then you may leave; we pray that you will never forget us, and we will honour you and your ancestors till the end of time. Blink, one day, we hope that you will return. Our history states that you will never return, but we see something in you that was never mentioned in the old book. Go forward with pride, go forward with our blessing and go forward to and put an end to the curse that has persistently tried to forever darken this world."

Blink had received the feast in her honour, and she, accompanied by her warriors, had left the next morning. They had set forth to make their way northwards into the great unknown. She felt deep down inside her that this was perhaps the sole reason that she was brought into this world. The recurring dream that she had been receiving since childhood may have some relevance to be unveiled in the venture ahead. Their ancestors had travelled across the vast ocean to reach this location many centuries ago. Blink, fully aware of the many insurmountable hardships that they had endured during the great crossing, provided her with nothing short of a massive dose of inspirational courage.

She had taken it upon herself to explain to every single member of her crew. Whatever the severity of the problems that arose to meet them, they would face them together, and together, they could defeat anything. Blink joined them in the motor launch and they started the journey North. One boat would race ahead, checking that the coast was clear, set up camp and wait for their arrival. They would rest and take shelter for a day or two, then repeat the process. If the advanced group came across any other groups, they would take the necessary course deviations required to avoid contact at all costs. Sometimes, this would involve several days at sea and when they came back inshore, again they would rest and recuperate. Blink was not exactly sure how far north they had to travel, but she was more than sure that they would have to arrive there fit, healthy and ready for anything.

Blink and her compatriots were slowly making progress, forever travelling northwards up the coast of South America. It was still relatively calm, and the currents and winds were mostly favourable. They had come across no hostiles on their journey; the odd distant exchange of gunfire sometimes was heard during the night. Blink hoped that it would remain this way for as long as possible. The last thing that she wanted was to be involved in a tooth-and-nail firefight before she met up with the one called Enunsha. The old woman in the hooded cloak had still not given her a precise location, but sooner or later, she would have to show her some form of a sign. Otherwise, they could be travelling northwards for just about forever.

In all the places that they had stopped over at, there had not been any recent signs of human habitation. She had seen numerous animal tracks but not one footprint and no signs of campfires. Blink thought that this was surely bound to change as they moved further up the coast. Her thoughts constantly worried her, and she thought that where people had gathered and established a settlement on the near inland areas of the coast, there was a distinct possibility of them participating in the abhorrent trade of piracy. Blink had reminded her crew to be on the constant lookout for wrecked crafts that showed signs of a struggle. She knew that if they travelled through the night, the time of the journey could be almost halved. She also knew that if they were to embark on that course of action, it would only leave them totally wide open to hidden dangers. In the coming few days, they would have to find some fuel otherwise, they would have to continue the journey by land. The worries about the dangers at sea, paled into insignificance when Blink compared them to the dangers that would exponentially increase if they were unfortunate enough to have to undertake the journey on the land. Blink settled in and drifted off to sleep, knowing with absolute certainty they would come across some fuel. The sentries on patrol would alert the camp if they sensed any unwelcome visitors approaching. She woke up just before dawn and assisted her people in preparing the communal morning meal, hoping that today Blink's crew were sheltering from the onset of bad weather. The storm had appeared out of nowhere and as she announced it to her crew, they had thought that she was delirious. Blink told them straight that she was not asking them to seek shelter. She was, in fact, ordering them to do so immediately. Almost as soon as Blink had reissued the order, the dark clouds had started forming almost above their heads. Luckily, there was a harbour close at hand, and on landing, they stormed ashore, half her crew checking that it was safe, the other half tethering the boats to a secure berth. In the two days that it had taken for the storm to pass, they had rested out of the gale-force winds and the torrential rain. Blink then knew that none of them would ever doubt her word again. She could appreciate that she was the youngest among them and by far the most inexperienced. Blink thought that she would not have been told of this journey by the old woman in the hooded cloak if she was not capable.

On the third day, the storm had abated enough for the crew to explore their surroundings. By chance, one of the ships at the other end of the harbour contained enough fuel to enable them to make most of the journey north. Blink thought it was too much of a coincidence and that perhaps the old woman in the hooded cloak had sent the storm to find the tanker. She gathered the crew together and formulated a new revised plan. The tanker would be checked, and if it were seaworthy, they would take it with them. As the vessel was slower, she would leave earlier and arrive later. To ensure that all was fair and equal, they would share all the duties; no one would be left to sail in the tanker for the whole journey.

They might lose a day or so in making the tanker seaworthy, but in the long run, they would save days, even weeks, in the time spent looking for other sources of fuel. Now alone, Blink prayed to the old woman to look over them and keep them safe, she said a prayer for her ancestors for their wisdom and their faith in the old ones. She heard a noise in the background; her crew had managed to get the rusting hulk working. Blink smiled, thinking that her grandmother would have said, "Never judge a book by its cover."

Blink and her crew we continuing their journey up the coast of South America, and the newly implemented plan of taking the tanker with them was working out fine. There had been no problems with the changeovers, and the refuelling schedules worked out just about fine. The overnight stops still had found no traces of recent human activity and they have encountered no problems whatsoever on their journey north. They had been travelling day upon day, and Blink still had no real idea when the journey would be over, but she had complete faith in the old woman with the hooded cloak, and her crew had complete unquestionable faith in her.

Somewhere near Texas, Enunsha had been up late and lucky for her, they had been roughing it, she had been plum worn out and had a quick nap with her clothes still on and had no awkward explanations to offer up to Abe. She did wonder why he was never in the dreams. The old woman with the hooded cloak had told her that the one called Blink would come and rescue her and her people. Enunsha wondered what the young woman could possibly do to save her from danger. She was a warrior, and even the dog soldiers were afraid of her; this would bother her for days. The ending also puzzled her: change, changes as it changes. There was so much she could read into this, but right now, she had some trucks waiting to get loaded up. Enunsha prodded Abe gently in the ribs, "Wakey, wakey honey, it is that time again, Jackson will already be looking at his watch, wondering when the next load will arrive."

Jackson was still pensively watching the grey-coloured ooze being discharged from the ends of the hoses. He relentlessly paced between the two filling points and talked to himself as he counted out the time intervals. Jackson figured that the stairwell would be just about full in about thirty minutes. They, by his calculations, were a full hour ahead of schedule; it could be a full day ahead and it would still not be happening quick enough. Jackson got another two discharge hoses shifted over to the lift shaft, instantly increasing the flow into the massive void. Perry had just about finished sticking the boxes into the required configuration. He walked over and asked Perry to gather up his squad, and he would show them all the next stage of the plan.

Perry was handed one rope, and Mike was handed the other; they watched as Jackson twisted and weaved them together. "That, guys and gals, is the double reverse Siberian hitch knot." They all looked at him as if he were the guest magician on a talent show, trying to outfox the judging panel. "Okay, I will show you all again." This time, he gathered all of them in closer, then slowly showed how the simple knot was done step-by-step. When he thought that they had finally mastered the process, Jackson left them to practise, returning to check the output from the hoses. When he returned, he watched as each of them performed the now simple knot. Jackson placed a small amount of the almond paste substance connected to the set timer in one of the spare boxes. He made them watch again as he placed it in the middle of the square-shaped pattern and covered it over with another full box. "I need you to wrap all this up in the plastic sheeting, then when complete, tie it up ready for lowering down the into the shaft."

Abe, Enunsha, along with her constant companion, Spotty, had arrived just delivering the replacement crew, food as well as coffee. Jackson grabbed a coffee and walked outside to smoke. Pete the Pumper was nursing his girlfriends, promising them all sorts of goodies if they didn't cause him any problems. Abe had thought he had heard him promising to get married to one of them along with starting family words, but pretended that he never heard a single word of it. He did ask Jackson about all the boxes now being lowered into the shaft.

"Well, these contraptions are boxes full of non-inflammable expanding foam. What you just saw being lowered down into the lift shaft will expand to ten times its volume. The almond paste will cause an explosion big enough to rupture the cans and apply pressure to the already poured cement mix. The applied force will push the mix into all the spaces that have been missed and the expanding foam will just add to the volume. The whole of the process with all the other boxes will only save us an hour or two, but we are at the stage where every hour counts." Abe and Enunsha just nodded; Spotty did not even look at him.

Jackson asked them if they had all the vehicles ready for the mass evacuation, and more importantly, they explained to everyone why they all had to leave. Enunsha did the talking, and she spoke to everyone, explaining the whys and, more importantly, the hows. "All I could tell them is that we have to move away and as we don't know where exactly, I just told them somewhere warm." Jackson just nodded, agreeing that was enough information for the time being.

The stairwell was now full; the last discharge hose had been dragged over and put in place to disgorge its contents into the lift shaft. Perry asked for his next set of orders; Jackson informed him that if they could, they should grab a couple of hours of shuteye. Still watching everything, he smoked and drank more of the rancid coffee. Peter the Pumper caught his eye and raised his cup, shouting, "Great coffee."

Jackson replied, "Sure is."

He wondered if Pete really believed that it was good coffee or if he was just shooting the shit. The next trucks had started to arrive, and Peter the Pumper jumped into action, dumping the coffee, immediately going to supervise his guys directing the grey goop down the extended chutes into the feed tanks.

Jackson was still constantly monitoring the grey sludge that plops out of the end of the discharge hoses. The wrapped-up packages of the expanding foam had all been completed and were numbered as per their scheduled time to be lowered into the shaft. Jackson had dismissed Perry and his crew, requesting that they report back for duty once their rest period was complete. He knew that the team would have carried out the next request immediately, but for this one, he really needed them to be on their toes and fully alert. Jackson knew that they had to relocate away from there, and the underground forces who had messed with them were still out there and could still be watching everything. The perimeter patrols had reported nothing and had been changed out regularly. Jackson thought that the bad guys could still be out there; the problem was that they could be hiding anywhere; before the group moved, he should at least scout out the surrounding area.

The next delivery arrived, and Jackson took a break from thinking, watching as the trucks moved into position to add their cargo to the feed tanks. He calculated that it was time to lower another package down into the lift shaft, which he did by himself. He looped the rope over the distorted elevator door frame, took up the strain, and then gently eased the next package over the side. The rope was fed over and into the void, and eventually, he felt a slight change in the weight. Jackson unhitched the rope from the frame and tossed it down into the lift shaft. He still thought that it was taking far too long to fill and wanted to get all of the people out of this god-forbidden place as soon as possible.

Perry had arrived, and so had the food; Jackson was so tired he could not taste what it was that he was eating but ate it anyway. Perry was going to mention that it would be a good idea if he had some rest, but he knew that it was not going to happen. Jackson downed the coffee and had several more while he and Perry looked over the map now placed in front of them.

Jackson pointed to the areas that he had marked out earlier, "I need you to go and check over all these areas to make sure that when the time comes, it will be safe for our convoy to travel through. You know the script: if you were going to set up an ambush, where would you set up? I hope you don't find anything. Nevertheless, I still need the whole area checked out."

Perry asked a few questions, and then, receiving all the information that he required, he gathered up his squad then led them out. Jackson returned to inspect the output of Peter the Pumper's machines, and this time, he actually heard the whoomph of the explosion. He rigged up the next package and gently lowered it down the lift shaft.

Abe, along with Enunsha, had arrived later; after passing out all the food and beverages, they had decided to go to pay a visit to Jackson. As they did not see him pacing around the place, they asked about it, and no one had seen him for quite a while. Spotty had found him slumped in the corner, fast asleep. Abe was all set to wake Jackson up but Enunsha persuaded him just to leave him be. They found some covers and gently laid then down on top of him and made it as comfortable as possible. Enunsha, without a doubt, knew that Jackson would be displeased about falling asleep on the job, but she was of the opinion that he was working non-stop and that, like it or lump it, he needed to sleep.

Enunsha had spotted all the loaded boxes containing the expandable foam; between them, they noticed the numbers. Jackson had not left any notes as to what the time sequence equated to, as in the time in between lowering them into the lift shaft. Nor did they know how long he had been sleeping for. "Abe, we can't take a chance and just hope that everything will be okay and these boxes won't explode and cause chaos."

Abe knew that this was a valid point and agreed. "Why don't we just get rid of them all, and even if we get it wrong, at least we have made a decision."

One by one, they manhandled the packages over to the opening of the lift shaft and lowered them down. Above all the noise, they could still hear Jackson snore away. They wondered if anyone had ever had the gumption to inform him that they were surprised that the devil himself had complained that he was so loud that he could wake up the dead.

Jackson had finally stirred back into life, and Enunsha delivered a round of applause. "I imagine that if you ever fallen asleep on public transport, you would have received a standing ovation when you awakened," Jackson asked if it was really that loud.

"Put it this way, you were louder than all the machines, and even Peter the Pumper was complaining that you were upsetting all of his girlfriends." He said sorry for falling asleep and wanted to know what he had missed. "We did not know what the time scale was for the boxes of expanding foam and did not want them to explode up here, so we made a decision then lowered them all down. None of us wanted to wake you. Even though you snore like the devil on heat, we figured that you must have needed it."

Enunsha handed him a coffee; Jackson thanked her and lit up a cigarette. Spotty did not like the smell of the smoke and wandered out of range. Enunsha walked with him as they went and inspected the progress on the lift shaft. She filled him in on the details regarding how many loads had been delivered to the pumps, and Jackson calculated the pending volume. "Later today, I think we should be about complete, and then we can get out of this place for good." He asked if the escape vehicles were all prepped, loaded and ready to leave.

Enunsha replied that everything was ready but added that everyone was asking where they were going to travel.

Jackson nodded, "I have Perry, along with his guys, out checking the route. Hopefully, they do not find anything. I intend to take us all South to an old army base down by the border. It will not be luxurious accommodation by any means, but we will be able to make it completely safe and secure." He saw her looking as if she was going to ask another question. "I know it will be a ball buster of a journey, but we now, honestly, have no choice." Jackson pointed to their recent upgrades, "They will not be too happy about the unsanctioned modifications, but we had to do something."

Jackson asked if there were any more of that special coffee on the go. Enunsha delivered a refill from the flask, and he asked her what Abe was doing. "Oh, he is out checking and shooting the shit with the teams on guard duty over at the perimeter. He thought it would be okay to go and speak to them."

Jackson agreed, suggesting that they go and join them. Peter the Pumper was observed in mid-conversation with his girlfriends, and neither of them had the heart to break up the intense lovey-dovey talk. The pair of them had distinctly overheard, "Look, baby, we will just move to a state where polygamy is legalised and well above board. Lots of people live like this these days, and honestly, honey, there will not be any problems."

Enunsha and Jackson just pretended that they never heard one word of it. Jackson thought that Peter the Pumper might have been incarcerated in a special psychiatric hospital prior to the spread of the sickness. Enunsha was pleased that he was a resounding success at this job and thought that she would run away if he returned to his former occupation. Just the thought of relocating Poison Pete back to the kitchen would give her and the rest of the entire camp endless nightmares and the possibility of potentially lethal food poisoning.

Abe had joined up with Jackson. As they looked into the lift shaft, they could clearly see the grey gunge rising up to meet them. They both knew that they could have left it half-filled, and it would have been just as effective. In filling the shaft to the very top, they were delivering a clear, concise message to the yet unknown underground group that they were prepared to hit them back. Jackson knew that they had not seen the last of them, and in the future, there would be additional grief. He hoped that it was they who suffered, and Jackson intended to give this group the upper hand in any action that transpired. Abe had delivered the latest update. The patrols on the perimeters still had nothing to report, and all the transportation was fuelled up, loaded ready to go. Jackson rechecked the level in the shaft, informing Abe to tell the people that they would be moving out at first light.

"Make sure you give them a good meal tonight and tell them that tomorrow will be a rather long day; the more rest they get, the easier the coming days will be for them," Abe confirmed that he would carry out what was required and asked Jackson if there was anything that he needed. "Lots of good luck with the possible addition of divine intervention." Abe smiled, hoping that it did not come down to that.

Peter the Pumper had not got the heart to tell his ladies that he would be leaving them in the morning and continued to sweet talk all through the night. Jackson was not worried about him; he just thought that he had some furniture missing upstairs. He also thought that he had done a great job in organising the pumping of all the sludge non-stop. The more Jackson thought about it everyone had contributed to a great overall effort in kicking back at the people who destroyed their future. Enunsha was the lead driver; she sat at the head of the convoy, waiting for Jackson to finish up. He had just witnessed the grey sludge reaching the top of the lift shaft and called for an immediate halt to the work. Jackson had run his finger across his throat twice in rapid succession, indicating to Peter the Pumper that it was time to say the final goodbye to his girlfriends.

As he made his way down the line of trucks waiting patiently to discharge their cargo, Jackson informed the drivers to leave the engines running and dump their loads where they stood. He cajoled and told the drivers to get on the transport that was waiting to take them all out of there. Jackson made sure every one of the workers, the perimeter patrol, was all accounted for and jumped in beside Enunsha. He calmly instructed her to take them out of there. Jackson gave her the details of the route they were heading in, taking in the view as they travelled towards the border region. Enunsha, Abe and Spotty had wondered why their bus was nearly empty. Jackson checked the map, asking her to pull over up ahead. Enunsha indicated to let the drivers know what was happening, and no sooner than she stopped, two of Perry's troopers climbed aboard. As Enunsha put the machine into gear and drove away, Perry's troopers informed Jackson that there was nothing at all to report. They continued driving for most of the day, occasionally stopping for everyone to pee and stretch their legs. On the last stop, they pulled into a truck stop and were met by another couple of Perry's troopers. They rested for the night there; the whole camp was pleased to know that Poison Pete was not doing any of the cooking.

Jackson and his convoy were still en route to their new home; they had collected most of Perry's troopers along the way. The good news was that none of the secret underground dwellers had surfaced. All the incoming reports were negative on hostile activity. Jackson knew the people were getting impatient and sick to death with all the overnight stops and temporary accommodations. With Enunsha at his side, Abe mentioned this fact to him several times; he would say that the hardships wouldn't have to be endured for much longer. The next day Perry is picked up, informing Jackson that all is good and the new accommodation has been prepared for their arrival. As they had all celebrated Christmas on the road, Perry had arranged a reasonably decent meal for their arrival.

The spread was not exactly traditional Christmas fare, but the chilidog's burgers accompanied with the real French fries were enjoyed by all, including Spotty. Jackson showed Abe and Enunsha around the former marine base, "Everything we need is here; we even have access to the ocean."

Enunsha asked what they would do for food, "I thought you were going to ask about that; please follow me." Jackson led the way to the vast storage area. "All of this works on solar power, and there is enough food in the freezer section alone to feed a full battalion for several years."

Abe piped up that they were not a battalion; Jackson looked at them both and let them matter-of-factly into his secret plan. "If we are going to survive, we are going to have to train all the people. Because if we don't, the people who fucked us over at the power station are going to arrive one day and wipe us off the face of the world."

Abe thought that Jackson had been planning this out for quite a while. "Don't fret about it for now, come and I will show you the new quarters; they are not what you would call five-star, more like four and a quarter."

Chapter 25

Gareth and his group, for once, had an easy day; the people from the harbour had not ventured out to investigate them. He knew for a fact that they had vastly superior numbers. The various types of weapons that they now possessed would render any aggression from Leena's crew utterly hopeless. Gareth did not want to attack them, hoping that Alwyn, Cinds' and Scruffy would have convinced them all that it was time to go. In failing that, by the goodwill and trust that he had displayed, they had an alternative choice of helping them acquire a suitable sea-going vessel and shipping him along with his crew out into the great unknown.

He never asked Leena how many people she had, how long they had been holed up here. Gareth had only highlighted the imminent danger that she and her people were undoubtedly facing in the very near future. It was not his choice. They had tried to be civilised from the very beginning, and the growing collection of the horrid tales from the south had spurned them into action. Gareth had tried hard to convince King David that they could work together, putting on a real show of strength. KD 1 had hardly listened to his appeal for a joint fighting force. Gareth had told him about the trained regiments of soldiers plus all the weapons they would bring to bear down upon them. Perhaps KD1 hoped to buy his way out or negotiate some pact offering a state of peaceful coexistence. The so-called liberation army will annihilate him along with all of his loyal supporters in less than a day. All of his accumulated wealth of gold and precious stones will still remain as worthless as it is now.

Alwyn had at last arrived back at their makeshift camp, "We have a deal, and believe it or not, you have Scruffy to thank."

Gareth was amased, fully aware of the fact that Scruffy had the vocabulary range and the associated diplomatic skills of an amoeba.

"He is related to a quite a few of them; they are all fucking cousins." Alwyn was going to add that his old professor would be performing cartwheels as he would have thought that, not only did he now have the fabled missing link in mankind's evolutionary chain. He now had full access to the whole of the missing fucking tribe. "Leena has invited everyone to come down to formulate the plan and have some hot food."

Gareth nodded, agreeing that it was all good news and rounded up his crew, spreading the word. 'Looks like we are going to the land that still eats their unborn after all.'

The convoy drove into the harbour; the whole of the main drag was now full of assorted vehicles; some of Leena's people came out to greet them, directing them where to park up. Gareth informed Leena that they should post a guard post at each end of the village, and in the newfound friendship, it should be a mixture of both groups. Leena agreed; in no time between them, they had sorted out who was going where. Once everyone had dumped their vehicles, Gareth along with his team were directed to the seafarers' club. Leena told him that for now, they could all eat, and then they could sort out all the other details later.

They walked past Scruffy, who was in deep conversation with his long-lost relations. "No, Aunty Violet was three doors down. That fat cunt, who made a mint in the middle east that had sold his council house to his son with, in his opinion, a generous five percent discount, stayed two doors down."

Gareth asked Alwyn if they were all really related. "It seems that Scruffy's father was humping anything that wore a skirt in the whole village. Oh, and before you even think of asking, I was from another area and as far as I am aware, we are not kith nor kin."

Leena had gone on her rounds, ensuring that all of Gareth's people were being fed and watered. Everyone here knew her by name. Surprisingly, there were no shouts of ' all hail Queen Leena' as she went from group to group. Even Alwyn for once seemed relaxed. Gareth was pleased that he and Cyril had put their differences well behind them; now, they actually spoke to each other civilly. Gareth thought that for sure Cinds must have had a quiet word with each of them to persuade them to cool their jets. She was a go the one who held everything together. Without her, he thought that the entire group would have faltered and then died.

"Are the lights on? Is anyone at home?" Leena had appeared with a couple of beers and a big map of the British Isles. "Okay, sailor, word is that you want to take me away from here then transport me faraway to a tropical island somewhere. That has a beach as far as the eye can see and has twenty-four-seven, constant sunshine all year long."

Gareth thought that she looked different now that she was not pointing a gun at him. "I guess that that island you are talking about will be in the far distant future otherwise, you would not be trying to entice me into looking at a map of the British Isles."

Leena pretended to look shocked, "Oh, honey, you caught me out and here's me thinking I was a femme fatal just about to lure you into my meticulously planned entrapment." They get down to the business of calculating what they need and where they need to go.

"I have by my recent calculation counted that you have one hundred and two able bodies, added to my motley crew, that gives us a grand total of one hundred and thirty-nine souls to put on boats. We don't have anything like that around here, but some other harbours a few miles north of here may have something more suitable. Gareth if you could sort out all the weapons, I will sort out all the provisions. We can do all the other stuff that is going to be required together or allocate some of our people for that task."

Gareth was all ears and could listen to her talk all night. He asked her to continue, and Lena blasted out the items that they would have to take onboard, like fuel, charged batteries, and jumper leads. He asked her to stop, and they would get a list made up and then compare the items required against the items that they may already have.

"I think that Alwyn and Cinds' can do this. He is shit hot with a pen and pencil. When I met him at first, I thought he was writing a fucking God-dam book." He took her over and reintroduced her to the dynamic duo; Gareth gave them the next task. Leena shouted a couple of her people over, filled them in with the details, and with the introductions over, she asked Gareth if he would like to go for a walk.

As they strolled around the harbour, she informed him that they would be more or less heading to somewhere on the west or east coast of Scotland. As the weather will have changed by the time they leave, the Atlantic is less than friendly at that time of year. "Cape Wrath is a particularly dangerous spot, full of rocks and unpredictable currents in the summertime. As you can guess, it is not a recommended winter sailing route, and we should avoid it at all costs. There are plenty of places we can shelter in, and maybe some of the locals, if they are not too busy eating their children, could tell us where we could find another group with the same outlook as yours. Gareth, for the record, I am not saying that I do not want to sail around the top of Scotland, even the sailors that are born and bred in that area avoid this stretch of water in the winter."

Both of them agreed that they would not decide on the final destination until they had the ship or ships fully equipped and ready to sail. Leena had promised to teach him how to read the weather, and just out of curiosity, she asked him if he had ever been on a boat; before he answered, she told him that a paddling boat in the local pond did not count.

Gareth confirmed that he was one hundred percent a confirmed land lover and asked her why she had aired that question. "Nothing really, just that your face was starting to turn several shades of green at the mere mention of unpredictable ocean currents."

He freely admitted that he was not looking forward to the journey and asked her if he had to learn sea shanties as part of the deal for a safe passage.

Leena did not answer, just smiled, thinking that she was going to have to add lots of buckets for Gareth and company to puke into.

As it was getting late, Gareth said that he should go and sort out where he was going to be Roger the lodger, for the next few days. Leena shook her head, "You don't have to bother; I have already made the arrangements."

She did her unofficial tour guide, leading him through several of the narrow-cobbled streets. Drawing to a halt, Leena opened the door, informing him that this was where they would be staying. "I don't know about you, but being in charge sort of makes life a little difficult, as everyone is constantly watching and commenting about everything you do, every decision that you make." She led him to the bedroom, stating for the record that he should consider this as part of the terms and conditions for his safe passage, then started to undress. Gareth had no problems with the adhoc agreement.

The next morning, he and his group had been out in the fishing boats. Gareth was puking his guts up five minutes after being introduced to the undulating motion of ocean waves. Leena shook her head and cancelled the planned trip to sail out of the harbour. He had purposely not consumed any food prior to the journey, but it had not made one blind bit of a difference. Gareth thought that he was dying and made Leena promise that she would not bury him at sea.

She offered him a sweet cup of tea, and he asked her if she was really trying to kill him. Leena told him to stop moaning and just drink it, "Sooner or later, your body will acclimatise to the new surroundings, and your brain will be able to compensate, sending the message out to the rest of your body that all is okay."

Gareth asked if she thought that was really true. Leena replied in all honesty that it was a pack of lies, but he would hurt himself if he continued to retch on an empty stomach.

She then taunted him with "land ahoy" and various offers of inviting him to join in and sing sea shanties.

Gareth confided in her that she was truly the evilest woman he had ever met.

Leena burst out laughing, confessing that all the sailors throughout her life had told her exactly the same thing.

He did what he was told and immediately was leaning over the rail adding a new food supply for the creatures that dwell below the waves.

In between the vomiting, he had asked how long she was going to subject him to this torture, and Leena had simply informed him that it would continue for however long it took.

Storage space, as well as bunk space, will be limited on the vessel, and he had to take that into consideration that no one wanted to have the pleasant planned voyage on the open sea disrupted by all of his people puking everywhere. He is handed the next cup of sweet tea, and now looking greener than green, he drinks it as fast as he can. The liquid barely has time to reach his stomach and he is holding on for dear life as he takes another turn at feeding the fish.

His entire crew had been out in a boat today, and almost all of them had succumbed to the sickness. The only one who did not have any problems was Cinds'. Later that night after they had berthed the boats, she was the only one of the newcomers in the galley eating. All the others had all stumbled off for the relative security of their beds, feeling worse for wear and tear at their introductory free sailing lesson.

Leena asked her if she had done it before, and she confessed that she had indeed done a stint in the Navy. Cinds' admitted that she soon got sick of all of the rest of the ships' company trying to get into her pants, and she had packed it in.

She asked how Gareth had taken to the water, and Leena informed her that he was so worn out by the seasickness that he had fallen asleep before they had returned to the harbour. "He will do better in tomorrow as I have planned that we go out at first light."

The search for a suitable vessel was still underway, and Leena, in the meantime, had all the items that they would require gathered and then stored. She hoped that when the vessel arrived, it would be a quick turnover simply involving loading her up and leaving as soon as possible.

They could always supply Gareth and his would-be sailors with sea sickness tablets if it came down to it. It would not really matter if the little tablets were way past the sell-by dates; the psychological stamp that would be imprinted on their brains would convince them all that they were now in possession of temporary immunity. They discussed the voyage ahead, which was very much dependent on the vessel and the weather that awaited them.

Leena had emphasized time and time again that at this time of year, even the Irish Sea could be unforgiving and totally unpredictable. "We would just have to wait and see what the conditions are; other than that, we will sail for as long as possible until Gareth finds what he is hoping exists in the northern regions of this country."

Gareth has at last managed to find his sea legs, and although he still did not particularly enjoy going out on the boats, the thought of it no longer made him want to puke. Leena had taken to calling him skipper; he did not know if this was a compliment or if she was referring to something else entirely. Today, he was in charge, and she informed him that they were going out into the sound. At first, he thought that it was something to do with music but then realised that they would be going out into the open water. "Don't worry; you will be fine; if we had a bath, you would experience the strange sensation of being in a boat, but as we don't have one, you can just take my word on that."

The larger boat or ship had arrived. Leena had explained the correct term and the type of vessel it was but he could not remember. All he knew was that it was big enough to take everyone and all of the kit they needed to take with them out of there. He hoped that the loading was finished soon and they would leave before the liberation army or whatever they were calling themselves arrived. Up till now, there had been no reported sightings or any news relating to them, but deep down inside, he had this uneasy feeling that they were coming for vengeance.

Cinds', Alwyn and the rest of his crew had taken to the water like they were born for it. Only Scruffy and himself were the star pukers. Leena had told him that one of her crew had wanted a vote on placing the two of them in a separate boat and towing them for the whole journey. She had added that as soon as they had stopped turning green at the mere mention of the sea, the proposed vote had been rescinded, but she added only by a narrow majority. Gareth knew that she was taking the piss, and all of his exploits on the ocean waves had amused her no end.

He checked everything according to her rule book, ordered the ropes to be untied and gently steered away from the harbour. Gareth checked the course heading and carried out the minor adjustments by turning the wheel accordingly. He kept his eye on the instrument reading and increased speed, taking her up to the required knots.

Leena said nothing and closely watched her protégée; maybe in another life, they could have been sailing to an unpopulated island somewhere in a warmer climate. She had never asked him, and he had never asked her what they had done for a living in the old world.

They had today, and all was going well. They had tomorrow; after that, it was all an uncertain adventure, neither of them knowing what the future had in store for them. Now, in the big, wide ocean, Leena ordered him to lock the engines into hoover mode; Gareth did not know what this was. She showed him how to keep the engines ticking over and dragged him below to make him earn his sea badge. Gareth thought that perhaps he would take to liking sailing after all.

On returning to the harbour, Leena and Gareth had just received bad news: the so-called liberation army had arrived in force and was now destroying everything in their path. Both of them agreed that it was now time to leave; they called their people together, telling them that the time had come and they must leave immediately. "We will be leaving within the hour; only take what you can carry, and sorry, that is all that you will be allowed. Time is of the essence, so let's move it."

Gareth had pulled some of his team aside, "Have you got everything that was required?" Alwyn nodded, acknowledging that everything he and Leena had requested was prepared and ready. "Okay, once we start loading on all the people, set it all up, and I will see you on the ship."

There was a flurry of activity as all of the passengers were directed by the crew to board the small boats that were going to ferry them across to the ship in the middle of the harbour. Alwyn, Cinds' and Scruffy had started working at the other end of the pier and moved from boat to boat. As Scruffy was the strongest, it was his job to unhitch the ropes and push the small vessels out into the water. They had to stop and rethink as the boat they had pushed out had just returned to the pier. Leena, noticing their predicament, sent a couple of her people over to show them how it was supposed to be done. Ten minutes later, with the engine fired up and the wheel locked in position, the first of the doomed boats were heading, under their own steam, out into the open harbour.

All the other small boats that had ferried the passengers to the ship were tied together and laid at anchor for the arrival of Gareth's and Leena's helpers. Gareth was worried about the time and was tempted to shout out, "Number five, your time is up!" Eventually, the last remaining passengers departed from the pier and then sailed towards them.

They tied up to the small flotilla of now abandoned boats, and fifteen minutes later, with all the work completed, the last of the combined group climbed aboard the ship. Leena gave the signal; the ship's engines slowly increased speed, and the vessel steered towards the harbour exit. The homemade devices that Cinds' and company had placed in the newly abandoned boats started to detonate, and one by one, they surrendered to the water then sank to the bottom of the harbour. Some of these boats had been in the families for generations, but the thought of leaving them to rot, tied up at the pier, did not go down too well with the soon-to-be ex-owners. They had held a meeting and asked Leena to arrange to have them all scuttled in the harbour. As the last one sank under the waves, the locals took a final look at the place they had called home as their ship manoeuvred out of the harbour into the Irish Sea.

Gareth joined the captain on the bridge, and Leena was giving course adjustments to the woman at the helm. He stood to attention and saluted her; Gareth was quite surprised that he never got piped onboard.

Leena had her back to him but could see his reflection in the glass and snapped, "Any more nonsense from you, and I will have you keelhauled." She turned to face him, "Please check that everyone has settled in okay and make sure that the people in the galley have hot tea on the go."

Gareth just looked at her, "Don't even bother thinking about saluting; see you later." It had taken him ages to get used to being on the open water; Gareth about turned and headed towards the galley. He knew that this was a journey into the great unknown, but at least they would evade being captured by the so-called liberation force, who, by all accounts, just intended to kill everyone they came across.

After carrying out his orders, he was now on the bridge and remained silent as Leena handled the helm; she moved it ever so slightly every time the forward-facing spotters indicated that they saw something ahead of them in the water. It could be a slightly different wave movement, a discarded plastic bag, or a differently shaped wave. All of them could be a reason for something else and the very reason that could rip the hull apart. He fucked off, returning with a cuppa.

Leena took hold of it without taking her eyes from the water ahead and around them. Her eyes were still glued to what was out in front of her. Leena was still issuing the small course adjustments to the helmsman. She was looking at the huge expanse of ocean in front of them, and she was very worried. She ordered a change of speed and an immediate alteration to the course heading. Gareth had carried out his last task without any complaints or questions. He couldn't understand why she never said anything, and he followed her. Leena was scanning the area that, moments ago, they would have sailed right through.

Gareth did not know what she was looking at; Leena handed him the binoculars. He saw the wreckage lying just under the water and now understood why she was not speaking and was in such a hurry.

Leena said in concern, "As the light is fading, we will need to stop. I don't know how much of this area has been used as a dumping ground, and it is too dangerous to continue in the dark." The harbour was miles behind them, and they were far enough out in the open sea for anyone to spot them from the shore. Leena issued the orders for an all-stop on the engines, "We will wait it out till first light, and when we continue again, we will need to place some people on the prow and keep a sharp lookout for any more partially sunken wrecks."

Gareth understood and asked her which of her people she wanted for the duty. Leena rattled off a list of names, and he did not salute her as he went to locate the required personnel for the task.

Leena thought that if they had collided with one of the wrecks, they would be scuppered as the ship did not have any lifeboats. It had a few of the emergency type of inflatable boats but nowhere near enough to save everyone. She sipped a brandy to calm down and thought that they would have to do better in the future if they were going to survive. They had not been in the open water for that long, and they had not been travelling at full speed. Leena wondered what the rest of the inner coastal waters would be like; there could be all sorts of sunken and abandoned vessels just lying out there, drifting about untethered at the mercy of the currents and tidal movements. Her nominated watchers have now reported to the bridge, and Leena informed them what task they would be undertaking at first light.

Gareth, fully aware of being unable to be of any help in here in the bridge went off to see if anyone else required his assistance. With nothing better to do, he went down into the galley come rec room. As he scanned the room for a familiar face, he spotted Cinds' and the gang in the corner. Gareth pulled up a seat, joining in the conversation, and they got around to where they were going and, more to the point, when they were actually going to arrive there. All he could say for sure was that they were heading to the safest place he could think of, and he hoped that when they reached the coast of northern Scotland, they would be able to connect with another group. "In order to start fighting back, we have to join up with a larger group. At present, there are just not enough of us to make a difference; we could carry out hit-and-run operations, but eventually, we would run out of room to manoeuvre and people. I think that amalgamating with others, just like us, is the only way forward."

Cinds' asked him, "What if we don't find another group?"

Gareth admitted that they would be well and truly fucked. Alwyn asked if that translated to that they would need to leave the UK, Scruffy added his ten pence and informed the table that it would be safer if they left the planet.

Gareth replied that he hoped it did not come to that and made his way back up to the bridge. Leena was shouting orders to the engine room; it looked as if there was a problem developing with one of the engines. She told them to shut it down immediately and try to find out what the problem was.

Leena noticed that Gareth had returned and said, "If we hit rough water, we will struggle with only one engine. That means we either fix it and hope we have calm seas, or we pull into a sheltered area and carry out the repairs there. Before we do anything, the guys in the engine room will have to find out what the problem is and the hope that we have the all of required spares to resolve the issue."

Gareth thought that translated to buggered if we do and buggered if we don't. The light was fading in about an hour, and they would be stopping for the night. Gareth made himself useful and went down to the engine room to enquire if they needed any other mechanics to assist them during the night. He had taken the liberty of going to get his guys and take them down to introduce to the crew down below. If the mechanics were okay with it, he would leave his guys down there with them, and they could speak in engine talk.

Chapter 26

Miasnikov had now just about finished with Hull; someone he had found a brochure about the entertainment delights that were waiting to be discovered in the allegedly sunny all year-round Blackpool. He wondered if this was true, and at the very least, he hoped that it was just not another shithole of a town like the one he was just about to burn to the ground. His people had rounded up all the available stragglers, and after the vetting process, he had sent the ones that were still breathing down south. The happy prisoners would now be on their way to the various entertainment packages that awaited them with open arms down by the capital.

He thumbed through the brochure, and a tune came into his head; it was almost something that you would hear the international brigade of brain-dead football supporters sing. The ones who devoutly followed the various third-rate teams that proclaimed to be a professional club but had never actually won anything. Miasnikov admired their tenacity in their unquestionable belief that their chosen team was the best in the world and just put it down to bad luck and numerous unscrupulous referees why they had never won anything. "We're all going to Blackpool, oh we're all going to Blackpool, da-na-na na, da-na-na na." He had to stop himself, or he would be singing this all day long, and what would his people think of him then?

Vladimir chucked the brochure aside, then gave out the order to commence burning the town. It had not been an exhilarating post but he at least provided some entertainment. These details he intended to put into his warts-and-all revealing memoir. There was one thing about raising a town to the ground: it always gave him an appetite. He hoped the next stopover would provide him with some decent fare, nothing too rich, nothing too bland just some good old English cooking, if there was such a thing.

Hull was aflame, and now, on the outskirts of the once fine city full of listed buildings, lit up the sky. Informing everyone and anyone who could see the grand spectacle, that ready or not he was coming, he was coming to flush you all out.

Miasnikov thought that they would come in contact with Olga along the way, and that should be soon, as she should have dropped off her passenger and now be on the return journey. He also wondered how JJ was progressing in Wales, with the wall-to-wall of mutant rebellious sheep attacking him on all fronts. Miasnikov had changed his tactics and stopped rushing into towns and villages to clear out any of the would-be resistance fighters. He had taken a liking to having all of his artillery set up and then being seated a safe distance away to avoid the deafening noise. Miasnikov enjoyed his lunch, and as the waiter poured a glass or two of fine wine, he viewed the destruction through the binoculars. Vladimir even had a runner on hand to relay any required coordinate changes. Miasnikov usually let the salvos continue until he had finished eating, mounted his tank, and led the armoured division on the wanton destruction of the village or town.

He had issued orders not to even look for people, ordering that every house or building was to be viewed as a legitimate target. Miasnikov had trucks full of ammunition and was aware that there were more than ample stocks available at all of the various storage depots located throughout this country and the best part about it all was that they were all free issue.

The office block was, as far as he was concerned, an eyesore, nothing but a blot on the once rather picturesque English town. He directed all the tanks to acquire his selected target, on the issued order they fired simultaneously. Miasnikov was delighted with the achieved results. Now, with the offensive building nothing more than a smouldering heap of rubble, he advanced the division forward. His men had been positioned on the outskirts; some days, he placed them in the south, and other days, he placed them in the north. Either way, they always got some shooting practice in.

Miasnikov was still very disappointed in the fact that of the great British public's reticence in not having the gumption to face him and have a good old-fashioned battle.

On completion of removing this soon-to-be-forgotten place from the map, he calculated the distance involved before he forced his troopers to give him a hearty rendition of "Oh, we're all going to Blackpool, oh we're all going to Blackpool da-na-na na, da-na-na na."

He wondered if he should get all of them scarves and pendants to wave and twirl about in the pretence that they were a visiting team of football supporters coming to enjoy the friendly rivalry. Miasnikov thought that it did not really matter what they thought. Sooner or later, the local inhabitants would realise that they were an invading army heading their way to render their town uninhabitable and eliminate as many of the people as possible.

Miasnikov had eventually reached Blackpool; he had obliterated every town that he had passed through to reach this much-hallowed place. As he was in awe of all the entertainment venues on display, he had ordered a halt to the destruction. Miasnikov wanted a tour of all and everything that was on offer; he had ordered his troops to follow him when he saw something that was of interest, something that caught his eye for the obligatory certain modifications. Miasnikov requested a hearty rendition of "Oh we're all going to Blackpool, oh we're all going to Blackpool Da na, na, na, Da na, na, na." He did not have a clue as to what da, na, na, na meant, but he doubted that anyone else on the planet knew either.

Miasnikov loved the way his troopers waved the football scarved around like medieval warriors trying to intimidate the opposing clans prior to the onset of battle. If he had a plentiful supply of prisoners, he would re-enact a battle right now between rival football supporters. He did not give two fucks that his side would have a miss match of scarves displaying various clubs, and he could not care less what the home team's choice of colours would be.

He thought that this idea had an almost endless list of possibilities. Miasnikov was bemused that if he was unfortunate to be in Glasgow rather than sunny Blackpool, he would only have the choice of two colours. This whole concept, he had never fully understood, and he did not think that the primitive bipeds had fully got to grips with it either.

The alleged, prime species on this planet had, for centuries, fought with each other over this issue. Even in a city in ancient Rome, he couldn't quite remember the exact name but what he could recall was that one night they had a chariot race. The blue team beat the red team or the purple team, anyway whatever the fuck the colour was, the losing team went nuts, and thousands of people died that night. These humans thought that they were special, sophisticated and advanced, but they would switch back instantly to primitive biped mode, and as soon as the referee blew the whistle, they would be sharpening their weapons. He thought for many of them, it did not really matter if they won. It did not matter if their team lost; it was genetically imprinted tribalism that many of them would never be able to escape from.

They could be stock brokers, bank managers, hedge fund consultants, but as soon as they put on the colours, they were fucking raging lunatics. They would gather en route to the venue. The numbers steadily increased at every junction, and the tribalism meter would rise slowly but was always guaranteed to go into the red. By the time they had entered the venue, the scene was reminiscent of the latest batch of clones with extreme tunnel vision and intense hatred of the other team. If any of their relations supported the other team, they were hated equally as much as the rest of the opposing clan.

Miasnikov had been inadvertently drawn into the infectious hype and gave his troops orders to wreck the shops along the front. Soon, the made-in-Blackpool ornaments, the ones that you suddenly lacked or no longer held any interest in after your immediate purchase, or the ones that were delivered to relations and close friends as presents. These were the ones that were binned as soon as the bearers of the gifts left the house. They were all then crashing through shop windows and car windows. Some of the larger items, along with lots of the smaller ornaments, were just being taken out on the street and being ceremoniously reduced to trash.

These items bearing the indigenous slogans "made in Blackpool" were allegedly made in the far east, and even the people who made them could not understand why anyone would even think about buying this crap. Miasnikov had joined in and was in the process of jamming a replica model of Blackpool tower down someone's throat when he was informed that he had just been delivered a dispatch from the Baroness of Kindeace-Shire.

Miasnikov stomped and booted the replica tower until the pointy end made an appearance through the back of her neck. He then called for a change of chant, and his fellow tribal group joined in with a heartier rendition of "We are the champions da, na, na, da na, na."

He was blissfully unaware of what they were the champions of but quite liked the little tune. As he opened Lesqueths latest communique, no doubt just the latest episode of tongue-twisting, unproduceable fucking long words. He continued to hum and dance along with, "We are the champions! Da, na, na, na. Oh, we are the champions! Da na, na, na."

The other families would soon be joining him, they have sent emissaries proclaiming greatness to their glorious leader, the Baroness of Kindeace-shire. They had moved up from the south, destroying city after city. Miasnikov was not put up nor put down with all the news. He thought that destroying one British city was exactly just the same as destroying any British city. There was no distinction between any of them as they were all equally as ugly and equally depressing as each other. If they had given him some notice, some reasonable notice he could have arranged some spectacular entertainment for them.

As he waited to greet them, Miasnikov was flicking through a brochure that contained all the famous attractions that unbelievably attracted visitors from all over the world. He thought that this could be a little porky pie; perhaps even the editor of this brochure had a very sharp pencil and creative licence just to write anything he damn well pleased. World famous or not, Miasnikov thought that once all his modifications were installed, this place would potentially have the most innovative fairground rides in history. The ghost trains were crying out for an urgent revamp. The loop carts that were all joined together and hurtled about, he thought that the track could be extended all the way out to the end of the pier. He noted that there were a few piers there, and he was not particularly bothered about which one would be featured. Anyone of them would do but took a mental note to enquire which one was situated in the deepest stretch of water.

Miasnikov could spend weeks there just listing everything that he wanted changed. The tower was fairly interesting and perhaps he could do something with it. "The Tower of Fire," "The Death Tower Comes to Blackpool," and lastly, "Save one of your loved ones from the Tower of Torture." This could be a game show and he would require a captive audience, perhaps even include a death wire that was not just a zip wire. The list was endless; he was so excited at the prospect of unlimited entertainment that he thought he would have trouble getting to sleep at night.

Miasnikov then settled in the cleaned hotel suite and opened Lesqueth's dispatch.

He was duly informed that Bartram and his sister had not been in contact for some time, and he had to deploy a unit to go and investigate. He, if he got away with it, would inform Lesqueth that it could be a simple case of them shagging non-stop and Bartram forgetting what day it was, never mind him remembering to send regular reports. The Baroness also reminded him that an up-to-date report on his recent activities was expected within the next two days. This section had been underlined, and she had added no excuses that it would be tolerated in brackets. Miasnikov pulled the cords the rang the bells throughout the hotel, informing every one of his staff that he required something.

He had been told which cord represented the various services that he required from time to time but he had not paid any attention and had pulled them all. They all would arrive, and one of them would be the note taker; another would be his runner who delivered instructions to the various units serving under his command. They all arrived at the same time; the scribe was told to construct a story about what his units had achieved since reaching Hull. While she scribbled away, the runner was ordered to send a unit north to inform Bartram that he had to send a fully detailed report immediately, without fail, to the Baroness. Miasnikov wanted food, vodka and for them all to fuck off and give him some peace and quiet. He informed the scribe as she was on the way out to draw up the various orders, plus the reports, and he would check and sign them in the morning.

Miasnikov was now thinking how the new name would sound, "Escape from the Tower of Death." He thought that this new name was just about perfect and slurped on some vodka while he imagined what delights he could install and then terrorise the contestants with. The death slide could be the number one, the major attraction in this new exhibition. To make it a truly resounding success, he would have to invent something totally new, and it would have to be exquisite and spectacularly nasty. He wondered if his little sister, sweet and considerate Irena, would give him permission to borrow the pair of Siberian tigers for a couple of weeks.

Vladimir could use crocodiles and alligators or construct a pit and fill it full of poisonous snakes but very much doubted that any of his favourite animals would still be found alive in this God-forsaken country where they think fried everything was a pure unadulterated fucking delicacy. Miasnikov was transferring the ideas from his head to the once-expensive wallpaper. He had just drawn a big black sloping line down the length of the wall when there was a knock on the door. The food had arrived; he looked under the silver platter, shook his head and told them to take it away. "If the next attempt is not a vast improvement, you and the culinary delights will be leaving via the window."

He slammed the door in their face, concentrated, and then returned to sketching up all the envisioned ideas for his masterpiece. Irena's tigers would, however, be an added bonus; perhaps he could just confiscate them.

Miasnikov had been awake since dawn; he looked at all the detailed modifications required to be installed the once-famous tower. Without a doubt, he thought that it was a true masterpiece whether anyone would be able to decipher his unique style of sketching while under the influence of copious amounts of vodka remained to be seen. Miasnikov was full of self-praise and intended to get the construction work started today. The paperwork had arrived for his perusal and signatures. Lesqueth's report was pages long and, at his insistence, was full of all the managerial speak that he truly despised. Miasnikov initialled every single page and signed without complaint on the dotted line. "I want this sent immediately, without delay."

The woman who had replaced Anna stood at attention, saluted and left immediately. She had left the details of the unit that had been sent out to remind Irena and Bartram that they were duly obliged to keep in contact. The more he thought about it, the tigers would be far happier with him. His morning meal was due to be delivered in the next few minutes, and he opened the window in anticipation of another rancid plateful of unidentified, undercooked animals that were meant to represent a full English breakfast.

He was astounded and, for once, sent his congratulations to the cook. He ordered them to close the window and tucked into his nearly perfect meal. Miasnikov summoned the mechanics and the other technical people who would transform his half-arsed ideas and turn them into a stark reality. As they arrived, he made them wait until he finished eating. They all stood at attention in line, wondering what he was going to come up with next. Their boss was completely unpredictable, and they received no hint or no clue as to what he wanted this time; no doubt it would be another hair-brained scheme. That was almost impossible to create to his delusional envisaged concept of engineering. They often lacked the basic rudimentary understanding of how things actually work and perform.

Miasnikov stood and placed his hands on his hips, belched and started his impromptu meeting. He pointed to the wall that they all had thought was graffiti from the under-five age group that had escaped from the local asylum. "Ladies and gentlemen, this is my next creation, 'Escape from the Tower of Death.' As you can clearly see from my more than informative, finely detailed sketches, I have supplied you with an image of what I want you to create and where I would like the specific enhancements placed. In the clouded-out sections, I have painstakingly noted what delights are expected to be revealed at these points."

He advised them to take all the notes they required, and reminded them that out of all the technological wizardry that he had made them build previously, they were all nothing compared to this engineering marvel. "I would like to think that without any undue interference, you will carry out all that is required with due diligence and utmost haste. The heads of the other families and all their troopers will be arriving soon, and I would like this project to truly represent what we are about and what we can achieve."

The general was knocked out of his stride by a knock on the door; he pointed for someone to open it. He noticed the uniform of Lesqueth's despatchers; Miasnikov dismissed the mechanics and the other fixers, reminding them to commence work straight away as they left his room. He signalled the dispatcher to come forward. Miasnikov held his hand out for the expected paperwork. The dispatcher stood and announced that there was no mail and that she was there to inform him of the serious news. She asked for permission to speak, "JJ and his entire force have been eliminated, and a dispatch is on its way to our esteemed leader, the Baroness of Kindeace-Shire. Due to the seriousness of the news, we thought that you should be notified immediately." Still standing at full attention she waited for his reply.

Miasnikov pulled all the cords continuously until his assistants started to arrive, "Summon all of my commanders and have the maps set up in the grand dining hall immediately."

The dispatcher who had arrived from Wales was interrogated, and once she had passed over all the information, he ordered her to go and get some food and rest. His scribe listened to the partially understandable words spewing out his mouth and translated them into something resembling actual words for his urgent message to be delivered to Lesqueth as soon as possible. Miasnikov stated that he was going to assemble his forces and capture the rebels in Wales who were responsible for the demise of JJ and his forces.

He then stood before his commanders in the dining room and addressed the situation. Miasnikov laid out the plan before them; he pointed at the location where JJ was located.

He drew arrows on the map to inform them of where they would attack from and where they would meet up. The coordinated battle plan would involve the remaining families coming up from the south who were presently being contacted to change the previous plan. The commanders were informed that they had moved out at first light, and he wanted the ringleaders captured alive. Miasnikov would have to wait to see the fruition of his plan for the "Tower of Death" but very much hoped that when he returned from Wales, he would have an ample supply of volunteers to entertain him in Blackpool.

The Baroness of Kindeace-Shire has just received the news about JJ. She ordered her new aide to get her a brandy. Lesqueth said a prayer to the fallen, the vanquished and the fallen. His body would have to be recovered and buried with all the full military honours bestowed on a great warrior. The Baroness wanted to know all the details, where it happened, how it all went down, and how could simple inbred farmer's sons and the misspent youth of permanently bitter miners managed to defeat her forces. She demanded the presence of her scribe, Miasnikov would have to be sent to Wales. Lesqueth suspected that he had all sorts of entertainment planned to take place in his new temporary headquarters, but for now, all that would have to be curtailed for another time.

The scribe was informed that she wanted Wales raised to the ground, every town, every city, every village had to be destroyed. If there happened to be any prisoners captured, she wanted them sent down to her for interrogation. The Baroness wanted the dispatch sent immediately and the driver to return immediately with the reply. Every other commander under her control was also sent a direct change of orders and instructed to meet up with Miasnikov and pull out all the stops and obliterate the country that had taken JJ away, well before his time.

She thought that JJ should be buried where this country had interned all of their kings, queens, and prime ministers. On reflection, Lesqueth thought about digging up all the old bones and all the work that it would entail. The Baroness of Kindeace-Shire had a complete change of mind and was now intent on building a mausoleum, something that would last for centuries, reminding everyone that true heroes did, indeed, exist. In her and her future family's eternal reign, she would show future generations that heroes are never forgotten. Miasnikov was sad, not about the loss of JJ but about having to nip in the bud his new entertainment package. He had thought that it was going to be the very best method of disposing of the unwashed and unwanted human debris that had managed to survive the great sickness.

Miasnikov had then more trucks and equipment than he could count and watched as the huge convoy snaked across the land. His troops had come across what was to be an international competition where armies from all over the world pitted their wits and their new technologies against each other. Due to the sickness, the event never happened, and they had just freely donated many more tanks and even some missile launchers to his cause. Miasnikov does not think that his troopers even know how some of them were operated, but still, they would have plenty of time to learn the new skills as they rained fire and death down onto the stubborn bi-peds. When it came to obliterating townships and the urban sprawl that infected all of this land, Miasnikov truly enjoyed being in the lead tank. He coordinated the artillery fire from the turret and got the odd chance of keeping his machine gun skills up to date in mowing down potential escapees trying desperately to flee the ensuing devastation and destruction. Miasnikov had issued a warning to all of his tank and rocket brigade commanders. If any of them failed to remove the munitions loaded with the florescent paint, he would transfer the offending crew and their commander to the live fire target group.

He was interrupted by yet another despatch from the Baroness of Kindeace-Shire; the driver saluted and stood.

Miasnikov read the message and scribbled on the back of it that his company was now en route to sunny Wales. He also stated that as soon as he had received the news, he had sent her a dispatch informing her of the change in circumstances that warranted a change to his standing orders. He underlined the passage that this was not a direct challenge, and he was only carrying out what she would have expected him to do. Miasnikov promised to keep her up to date and signed off. He stuffed his reply back into the envelope and ordered the driver to deliver it personally to their great leader. He stood at attention and saluted the despatch driver, wishing them a safe journey.

Miasnikov had relentlessly followed the trail of destruction that JJ had left in his wake. The town that was decorated with the pile of the dead beneath the clock tower was even, by his standards, quite impressive. He followed the route JJ had taken by the burnt-out vehicles and the newly dug graves. Miasnikov thought that JJ had come into contact with more than just rebellious sheep, and he was very much looking forward to being introduced to all of them. His forward group had located where the final battle had occurred and they had started to dig the graves when Miasnikov had arrived.

The rebels had no insignia, no uniforms, and just looked like normal civilians. He ordered that these people had to be left out in the open for the animals, insects and weather to reduce them to a pile of bones. Miasnikov summoned his commanders, and over the displayed map, he issued his orders, "Somebody out there in this wilderness knows something, and you are going to find them."

While his troopers scoured the outlying regions, Miasnikov destroyed every single village and town that he came across. Each and every single dwelling received a gift from one of his tanks. He issued no warnings, no come out with your hands up. They just drove in, took up position and blasted away. In the last few days, they had seen no one; not one solitary figure had been spotted trying to evade them. If anyone had attempted to approach him, it would have done them no good. Miasnikov had issued a firm request to shoot everyone on site. At last, they had reached the outskirts of the last city, it was surrounded, and Miasnikov and his forces had every exit covered. The artillery and the rocket launchers would commence the bombardment at dawn. He realised his potential life-threatening mistake in that the Baroness was expecting prisoners. Immediately issuing new orders for capturing some of the indigenous people for questioning. He scanned the view in front of him: just another ugly city crying out for destruction, and this country had way too many of them.

Miasnikov was deep in thought; he rated JJ very highly, and he was trying to figure out how a nation of interbred sheep lovers and a horde of the bitterly unemployed had managed to defeat him. JJ had received all the training, he had all the necessary skills, unquestionable leadership and could be ruthless when and where required. His thoughts were interrupted as one of his commanders' approached; the woman stood to attention and then saluted. After getting permission to speak, she announced that a delegation from the city had approached and they were requesting a meeting to negotiate an accord. The commander was just about ready to dispose of them when she had received the newly issued memo relating to capture of prisoners. Miasnikov ordered her to allow them to enter the camp and to personally escort them to the negotiating table. He should at least hear what they had to say; perhaps they were there to betray the bastards who wiped out JJ and his troops.

He waited patiently for them to arrive; the boxes arrived before them, and Miasnikov wondered what they contained. He did not go near them and would allow the agents or diplomats from the city to reveal the contents when they finally arrived. Vladimir would quite happily just torture them as soon as they sat down, but due to the nature of the crimes committed, he was required to adopt a slightly more delicate approach.

KD 53 had been given the task of negotiating; he cautiously approached the commander of the invading forces with KD 14 and KD 18. All three of them bowed to Vladimir simultaneously, and KD held his staff upright and much to Miasnikov's utter disbelief, all three of them shouted out, "Hail King David."

Lesqueths commander thought that there could be room somewhere in his future presentations for these theatrics and waved his hand for them to get on with it. KD 53 stepped forward, bowed again and motioned for his assistants KD 14 and KD 18 to open the boxes. "The esteemed King David has asked me to present these gifts to you in the hope of establishing a peaceful coexistence. King David wishes to convey his sincere condolences for the recent loss of your forces and hereby states for the record that he nor any of his militia was involved."

KD 53 put his hands in the boxes and displayed some of the items. "These priceless gems are some of the finest available in the land and the bars of gold with King David's personal stamp are a gift from one leader to another leader. King David realises that, as you are aware, the world will return to normal and hopes that you accept this sum of great wealth as a token of his upmost belief in a peaceful coexistence between our great nations."

Miasnikov was bewildered at the presentation and wondered what dangerous mix of pharmaceuticals they had been overindulging in actually thinking that these shiny baubles could actually be worth anything. He raised his hand and requested some food. Miasnikov ordered KD 53 to refrain from speaking and sat him and his strangely numbered assistants at the map table. "While I am eating my dinner, you are going to point out where exactly your base is located and all or any information leading to the capture of the rebels."

Miasnikov picked away at his food, looked at the presented gifts and was of the opinion that the boxes could actually be worth more than the contents. He heard them squabbling away as they were gently persuaded to disclose any viable information relating to his enquiries.

Chapter 27

General Vladimir Miasnikov finished his meal and was slightly pissed off. That it was just another plateful of discerning delights which could have been either animal, mineral or vegetable, he reviewed the information that had been collected while he was dining; shaking his head, Miasnikov requested a hammer. KD 14 was selected, and the tip of the office staff was hammered into one ear and out through the other. As he was screaming during the insertion of the attachment, Miasnikov stomped on his head several times. In the lull of the screams, he informed the two still alive KD's that he wanted the information and he wanted it right now. KD 14 laid motionless on the floor; the staff of the office reminded him of golf. The only thing missing was a number on the pole. Miasnikov reviewed the newly gleaned information, "So who is the Gareth D chap? And more to the point, where is he now?" By the end of the session both KD 53 and KD 18 had then been joined together with KD 14 on the ceremonial staff of the office bearer. Miasnikov thought that the pole looked much better with the new attachments, a little on the heavy side to carry about a bit, but still more appealing to the eye.

"Get them placed on the outside of the truck that will be delivering the new batch of prisoners to the Baroness."

KD 53 had fainted several times during the intensive questioning. Miasnikov had lied through his teeth, promising all sorts of incentives and acquiring all the necessary information. He waved them bye-bye as his commanders appeared for the new orders. On the full-scale map, he pointed to areas that they were going to visit. "I have been recently informed that Gareth D and all his merry-men reside in this village. As by all the signs of destruction that they have left in their wake, be advised that home-made explosive devices are their preferred method of attack." Miasnikov pointed to various highlighted parts of the map, "Approach these areas with caution. If you manage to apprehend any prisoners or round up some sheep, send them in first."

He moved to the next area on the map, "This is where King David and his followers are located. Block these roads and have the trucks waiting here and here." Miasnikov pointed at his commanders, "You will commence the attack from this location. I want prisoners, and I want lots of them." His voice changed slightly as he reminded them, "Please do not even think about disappointing the Baroness. Okay, ladies and gentlemen, you have your orders dismissed." Miasnikov was looking forward to reintroducing King David to the delegation that he had dispatched to formalise the peace accord. He was still perplexed at the so-called Kings' thinking process. The paltry baubles and brightly coloured metal did not hold any sway in this new world. Vladimir ordered his driver to get the vehicle ready. He wanted a ringside seat to enable him to watch King David's demise as the events started and his empire started to unfold.

Miasnikov was in position and waiting on the first arrivals. It would be dawn very shorty, and for King David and his crew, it would be arriving with more than a new day. He summoned his assistant and ordered her to set up his temporary viewing stall. As she scurried off to set things in motion, Miasnikov scanned the horizon with the high-powered binoculars. The kingdom in front of him was still in total darkness; not one single peep of light was on show.

He thought that King David was very clever and knew something that he did not. Or he was a very fucking stupid individual and had no idea of the events that were going to unfold very shortly. The assistant informed him that the viewing stall was all set up; Miasnikov followed her, took a seat and browsed the menu. He selected a bottle of wine and was having the first slurp as the artillery barrage opened up. Miasnikov put on his battery-operated noise-cancelling headphones and watched as the incoming salvo brightened up the otherwise dull morning. He cross-referenced the spreading trail of devastation on the map in front of him. Miasnikov sent one of his runners to inform the snatch squads to get ready. King David must surely realise that there would be no peace accord after all, and it was time to evacuate.

The now empty bottle was thrown at full force towards his assistant, indicating that he required a refill. Miasnikov did not even look at the label; wine was wine, and no matter how much of the stuff was consumed, he still thought that it was one of the vilest creations ever to have been invented. He cheered and raised his glass to the rockets that blasé across the sky. The rocket battalion had missed their assigned targets, but at least they had finally managed to figure out how the equipment worked. Miasnikov summoned a runner to go and warned them to reset the coordinates immediately or else face the consequences of being transferred to the live target company.

Vladimir had just been informed that the first batch of prisoners had been secured and asked if he would like to inspect them prior to transporting them to the Baroness. Miasnikov informed them that he did not want to inspect them, but once they could supply him with the final number, he would come and maybe kill a few of them. Vladimir would really like to see King David chained up beside his envoys before he set off on his final journey.

King David was still in his bed; he had stayed awake until the early hours, hoping that KD 53 had returned with a treaty. The sentries on duty had reported no signs of any activity; it was only when the shelling had started that he realised that it was time to leave. King David had changed into normal clothes and instantly reverted back to his former self. Steven Donaldson had abandoned all his pseudo claims of royal existence, along with all his subjects and attempted to do a runner. His concubines and wives had asked him what he was doing; he had curtly told them to fuck right off. He never even said goodbye as he left.

The way Steven had seen it was that he did not have a local accent, therefore he would be able to talk his way out of any trouble. The former King David did not inform anyone of his intended departure and just helped himself to the first available vehicle. As he drove away at breakneck speed, he ignored his former wife and anyone else who had noticed him attempting the vanishing act. The first road that he intended to use as his exit point was blocked off. The former sentries swinging from the trees clued him up so quickly that he had to reverse out of there. King David had not been behind the wheel of a vehicle for quite a while, and it took several attempts to find the hidden gear. He reversed into several objects on the way out and never once looked back at whether he had run over any of his former subjects. As far as he was concerned, it was no longer anything to do with him, and he was merely a lost tourist.

King David tried every single escape route he could think of, and up till now, they were all barricaded off and now manned by dead sentries. The former King David thought that he would find some group along the way who would believe his tales. Then, they allowed him to join their group. The last road out of town now lay ahead of him, and with no visible obstacles in sight, Steven pressed hard on the accelerator. He was delighted with himself to be escaping. Steven was now on the main drag, the highway out of there, and as he hit the dual carriageway, a huge block of concrete was in the process of being dragged across the road up ahead of him. He had slammed on the brakes, but his reaction time was way too slow; he had left it way too late and crashed head-on into the obstacle.

Miasnikov had been informed of the total count of prisoners captured alive, the runner who had been given the task of passing on the information that King David had not been found. Vladimir could kill the messenger, but that would not be right, as his commander should have had to courage to pass on the news themselves. Miasnikov took the opened bottle of wine with him as he was driven to view the captives. He was amazed that they were all still wearing their allocated KD-numbered shirts; well, that was all except one. He asked the commander why this one had not gotten a KD identification number and why was his head wrapped up in bandages?

Miasnikov asked for a megaphone. He switched it on and did the normal squelching with the volume selection, and when everyone was wincing at the feedback, he lowered the volume. "Testing, testing, one, two, three testing. I would like to give King David the opportunity to make his presence known to me or my troopers. You will be treated fair, and I promise not to kill you. If you do not come forward, we can do the following: I can start killing your people, or your people can point you out."

Vladimir Miasnikov asked for a bladed weapon, anything that was sharp or had a point on the end. He had said this loud so that everyone could hear him. "Okay, I am going to count to three, and then I will start killing, King David; let yourself be known, or somebody point him out."

He only reached the first number when everyone present had pointed at the chap with the bandaged head.

The general instructed his guards to bring him forward. As he was forced to move, Steven Donaldson declared that he was a lost tourist and this was nothing but a set up.

Miasnikov punched him in the guts and started to remove his bandages. King David had a little bruising, a few cuts, and a broken nose; none of the injuries required to be covered up. "When I was in deep conversation with your envoy KD 53, I did get a valid description of you and what your voice sounded like. "All Hail, King David indeed." Miasnikov booted him in the balls, and as he bent forward, he kneed him in the face. He then ordered his guards to put the now unconscious KD 1 in the same transport to accompany KD 53 and his former chums.

Miasnikov's advance unit had followed King David's directions and were now searching the camp. They had checked every building, every single shed, and they had found no one. The prisoners that had been captured en route had been used to open doors, and once they were inside, they were forced at gunpoint to search the area. At a safe distance from Miasnikov troops, they were instructed to open drawers and cupboards to retrieve any paperwork that might disclose useful information.

The prisoners did not always do as they were instructed, they had been told to be extremely careful and only move or open the objects that they had been instructed to. One of the prisoners had noticed a picture postcard on the desk, and without thinking, she had picked it up. As they lifted it up closer to read the caption, they failed to notice the fine wire connected to the cluster of grenades. The prisoner had just finished reading the caption, "Wish you were here," when all the interconnected grenades exploded simultaneously, killing everyone in the room. The other troopers had rushed to the scene, and now realising that this method of searching the abandoned property was dangerous and futile, they herded all the prisoners into the empty buildings and then called in the tanks to flatten the place.

The troopers agreed that they would report to Miasnikov that the camp was completely deserted by the time they had arrived there. They would also inform him that the locals that they had come across on their journey had refused to surrender, and they had lost some troopers in the resulting firefight. If Miasnikov found out the truth, he would blame the commanders for everything and punish them all. The level of the punishment he inflicted upon them would be dependent on the quantity of alcohol that he had consumed. Miasnikov's advance unit had one piece of useful information one of the prisoners had confessed that Gareth and his crew might have travelled to the port. They had located the unpronounceable place on the map, and fully aware that Miasnikov would expect them to go and investigate immediately, they travelled to this location as quickly as possible.

Miasnikov's advance unit had arrived in the early hours, and finding no prisoners en route, they had to conduct the search themselves. The furtive investigation took a long time to carry out as every item had to be thoroughly checked before it was touched and moved. The search concluded that Gareth and his crew had left the area at least several days ago. The quantity of abandoned vehicles that lined the small streets and the harbour devoid of any watercraft indicated that they had left on boats. The commander thought that they had just unearthed some buried treasure; Gareth's team, in their haste to leave, had inadvertently left a large map of the British Isles with various markings on it. Miasnikov would have to be informed of the newly discovered information, and by the directions highlighted on the chart, he would also note that Gareth and his crew were intent on travelling to Scotland. The commander summoned the current dispatcher and ordered her to deliver this information to Miasnikov as soon as possible. "Tell him that I think he will want to read it straight away."

The general had been enjoying himself; almost all of the major cities and towns in Wales had been pulverised. All that remained now in these places were smoking ruins of dust and demolished buildings. Vladimir was happy that all of his mechanised divisions had improved their targeting skills. His artillery commanders were now almost capable of dialling in the new coordinates without being ordered. He was now leading the tank battalion forward; they were now all lined up along a residential street. In the old days, this would have looked like the mechanised machines had a short stop before continuing to their regimental base or en route to a training exercise. Miasnikov delivered the order to the gunner, and the turret rotated towards the rather nice house. The gun had already been loaded, and Miasnikov delivered the final incremental changes before ordering them to fire. Every single tank lined up in the street had followed his example, and they continued until every house had been levelled. Miasnikov drove across the children's playpark, crushing the slides along with the swings beneath the tracks. He travelled through a rather once-ornate garden and straight through the house to arrive at the next street. He directed his tank to the bottom of the street, waited until the rest of the battalion was in position and continued the destructive process.

Miasnikov wanted to complete this task of leaving this country completely in ruins and return to his beloved Blackpool as soon as possible, even though he very much enjoyed creating the ensuing destruction. Vladimir, given the choice, much preferred inflicting unrestricted torture on the hapless survivors. He wondered how the mechanical people were progressing with his unique plans for the Tower of Death. Miasnikov had plenty of time to think up many new delights to enhance the various fairground attractions and couldn't wait to show them to his modification team and get his new ideas up and running. As for willing constants for his new contraptions, Miasnikov thought that Lesqueth would approve of his unique way of disposing of a few prisoners, especially the ones that had been rounded up in Wales. Vladimir wondered if the different accent would still scream the same way as the other members of the indigenous species belonging to this country. Miasnikov whistled as he jotted down an idea that had just popped up in his brain; this time, he was imagining the sheer terror that he wished to adopt into the ghost train.

The general would like to apply for a permanent posting to Blackpool, but he doubted that the Baroness of Kindeace-Shire would agree to his request. He thought that by the time he had completed all of his proposed modifications, it would be his dream location. Miasnikov in now thinking that if the Baroness rejected his application, he could simply work around it. All he had to do in the future was relocate and transfer the newly captured prisoners.

Miasnikov's advanced patrol had been sent forward into the darkest Scotland to contact Bartram and his estranged sister Irena, who had travelled for days on end. Several times along the route they had been attacked by the irate locals who were under some misconception that they were now in charge. At one point, the indigenous tribespeople of that region had even tried to stop them at their rudimentary checkpoint. Needless to say, it did not turn out to be good for the locals. The mini convoy had accrued little in the way of damage to their vehicles, and by the luck of the gods, they had suffered no fatalities.

Commander Essmie had found this whole country dull, damp and dreary, and in the winter, it was worse than that. The troopers on this mission could now all fully understand why, centuries ago, the Roman soldiers stationed here had complained that they had been sent to the far end of the world. As the mini-convoy came around the sweeping bend in the road, they spotted yet another roadblock in the distance. The leader of the advance patrol ordered a complete stop. She opened out her antique spyglass, that had been generously bequeathed to her by a museum down south and observed the spectacle in front of them. The commander requested the .50 cal heavy machine gun should be brought forward. The gun crew jumped to it, and five minutes later, the barricade was being shot to pieces as the large rounds tore through the vehicles blocking the road.

Now that they had introduced themselves, she ordered them to advance slowly. The commander had not seen anyone trying to escape the ensuing heavy machine gun fire, and either they were all now dead or hiding, pretending that they were not there. As the mini-convoy approached, a pair of the rebels broke cover and made a run for it. They did not make it very far before each of them was cut to pieces. The tattered remains of the blockage were firmly pushed out of the way as Miasnikov's advance patrol moved forward. The drivers were curious as to why the local planners had never built a road straight. Every single one up till now had been twisted and turned, even when the surrounding countryside around them was as flat as a pancake. The driver asked the commander the question, and Essmie told them to shut the fuck up and pay attention to the road in front of them. They had now been able to join on to the motorway; someone must have carved a path through the endless sea of abandoned vehicles.

Even though this was only a relatively short journey taking them from the outskirts of the city to the town where

Bartram's castle was situated, Essmie had warned the troopers that this was an ideal place to launch an ambush, and they had to be prepared to shoot their way out if necessary. The commander checked the map; the slipway leading them into the outskirts of the town should just be up ahead. Essmie remembered the road number, closely watching everything in front and around her. The one thing that she had noticed was that there were no animals in this area, no birds, nor any stray cats or dogs. She spotted the turn off up ahead, signalling to let the other vehicles aware and drove up the small incline that would take them into the town. On both sides of the street, burnt-out houses and cars lined the path in front of them. The town was devoid of all signs of life; they passed what looked like a medieval church; miraculously, it looked completely undamaged. No doubt, it would be full to the brim with the skeletal remains of all the people who had sought shelter in there when the sickness had rapidly descended upon them.

Essmie watched the map, following the seemingly never-ending twisted roads that would take them out of this cold town into the outskirts. She was perplexed as to why a high-ranking member of the Baroness of Kindeace-Shires' inner circle would have chosen to stay in this almost barren place, when they could have picked one of the many warmer and pleasant areas down south. She caught a glimpse of the surrounding hills through one of the spaces created by the gap of the demolished building and it did not make the area look any prettier. Essmie thought that the whole place had a gloomy, almost desolate feel to it, and even if the temperature were in the high thirties, it would still feel freezing cold.

By her calculations they should be coming into contact with some of Bartram's security detail, a roving patrol or a manned-up checkpoint or two. Essmie was fully aware of the security standards that they are meant to be adhered to, when stationed in an outlying district. The convoy went up a hill, down a hill, and then at the top of the next one, she saw the castle over on the right-hand side. Essmie's convoy had still not encountered any checkpoints; she signalled and pulled them to the side of the road. She gathered them together, explaining that something was not quite right there, and then issued the revised plan.

They drive at full speed to the castle, and not one living soul was spotted, no guards to wave them down and check their credentials, no checkpoint, absolutely nothing. They drew to a halt at the castle, and as per her orders the troopers spread out, conducting a quick recce on the immediate surrounding area. There was no sign of any recent habitation;

Essmie, trying to attract attention, banged her fist on the tattered doors. The attempt at contact went unanswered; she ordered the troopers to force the doors open, and then they saw why no one had answered. The skeletons were firmly attached to the walls with nails lined both sides of the staircase. Some of them still had on their uniforms, displaying the Baroness of Kindeace-shire as well as Miasnikov's insignias.

Essmie led her troopers up the stairs; as they reached the top they were astounded at the sight before them. The animals that Miasnikov had issued orders to confiscate were, for some strange reason, stone tigers. The faded patches of shrivelled skin that once were the proud family emblems tattooed on their brethren's backs were now all roughly draped over, adoring the framed artwork. One of the framed pieces of art stood out from the rest; the human skins had been placed over the frame very neatly. Essmie thought that those once belonged to Bartram and Miasnikov's younger sister, Irena. The commander ordered a search for the bodies of the former rulers of the castle.

Commander Essmie was summoned by the shouts coming from below; the troopers had found the remains of several people in the pile of ashes outside. The skeletons still had nails in them, declaring loud and clear that they were crucified and then burnt alive. Essmie ordered them to bury the remains of Bartram, Irena and the one that they could not identify. The commander was not looking forward to reporting this news to either the Baroness or Miasnikov.

Thousands of miles away on the West coast of America, the great Indian Nation was on the search; none of their scouting parties had found any recent signs of their brethren and the Southern tribe had not turned up for the annual meeting. The nation had split into two main tribes but had agreed to meet up once a year to discuss everything that they had witnessed and what they had planned for the future. In them not appearing, this had raised great concerns among the elders, and the council had then proposed that they should go and look for them. The Northern tribe had searched nearly everywhere on the continent for them, and now they had ended up on the West coast. This place was full of many unpleasant reminders from the past and it was with a great feeling of despair and foreboding that they had ventured into this area.

Much of the country of Merica had been taken from them in this place; all the treaties that were signed had ended up not being worth the paper on which they were written. The ratification of the documents was resigned and renegotiated, and in the end, they had nothing left. Many of their people had perished there from the ensuing fighting and the many diseases that the Europeans had carried over and then gifted them with. They had fought long and hard, and when they had lost too many people, they were placed into the dreaded reservations that did not have enough natural resources to sustain them. This whole area was full of many ghosts from the past, and even their horses did not like it here.

Day after day, they searched for some signs of recent activity, all the messages that they had located were old. The elders thought that some catastrophe must have taken them away to the spirit world, as there were no longer any able-bodied whitemen left in the country to fight against them. They had crossed the deserts, crossed the barren lands and they still had found nothing. At the last meeting, some of the tribes wanted to split up to enable them to search a wider area. The elders had disagreed on the thinking that if there were any danger, it would be to their benefit to be in a group of many, rather than in a group of a few. Again, they searched for weeks and weeks upon end without finding any sign of their missing kin. The forward scouting party had failed to return one day, and the elders stated that they must follow in their footsteps to confront the evil that could have taken them away from them.

The whole of the tribe followed along the route that they had taken, and again, no sign of their missing brethren had been found. There was nothing in this land that could have made them just simply disappear into thin air and they had continued searching. The weeks turned into months, and they checked every valley, climbed over every hill and still no signs of their brothers were displayed anywhere in this unforgiving landscape.

In the twenty-first century, the armament companies supplying the latest technology to warring nations had spent a massive amount of expenditure and research into drone warfare. These new weapons were semi-autonomous and required to be controlled from a central control point. This could be located thousands of miles away, but with constant satellite surveillance, there was no time-lapse, and it was an eye in the sky in real-time. The richer countries had developed their own private systems primarily for their own use only. These systems were never acknowledged publicly to be in existence, nor were they ever sold to allegedly friendly nations. The fully autonomous system had been developed by one of the untraceable subsidiary companies owned by Baroness of Kindeace-Shire. This company was completely untraceable, and even her closest inner circle was unaware of its existence.

The sensors placed in the outlying reaches of the company's location had picked up the unauthorised movement, and the system activated phase one. This sent a coded message out to the autonomous drones, and on receiving the signal their systems automatically proceeded unhindered into phase two. The Northern tribe of the Indian Nation was secretly monitored from the start of the groups' passage until the last man and horse had crossed over the invisible line.

This fully autonomous system passed nano-second bursts of predicted coordinate information to each unit. The underground munitions reconfigured their positions according to the latest longitude and latitude displays. The sensors were the entry points that relayed their information readouts constantly in short bursts to the sensors located at the exit points. A general time was issued to all the underground munitions and they proceeded into phase three. The weapons were now all fully activated and armed; as seventy-five percent of the buried drones confirmed the trespassers' presence, they proceeded into phase four. The whole of the Northern tribe of the Indian nation was wiped out in seconds; the underground munitions' first charge sent them three-quarters of a metre into the air. The second charge detonated the main explosive, and the undetectable, hardened, multi-shaped plastic projectiles decimated everything within a five-meter radius. The front and back sensors initiated phase five, and a drone rose from the ground and flew around the surrounding area, checking that all the trespassers were dead. Any objects that displayed a heartbeat were eliminated instantly by the airborne fully autonomous drone.

In the underground control centre of the base of the LAMF army, the drone field was deactivated, and the secret exits were opened up. The men and machines set about their dedicated tasks; the Northern Indian tribe was buried under the soil beside the Southern tribe. All the used munitions were replaced, and the surface was remodelled to hide all traces of the carnage.

Lesqueth Bretton, the Baroness of Kindeace-Shire, had followed in her father's footsteps and had set up various contingency plans throughout the world. The UK had not been a major player in global affairs for a considerable time. She thought it only prudent to ensure the survival of her family by clandestinely taking over several of the major armament companies in the USA. None of her closest confidants were aware of their existence nor of the presence of her secret armies located around the globe. As far as she

was concerned, she alone would set the future for this family
and this world.

Chapter 28

The person formally known as King David or Steven Donaldson was now awake. The bizarre feature above him freaked him out, and he thought that the beating he had received must have been quite severe. Steven had taken some time to recognise the figures above him. The former holders of KD 53, 14 and 18 were almost staring down at him from above. The staff of the office held all their heads in place as their limp bodies swayed in perfect time with the moving vehicle. He had asked the guards a question, but they had completely ignored him and had not even looked in his direction as he had spoken. If he was still King David, he would have maybe exiled them for the displayed arrogance, perhaps even allocated them a shitty job for life, and the more they ignored him, he could have ordered their execution.

King David again asked the guards, "Where are we going?" and was promptly awarded with another beating. The clubs that they were using were recognised as being police-issued weapons. They pummelled him, hitting him repeatedly all over his body. Now, the unconscious Steven was quiet; the guards were thankful that the prisoner was silent. They laughed at his audacity in proclaiming that he was a King and that they should treat him with all due respect. The convoy comprising King David and all of his still-alive followers was heading towards London. Their glorious leader, the Baroness of Kindeace-Shire, was sure to have many wonderful delights prepared for their arrival.

All of King David's former subjects had been crammed into sealed trucks. It made no difference if they held a former rank or position; they were all equally mistreated. First, their hands were positioned behind their backs, and then the plastic cable ties were placed over and roughly tightened. A severe beating was then administered by the double line of baton-wielding thugs as they were forced and prodded to march down through the line into the waiting vehicles.

Steven Donaldson had woken up a few times during the journey but did not feel the need to ask any additional questions. The guards talked away quite happily to each other; King David had no idea what language they were using and, therefore, did not know what they were discussing. He thought that he had been in this vehicle for hours upon hours; he guessed that they must be journeying south; otherwise, they would have reached their final destination. His former delegates KD 53, 14 and 18 were starting to stink the place out. It was not just the stench of shit and stale piss but that peculiar smell of dead rotting flesh that almost clung to every exposed pore on your being. The trio was still swaying backwards and forwards, perfectly synchronised with the vehicle's movements.

As they came to a sudden stop, KD 14's rapidly decomposing corpse dislodged itself from the head and fell on top of King David. He screamed relentlessly, shouting that the dead were attacking him. He received, as far as the guards were concerned, another more than well-deserved beating. He was still kicking and screaming as he was roughly dragged from the vehicle and dumped unceremoniously on the ground.

All he could see in front of him was a pair of highly polished boots. "I am the ruler of this country, and sorry, I have to ask: was your journey down here pleasant? Did my people treat you well?" The ex-King David replied that they beat the shit out of him every time he asked a question, and he was chained up like a stray dog.

Lesqueth delivered a full-force kick to the area of his stomach region, telling him to stop whining and to stand up when he was speaking to her. Steven Donaldson moaned and groaned as he forced himself to stand in the upright position. The first thing that he noticed was all his concubines, KD

1A, B, C and D, were spaced out 3 meters apart from each other and were all firmly chained to a small post embedded in the ground. Lesqueth walked over to them, gently touching each of their faces as she passed. "Well, now, you do like the pretty ones; I wonder if you will be able to recognise any of them by the time we finish our little quiz. JJ was one of my closest associates, one of my best commanders, and you and your people allowed him to die."

King David blurted out that he nor any of his people had anything whatsoever to do with the killings.

The Baroness of Kindeace-Shire looked at him and calmly walked over to the woman with KD 1A emblazoned on her tee shirt. Lesqueth reached into her inside pocket and retrieved a container. The Baroness stared her straight in the eyes, removed the cap and then proceeded to pour the contents over her head. KD 1A tried to pull herself away from the liquid but only managed to increase the area of spread. Lesqueth totally ignored her urgent pleas to show some compassion and bestow some mercy upon her. The Baroness of Kindeace-Shire lit one of her small cigars and, as she exhaled, set KD 1A on fire. Lesqueth watched her burn without showing any trace of emotion or feelings and did not wish to compete against the volume of her loud yelping. She patiently smoked and waited until the unwelcome noises that emanated from her ceased completely.

The Baroness came over and stood beside him; she almost hissed as she whispered in his ear, "That was fun and just think of how much entertainment you and yours are going to provide me with on this fine day."

King David attempted to speak, but Lesqueth delivered a perfectly aimed headbutt and as he laid on the ground holding his now distorted nose.

"The next time you attempt to interrupt me, I will remove your tongue and nod if you understand."

King David nodded repeatedly.

"In future when I ask a question, you will throw yourself on the ground and grovel for permission to speak, nod if you understand."

Steven Donaldson nodded just once this time, then stood up.

"I want you to tell me everything you know about the people, the group who attacked my forces, that had arrived in your country with nothing but open arms of friendship to deliver you and yours: salvation, liberation and hope in these uncertain. times."

King David, as previously instructed, threw himself to the ground, praised her to no end and begged for permission to speak.

Lesqueth politely informed him that he had to work on his begging and grovelling presentation skills as it was really not quite convincing enough. The Baroness had KD 1B in her sights, and as she was walking away from him, "Did you know that my father at one time used to own several demolition companies? Hmmm, I don't suppose you did?"

Lesqueth reached into the magic pocket again, and this time, she produced a single stick of dynamite. As she approached KD 1B, the Baroness told her that she would want to examine her tonsils, that she had a very good patient, and to open her mouth as wide as possible. Lesqueth clamped her hand on her face pretending to be interested in the displayed opening. The other hand quickly forced the stick of barbed dynamite as far down into her throat as possible. A quick flick with the lighter, and the fuse started to burn. KD 1B tries to dislodge it by frantically moving her head about, but it did not budge. Lesqueth had just managed to reach King David in time; she had grabbed his hair and forced him to watch as the explosion blew her head apart. KD 1C and 1D stood with their eyes wide in shock and shook uncontrollably at witnessing the abject terror, wondering how long they had to live and by what means the certifiably insane ruler of this land would devise for their swan song.

KD 1C & D didn't have long to wait as the Baroness pushed King David to watch as she cut their throats. Lesqueth asked Steven more questions and informed him that if he waffled or withheld the truth, that inability would create some problems. "Where is Gareth hiding and how many people in his group?"

The Baroness had now attached a rope around his neck and dragged him along to the unidentified structure covered in tarpaulin. Lesqueth let go of the rope and instructed King David to remove the covers.

The Baroness of Kindeace-Shire sighed and marched over to him; she kicked his legs out from underneath him, then kicked him in the face several times. Lesqueth summoned some of her guards, and they removed all the coverings in minutes as she waited for Steven Donaldson to recover enough to stand up. The Baroness ordered a round up of a group of King David's subjects. Her guards pushed and squeezed as many as possible into the plain-looking metal shed. None of them wanted to go in willingly, but Lesqueth made them have a change of heart as she shot a couple of the most troublesome objectors in the head at point-blank range. The row-upon-row of oxy-acetylene burners was set and positioned flush with every surface inside the shed. They were on the ceiling, on the floor and on every wall, and even a smaller than small church mouse could not find a safe space to evade their reach. King David was now starting to stir, and Lesqueth pulled on the rope to force him to stand upright. "How nice of you to join us, and guess who is in the shed?"

All of the equipment had been checked, and the control knobs pre-set; Lesqueth nodded, and the oxy-acetylene quads were opened fully. The Baroness coldly looked into his eyes and pressed the ignition button. There was a momentary panic as the occupants of the enclosed space heard the gas escaping. They shouted, screamed and tried to evade the intense heat as the burners sparked to life. The panicking and the pleas for mercy didn't last for too long, as the three-thousand-degree temperature and the three-foot-long flames fired into the cramped space incinerated all of them within minutes.

King David was speechless, but Lesqueth was absolutely delighted with herself. "What do you think we should do now? Any ideas? Well, don't you be worrying about that for now."

All the remaining people from his kingdom had all been laid out in two rows, pinned securely to the ground. King

David was forced to sit with her in the cab of the tracked bulldozer. Lesqueth made her best hunting horn imitation, pretending to alert the hounds to the chase. The bulldozer inched forward, and the one-hundred-tonne tracked vehicle crushed every single head. Steven Donaldson was now the only one left alive, and he knew that she was never going to set him free. King David would just like to die right now. The Baroness of Kindeace-Shire reversed the machine and manoeuvred backwards and forwards all down the line, leaving nothing but a mass of unidentifiable flesh and bone. A cage had just been dropped off in the middle of the carnage. Lesqueth dragged him over towards it, removed the rope from around his neck, made him strip naked then pushed him inside. The Baroness locked the door, threw the key into the mass of scattered flesh and bone, walked away without uttering a single word.

The Baroness of Kindeace-Shire was reading the latest communique from the keeper of the records; she had noticed a slight change in the colour of the medium used for writing. Lesqueth wondered if Memo was now an active participant in assisting the brethren in the stationary department. The fine, ornate calligraphic script praised her wisdom and her greatness and wished her the longest and most glorious reign to be bestowed upon her by the gods on high. Tesporo was kindly remembering her of the most generous offer of fifty-four able minded bodies to commemorate the passing of the green comet that has not been seen for 50,000 years. This was last seen when their ancestors were making the long walk out of the unforgiving desert region and venturing into the fertile lands to plant the first seeds of civilisation on this otherwise barren planet.

Tesporo had also added a detailed drawing of the planned celebration; it listed everything that was required. Lesqueth quickly scanned the list. She had no idea why he needed so many heavy-duty cranes and lots of bunk beds, but nevertheless approved his request. The Baroness had informed Tesporo that, at present, there was an abundance of Welsh prisoners and could assure him that they could scream just as spectacularly as the last batch of volunteers. The Baroness added that at the end if he required any more assistance, all he had to do was ask and pass on her warmest, most sincere regards to the memo.

Lesqueth had just received the news about Bartram, as well as Irena and she guessed that the other skeletal remains belonged to Ernesto. This form of execution had the Hidden written all over it in bold capital letters. The Baroness had thought that they were gone, gone forever. Now, she had to reconfigure all of her plans; it might come to nothing, but she did not want to take any unnecessary risks. All the progress that the Baroness had achieved could very be very soon null and void. The Baroness of Kindeace-Shire drafted a set of instructions to Tesporo, then summoned her dispatcher. "I want you to have this delivered to the keeper of the records immediately." Lesqueth handed over the urgent message, "Report back to me as soon as you have the reply."

The Baroness knew for sure that Miasnikov would go utterly and completely berserk when he heard the news. Lesqueth knew that he would leave a contingency force in Wales, and then Miasnikov would assemble the rest of her armed forces and advance into Scotland. She had no intention of stopping him. Lesqueth thought that even if she ordered him to return to headquarters to coordinate a planned offensive, he would just blatantly ignore her. The Baroness of Kindeace-Shire summoned her driver, giving them directions to drive to her family home. Miasnikov could very well be successful, defeating the old enemy once and for all. These people had vanished for centuries, and now, all of a sudden, they have resurfaced. Lesqueth wanted them all completely eradicated and forever removed from this plane of existence.

The crimes that they had carried out at Stanley Castle were a crystal-clear declaration of intent, and the Hidden were letting her know that they were not gone, they were still here. It was possible that Miasnikov and her forces would be wiped out in Scotland and that would curtail all of her plans for the future. The Baroness of Kindeace-Shire had never envisaged that this day would come. Lesqueth opened the secret compartment, delivering the three-word coded message: "Across the pond."

About The Author

This is book number 5, and if you send a nice, pleasant email, you will get a nice, pleasant email in return. croftengrebe@gmail.com.